A Contemporary Asshat at the Court of Henry VIII

MaryJanice Davidson

A Contemporary Asshat at the Court of Henry VIII

Copyright © 2020 MaryJanice Davidson
All rights reserved.
This edition published 2020

Cover courtesy of Recorded Books
Cover image of King Henry VIII: public domain
Other images from Shutterstock
Cover design by Joie Simmons

ISBN: 978-1-68068-183-3

This book is published on behalf of the author by the Ethan Ellenberg Literary Agency.

You can reach the author at:
Facebook: https://www.facebook.com/maryjanicedavidson
Twitter: @MaryJaniceD
Email: contactmjd@comcast.net
Website: https://www.maryjanicedavidson.org

Gorgeous series
Hello, Gorgeous!
Drop Dead, Gorgeous

Standalone Stories & Short Stories
Beggarman, Thief
By Any Other Name
Carrie
Keep You Brave And Strong: A Hurricane Harvey short
    story
LTF: A Satirical Romance
Medical Miracle

Collections
Doing It Right (Thief of Hearts, Wild Hearts)
Dying for You (The Fixer-Upper, Paradise Bossed,
    Driftwood, Witch Way)
Hickeys and Quickies (Unwavering, Medical Miracle, My
    Angel is My Devil)
Really Unusual Bad Boys (Bridefight, Mating Season,
    Groomfight)
Under Cover (Sweet Strangers, Lovely Lies, Delightful
    Deception)

Anthologies
"Letters To My Readers" in Wicked Women Whodunit (with
    Amy Garvey, Jennifer Apodaca, Nancy J. Cohen)
Bad Boys With Expensive Toys (with Nancy Warren, Karen
    Kelley)
Bite (with Laurell K. Hamilton, Charlaine Harris, Angela
    Knight, Vickie Taylor)

Valentine's Day is Killing Me (with Leslie Esdaile, Susanna Carr)

DEDICATION

For my daughter Christina, who knew how much I wanted to write this book, and how much I didn't want to write a 16th century heroine, and told me how it could be done. So I'm thankful, but also irritated I couldn't figure this out on my own.

TABLE OF CONTENTS

PROLOGUE

King Henry VIII is a fat bastard.

And no matter what, I'll always hate him.

I hate his mean piggy eyes, I hate his sweaty jowls, I hate his smell, his politics, his casual brutality. I have to constantly remind myself that killing him would be bad. No matter that I'd probably never be caught. No matter that'd it be easy, and deeply satisfying.

And I have to keep thinking that because I'm in his company a lot—he likes me.

All this because I get migraines and know the Heimlich maneuver.

PROLOGUE THE SECOND

Because this isn't your mother's historical fiction. Or even your grandmother's.

Even before I met Henry Tudor, I didn't like him.

I blame my mother. She was a Tudorphile. And not just any Tudorphile. She was hot for Tudors the way Henry VIII was hot for spit-roasted boar and legitimate sons. When other moms rhapsodized over *Barefoot Contessa* or *Game of Thrones* spinoffs, my mom would watch and re-watch every movie, miniseries, and History Channel special about any Tudor, from *Tudor Rose* to *The Private Life of Henry VIII*.

When I subtly expressed—via fake throwing-up noises—my loathing of whatever Tudor drama she was re-inflicting on me, she explained that this was important research because our family came from England and she just knew there was royal blood waaaaaay back in the family line. Explanations that technically almost everyone came from England, just like technically almost everyone came from Africa, would fall on totally. Deaf. Ears.

Come to think of it, that should be chiseled on my tombstone: *Her explanations fell on totally deaf ears.* In letters an inch deep so they won't wear off for a couple of centuries.

CHAPTER ONE

It's really not that complicated.

On my end, at least.

It goes like this: in the wee hours (I hardly ever get the call at noon), I.T.C.H.—Information Technology for Culture and History—reaches out to tell me we've got another Lostie. If I have time, I take a shower; there's no way to predict how long I'll be gone or if I'll have access to niceties like hot running water and shampoo.

I grab my gear and hustle my sleepy self to their woefully underfunded, understaffed Secret Lab. (Yes. They really call it that. Discussions on the intense lameness of this have fallen on deaf ears.) Then we all yell at each other for a couple of minutes, me about the sheer madness of their continual tinkering with tech they've proven they don't understand, and them about me wasting time yelling at them about tinkering with tech they don't understand.

Then I jump.

That's the best and worst part.

I don't pretend to understand the tech, and neither do the techs who invented the tech. I don't know why time travel doesn't hurt, or why it doesn't play with my brain. I don't know how I can stand on the platform and take one step and find myself in the same general area five hundred years earlier, as easy and painless as stepping off a sidewalk.

And since I don't understand any of that, I focus on what I do understand: finding the Lostie and bringing them back to the present.

And almost every time, finding them isn't the hardest part. Rescuing them is. All I have to do is follow the gossip, or the sermonizing or, sometimes, the screams. Then: *voilà!* There they are, sometimes about to be burned for witchcraft. Or tortured for being a witch. Or imprisoned for inadvertently breaking the law, tortured, and then burned as a witch. The 16th century enjoys Ku Klux Klan/ISIL levels of intolerance.

So, the first thing: I have to hit the ground running. Literally running, because I appear out of nowhere, and for half a second you can see the lab and the techs gaping at me through the transfer window. If there are any witnesses to a sight that would freak people out in *my* time, never mind five centuries earlier, I have to get away. Quickly.

Fortunately, the gate tends to dump me beside the same enormous willow tree, and the long fronds do a great job of concealing me until I am ready to be unconcealed.

More fortunate: the lab was built on what has historically been an under-inhabited area, which is a good trick in Great Britain, one of the more consistently settled places on the planet. It's on the bare outskirts of London, and "civilization" isn't far away. This is good news for me, because it means I usually end up in roughly the same spot. The bad news: the gates the Losties fall through can spit them out anywhere between here and twenty miles from here.

So the trick is to get going right away and keep an intent-yet-distant look on your face, as if you know what you're doing but you're in a rush and thus a bit preoccupied, no time to stop and chat, so very sorry. Like a party where you don't want to get hit on by random people, you're looking for the guy your friend swears will be, like, *perfect* for you. Focused, yet distant.

This time the only witnesses to my abrupt appearance were several ravens perched in the willow tree. This was better than being spotted by people, but only just. Ravens are creepy, creepy birds—intelligent, predatory meat-eaters. Wolverines with wings.

I glared at them, hiked up my skirts a bit, and set out at a ground-gobbling trot. In no time at all, I was making use of the 16th century version of Hertz.

Important tip: in the past, as well as the present and probably the future, having money makes everything easier. In this case, the smith was happy to sell me his best horse.

"But I don't want to buy it."

"It is yours, m'lady!" This with a dramatic flourish. Since he was a foot taller than me, with the build of a linebacker, grimy from head to toe, and brandishing a hammer, this could have been terrifying.

"Yes, thank you, but I'm not buying the horse. I will bring it back. I promise."

He made a show of listening (my Midwestern American accent befuddles most people here *and* in the 21st century), then shrugged and proved he wasn't listening. "I have other horses," he assured me, pocketing gold. "When y'return, you may buy any of those you wish."

"Yes, but I'm not buying, I—thank you." How many times was I going to have this discussion before I wised up?

It was tricky enough getting me and a Lostie through the gate; I didn't want to think of the logistics of hauling back a horse.

But as annoying as this recurring argument was, it could have been a lot worse. As usual, my clothes had done most of the talking for me. As for my accent, people who didn't sound like everyone else weren't unheard of in 16th century London.

Rule number one: dress like you're somebody. Not royalty—that was a test I would flunk. But nobility? I could pull that off with the right clothing. And because Henry VIII liked me. Discomfiting as it was to be in the good graces of a narcissistic sociopath, it gave me the confidence to pull off the attitude I needed to stay unburned. Even if, during trips like this one, I never crossed paths with His Royal Grossness.

So my deep blue gown looked like it was pulled together by a skilled tailor, hugging my figure until just past the waist, then dropping to the ground in a series of folds that looked artfully crumpled (this was a cut considered "old fashioned", hilarious given where I was). My wide detachable sleeves were turned back to show a lighter blue silk lining (as uppity a cloth as I dared wear—only royalty and high nobility were allowed to wear it), and draped so low and cut so full I could have a boulder strapped to each arm and no one would notice. I had a chain around my neck that looked like gold, and my low-slung belt was good for more than decoration; I'd attached a pomander to it via another gold chain. My hair, a color exotically known as brown, had finally grown out enough to be pulled back and stuffed under my black velvet headdress.

If my clothes had been truly authentic, I would have needed at least two maids to help me get in and out of them, and another one to tackle my hair. If *I* were authentic, I wouldn't be wearing my Notorious RBG underpants; I wouldn't have any underwear at all. If you were a woman in this day and age and you had to pee and you didn't want multiple maids crowding into the privy to help you, you lifted your skirts and went. No underpants. Gross, yet practical. And before you suggest that getting caught with 21st century panties could get me in untold amounts of trouble, if whomever caught me knew what kind of underwear I had on, I was already in a lot of trouble.

"Besides, my underwear is nobody's business," I said, before I remembered that was an exceptionally dumb thing to say out loud.

Fortunately, my accent foiled the smith, who just blinked and said, "If you'll allow a 'pertinence, m'lady—"

"Oh, sure." I patted the horse's broad velvety nose and smiled. Horses were growing on me.

"Why are you traveling alone?"

I was ready for that one. "I'm not. My husband is just up the road."

"Take every care." His mild curiosity satisfied, he tipped me a casual salute, and in next to no time was boosting me into the saddle on a pretty roan mare with a back like a dining room table. *Oooh, sore thighs tonight. Guaranteed.*

I had been surprised to find that riding a horse isn't just work for the horse. Your arms, hands, legs, back—they're all in play. It's not like the movies, where everyone effortlessly rides for hours while having a good time. At worst, once they climb down, they stretch a bit and then they're back in business.

Nuh-uh. Being in the saddle for any length of time is exhausting; soon I would be able to crack golf balls with my thighs. But short of renting a carriage complete with a team and driver, my options were limited. My kingdom for a moped.

I got lucky again. My Lostie had stumbled across one of the few people from this time who wouldn't be horrified by someone popping out of nowhere dressed in never-seen-anything-like-it clothing and talking crazy: Thomas Wynter. I hadn't been riding two minutes before he loped (he was a human-shaped gazelle; 85% of him was legs) out of The Gray Horse and waved me over.

I grinned at him, I couldn't help it. It was always nice to see Thomas Wynter, and not just because I liked redheads with great forearms.

"And here you are again! And as lovely as ever, if you will allow me, Lady Joan. As always, you seem not to age a single day."

I'd aged weeks, actually, but Thomas thought we'd known each other for years, ever since the Field of the Cloth of Gold.

"You need a husband," he reminded me. It was a recurring theme. The smith would have been shocked to learn I'd lied, was in fact single and ready to mingle. "You spend too much time on your own, unless you are shepherding one of your lambs."

Lambs. Ha! Bewildered hair-trigger feral cats was a little closer to the truth. "You're the one lying in wait for me outside nondescript taverns," I teased. "You need a wife."

"Aye, I do."

"So you loitered to wait for me?" I'd pulled up by now, and Thomas caught my steed pro-tem by the bridle and held on, petting the horse's nose.

"Aye," he admitted cheerfully. "You're drawn to people like this, no need to deny it. Once I saw this poor lass, I knew you would be along directly."

"The poor lass" was accurate. She'd crept out of the inn a few feet behind him, swathed head to toe in a heavy dark wool blanket. That likely elicited comment, as it was August, but not as much comment as her clothes would have: shorts, probably—her legs were bare. Maybe a t-shirt. Flip-flops?

She blinked up at me with light brown eyes, squinted a little against the summer sunshine and rubbed her earlobe, which was bloody and torn where someone had yanked her earring. She had dirt on her forehead and her hair was a messy blonde cloud. Her hands were fisted in the blanket, holding it tightly around her like a fuzzy shield. "I'm having the *weirdest* dream."

"It's all right, I'm here to take you home."

She was already shaking her head. "You don't understand. I'm not supposed to be here. I have to wake up."

"Amazon. Tablets. iPhone."

"Oh thank God!" Yes, that always did the trick. And Thomas, bless his gingery heart, thought it was part of my charm.

"Your words soothe them, as when the monks chant," he observed.

Sure. Exactly like that. "Thomas, give her a boost, would you?"

"Of course, my lady." And he did, lifting my Lostie almost as easily as the blacksmith had tossed me. Thomas was in excellent shape for a man who self-identified as a scholar and spent most of his time reading. In addition to those nice long legs, he had agreeably broad shoulders (if you were into that), and his hair was a deep, rich auburn, so dark in some lights it was the color of grenadine and Coke.

(Mmmmm. Cherry Coke.) His bright blue gaze never left my face.

I'd only seen him wearing a hat once, the day we met. Today he was hatless, dressed in black, and his wonderful dark mop made him easy to spot. Sixteenth century clothing, like clothing from any time period, was a code people in the know could crack. Thomas' black doublet, full sleeves, venetian hose, and ankle boots all said, "I spend most of my days reading and writing; I don't *have* to do manual labor in order to eat, though sometimes I do for fun".

I blinked and decided it was time to get back to business. "I'll take her to the doctor."

"Or a priest," he suggested, still absently patting my Hertz horse's neck.

Oh. Yes. Yes, that will fix her right up.

I found a smile. "You're going to get a reputation. Soon everyone will think you only come to stay at the inn to catch strays."

"You are the only stray I wish to catch," he declared.

Aww. Sweet! Probably. "It was nice seeing you again."

"I quite agree! Dare I ask if once you have tended to your charge, you might—"

"I apologize, I can't. Next time," I lied (again).

He quirked half a smile at me. "No need to tease, my lady. If you keep to your pattern, I won't see you again for months, perhaps years."

It bothered me to turn him down, partly because he was always helpful and I owed him a lot more than a tankard of ale. Plus, he was gorgeous, single, liked me, probably didn't think I was a witch, watched for me, and thought my essential weirdness was charming. The irony: I couldn't get a second date in the 21st century, but I was catnip in the Tudor era.

But it was safer for both of us to turn him down. Nothing could ever come of it. Every minute I was here, I was exposed. Lingering for the 16th century equivalent of a tall double foam wasn't just indulgent, it was dangerous.

"I'm sorry," I began, hating how halting my tone was. "But—"

Steel fingers seized me by the upper arm.

"Ye-ow!"

"Will you shut up with the fucking chit-chat and get me the fuck out of here?" The Lostie had hissed this into my ear so rapidly, all I heard was, *shupfuckchitchatgetfuckouttafhere.*

Annnnnd my cue. "Goodbye."

He swept me a graceful bow. "Farewell, Lady Joan."

I didn't look back as we trotted back to the smith.

I never do.

CHAPTER TWO

Sixteenth century Hertz was delighted to see me. I was delighted, too. I hadn't been here more than an hour, my Lostie was (relatively) safe, and I wouldn't be saddle sore in the morning. It didn't take long to nag the smith into giving me back all but one of the coins I'd paid him.

"But milady, you bought her!"

"No, I rented her. Like I told you. Now you can sell her again."

"But—"

"Trust me."

Then I took my Lostie by the hand, gave Hi-yo Silver a goodbye pat, and set off for the entry window.

My Lostie (real name Sarah Watkins) told me a now-familiar tale: minding her own business, realized she didn't feel well, saw something bright, next thing she knew, her phone couldn't get wi-fi and her apps didn't work. Everyone looked weird. Everyone sounded weird. She was yelled at and grabbed and had no idea why. Etcetera.

"I know it sounds crazy—"

"Not to me." I got a watery smile for that one. "Don't fret, I'll have you back in no time." Probably.

This was often the most stressful part of the ordeal. We were seconds from making our escape, but it could take a few minutes to spot the gate. And of course the more time it took, the higher our risk of discovery. It was like playing *Beat the Clock*, except if you lost, you risked being messily murdered. If we had to linger longer, I was going to get her to stand beneath the willow with me. The fronds were so thick we'd be difficult to see from the road, and the locals didn't care for the *salix alba* in their midst. They thought it was haunted.

Today, like everything with this Lostie, it was easy. I spotted the shimmering gold squiggle after thirty seconds. Squinting at it made me dizzy and nauseated, because the gate looked exactly like my migraine aura, and the aura always meant hours of pain were on the way. I walked straight toward it, tugging Sarah with me.

"Time to wake up, time to wake up," she chanted, which was off-putting. "Timetowakeup oh God pleaseletmewake—huh?"

That 'huh?' because we were back in the lab. Which in its own way was probably just as startling to poor Sarah, but at least…

"Oh thank God!" She was staring down at her phone as if it held the answers to every question in the universe. "My feed's back!"

…she knew she was back in the present.

"Ta-dah! Or something." I waved at the assembled techs, who loved playing it like time travel was no big deal and fooled no one. "Hi, guys."

"Dammit, Joan! I bet it would take you another forty-five minutes. I owe Warren twenty pounds."

"I hate you, Karen," I said sweetly.

"What the *fuck* is going on?" Sarah screamed, because that's what Losties do.

"Have fun, you crazy kids," I told them, and left, because that's what I do. When I wasn't wishing for a swift death while in the grip of a migraine, but that's another topic for another time.

CHAPTER THREE

(A nd that time is now!)
I've been having migraines since I was fourteen. It hasn't been fun.

It's not just the headache and the nausea. It's the bag of hell that comes with it:

sensitivity to light ("Turn off that light before I throw—too late.")

sensitivity to sound ("Turn off the TV before I throw—too late.")

aphasia ("Turn up that beaver before you jump—now later.")

and a crushing pain that feels like someone is jabbing a pencil an inch deep into the side of my skull over and over and over and over and over.

People used to kill themselves to be rid of them back in the day. Most of them were women, who had been soothed by their "doctors" into thinking the problem was in their head, no pun intended.

If you suffer through them, you know how bad the pain can get. And if you're willing to medicate the problem, you'll try damned near anything. Imitrex. Stadol. Zomig. Frova. Axert.

And Maxipan (which I definitely didn't first mispronounce as Maxipad). It was a new drug, neither an opiate nor a triptan nor an ergotamine. It was plodding its way through human testing, and the reason I was able to try it was because my best friend, Lisa Harris, M.D., had won the Online Poker Series when she was eighteen.

Lisa was a prodigy, those children you read about who are composing sonnets at age four and graduating college at thirteen. As she herself would describe her life, "I was born of a long and distinguished line of trailer-dwelling substance abusers." She never knew her father, and took care of her mother until the lady overdosed on a diabolical cocktail of methamphetamine and Oxycontin. We met as kids when we were both desperately ashamed of our home lives and desperately determined to hide the details from the world; to say we clicked is to say Godiva makes chocolate.

Long story short: once her mother was in the ground, Lisa took some of the money she'd won online and bought a ticket to Vegas. Six months after that, she was using *those* winnings to pay for the number one medical school in the world, Oxford University.

Do I have to tell you she sailed through? And graduated at the top of her class, then went straight into a Neuro residency? And kidnapped me, sort of?

She wanted to study the effects of addiction on the brain, which was understandable. And then fix the brain in question, which sounded impossible. She was, essentially, determined to find the cure for addiction. Along the way, she learned quite a bit about migraines. (She also frequently repelled me with casual chit-chat about teratomas, echinococcis, and naegleria fowleri, all terms I wish I hadn't Googled.)

All that to say she had great sympathy for my suffering and got me into the Maxipan study as soon as she heard about it. "This is the most promising drug in thirty years," she promised, "and the friggin' NIH is still holding it up. Pre-clinical's been done for years, buncha bureaucratic cockheads."

"I don't understand anything you just said."

"Don't sweat it. I'll get you into the group that isn't snarfing down sugar pills."

"But I love sugar pills."

"Shut up and sign this."

Lisa could be, um, abrupt. But that was fine. We weren't the type of friends who went shopping together, or gossiped about our love lives, or indulged in other stereotypical chick pal behavior. We clicked at once, and bonded over our very different but equally strange childhoods. When she found out she was Oxford-bound, she arranged for me to join her. Typical of Lisa, she didn't ask. Just bought my ticket and e-mailed me the receipt. That's how I found out I was headed to Oxfordshire, population 175,021, sixty miles from London.

That was fine with me. Does that sound passive? I can see how it could be construed that way. But I'd been drifting for the last few years, my studies were stalled, my parents were gone, there was nothing keeping me home. I was more than ready to leave Wisconsin and see a bit more of the world. England sounded swell.

And it was. Twenty-first century England, I mean. Sixteenth century England, not so much. Although, I have to say... the food is amazing.

CHAPTER FOUR

Renaissance Festivals are equal parts wonderful and terrible.

Nothing embodies those dichotomies better than what I was wearing (stifling, period-appropriate clothing) and what I was craving (a turkey leg).

"I'm not following the math," Lisa said, which was a lie (she aced college trig in 7ᵗʰ grade). "Letting your boobs hang out = turkey drumstick?"

I examined said boobs in the mirror. The corset *was* pushing them a little high; they were yanked so far up, my chin could give them shade. "It sounds silly when you say it like that."

"That's the only time it sounds silly, huh?"

I ignored the sarcasm, left my room and searched for my purse. I found it in the kitchen, which was not okay, since it belonged in the bathroom. "First, stop snacking out of my purse."

Lisa actually pulled off looking wounded, like *I* was the junk food craving roommate with low impulse control. "But you've always got something defuckingliscious in there."

"Second, stop making up words. Third, this is very simple. If I'm in costume, I get a discount. Turkey drumsticks are almost ten dollars apiece. I would also like to wash them down with a few Cokes, and then perhaps a hot fudge sundae for dessert."

"How medieval!"

"And I'm on a budget."

"If you're on a budget, why spend three hundred bucks on ... oh my God." An expression of vague horror was creeping across Lisa's face. That was rare; in medical school, Lisa had occasionally showed up at my place with brains on her clothing. And once, memorably, a foreskin.

"You already had it!" she was saying. "You ... you *brought it with you*. You only brought two suitcases to the other side of the world and one of them had that dress!"

"My mother," I replied. That was all I said, and all I had to say. She'd never met my folks—she couldn't have, we met during The After—but we talked. Of course we talked. Complaining about our weird childhoods was our favorite thing. "I have to go. Thanks again for the car."

Lisa waved me away. Her thoughts on money were the same now as when she didn't have any: it was a tool. The more you had, the better. If you didn't have much, make do. There were professional chefs who didn't have her gift with ramen noodles and leftover pizza.

One of the first things she'd done when we moved here was buy a car (she'd found us a house to share before she bought my ticket) and she was generous with it. I never even had to ask; she didn't care if I drove as long as I filled the gas tank when I was finished. It was a side of her she tried to keep hidden.

The niceties over, I headed for the U.K.'s version of the American Renaissance Festival: the Medieval Festival at Herstmonceux Castle. For some reason, the unofficial weather rule at these venues was always one of two choices: too hot, or too chilly and muddy. Today, too hot had won the coin toss. Given that I had heavy cloth touching every part of my body from neck to toes, that was unfortunate.

But a tall Coke with lots of crushed ice would fix that in no time. Go to Hell, authenticity.

But I'd no sooner started sipping (after enduring the authentic barmaid behind the counter shout the *de rigueur*, non-authentic "Ten pounds for the king!") when it started. And I know it's a cliché, but it's also accurate: my stomach sank.

As always, at first there was no pain, just disorientation, because out of nowhere I'd see squiggly lines on the edge of my vision. Those opaque lines would eventually grow and crowd each other until I could barely see out of my right eye. The sun instantly seemed several million miles closer. And sounds instantly seemed several million decibels louder. Which meant the aphasia was *en route*.

I didn't always suffer the aphasia phase, thank God, because in a way, that was the most maddening symptom. I knew exactly what I wanted to say, I could even picture the words in my mind, but the only thing that made it out of my mouth was gibberish. And the harder I tried to focus and speak coherently, the worse it got. It was like downing three tequila shots and then trying to sober up with daiquiris: doomed to failure.

I had about half an hour before I was doomed to incoherence and could not be trusted behind a wheel. Any wheel. Under any circumstances. The phrase "do not operate heavy machinery" more than applied.

It was an hour's drive back to the house. Which meant I could look forward to lying down in the backseat of Lisa's car on a sunny day, to sleep or just endure until the pain eased. Then I remembered the new drug she'd started me on, fished the small bottle out of my purse, got it open after a brief struggle (where was a dexterous first grader when you needed one?) and obediently popped a pill.

Ah! Candy coated, excellent. The worst part about meds is forcing what feels like a piece of round chalk the size of a quarter down your throat.

Down it went, chased with Coke. At least I didn't need a bathroom, and thank goodness. Back in the day, if a visitor asked a staff member where the bathrooms were, their response was to seize the unwitting person's hand and haul ass toward the porta potties while shrieking, "Privy run! Priiiiiivy run!" This was considered a wonderful (authentic!) way for employees to interact with guests, until the first heart attack. Now the employees just quietly point in the general direction of the land o'loos.

I started toward the field they had converted to a parking lot, and then the squiggly lines on the edge of my vision seemed to get much brighter, so much so that I could barely see and...

... then I wasn't there.

CHAPTER FIVE

Someone had moved all the cars out of the parking field. And replaced them with thousands of people. Which was amazing…think of the man hours! The coordinated effort! The—

(What is happening?)

And where did all the horses come from? I had to hop aside before I was clip-clopped into oblivion. At least the migraine aura had receded; for a second it had seemed as if those bright jagged lines had swallowed my entire world.

They also moved the play jousting arena. And—whoa. The guys doing it this year were a lot bigger. And wearing a lot more armor. And their horses didn't look like anyone should try to entice them with sugar cubes. Quite the no-nonsense ensemble this year.

And tents. Many more tents than I'd noticed earlier. If the festival normally looked like part of a small town, now it seemed more like a small city.

Which made no sense.

So it had to be the meds.

And since I didn't feel like I was about to vomit, and since the aura wasn't getting bigger, and since I had no idea where the car was, and since this was shaping into a weird day, I figured I might as well do some exploring. Perhaps a turkey drumstick would ease my pain. (Sadly, my Coke had gotten lost along the way.)

I followed part of the crowd, marveling: the Medieval Festival at Herstmonceux Castle really stepped it up this year. And in next to no time, I was watching two male actors (crowns were the dead giveaway) pretending to wrestle. Then it clicked, and I realized what they were reenacting. I was right in the middle of one of the most expensive pantomimes in the history of human events, the Field of the Cloth of Gold. To wit (whatever that meant), Henry VIII's impromptu wrestling match with Francis I. Which was worth watching if for no other reason than because Francis I had famously knocked Henry VIII on his ass. Even as the watching crowd gasped and groaned, I couldn't take my eyes off the men. The actor playing Henry VIII was very, very good. When Francis threw the English king on his rump, the looks on the mens' faces were hilarious. Henry: flabbergasted outrage. Francis: smug squared.

Henry had the look of a man whom no one had laid a hand on without permission since his father died. It was the look of a man whose ass is kissed so often and so hard, the thought of being knocked on it is insupportable. It was enough to make you laugh, and I did. For some reason, I was the only one in the crowd who saw the hilarity.

Queen Katherine (the first of three Cathys he'd marry) and Queen Claude quickly intervened, gently but completely separating the men under the guise of "oh, gosh, wasn't that fun, time for a drink, maybe? and no more wrestling? boys? okay?"

It worked (*authentic!*) and the kings allowed themselves to be led from wrestling and toward treaty signing. The show was over, so I wandered outside the big-enough-to-be-its-own-castle-sized tent.

The smell hit me all over again; a powerful mix of food, fire cooking the food, too many people, shit, horses, and more people. I shrugged it off; everything smelled like too much when I was in the grip of a migraine. At least the pain was holding off. Which was a blessing indeed, because it let me focus on my surroundings. They were worth the focus, since everyone I saw was putting every effort into making it seem just like …

Um.

Where are the power lines? Sure, we were in the country, but I couldn't see a single utility pole. Just a cool blue sky broken by clouds …

Also: where were the lights? Though it was midday and lights weren't needed, I couldn't see anything that would work when it finally did get dark.

(Even the … huh.)

Even the signs were authentic. No plastic, no metal, they were all made of wood, and the archaic misspellings were an interesting touch. Some were so misspelled I couldn't read them.

(There weren't this many people around before you took that pill.)

Oh, of course there were.

(Nobody moves 400 cars in twenty seconds.)

Well, that was harder to argue. But what was the alternative? That I had magically been transferred from 21st century Great Britain to 16th century France? That was beyond ridiculous.

(Jesus Christ who put a harbor there?)

I rubbed my forehead and looked again. I might swallow the argument that someone had moved four hundred cars and gotten rid of all the metal and plastic and electric lights and power lines while my back was turned. But then they … dug a harbor? And quickly produced a bay for the harbor they dug? And immediately filled it with period-appropriate ships? But not a single modern boat?

"Dammit," I managed, and barely recognized the weak thready voice as my own. "What's happening?"

"Are you well, fair lady?"

"*God* no," I managed, and turned to face who'd asked.

A good-looking teenager had separated himself from the teeming throng and was reaching for me, not quite touching. He was lean and tall, with hair the color of a Cherry Coke, a beverage I would dearly love to be guzzling right now. He was simply dressed in dark colors, hatless and, going by the sober clothing, an apprentice to a scholar

(an actor pretending to be an apprentice)

(no, it's real, this is real)

or a clerk-in-training. A job requiring brains, and only occasional brawn.

I stared at his hair and thought, I wish I had my Coke. I used it to wash down the meds and then I lost it when I…when I

(traveled back in time)

ended up here and I really, really wish I still had it because I could because I

(meds?)

"Oh thank God," I told him. We were exactly the same height, so I was gazing into a pair of startled blue eyes. I'd grabbed his hands at one point and was hanging on so tightly he winced. I let go at once. "It's the meds!"

He was rubbing his knuckles, but at least he wasn't shouting for a constabulary. And I had to award points for his composure, when mine was in rags. "Who are the meds, my lady?"

"Of course it is! Oh. I thought you were going to ask something else. It's my new migraine medication. It's not even on the market yet, and I can guess why." Lisa was going to burst a brain cell when I told her about the hallucinations. "Your accent is awful, by the way."

"Perhaps you would like to be bled," he suggested.

"I can't think of anything I'd like less. Did you hear what I said about your accent?"

"Yes, my lady."

"I like your costume."

He looked down at himself and seemed almost surprised. "Ah. These ... these are not technically mine."

"Well, no. It's a costume. And you know what's silliest?"

"No, my lady."

"This!" I made a windmilling gesture with my arms and he leaned back so I didn't clip him on the nose. "It's all for nothing! This is supposed to fix it so England and France are best friends forever. And it's a joke. One that goes on too long, like Family Guy."

"I do not understand."

The more he talked, the better I could understand what he was saying. To be frank, at first he sounded as if he had jammed walnuts up his nose to fight a head cold.

"Okay, it's like this. He—what?" I caught a couple of the locals staring at me. "Don't stare; it's rude. It's for a masque." The one that will never take place because this is a migraine-induced hallucination. The teenager with hair like lustrous Coca-Cola gestured and we headed in the other direction, gradually pulling away from the crowd. "You know what this is? All this? It's two weeks of dick-measuring. That's all. That's the entire point."

"And Dick is ...?"

"Shush." I was on a roll, giddy from the high of whatever experimental drug my roommate gave me. "Henry and Francis are just trying to impress each other. That's it. That's all this is. It's why there are five hundred horsemen and three thousand soldiers for each monarch. It's why there are jousts. Banquets. It's why people are wearing cloth of gold, and why that cloth is decorated with pearls the size of jawbreakers."

"Jawbr—?"

"Shush. It's why there are two thousand eight hundred tents for the peons. Thousands of retainers. And one addled college student. I mean, there's glamping, and then there's this."

"I do not understand any of that," he admitted.

"Is that because of my horrible American accent or because I'm deep in migraine aphasia?" Most of the locals I'd met in the U.K. were perfectly polite, but Lisa and I were aware our accents were a bit "nails-on-chalkboard" to them.

"Nor that," he added.

Oh, who cared? I was going to enjoy this mind-trip while it lasted. I normally had all the coherence of a drunken hyena when I had a migraine. Being able to babble was kind of fun. The lack of pain was even more fun.

"All the players are here, too," I marveled. "Two kings, two queens. Suffolk. Buckingham. At least two Boleyns. Wolsey. And—"

"Cardinal Wolsey," the teenager corrected me, sounding testy. Which was odd; out of the provocative things I'd been blaring, why did that get a rise out of Coke Hair? When I paused to look at him, he added, "My father."

"Oh. Is that why you're here?"

To my surprise, he ducked his head and flushed blotchy pink from eyebrows to chin. "Yes. But not for the reason you think. If he sees me I'll—I'll be in rather a lot of trouble. But..." He raised his dark head and looked around. "Who could miss this, if there be any way to attend? Who would ever leave, if they could remain?"

"Oh. Well, if you're only here for a show, and have no expectations of lasting peace, and don't think too hard about the waste of time and money, then this is the place to be." He grinned, so I decided to lighten up. "Tents!"

"Jousts."

"Multiple royal persons!"

"Multiple composers."

"Multiple priests!"

"Feasts."

"Multiple courses!" I had forgotten about the food. Oh, very well, maybe the charade wasn't a complete waste of everyone's time. Maybe this army of hangers-on could actually contribute to the betterment of society, to wit, geese, capons, veal, venison, mutton, lamb. For appetizers. Do not get me started on the many, many desserts. Syllabubs. Strawberries swimming in cream. Sugared almonds. Simnel cakes.

All this, not to mention a disposable castle, thousands of sheep (mutton!), thirty-some priests, at least two court composers (which was to be expected), two monkeys (which was not), and thousands of retainers.

"So we agree: there's a lot going on."

"Yes," he said, smiling.

"And it's a good show to see."

"Oh yes!"

"And it's still all for nothing. Within three years, they'll be at war. Again. Wolsey will set up an alliance with the queen's nephew, and Charles will break his engagement to Princess Mary. Huuuge waste of time and money, all of it. Also it occurs to me that I've done nothing but babble."

"I like listening to your babble," he said, and blushed again. Adorable! "And I am remiss. Thomas Wynter." And he sketched a shallow bow, so quickly and carelessly it was like a handshake; he didn't have to think about it.

"What?"

"My name. Thomas Wynter." He didn't bow again, thank goodness. "Might I have yours?"

"Oh. Right. It's Joan Howe."

"Like the saint?" he asked with a shy smile.

Adorable! And a bit deluded. "Like my late great aunt."

"If you will permit me, your clothing…unusual. Is it a masque?"

"Sure." The full-color cast-of-thousands masque going on in my head right this minute. "It's—what're you…?"

He'd paled, taken a few steps back, then jogged toward the nearest cluster of tents. When I saw the donkeys, I got it: Cardinal Wolsey was nigh. On his donkey. (His donkey was also nigh.) I barely got a glimpse of the man, he went by so quickly, and in the company of so many—that donkey was like a greyhound hybrid.

And something else: my subconscious was a twisted, sick place. Sure, I had often suspected as much, but it was sobering to get proof. Out of all the things I could have hallucinated, both positive

(Rome! Gotham Bar and Grill! National Strawbery Festival!)

and negative

(food poisoning after Taco Bell! squirrel stew!)

my mind seized on the Field of the Cloth of Gold? Something I was heartily sick of hearing about before I was in training bras?

And don't get me started on my field of study. I'm not going to get into it, but suffice it to say that part of me has never left the living room where my mom and I watched all things Tudor. Not least because whenever I had to write a book report or a paper, I invariably chose the Tudors, supplementing my living room "research" with actual research. Yes, I'm lazy.

Since Wolsey's bastard had cut our chat short, I decided to head back toward the trees lining the parking lot. Not that the parking lot was there, but it was someplace to go while I tried to figure out why my mind was working the way it had.

I was so busy contemplating my disgusting subconscious it took me a few seconds to notice the sparkling spots were starting up again. Did that mean the meds were wearing off? Or that the sun was in my eyes? Or that the migraine was finally settling down to bring the pain? I took a few experimental steps toward the sparkles and

came

back.

CHAPTER SIX

"—lost *another* one?"

"Er." For some reason, I was in a lab with frantic men and women rushing back and forth. The Field of the Cloth of Gold had vanished, if it had ever been there. Well, of course it had *been* there, just not... you know. Recently.

"—can't keep track of them!"

"Hello?" There were screens everywhere, a staggering amount of tech, white coats, nametags, paperwork, half-empty Starbucks cups, and—was that a microwave? They could afford state of the art equipment but not a separate kitchen? Was it even safe to be around this stuff with a cup of coffee in one hand?

"How the hell are we going to document this?"

"You're worried about documenting? Now?"

Is this insanity? I might be insane. Which is kind of interesting. And, according to my late mother, inevitable. Hats off, Mom, you called this one.

But I wasn't the only one who had succumbed to insane hysteria, given by the people sweating. And yelling. And running. And yelling. None of whom had noticed me.

"I'm confused," I managed in a small voice.

"How about you worry about *your* paperwork?"

"Fuck your mother, Warren!"

I tried again. "I am very confused!"

"Nice, Karen. Reeeeal nice. Did they ever mail your diploma, or did the online college just send you an e-card?"

"I am very confused right now!"

Karen's response, which seemed as if it would have been acerbic, was cut off as she stared. They all stared. I didn't want to be left out, so I returned the gapes. *Things to remember: to get their attention, shriek until if feels like you tore something in your throat.*

"Holy shit, this one came back," Karen—a dainty, big-eyed blonde all but swimming in a lab coat too big for her—managed in a voice that sounded like she was losing all her air.

"Damn right! Wait, 'this one'?"

"What happened? Who did you see? Where did you end up?"

I stepped down from the dais (later I was to learn it was called, without irony, the launch pad). "I was really hoping you guys would be *answering* that set of questions."

Another lab wretch darted into the warehouse-sized, frigid room from somewhere, skidded to a halt when he saw me, and said, "Holy shit, this one came back."

"That is a worrisome phrase I don't like hearing one bit," I announced. "Certainly not twice."

While I whined, I was looking around the lab which, even if it hadn't been chock full o'time travel tech, would have been interesting. I was in the middle of an enormous circular room and hadn't a clue what all the machinery around me did, but it looked impressive. There were at least three short flights of four to five stairs leading up deeper into machinery, there were red and purple lights coming from…somewhere…and everything was blinking and beeping. I could see enormous flat screens dominating the far wall and it looked as if they were all set to different news channels around the country, covering disappearances, accidents, the Tower of London, and ... the Medieval Festival at Herstmonceux Castle?

And I noticed something I wouldn't have thought possible: the lab was strangely beautiful, like how the Christmas tree looked when you ran out of one kind of lights (white, plain) and had to add a different string (colored, blinking) halfway through. At first you thought it'd be a mess, but then you see the modified chaos and step back a little and ... it's nice.

"Are you okay?"

I looked at the one who'd asked—the fellow who'd been squabbling with Karen—and replied, "I have no idea. Back from what? What's going on? And unrelated to anything that just happened, you have booze here, yes?"

As it happened, they did.

Chapter Seven

I was always terrible at science. Any science. All science. I didn't even like science fiction. So everything Dr. Warren told me was *soaring* over my head.

"This is incredible," he kept saying, "you're incredible, I can't believe this!" Before I could ask, he slopped more vodka into my ginger beer.

"So it was a mistake?" This, out of all the scientific jargon, was the part I kept going back to. It sounded so ... anticlimactic. "An accident?" Like taking a right instead of a left? Or dropping a glass? Or inventing the cure for polio? Wait, that was on purpose ...

"It sounds insane, right? We weren't even trying to invent time travel!"

"What *were* you—"

"Matter transition! Not—" He made a gesture that encompassed me (sitting across from him in what I assumed was the break room) and the open doorway behind me (which led to the lab I'd fallen into). "Not what we got."

"Matter transition?" Argh, science. "Do you mean teleporting?"

"Something like that. We thought we were sending matter somewhere else—"

"You were," I pointed out.

"Yes!" He nearly shrieked it, because he was an excitable fellow. Cute, too, which wasn't relevant, but I wasn't a stone. Mussed brown hair, and he needed a haircut because he was constantly shoving his shaggy bangs out of his dark eyes. He had long lashes that are always wasted on men, and was pale—which I'd expect from a lab geek—but not sickly. He was about six feet tall, with great forearms.

Yes. I admit to having a thing for muscled, slightly hairy forearms. Especially when the owner of said slightly hairy forearms has unbuttoned his cuffs and pushed them to the elbow while gesturing wildly and peppering his chitchat with "I can't believe you made it back alive, you're wonderful!"

Except, because he was from New York (state *and* city, if I had to guess), it came out "yuh made it back uh-live, yuh *won*-dah-full!"

I giggled; I couldn't help it. "I'm sorry," I said at once. "It's been such a long day." Understated understatement. "A strange, long day with too many surprises and not enough grain alcohol. And it's been some time since I've heard an Ameri—"

"New York."

"Ah-ha! I mean, oh?" I forced a casual cough: *ack-kack!* "Are you from the United States? I definitely didn't notice you were dropping your Rs all over the place."

He grinned as he shoved his glasses (black horn rims that only Buddy Holly and tall, cut scientists could pull off) up. "Sure you didn't." *Sure yuh dint.* "I like yours, too. I keep hoping you'll say 'you betcha' or 'oofta'."

"I. Will. Die. First." Thanks to the classic *Fargo* TV show (and the older, classic-er movie), my Midwestern twang was actually considered desirable in some circles. This never—repeat, never—failed to send Lisa into hysterics.

("We sound like farmers with head colds!" she'd shriek, pointing at whomever made the mistake of complementing our accents. "And you know it! *You know it and think it's cute, oh my good God that's hilarious!*")

"Listen." Warren ("Naw, not Dr. Warren. Just Warren. Because I hate my first name.") had leaned forward and squeezed one of my hands. I realized I was still sticky from the Coke I'd lost when I fell through time. Jumped through time. Collapsed into time. "I'm just so glad ya made it back. I can't tell ya how exciting this is for us. I've got so many questions."

"You're not the only one. Can we—" I cut myself off as one of his mad scientist colleagues—Karen, the tiny blonde dwarfed by her lab coat (and the one who had told Warren to have marital relations with his mother)—hurried in with what looked like a ream of legal paper.

"Hello again," she said. "Sorry you had to wait so long."

Was I waiting? I thought it was just that I hadn't left yet. "For…?"

Warren leaned forward. "For the paperwork," he said quickly.

"It…" I trailed off as she dropped the paperwork in front of me—thud! "It almost sounds like you think *I'm* going to be filling all this out. I'm going to share something with you: I hate paperwork." When Warren opened his mouth, I added, "Don't say 'everyone does' or 'I hear you' because you mildly dislike paperwork. I. Hate it." Like plague. Like famine. Like when they censor the sex out of a movie but not the over-the-top violence.

"We can—you won't have to do it by yaself."

I squinted. "Jesus, what font size is that? Eight?" I must have sounded pretty aghast, as they both winced. "And it's single-spaced? *Single-spaced?*" Apparently, I escaped persecution in the 16th century only to be blinded in the 21st.

"Ah. Well…"

"You see the irony, right? You guys have invented time travel but haven't mastered electronic documents?"

"A task for another day." Karen coughed into her fist. "For, um, legal purposes—"

I could feel my eyebrows trying to climb off my forehead. "Legal purposes? Involving accidental time travel? So there's precedent? I don't think there's precedent." There'd better *not* be precedent. "I can honestly say that when I left home this morning I didn't think I'd fall into the 16th century and then need a lawyer."

"Oh no-no-no," Karen hastened to assure me. "It's just— we need—"

I'd managed to squint through the first paragraph and almost laughed. "You're trying to get me to sign non-disclosure agreements."

"An NDA, yes, for your protection and—"

"Yours, I imagine," I replied dryly. "First, when anyone in Corporate tells you the non-dis agreement is for *your* protection, they are lying. Second, why does a random think tank in the wilds of the London suburbs need legal protection?" I looked up at both of them. Warren, who seemed pained, and Karen, who seemed a combo of thrilled and terrified. "Oh."

They just looked at me.

"I see." And wished I didn't. My dazed relief was starting to shift into anger. "How many have you lost?"

Warren took a breath. "We think—we think three. Not counting you."

My eyebrows arched so fast and so high it actually hurt a little. "You *think*?"

Again, the Doctors Frankenstein traded a glance. Then they turned their attention to me, and I saw it in their faces in a way I hadn't noticed before: they were scared. Actual certified geniuses were frightened and tiptoeing around me—literally. *Even though I'm back, I don't think my troubles are over. And they don't, either.*

I sighed. I had a trick for dealing with non-dis agreements, so I'd just employ it. As for the rest of it... "You should just gird your panties and tell me."

"Okay. Well." Warren freshened my juice with extra booze, because he was a god among men. "Here's the situation."

CHAPTER EIGHT

M an has long invented things by mistake.
Which is why I'm a part-time time traveler and potato chip connoisseur.

The pacemaker, penicillin, bubble gum, X-rays, maxi pads, potato chips... all screw-ups. (In the case of the latter, a delicious screw-up.) Which brings me to the Information Technology for Culture and History, and yes, that spells I.T.C.H.

To make a long story slightly less long, a gaggle of physicists and researchers and experts in quantum mechanics decided to put their mad scientist brains together to form one gigantic mad scientist brain and solve that pesky "how come we can't teleport like they do in *Star Trek*?" problem. Because, as Warren explained to me, teleportation was the new alchemy.

"But alchemy was a failure. No one ever figured out how to turn metal into gold."

"Well, yeah," he admitted. "But they sure had fun trying to make it work."

Wasting fortunes and lifetimes on the impossible = fun, apparently.

"And we're not all about work here. We stream sci-fi flicks on Fridays! And the company retreats are amazing. And there's the sundae bar. We get great funding."

Warren took my bemused expression for interest and went on to explain, "At first, we could only teleport information. But then we had a real breakthrough involving something-something quantum entanglement. And that of course led to something quantum teleportation, and at first we were worried about something something, but that turned out to be a minor problem, and it was ultimately moot because wormholes something but worth the trouble 'cuz it led us to something something." I must have looked glazed, because he paused. "Not going too fast for you?"

"Not at all," I lied.

"Great! So anyways, we knew we were on the right track with the something quantum something. Or so we thought! But we were actually sending things back in time."

Was I a 'thing' now? "But you weren't getting the things back," I guessed.

"Exactly!" He beamed, which I didn't deserve. I wasn't getting it, not really. "I don't have to tell you we were getting damn discouraged. But we kept at it, y'know? We figured 'what's the worst that can happen?'"

"Like when Tesla kept teleporting top hats and cats."

"Sorry, what?"

"Next Friday, stream *The Prestige*. And in response to 'what's the worst that can happen', stream *The Fly*."

"Even now, we're still figuring it all out. There's so much we don't know!" *That* part I understood. "Opening the first slide was like knockin' over the first domino."

"Except they're dominos that sometimes scoop people up and dump them in the past."

"Well. Yeah."

"And I'm the only one who rode the domino back." I made a mental note to use another analogy, because the domino thing was dumb.

He nodded. "Yes."

"So would you say it's *Terminator* time travel or *Back to the Future* time travel?"

"What?"

"Please tell me it's not a *Twelve Monkeys* scenario," I fretted. "Or—oh God!—*Groundhog Day*." The thought of reliving any single day of my adolescence, or my senior prom, over and over made me break out in goosebumps. "If it's *Groundhog Day*, be prepared for me to have a severe freak out."

"No, I—we—" He trailed off and shook his head. "Well, I'm not sure. Definitely not *Groundhog Day*, though. But listen, I've gone into this about all I can until you ... you know." He nodded at the ream of paper with my name on every page. "So if ya could—"

"Yes, we should talk about that."

"And we can! I'll answer as best I can once you—"

"Shush."

Warren blinked his baby browns at me. (His peepers were the exact color of a Godiva milk chocolate open oyster, which under less weird circumstances would have been distracting in all the best ways.) He'd been expecting any number of reactions—hysterics, shock, vows to hire a platoon of lawyers, perhaps a fist to the nose—but not that one. "Did you just shush me?"

"First, I'm not blindly signing these." I tapped the pile and briefly regretted biting my fingernails last night. "I'll be taking this home and reading every page." And giving myself another migraine. "And from what I've skimmed, I can tell you right now I won't submit to a physical or lab tests of any kind." I'd spent years avoiding doctors (as well as Wisconsin Child Protective Services), and it was a habit I wasn't inclined to break. Especially when *I* hadn't done anything wrong.

"But—"

"It's my fault," I said kindly. "That you think this is a debate. It's not. I'm explaining what I will and won't do. It's not a discussion. It's a list."

"But—"

"Fine." That was a new voice, from a redhead who was built like a fire hydrant: short, blocky. Possibly full of water. He was pouring himself a cup of coffee. From his post-gulp grimace, a bad cup of coffee. "That's fine."

"Ian, we—"

"She's not our employee or our prisoner or our property, Warren." This in an exasperated tone that immediately endeared him to me. "We can't make her do a thing. We certainly can't make her sign anything. We should consider ourselves lucky if she doesn't sue."

Fat chance. A lifetime of avoiding authority figures and, by association, lawyers pretty much guaranteed I wouldn't sue. No need to share that, though.

Plus my new hydrant-shaped friend had a Scottish accent, so I could have listened to him talk all afternoon. Speaking of afternoon… "How long?"

"Sorry?"

"She's wondering how long she was gone," Smartguy McRedhead said. He turned back to me, blinking hazel eyes, under which were a pair of spectacular under-eye bags that were so dark he looked like he'd been punched (twice). The think tank gang had been working hard and skipping naps, no question.

In fact, I was just now noticing how they were all various degrees of rumpled, and/or pale, and/or haggard. Trying to bring people back from the past via a gate you accidentally opened and can't control must be exhausting. "Don't worry, lass. That particular drop was only an hour or so. Oh. Apologies." He stepped up to our cozy (and sticky—somebody really liked making a mess with their sugar packets) table and extended a hand he could palm a basketball with. "Dr. Ian Holt."

"Joan Howe. So you can tell how long I was gone, but not who else disappeared, and you can't control where the—the slides, you called them? You can't tell when they'll open, or where they'll dump people or when they'll bring them back or even if they'll bring them back."

He shrugged. "It's complicated."

"No, making a soufflé that doesn't collapse on itself is complicated." And I'll have you know I perfected the art of the elusive soufflé in just under seven months. "This? All this?" I gestured to him, Warren, their colleagues, the breakroom. "It's impossible."

He shrugged again, and showed me a rueful smile. "We're living in the age of impossible."

"No, *you* are. I'm just an innocent bystander who wasn't paying attention to the construction going on and fell into a manhole." How does that happen to the same person literally *and* figuratively? (It wasn't all bad. The City of St. Paul cut me a nice check.) "How do you know when someone goes missing?"

"Missing person reports."

I just looked at them.

"I know how inadequate that sounds."

"Not sounds. *Is.*"

"The first slide opened just over two weeks ago. We've been working around the clock ever since. Which is why we were so relieved to see you show up safe and sound."

Sound might be inaccurate. "So you hear 'local woman goes missing' and write that name down somewhere—"

"Wow," Warren said, looking glum. "Sounds really bad when ya put it like that."

"—but what are you doing to get the others back?"

"Everything we can," Warren said, and he was so earnest I believed him. Of course, later I found out "everything we can" meant "we're utterly clueless".

But that was a lesson for another day.

The rest of my "visit" was anti-climactic. My brain was buzzing with everything I'd seen and everything they'd told me, and also the caffeine (I'd switched from booze to my elixir of life). They all wanted to get back to whatever it was they were doing before I fell into their lab and I wanted to go home.

"We can't make you keep this quiet, of course," Ian said. "But we'd sure appreciate it, lass."

"Who'd believe me?"

They saw the sense in that because they nodded in unison. "We'll be in touch."

He probably hadn't meant that to sound vaguely ominous. "Er—why?"

"To pick up our NDA if nothing else," Warren teased. "And to make sure the teleportation process didn't give you a tumor."

"Jesus."

"Sorry, bad joke."

"Yes, it was." And now I had something new to worry about: the possible side effects of time travel while taking new medication, followed by booze and paperwork and Cokes with lots of ice.

They walked me down a long corridor that would have been a mezzanine in any building not engaged in perfecting time travel. I realized that half the lab—which I was now looking down on—was underground, for science-esque reasons that were beyond me. We came into a pleasant, comfortable lobby filled with natural light and an abundance of plants that wouldn't have been out of place in a bank lobby. They even had a receptionist, and the walls were covered with Employees of the Month and pictures of everyone at various retreats. Because when they weren't meddling with the space/time continuum, they were big on team-building exercises.

We all shook hands and into the cab I went. I'd need to pick up my car, preferably before I had my nervous break-down. I looked out the back window, but they'd scurried inside, and the building was fast receding. (Well. The *building* wasn't receding. Obviously. Just the cab, just me. But that's how it felt. And looked.)

So that was that. An exciting interlude that was already starting to feel like a dream. Not a bad dream, but one you kept thinking about. And one that was definitely over.

CHAPTER NINE

I love living in England for the same reason I hated living in Wisconsin: history.

I'll elaborate. Lisa rented us a "cottage", which is British for "amazing house/mansion built long ago in the country and out of the financial reach of most citizens". I don't know about you, but when I think "cottage", I think "Dad's tool shed, which looked like a battered tiny house and smelled like oil and cut grass and, one summer, skunk and marshmallows".

Not at all what Lisa and I are borrowing. The ad said it was a cottage "brimming with charm", and it was. It was also brimming with bricks, exposed woodwork, and fireplaces. We always used the side door, which you could get to by walking through a little garden (don't get excited—"garden" is Brit for yard; they'll refer to the mangiest, tiniest, saddest yard as a garden just to dash your hopes) to a white door that led into the kitchen.

The kitchen was also white, with red appliances and black, exposed beams, and the *de rigueur* Aga, along with a tiny kitchen table that seated two, which Lisa and I used as our *de facto* dining room. (The actual dining room was my office and Lisa's dissection lab/lair.) The kitchen led to the living room, complete with fireplace, built-in bookshelves stuffed with books (a fire hazard of staggering proportions), and some uncomfortable chintz-covered chairs. Every time I sat in one, it creaked and I would think, *Am I about to shatter a chair someone made in 1525? Will it take me down with it?* It could be nerve-racking, so mostly I just lolled on the couch.

All three bedrooms were upstairs and as they were decorated roughly the same (the walls painted white and the exposed beams painted black, so it was like sleeping in a zebra) and were roughly the same size, I took the one at the end of the hall, and Lisa grabbed the one on the right.

They were small—room for a double bed, a dresser, and an end table but not much else, with windows overlooking the back yar—garden, which was all we required. Neither of us were in the habit of, um, regularly entertaining visitors. Or stuffing closets (except there weren't any, just beautiful ancient wardrobes paneled in dark wood). So there was no need to turn random bedrooms into sensual dens of seduction. Plus we didn't have enough linens for that.

As for me, since The After, I liked things sparse; the only things on my walls were my father's aikido medals and my Michael Scott poster ("Would I rather be feared or loved? Easy, both. I want people to be afraid of how much they love me."). My other valuables—my parents' wedding rings and a .38 pistol I'd had shipped to myself once we were settled—I kept in a locked, fireproof strongbox beneath my bed. The gun was exceptionally illegal and I didn't want to know the strings Lisa had pulled or the cash she threw around to get it here. But we both felt safer knowing it was in the house, which was just dumb given the low crime rate. We were more likely to get struck by lightning than shot in the U.K. But that's the American mentality for you. I just didn't feel confident taking on an intruder with a spatula or a cricket bat.

There was an enormous bathroom next to my room, with a tub long enough and deep enough for me to submerge

and float (bliss!), a double vanity, and a towel warmer neither of us could figure out how to work. We used room tem-
perature towels, like savages.

So I was lucky enough to stay in a beautiful temporary
home in Henley-on-Thames, twenty miles from the university and zero miles from my job. In addition to being
my fairy godmother with a black American Express card,
Lisa had also gotten me a job as a medical transcriptionist,
which meant I transcribed tapes from medical exams, hospital intake notes, and the occasional autopsy, could do it in
my pajamas with my laptop, and set my own hours.

Must be costing a fortune, right? I probably had to tran-
scribe my fingers to the metacarpals? No. Lisa wouldn't take
a penny in rent from me, not so much as a farthing (they
still had those, yes?). She pointed out that whether I had
joined her or not, she still would have rented a house.

"Yes," I agreed, "but not a lush ancient three-bedroom
house that looks like something out of Masterpiece Theater."

"Shut up," was the logical rejoinder.

"No, *you* shut up!"

But after days of courteous discussion

("No, *you* shut up!")

we agreed that she was in charge of rent and utilities
and picking fights with our landlord (I was honestly starting
to feel bad for the guy), and I was in charge of grocery shopping and food prep. The post-meal clean-up chores would
be settled in the traditional manner, via Rock/Paper/
Scissors or a death duel. Since Lisa's idea of a nutritional
meal was a bowl of Cocoa Puffs with a V-8 chaser, it was a
hierarchy I could live with.

Money *was* going to be an issue, though. Much as I
enjoyed working from home, the pay wasn't wonderful, and
I was only working about twenty hours a week. Thanks to my

folks' careful planning, I didn't have much student debt but had yet to snag my degree. And I hadn't had much money when I'd followed Lisa to England.

Basically, I was one accident/car repair/unforeseen horror away from a negative bank balance. And since The After, I never liked living with an axe hanging over my head, even if the axe was figurative.

But I'm getting off track—all that to say I was mighty pleased to pop through the side door, even if it meant happening on Lisa caramelizing a strawberry Pop Tart over her Bunsen burner.

I greeted her with, "We talked about this."

"Naw. You talked about it."

"I'm sure it was an actual conversation."

"Naw."

"Dammit." No energy to be had for this nonsense. I opened the fridge and smiled at the delightful array of nom-nom-nom.

There was a hiss behind me as Lisa took a bite of her Pop Tart while it was still lava-hot. "Thet any thurkey drumthticks?"

"Hardly." That was the worst of my ordeal: I'd been cheated of the wonderful food. "I got a migraine before I even finished my Coke."

A clatter behind me. "You did? When was the onset? Did you take a Maxipan?" And at my giggle, she grumbled, "Grow up, idiot."

My giggle shriveled up and died as I realized this was the last thing I should be discussing with Lisa. She'd either think I was hallucinating (hello, 72-hour psych hold) or I was telling the truth (hello, violated confidential agreement).

I didn't like lying to her, would make an exception. I barely understood what had happened myself; I certainly couldn't explain it to anyone. Plus, I'd given my word. There was a time when my word was the only thing I had that was worth anything.

So I stuck with the basics: "Yes, I took one, but it didn't work."

By now I'd turned around, my arms laden with string cheese and Tim Tams, and saw she had unfolded her tablet and was fiddling with it. "You took it as soon as you saw the aura?"

"Yes." *Oh, string cheese. Whee have you been all my life?*

"With a Coke, I'm betting?"

"What else?" I would bathe in Coke if it wasn't impractical and sticky. The fact that doctors actually recommended it (drinking it, not bathing in it, as the sugar and the caffeine were known to ease migraine symptoms) was icing on the Coke.

"What time?"

Oh, around 1520. "Uh … about one o'clock."

She looked up from her notes with raised eyebrows. "Try to be more precise in the future, okay? 'About' isn't scientific. I know the aura's distracting, but next time whip out your phone and note the date and time. Even if you just say it out loud as a voice memo. It's important."

"Okay. Sorry."

She nodded, more sympathetic than annoyed. "And don't be discouraged. Not working this time doesn't mean it'll never work. That said, I'm sorry your Costumed Nerd Day got fucked. Couldn't have been any fun just hanging around waiting to feel better."

Well. Parts of it had been fun. Chit-chatting with Wolsey's bastard had been fun. But again: nothing I could discuss with my roommate. So I settled on, "It wasn't terrible."

Lisa bit into another Pop Tart with dark pink frosting the exact shade of her close-cropped hair. It should have looked silly in contrast with her angular frame, almond-shaped dark eyes, and olive complexion, but she pulled it off. She looked like an edgy Easter egg chick in all the best ways.

We ended the day as we often did, bragging/bitching about our day while devouring processed snack foods, and it took me months to realize that by keeping Lisa in the dark that night (and all the nights that came after), I had made the second biggest mistake of my life.

Hindsight, thou art a bitch.

CHAPTER TEN

I've never been a fan of the grid. So I didn't acquire a cell phone until three years ago, under duress.

Which is why I was alarmed to hear the thing click at me while I was transcribing a gerontology exam. Only three entities had that number: Lisa, me, and AT&T. And I could see at a glance that it wasn't any of them.

So I answered with my best reanimated corpse impersonation: "…"

"Hello? Ms. Howe?"

"…"

"Hello? It's Warren? From I.T.C.H.?"

"Hi!" Right. The paperwork. So four entities had my number. They must have read it and realized I hadn't taken it seriously. The jig, she was up. "I mean, hello. How are you?" Why was I so excited? It wasn't like he was going to ask me out. "And I think I know what this is about, but let me explain. Back when—"

"Oh, thank God, you're there. Could I get you to come—"

"Yes!"

"—to the Institute? We've—there's a problem."

"Dammit."

"What?"

"I said sure. What's wrong? Or is it something mysterious that you can't talk about over the phone?"

"It's incredibly mysterious and I can't talk about it over the phone."

Right. Made sense, actually, given what they were (accidentally) up to. "Well…" I looked at the notes I was transcribing. I was right in the middle of Mr. Benniman's benign prostatic hyperplasia. On the other hand, clinic notes weren't due back for days, and I'd already gotten through Mrs. Barclay's inflamed urethra and Jenny Fitzpatrick's cyclic vomiting syndrome. Plus, Warren had those terrific forearms. "Sure, I'll have to call a—"

"We're sending a car. And thank you, Miss Howe!"

"Joan."

"Thank you, Joan! See you soon!"

Warren was a screamer, apparently.

"You—*what?*"

"She's not getting it." This from Karen, who added insult to insult by not bothering to lower her voice. And why did her voice always sound like a slowly deflating balloon?

"I'm getting it, Karen," I snapped back. "I just can't believe what you're asking. So I'm repeating myself to express flabbergasted surprise and not a little trepidation. Any other human behavioral codes you need me to translate?"

She mumbled something that sounded like "*you're* a behavioral code", which was senseless. Which meant I'd probably heard her correctly.

"We're sorry." Warren held up his (bare! short-sleeved shirt!) forearms in a placating gesture. Or he was motioning for someone not to park there. "We know it's a lot to ask."

"Expecting me to pick up your dry cleaning for a month is a lot to ask. You're asking me to risk death by attempting the impossible. There's a significant difference."

He was nodding so hard my head ached in sympathy. "There is, there is, you're right."

"Stop agreeing with me. And roll your sleeves down, it's distracting."

"What?"

"Just explain what happened."

What happened was, another poor idiot tumbled into the abyss and was probably stumbling around the early 16th century, terrified and hoping they were going to wake up soon.

"And...?" Because it couldn't be what I was thinking. "What, you wanted a time travel consultant?"

"Not... exactly."

There was a silence that felt like it went on for an hour, because I was damned if I was going to break it. If they were going to propose what I assumed they had in mind, I had no intention of making it easier by bringing it up first.

Karen cracked like an egg hurled at a sidewalk. "Look, we need you to go back through the gate and try to find her. And bring her back."

I just looked at her, so Warren jumped in. "You're the only one who pulled it off."

"Out of sheer stupid luck."

"And you actually know a bit about the time period—"

"No, I know what movies and television and fiction books had to say about the time period. I'm not a historian." Yes. *A historian*, I said it like that. With a hard 'H', because I refused to say *uh nistorian*.

"But all that aside, the main thing is—"

"Because I didn't die, you've decided I'm qualified."

"Well." Warren's gaze darted everywhere but my face, but he finally gave in and looked straight at me. Which was more distracting than his previous shifty-eyed nonsense. "Yeah."

"You're all clinically insane," I observed.

"Irrelevant." This from the boss, Dr. Holt, whose eyes looked redder and his skin grayer than when I saw him last week.

I sighed. Had they thought to lull me into a sense of security by having this meeting in the break room? Because it wasn't working, not least because the room smelled like scorched toast. "And one of you bums—the ones who created the problem in the first place—going after her is off the table because…?"

"Again: you're the only one who made it back. And there aren't that many of us left."

"What's that supposed to m—"

"It's not that complicated," Karen put in, and I was really starting to dislike the woman. "Just do what you did before and you'll be back."

"But I have no idea how I got back," I protested. "I just saw lights and headed for them. Like a moth! And why is it on me to play fetch? I don't even have a college degree."

"You listed 'student' on the first page of the NDA," Dr. Holt pointed out.

I *knew* I shouldn't have finished filling out that paperwork. "Because I am."

"You're still in college?" From guess-who.

"Still? I'm twenty-six. I'm sure it seems quaint to you—you've probably all got Masters and Doctorates—" Nods and *faux*-modest shrugs all around. "—but I'm a part-time student. I'm only one semester away from graduating." Or two. Or four.

"What degree are you studying?"

Tricky ground. Once upon a time, when people asked about my degree, I would tell them I was studying social history. Then this would happen:

"Wait, like social justice?"

"No, social history."

"What's that?"

"Historians know what really happened. Social historians know the versions we wish happened."

"What?"

"You know—historiographic revisionism. Like how *The Tudors* isn't really historically representative of the Tudor period due to the waxed legs and shaved armpits and perfect teeth."

"What?"

Lisa calculated that in four years I had spent a little over three and a half hours explaining this to people. So now this happens:

"What's your major?"

"Law."

"Oh, okay."

"My studies aren't the point," I said, dragging us back to the point. "My point is that everyone in this building is probably smarter than I am."

Karen nodded, because she was loathsome. Warren just stood there and stared. Actually, most of them were standing and staring.

"That's a fair question. The answer is, everyone here is vital to fixing the problem," Dr. Holt replied, but not even his soothing Scottish burr was soothing me. Nothing soothing could soothe me. Not even chocolate cake. "As you know, we're working 'round the clock." Yes, and without brushing your teeth or changing your shirt, but I wouldn't point that out. "It's your choice, of course, Miss Howe. But I can't spare anyone."

"Except me," I said dryly.

Holt inclined his head toward me. "Quite right, lass. And if you don't go, Dana Edwards will almost certainly be trapped forever in the 16th century, if she's not dead already."

He told me her name! Dirty pool, Holt. "That's quite a pep talk."

"And we'll pay you ten thousand pounds."

Much better pep talk. I did the math. If I came back unscorched, I'd have a tidy sum to bank. It would also go a long way toward solving my dollar dilemma. From adolescence, I'd never been able to relax unless I had a four figure savings account. I was probably the only 8th grader in my district who worried about that.

The key words, though: *if* I came back.

"Ten thousand pounds," I said, and let them hear the skepticism, because holy hell, that was a nice bundle. "That's what you think my life is worth?"

"No, that's how much we can afford," Holt said bluntly.

I snickered. "Points for honesty." *Was I really considering this?* "How about this? I get paid even if I don't find Dana and bring her back."

Karen opened her heavily Chapsticked mouth (she really laid it on, did she like the taste?) and Warren jabbed an elbow into her side. "Deal," he said quickly, ignoring her glare. Holt nodded. "You're taking the same risk either way. I think that's a fair exchange."

"And I want booze and accolades upon my return," I announced. "Don't skimp on either."

Holt actually smiled. "Agreed."

Huh. That was easy. From this day forward, those will be my terms for any errand.

CHAPTER ELEVEN

All this to explain why I was sweltering in ankle-length period clothing while my skull sweated beneath a stiff wig while searching for a dentist as I tried not to draw attention to myself or end up named as a witch/heretic/tourist.

And what was with the heat? It was spring! Was global warming a concern in the 16th century? Because that would be alarming.

Even more alarming: the people. It was easily as crowded as the Field of the Cloth of Gold; something was up in the enormous building before me. People weren't bustling to and fro; most of them were standing outside the church, clearly listening. If it had been, say, Times Square, they'd all be craning their necks and gaping open-mouthed up at gigantic screens. No screens here, so they just stared at the building as if they were waiting for something amazing.

Which probably meant the Lostie was on trial inside. Or tied to a stake inside. If they even did such things indoors…think of the smoke! Or she was babbling in tongues about dark omens like Amazon's latest takeover and vaccines to a spellbound audience.

Counting on my costume for protection, I began pushing my way past the crowd. "Excuse me…pardon me…husband, wait for me!" See? Everything's fine. I'm not alone, I'm supposed to be in that church, I've nearly caught up to my legitimate escort and husband, who is certainly not imaginary, and I'm not wearing hipster underwear from Target.

It was an enormous church with impressive stained-glass windows, spires jabbing the sky, and several pale statues decorating the outside. It was as richly decorated inside, with gleaming dark wood and the colorful glow from the stained glass splashing the floor. The place smelled like incense, smoke, and sweat, almost exactly like the basement of the church where I went to Sunday school.

I could see some smaller rooms off to the side, and before me was an enormous hall stuffed with people and candles (which was probably a bad idea, but hey: none of my business). The hall would have been dark save for the dozens of enormous windows; the natural light and creamy walls made the place seem bigger than it was, and it was already huge.

I managed to poke and prod my way forward until I could see. Most of these people were seated, which meant I had a great view of King Henry VIII and Catherine of Aragon.

Oh. I knew where I was. I even knew *when* I was. I had shoved my way into the Parliament chamber of the convent at Blackfriars. It was 1529, and Henry's first marriage was fizzling and dying. For many couples, that meant counseling. For Henry, it meant demanding an annulment and, when thwarted at every turn, forming his own church out of spite. Oh, and killing a *ton* of people who disagreed with him about his spite-church.

They'd apparently just finished taking roll, because Henry stood and launched into a short speech, the gist of which was: Catherine of Aragon was wonderful, Catherine of Aragon was crammed full of virtues, he hated the thought of leaving Catherine of Aragon but his tender conscience demanded it, very sorry to inconvenience everyone, especially Catherine of Aragon, and this definitely had nothing to do with Anne Boleyn.

I caught the highlights, so I didn't care about the specifics of Henry's self-delusion. His entire purpose was to convince everyone—himself first of all—that he was right and the world was wrong. He was doing a credible imitation of a man who has fooled even himself, and I didn't want to hear it.

No, I wanted to hear Catherine's rebuttal. I managed to get closer, no easy trick in a crowded hall while wearing what felt like sixty pounds of clothing.

Oh! The clothes. When I told I.T.C.H. I would go back, several techs ran off and returned with (authentic!) headdresses, kirtles, and bumrolls. Because this was England, not Los Angeles, it seemed as if everyone had a trunk full of period gear. Or were related to someone who did.

So while I was relieved my costume was protecting me, I had the impression I could be standing there in a tank top and few would notice. All eyes were on the lady.

Catherine was on her feet now, had crossed to where the king was seated and knelt before him. I was able to get a look at her clothes, which defined sumptuous. Her gown was the color of red wine, her kirtle was deep gold, her sleeves trimmed in dark fur.

Her headdress made her seem taller, even as she knelt—or perhaps it was simply her presence. Which was *spectacular*, by the way. And while she had been born and raised in Spain, her English was perfect, and I was amazed by how far her voice carried. I could hear her a lot better than I heard Hank the Tank's self-serving speech, which was all to the good.

"Sir, I beseech you for all the love that hath been between us, and for the love of God, let me have justice and right, take of me some pity and compassion, for I am a poor woman and a stranger born out of your dominion, I have here no assured friend, and much less indifferent counsel: I flee to you as to the head of justice within this realm."

Yes. Well. Good luck with that, ma'am.

"Alas! Sir, wherein have I offended you, or what occasion of displeasure have I designed against your will and pleasure? Intending, as I perceive, to put me from you, I take God and all the world to witness, that I have been to you a true and humble wife, ever conformable to your will and pleasure, that never said or did anything to the contrary thereof, being always well pleased and contented with all things wherein ye had any delight or dalliance, whether it were in little or much, I never grudged in word or countenance, or showed a visage or spark of discontentation. I loved all those whom ye loved only for your sake, whether I had cause or no; and whether they were my friends or my enemies."

True. It was all true. She loathed the French but had to make nice with them many times, because Henry was always looking for new allies he could piss away money on or with. She took Henry's side over that of her nephew, Charles, which probably felt like a knife in her throat. She'd supported him in everything and bitten her tongue for... what? Fifteen years?

"This twenty years—"

Twenty! My God. *Henry, you dick.*

"—I have been your true wife or more, and by me ye have had divers children, although it hath pleased God to call them out of this world, which hath been no default in me."

While she was blowing up the hall with hand grenades of truth, her dick husband was trying to get her off her knees (you could almost hear him thinking *"you're making a spectacle of yourself… and worse, of me!"*), but she was having none of it, and stayed planted. She was like a stately oak tree, if oaks were swathed in velvet and wore headdresses and spoke with a beautiful Spanish accent.

"And when ye had me at the first, I take God to be my judge, I was a true maid without touch of man; and whether it be true or no, I put it to your conscience."

In other words, *if I'm lying, here is your chance to say so. In a court of law. In front of hundreds of witnesses. If I'm lying, speak up right now and say so and put an end to this whole thing.*

He couldn't. Because he knew she wasn't lying.

"If there be any just cause by the law that ye can allege against me, either of dishonesty or any other impediment to banish and put me from you, I am well content to depart, to my great shame and dishonor; and if there be none, then here I most lowly beseech you let me remain in my former estate, and receive justice at your princely hand. The king your father was in the time of his reign of such estimation through the world for his excellent wisdom—"

Well, his wisdom and his greed. And his paranoia. And his deeply stingy nature. And his incredibly overbearing mother.

"—that he was accounted and called of all men the second Solomon; and my father Ferdinand, King of Spain, who was esteemed to be one of the wittiest princes that reigned in Spain many years before…"

Witty. Wily. Sneaky. Back-stabbing. Whatever you wanted to call it, Ferdinand of Aragon was more Machiavellian than Machiavelli. Literally.

"…were both wise and excellent kings in wisdom and princely behavior. It is not therefore to be doubted, but that they were elected and gathered as wise counsellors about them as to their high discretions was thought meet. Also, as me seemeth there was in those days as wise, as well-learned men, and men of good judgment as be present in both realms, who thought then the marriage between you and me good and lawful, therefore is it a wonder to me what new inventions are now invented against me, that never intended but honesty. And cause me to stand to the order and judgment of this new court, wherein ye may do me much wrong, if ye intend any cruelty; for ye may condemn me for lack of sufficient answer, having no indifferent counsel, but such as be assigned me, with whose wisdom and learning I am not acquainted."

Even my lawyers are on your payroll. Was the concept of conflict of interest not understood in the 16th century? I can't imagine it was a 21st century invention.

"Ye must consider that they cannot be indifferent counsellors for my part which be your subjects, and taken out of your own council before, wherein they be made privy, and dare not, for your displeasure, disobey your will and intent, being once made privy thereto."

Oof. Very nice. If nothing mattered more to Henry than Henry, a close second was what other people thought of Henry. She was calmly and respectfully calling him out in front of the world, and he could only squirm in his chair. You could almost feel the body blow to his ego.

"Therefore, I most humbly require you, in the way of charity, and for the love of God, who is the just judge, to spare the extremity of this new court, until I may be advertised what way and order my friends in Spain will advise me to take. And if ye will not extend to me so much indifferent favor, your pleasure then be fulfilled, and to God I commit my case."

Cheering would not be wise. Do not cheer. But ohhh, tempting. And I was willing to wager I wasn't the only one in the hall holding back.

When Catherine finished, she walked straight up the center of the hall, looking neither left nor right as people stood and bowed their heads. I dropped mine so fast I heard my neck creak, and peeked at her with my peripheral.

She had taken the arm of the usher, ignored the command to return, and the usher didn't know (in the poetic words of my father) whether to shit or go blind. He opened his mouth, probably to point out the town crier shouting "Catherine Queen of England, *come into the court!*", but the crier might have been a mute mosquito for all the attention she paid. She just said, in a low voice that carried perfectly, "On, on, it maketh no matter, for it is no indifferent court for me, therefore I will not tarry: go on your ways."

And out she went.

Mic drop, three hundred fifty years before the invention of the microphone.

CHAPTER TWELVE

And all of it for nothing. Seven years from now, she would die alone, starving, in pain, and miserably lonely. Her impassioned defense of her honor would go down as one of the finest speeches in history, the world would know Henry Tudor, Eighth of his Name, was full of shit, people would be reading about it and writing about it and making movies about it well into the 21st century, but that would have been cold comfort, even as the modern world—dammit!

I'd been so caught up in current events (so to speak) I'd momentarily forgotten about the modern world, and the Lostie, and the reason I'd entered the church in the first place.

I turned and started politely shoving my way through the crowd, furious with myself for losing focus. Fortunately, everyone was too busy being flabbergasted to pay me much mind, and in a few seconds I was on the street, no further in my—job? mission? weird new hobby?—than I had been ten minutes earlier.

"My lady Joan!"

Eh? Well, Joan wasn't exactly uncommon. Most likely a coincidence. I couldn't get distracted again. I had to—

"Lady Joan Howe!"

All right, what were the odds? I hopped back up on the church steps so I could see over the crowd and saw a tall, broad-shouldered man holding up his hand like he was waiting for the teacher to call on him.

"Uh. Hello?" As he moved closer I recognized the cute helpful teenager I'd met at the Field of the Cloth of Bullshit. "Thomas! Come to see the show?"

"Oh, yes." He came up the steps, whipped his hat off, and swept me a bow. If I hadn't recognized him, the dark auburn waves would have been a giveaway.

Of course. Wolsey was here somewhere; it stood to reason that his secret son would want a peek. I grinned when he came up from his bow. "Sneaky."

"Indeed," he replied with great dignity, and then he grinned back. "And while it is rude to mention a lady's looks, I am compelled to point out that you have not aged a day."

Wrong. I'd aged nine days. But for Thomas, it had been nine years. I had to say he'd sailed out of adolescence in spectacular manner. He still dressed like a scholar on the rise—mostly black, good material, well-cut and well-made—but now he had the body of a man in his prime who didn't spend *all* his time on books. If I didn't take care, it could get messy.

But he was the only person I knew here. "Thomas, I wonder if you could help me."

He'd plopped his hat back on his head but when I spoke, he pulled it off and placed it over his heart. "You have but to ask."

"My friend is lost. She's not well—nice touch with the cap-over-heart, by the way—she's not well and I think the crowds were too much for her. And she's not from around here." *At all.* "So she's likely to be disoriented." *Really, really disoriented.* "You haven't seen anything odd, have you?"

He looked down at me—he'd gained some inches in the last few years—and his lip curled into not-quite-a-smile.

"Aside from our king telling the world that his beloved wife, the Queen of England, has been his whore for twenty years, and the Princess Mary a bastard?"

"Yes, aside from that." Also: *whoa*. And his cutting remark reflected the mood of the crowd. There was a lot of head-shaking and dark muttering, none of it in the king's favor.

Thomas was already nodding. "There was a young woman running about earlier today, quite hysterical. Her clothing was strange and she seemed not to know where she was, so Master Cromwell had her taken to Bridewell."

Cromwell? Wolsey's right hand man and, very soon, the king's? Ridiculously intelligent by reputation, and stone cold, doomed to be betrayed by the king but only after a *lot* of good people were legally murdered? That Cromwell? I had no interest in crossing paths with him. And what the hell was a Bridewell?

My consternation must have shown, because Thomas put out his arm and said, "I am certain Cromwell means your friend no harm. He thought my father would like to meet her."

"He did?" Thomas Cromwell made a habit of fixing people up on blind dates? This detail had escaped my attention—certainly *The Tudors* on Showtime hadn't mentioned it.

"He believes she suffers from amentia."

Amentia. Sure. It was probably going around, like the flu.

"But," he continued, "my father often says such people are touched by angels and is always pleased to speak to them."

Touched by angels, yanked five centuries out of their timeline, tomato, toe-ma-toh.

There was a pause, broken by Thomas' helpful, "If you will allow me?"

I finally realized he was waiting for me to take his arm. "Oh. Oh! Yes. You'll take me to her? I—I'd rather not bother Thomas Cromwell."

"Of course. Ah!"

I realized I'd clamped down on his forearm. "Sorry! Sorry. I might be suffering from some amentia myself." Whatever that was. I glanced around to see how it was done, then loosened my grip until my fingers were just grazing his black sleeve. And away we went, off to rescue a dentist without drawing attention to myself while avoiding one of the smartest men on that side of the world.

CHAPTER THIRTEEN

Bridewell Palace was intimidating and large and beautiful and smelled only a little repellant. I was guessing that was due to the weather—their first hot day that spring, apparently, so everything that could be aired out was being aired out. The place probably smelled like a gas station bathroom in February.

The palace stood on the bank of the Fleet River, and Thomas and I strolled into the outer courtyard past any number of ladies and gents as if we had every right to be there, just another gentleman and his lady, not a cardinal's bastard and a 21st century medical transcriptionist who was dying, *dying* for a Coke.

"This is something else."

"Yes, it's an ongoing project of the cardinal's. And ideally situated while he tends to the King's Great Matter." Thomas pronounced it just like that: you could hear the capital letters. "Pray God this gets resolved while everyone still has their dignity."

"Too late." Plus it would drag on for years. And what was worse for Thomas was the fact that the clock was ticking on his father, too. I wished I dared warn him.

"Is it heresy to suggest I think God may well steer clear of the whole thing?"

He laughed. "Perhaps. But no fear—your heretical impulses are safe with me."

"And here you are again, Thomas."

My escort stopped, so I did, too. A stout, dark-haired man of medium height, wearing what I was beginning to recognize as the business casual of the 16th century, had hailed us. He was standing at the far end of the courtyard, partially hidden which I suspected was on purpose, as he had the look of an avid people watcher.

"Master Cromwell, this is the Lady Joan Howe."

Dammit! The second worst person I could have run into, and Thomas was introducing me to him.

Cromwell bowed and I tried not to wet myself in terror. (His reputation preceded him a smidge.) He was probably in his late forties, with layers of dark understated clothing that set off a pale expressionless face. Which is what I'd expect from a former cloth merchant. And he wasn't sweating, though his clothing looked heavy, and his cloak was fur-lined. Which is what I'd expect from a cold man who could sum up anything—cloth, contracts, a monastery, human lives—with a glance.

People who looked at his simple, understated clothing and knew of his low birth were making a mistake by dismissing him. Cromwell was no stranger to slitting the occasional throat, as he was a former mercenary. (And, even more intimidating, a lawyer.)

"Her friend has strayed—the young woman you helped into custody."

Helped into custody? *Dammit. Everything just got harder.* My consternation must have shown, because Cromwell was quick to add, "She was attracting rather a lot of attention and I feared for her safety, particularly as she was next to naked." He lowered his voice. "With all respect to your companion, she seems quite out of her mind."

I jumped in with, "She'll be all right once I get her back to her family. May I see her?"

Cromwell had tilted his head to the side. "Forgive me, my lady—your accent. Might I ask where you're from?"

Careful. He's been around. So don't say France. Don't say Italy. Don't say Belgium. Best not to say anything, really, but that might not be an option.

While I cast about for a convincing lie and considered faking a well-timed swoon, Thomas (the one whose arm I had, not the Thomas who was looking me over) teased, "For shame, my lord. Did your father not teach you it's rude to put a lady on the spot?"

This elicited a snort. "He was a blacksmith. Somehow he never broached the subject."

Thomas laughed, a cheerful sound that got a small smile out of Cromwell. Laughing with, not at, was a valuable social skill in any century. "This is why the lords do not care for you, Cromwell. You refuse to be ashamed of your low beginnings."

"That is not why they don't care for me, Thomas, but I thank you all the same." He turned to me and inclined his head. "I withdraw the question, my lady, and will shoe your horse to make amends."

"That isn't necessary."

"For the sake of my late wife, if nothing else, because she despaired of me learning to be a gentle."

Oh.

I cleared my throat. "I was sorry to hear about your family."

There was a beat, and then dark brows arched. "And?"

"Er." Was he waiting for the 16th century equivalent of a Hallmark card? What would that even be? A letter? A bard?

"Nothing about God's mysterious ways?" The tone was sardonic, but I didn't sense any malice. Just weariness. "Or how women are plentiful, and children easily brought forth?"

People say that to him? *No big deal, just grow a new kid with a new wife. Problem solved.* "I don't care for platitudes. And words don't change anything. Especially a stranger's words. We say 'I am sorry' when we break a glass and when someone's child dies. Sometimes it's just noise, no matter what the intentions are."

Now both Thomases were gaping at me. This had not been a good time to expound on my 'why saying I'm sorry is inadequate' philosophy. *Well, I had a good run. Cannot complain. Burning stake, here I come.*

"Too true," Cromwell said, and smiled. The expression transformed him. He didn't look like a man who would have the power of life and death over scores once Wolsey died of disgrace. He looked like a grieving family man who occasionally found something to smile about. Whose grief was still fresh enough that he was surprised each time it happened. "And far be it from me to keep you from your friend." He glanced around, and a shorter, younger man with reddish-brown hair and a red beard was at his side in half a second. There was a brief murmured conversation that I missed because Wolsey's bastard chose that moment to lean in and whisper, "He likes you."

"I am terrified," I hissed back.

He chuckled, as if I'd made a joke. "You? Ha."

"Oh, excuse me? We've met *twice*."

The whispering over, the young man who'd been at Cromwell's side (I found out later it was his ward and secretary, Ralph Sadler) left as quickly as he'd appeared. Even better, Cromwell was still smiling. "My assistant is bringing her around to the west entrance, and we have found her appropriate clothing."

"We'll make sure to get it back to you," I lied.

Cromwell waved that away, thank goodness. "She is obviously unwell, so I thought you might like to remove her from the public gaze in what little privacy I can provide." He made a gesture encompassing the gallery filled with gossipers, a sort of 'see what a madhouse this is?' shrug.

"Thank you," I replied, and I'd never meant those two words more. "And now I'm forced to admit that at least half the things I've heard about you might be false."

"And might not," he replied, earning a snort from Thomas. "It was a pleasure to meet you, my lady."

Friendly. Efficient. Helpful. Not unattractive. I might kiss Thomas Cromwell. "You, too."

With that, Cromwell took his leave, doubtless scurrying off to his next intrigue. I let my breath out in a gasp hard enough to make me sway on my feet a little. "I did not expect that."

"He has a terrible reputation," Thomas acknowledged, steadying me with a shy hand. "One based on fear, not familiarity. Anyone who has spent more than an hour at Austin Friars would see how kind he is. Even now, after..."

"Well, it was a pleasant surprise." By now I realized we had been doing the Sorkin walk-and-talk, because we'd gotten to the end of the gallery and were just a few feet away from where the court had settled in to dine. I had a good view of the king and queen as we worked our way past, and despite our urgency I almost stopped.

I hadn't noticed before; I'd been focused on avoiding attention and mentally cheering on the queen. But now I had the chance to take a hard look and was shocked by the changes in both of them in nine years. She looked twenty years older than she had at the Field of the Cloth of Bullshit, and Henry looked twenty pounds heavier. The king's enmity and impatience was plain for anyone to see—when he wasn't stuffing his maw he was openly glaring at her—as was her pain and pride as she stared at her plate.

I wanted to tell her to cheer up, which would have been as useful as telling Cromwell the Lord worked in mysterious ways when He casually murdered most of the Cromwell family with The Sweat. I wanted to tell her it would all be worth it in the end, but that would have been a lie, too.

And I wanted to tell her that she had plenty of people on her side, but in the end, she was her own best advocate, the one person who never wavered or faltered or second-guessed herself. She was the queen, Henry's wife, Mary's mother, Isabella's daughter, Charles' aunt. Those things were always going to be true. And nothing anyone said could un-do any of it.

Though her shitbird spouse would cleave the country in half trying.

Speaking of the Royal Shitbird, he had been so busy sulking he wasn't paying attention to what he was eating, because he dropped his knife, which hit the gold plate with a clatter, and clutched his throat.

All right. Nothing to sweat over . . . in fact, a perfect time to flee. We were almost out. The dentist was nigh. I had no desire to push my luck more than I had.

Okay, yes, Henry was turning red(der), and couldn't make a sound, and he was pounding one fist on the table so hard the cups were dancing, but Henry VIII doesn't—didn't—die in 1529.

So it was time to go.

Even though he was turning purple.

He wouldn't die for years.

His eyes were rolling back.

But, again: he wouldn't die until his son—who hasn't been born yet—was nine. A long time from now.

He doesn't even have the strength to pound the table...

"Dear God," Thomas breathed, which was an accurate read of the room. No one seemed to know what to do. Touching the king without permission was against the law, and everyone knew how paranoid this monarch was getting. No one wanted to reach for him and be accused of poisoning the royal gullet. No one wanted to pound the royal backfat and risk being charged with assault, either. Then there was the man's ego—even if you saved him, he might be embarrassed to have received help in public, and make the savior pay for it.

Even the queen could only sit, clutching a rosary and—guessing by her moving lips—praying. For him to be saved, poor noble idiot.

If he goes down, that's it.

He won't. He isn't supposed to die today.

Well, he is dying.

"Dammit!"

CHAPTER FOURTEEN

"**M**ove. *Move*." I shoved my way past too many court-iers and was at Henry's side in seconds. I seized him by the lapels and respectfully shouted into his florid face, "Up! *Up!*" He heaved himself to his feet as best he could and I clawed at his doublet—the thing was stiff and padded and there wasn't a chance in Hell of getting my arms around Henry *and* all his layers. I got the thing open, somehow wrestled it off him, got him turned around, and hoped

"Guards!"

"What is she—"

"Please, somebody has to—"

I wasn't about to get jabbed in the kidney with someone's partisan. I could hear people shouting but all my focus was on Hank the Tank.

I got my arms around him, made the universal symbol for hitchhiking, and jabbed my thumb, hard, to put pressure on his diaphragm.

Nothing.

I did it again, harder, with both fists, like I was trying to lift him up. I had a decent adrenaline high by then, because it worked—I managed to lever the king off his feet. Unfortunately, as I was now off balance, I couldn't stay on my feet and we (*timberrrrr!*) crashed to the floor.

It made no sense, but the shock when we hit dislodged the turkey leg or foot-long baguette or whatever he'd been inhaling. A wad of food shot straight up and out of his mouth and I heard it hit the floor with a wet thud.

I tried to take a breath while wriggling, pinned beneath him like a butterfly to a board, but I couldn't move and suddenly it was night, which made no sense, and I was falling asleep, which made less sense. It was too early to sleep. I wasn't even tired.

I think
I might be
in trouble...

CHAPTER FIFTEEN

Just a quick sidebar: five hundred years from now, I.T.C.H. impressed upon me four unbreakable rules:

1) Do not draw attention to yourself.
2) Leave nothing behind.
3) Tell no one in the past about the future.
4) No, really, *do not draw attention to yourself.*

CHAPTER SIXTEEN

"Ah! She has come back to us, praise God."

I cracked an eye open and observed Henry Tudor, whose color was significantly better than it had been a few seconds ago. Still, big trouble. Remember when I said Thomas Cromwell was the second worst person I could have run into? The first worst was holding my hand and beaming down at me.

"I—must have—" Been squashed like a bug. Been flattened like a pancake. "Swooned?"

"Small wonder in your terror for my life!"

Yes, that was definitely it.

"Do you think you could rise?"

That from Thomas, who was down on one knee across from Henry Tudor. His expression was pinched with anxiety, his eyes very wide.

"I—of course." I demonstrated, sitting up like Frankenstein's monster coming to life on the slab, and heard a chorus of relieved sighs. Lovely. I had the full attention of the room. I.T.C.H. was going to be pissed. (Angry. Not drunk.) And that was assuming I talked my way out of this and made it back. "Don't fuss. Everything's fine."

"Lass, I can barely understand you." Which was fair. I had discovered that people in the 16th century spoke recognizable English for the most part—context helped more than anything—though the usage and pronunciation would give any time traveler pause. But the more I heard it, the easier it was understood. I hoped the reverse was true. "Did you perhaps hit your head?"

"Your Grace, forgive my interruption … Lady Joan is a friend, but not from here." Which was both an overstatement (we've met *twice*, Thomas) and an understatement. (Cross the ocean, then cross the continent to the halfway point and wait five hundred years. That's where I'm from.)

"That explains the dreadful gown and hair," someone tittered, and I wish I.T.C.H would have warned me that the 16th century was a lot like high school. And how dare anyone disparage my ill-fitting wig?

"Her accent is charming, but takes getting used to."

"*Most* charming," Henry agreed warmly. "How did you do it, my lady? Dislodge the obstruction?" He let go of my hand and prodded at his stomach. "Oh, we shall be sore tonight! I've taken hits in the ring that were less painful." The court tittered dutifully while I focused on not rolling my eyes. "And you've torn a button from my jacket. But worth it and more, don't you agree, Catherine?"

For the first time, I realized the queen was holding back most of the lookey-loos, who were craning to see around her. One woman in particular, a tall brunette who looked entirely too smug—probably the bitchy wig disparager—was doing her best to get an eyeful. Queen Catherine let them have one more admonishing glare, then came and ponderously knelt beside the king and Wolsey's bastard.

Wolsey! I looked around but couldn't see him, thank goodness. The cardinal had likely decided after the queen's speech that it was a good time to get scarce, which was more than fine since the last thing I wanted to do was get Thomas into trouble.

"Indeed, yes," Catherine said. Her smile took five years off her face, which was just sad. Even though his death would have simplified matters, she couldn't ill-wish him. "With your permission, my lord king, I thought the lady could rest in my chambers."

"I can't!" I cried before I could think better of it. "I have to—" *Leap through a slash in time to head for the 21ˢᵗ century and charge my phone.* No, no. "My friend. The crazy one. I mean, the one touched in the head. I have to take her home. I gave my word." Also: $$$$$! Wait, technically that would be £££££. "I'm sorry but I have to go." I *was* sorry, by the way, but more because I was forced to defy them than actual sorrow at taking my leave. Because if they weren't inclined to let me go, I was bound to be a lot sorrier.

The monarchs watched me carefully while I garbled nonsense. "I think," Henry began, "she declares she must leave us. And what a shame it is. But perhaps we should meet your friend. Does she require a physician?"

Thomas must have read some of my panic, because he broke in with, "The lady Joan has holy visions."

I do?

"She does?"

"I believe angels guide her actions," he said, so earnest it was adorable. "We met at the Field of the Cloth of Gold, many years back, and I thought she was dazzled by the sun—"

No, just mourning the loss of my Coke.

"—but she was having a vision. She predicted that England and France would be back at war within three years, and that the Holy Roman Emperor would break his engagement to Her Highness the Princess Mary."

"That is astonishing!" Henry exclaimed, and the queen crossed herself.

"So if she believes the angels want her to bring her friend home as soon as possible..." Thomas trailed off, doubtless because he didn't want to tell a king with absolute power what to do. Especially this king. Also, Thomas Wynter was a card-carrying genius.

"Oh, of course, of course." The king was still smiling at me, his pleasant expression perfectly visible through the reddish beard, and his small blue eyes were merry. "Far be it from me to thwart the will of the angels"

Ha! Let's hear you say that three years from now.

"But could you tell me how you managed to do—whatever it was that you did? I confess to much curiosity about your method."

Well, I definitely didn't use a technique invented by Henry Heimlich in the 1970s. If that's what you were wondering.

"I—" I realized that thanks to Thomas' off-the-cuff excuse, I had the perfect out. "I don't know what I did. The angels told me you had to live."

"Of course." His Royal Ego nodded.

"They—they guided me. And the next thing I knew, I was on the floor and you were holding my hand."

I was half afraid Henry would laugh, then declare me a witch and find a random blacksmith to strangle me, Cromwell perhaps, then bury me at a crossroad. But far from laughing, he seemed awed and even grateful. "I shall thank your angels in my prayers, Lady Joan," he promised. "And you as well."

"As will we all," the queen added.

"Perhaps not all." I couldn't see the source, but I was guessing it was the bitchy brunette who wig-shamed me. Could it be Anne Boleyn? I was dying to get a better look.

Don't you think you've pushed your luck enough?

"When you have done their bidding, you will return to court." And though the king's tone was warm, it wasn't a request. "We would hear more about your gift and your home."

"I will return to tell you all about it," I lied.

Wait. What if it wasn't a lie? What if the king and I crossed paths again? Here was an unprecedented opportunity to foster good will for the future. Too bad it meant breaking an I.T.C.H. rule (again).

But I.T.C.H. wasn't here. None of them were here, and it sounded as if none of them would ever be. It was my neck in the noose, every time.

So then. Just in case.

"Your Majesty, before I leave to do their bidding, the angels want me to tell you a secret." I looked around the small crowd. "*Just* you. Could we please ...?"

The Tudor's beady blue eyes widened and he helped me to my feet, then led me to a small alcove a good ten feet away from anyone else.

This is a genius move. Or the move that gets me killed. Either way, get on with it. I leaned in, took a breath, was pleasantly surprised to find the king didn't stink, and whispered in his ear.

He pulled back and stared at me, aghast. "No, oh no! Say it should never come to pass, lady, I beg you."

"Shhhh! I mean, um, perhaps the angels are wrong. Maybe this is a test? But they wanted me to tell you, and you can never tell anyone else, not even your priest, until after. Of course, no one can tell the King of England what to do," I added, seeing the small eyes narrow, the small mouth tighten. "I'm just passing along their suggestions. But cheer up. Maybe it won't come to pass. Maybe I'm just insane."

Just like that, the pursed lips loosened and he was smiling again. "I would never wish such an affliction on thee, my lady. And I will do as the angels bid, and pray that they beg God for mercy for us all."

"Thank you." There was a pause, and I was reminded that there was a curious crowd right behind me and I had unfinished business. "If Your Majesty will excuse me?"

"We do excuse you. Come back to us soon, Lady Joan."

And I got it. I felt it: man's charisma hit me like a wave that drowned the sensible part of my brain. His focus wasn't just flattering, it was intense. I'd read that Henry VIII had the gift of making anyone feel special, whether they were a royal Duke or a blacksmith.

(*Authentic!*)

If anything, the books underplayed it. I wanted to smile back and hug him. I wanted to make him laugh. I wanted him to *see me* and then *keep seeing me.*

For the first time, I understood all the sycophancy and enabling that had turned Henry Tudor from golden prince to raging tyrant. People *wanted* to please him, to be his focus, to get his approval. Not because he was king. Because of *him.* He could have been a baker and still been interesting.

Not only did being around him make me (reluctantly) like him, it gave me even more respect for Queen Catherine, who knew exactly what she was up against, but fought anyway, right up until she died of it.

"Time to go," Thomas murmured, taking my hand and placing it firmly on his forearm.

"Oh yes," I replied. Truer words were never, etcetera.

"I've gotta be on my own nitrous. It's the only thing that makes any goddamned sense."

Found her!

CHAPTER SEVENTEEN

"It was above and beyond for you to help me." The three of us—Wolsey's bastard, the dentist, the part-time student/medical transcriptionist—were on the outskirts of London by now, on a road I was going to know well—The Gray Horse was just over the rise.

The dentist, a wild-eyed brunette with skin the color of good amaretto, had been bundled into an ill-fitting dark gray woolen dress and a cloth bonnet.

(*Authentic!*)

She flinched away from me until I got her attention with, "I'll bet none of these people floss. Which is so important when it comes to good dental hygiene and fighting gingivitis, don't you think?" Then I couldn't get her off me, poor thing. Even now, half an hour later, she was clinging to my hand and my fingers were dead white.

"Just... really, really decent. Above and beyond, truly." I was still babbling at Thomas, knowing the words were inadequate, but there was nothing else I could give him. "I know there would've been trouble if your father had seen you."

"To put it mildly." He grinned, pulled his cap off, and raked his fingers through that wonderful auburn hair, then clapped the cap back on. "But how could I leave a lady in distress?" He smiled at the dentist. "*Two* ladies."

"You're spinning this—"

"Spinning?"

"It's slang from the odd place I come from that you've never heard of." Of course! Sounded legitimate. No dissembling here. "You're talking like you weren't much more than an escort, but you helped me with Cromwell, and the story you told the king, that was bril—" I cut myself off as the realization hit. "It ... wasn't a story. You really think that. That I have, uh, heavenly visions."

"I apologize for sharing your secret," he said earnestly. "But our king is most learned in matters of theology, and I felt certain he would respect your gift."

Cripes, was there no end to my luck? So far I'd only run across people who were either helpful, indifferent, inclined to overlook my 21st century oddities, and/or who assumed the best instead of the worst.

And if I came back—not that I would—but *if* I came back to find another Lostie, I was less likely to be accused of witchcraft if people thought I was a holy fool. Or even a run-of-the-mill fool. Plus the King of England owed me his life.

And to think when I woke up I thought it'd be a regular Wednesday: transcribing someone's bursitis and sneaking avocado into the brownie batter so Lisa ate something green that wasn't an apple Jolly Rancher.

I ignored the odd-yet-compelling urge to tell Thomas the truth. "Well, thank you again. For keeping my secret until you didn't. Which is not a judgment! And this will sound mysterious and odd, but you need to go away now so the dent—so my friend and I can go home. The angels. Um. Are telling me to tell you that."

"Of course," he said at once, and bowed. "Until our next meeting, my lady."

"I don't think—"

"Do not dash my hopes, I beg you!"

Adorable. "Right. I withdraw the hope dashing." I turned to the dentist and pointed to the small rise in the road in front of us. "Home is yonder." Then, to Thomas, "It was wonderful to—ack!" Not only did the woman have a grip like an angry octopus, she could *move* when she wanted, which she demonstrated by dragging me up the hill. "Goodbye!"

"Farewell, my lady!"

Now came the tricky part. Once the rise was behind us, we stepped off the road after making sure no one could see us, and then I led her to the willow tree.

And then we had to wait.

Which did not go over well.

"What do you mean you don't know?"

"I mean I don't know." I shrugged and tried to project confidence, but I think it came across as helplessness. Which wasn't wrong. There were *so* many things I didn't know. Why did one jump drop me in 1520, and the next in 1529, for starters? Why was I in Calais for one jump and London the next? Bad enough I didn't know; *nobody* knew.

None of which I could share with this poor woman. "Look, I'm sorry. This is new tech—no one was doing this a month ago." I was pretty sure. "The techs will explain everything. Well. They'll explain what they can. And maybe I can fill in the blanks. And there might be some paperwork for you to sign."

"Paperwork! Are you shitting me?"

"They use a really small font, too." Might as well give her all the bad news at once. "It's bound to bring on a headache."

"I get enough headaches," she snapped. "Bad ones, the kind that make me throw up. I should have just left it alone, I should have just assumed I was having a breakdown and let that asshole keep smacking the kid."

"Can you narrow that down? What asshole and what kid?"

She described an older, arrogant man, most likely a nobleman from how she described the man's outfit and coat of arms: a white lion with an arrow in its mouth (*Who thinks these things up? Yuck.*) and three yellow lions, and what looked like a yellow and blue checkerboard. Apparently she had seen the "noble" kicking the crap out of one of his servants, intervened, and was taken into custody for her pains.

"If it makes you feel better, you did the right thing. From a moral standpoint, I mean." From the glare she sent my way, it wasn't comforting. "Look, I'm sorry, I know you don't want to hear this, but I've got no control... well, over any of it, really, but especially the time it takes to get back. It could be another five minutes, it could be hours. Everyone is figuring this out as we go along. But there's simply no way to—oh, hey, there it is!"

"There *what* is?"

That was disconcerting. "You don't see a ton of sparkling lights which are helpfully gate-shaped?"

"What the hell are you talking about?"

"Nothing." No need to take her hand; she hadn't let go of mine once. So it was simplicity itself to walk around the trunk and over to the sparkling gate and take her through it.

Easy money.

CHAPTER EIGHTEEN

It took the I.T.C.H. gang several seconds to notice my triumphant return with the dentist. This was irritating for several reasons, not least of which was it was the second time they didn't notice my groundbreaking unprecedented amazing return.

"For scientists, your attention to detail sucks." Still nothing. "Really, lab cretins?"

"OhmyGod." She'd finally let go of my hand, and I worked on massaging the feeling (and blood flow) back into my fingers. "Whatevenisthisplace?"

The boss, Dr. Holt, paused in mid-scurry to blink at me. "Huh."

(*Huh* is the definition of anti-climax.)

"Hey, you're not dead!" This from Warren, who was wresting paperwork away from Karen. He let go and she clutched the paperwork to her chest with a crow of triumph. Then, to Karen, "You know you're not going to read it, so why grab it? And that's ten bucks, Karen."

"Shit."

"You bet on me to *die?*"

"Not all of us!" Karen said quickly.

"OhmyGod ohmyGod you'reallytotallycrazy."

"Hey!" I replied, stung. "Don't lump me in with these heartless dolts who have to wager on matters of life and death in order to feel something." I turned back to the dolts. "And you'd better have my check."

Oh, and *don't* point out the irony. I'm aware.

CHAPTER NINETEEN

I love rain, and I love fires.

But mostly I love them together. Which is why I was so pleased to get home and find Lisa had kindled a blaze in the living room fireplace (she used a can of compressed air as a bellows, and could coax flames out of damp wood like some kind of grizzled woodsman), and was currently lolling in front of it like a grumpy-but-comfy cat.

"Hey, this is nice."

"Leave it to you to decide the fourth straight day of rain is 'nice'." She yawned and flopped over on her belly. "Why didn't I research this place before I moved us here?"

I could only snort, because she had. Cost. Visa requirements. Local customs. Economy. Political stability. Crime rate. Gun control laws. Expat etiquette. (Okay, Lisa didn't research that last one. That was all me. Then she ignored the memo I wrote her about it, because you can't tell geniuses *anything*.) She even got her hands on topographical maps of the area, for God's sake.

All that to say she was bitching simply for the joy of it, as opposed to it being a warning that someone was about to be verbally eviscerated.

I trotted back to the kitchen, kicked my shoes into the Shoe Hump, grabbed a Coke, grabbed my laptop. In seconds, I was sprawled on the couch and researching that wacky Tudor clan.

Well, no. I was buying a shitload of books on Amazon. And also Grether's blackcurrant pastilles, an addiction I had been unsuccessfully fighting for three years. And I was doing those things because the check for £10,000 was burning a hole in my wallet. I'd bank it in the morning; all I wanted to do until bedtime was loll on the couch, indulge in capitalism, and congratulate myself on 1) not dying, and 2) saving the dentist. And saving King Henry, I guess.

It had been a satisfying afternoon, not least because of the debriefing at I.T.C.H. Because you know the old saying: one woman's time travel debriefing is another woman's tea and scones.

Something like that, anyway.

CHAPTER TWENTY

Two hours earlier
21st century

"This is incredible! You *met* them. You actually went out and met Henry Tudor and Catherine of Aragon, holy shit!"

"Don't forget Thomas Cromwell," I prompted, not boasting at all.

"Holy shit!"

"Mm-hmm." I swallowed the bite of chocolate chip scone—so tender and studded with just the right number of chips, just delightful, who made these wonderful tidbits?—so I wouldn't spray crumbs all over Warren's terrific forearms. "It *was* amazing." Meaning me. I was the amazing one. *Me.*

Yes, I was a praise-hungry tart. But it was nice to relax in the break room with Warren, knowing I'd saved a life and lived to tell the tale, and had someone almost literally hanging on what came out of my mouth (he was leaning so far forward, I was worried he'd topple my cup of tea).

And the praise. I'll be honest: I liked that, too. Some people are the stars in the movie of their lives. I was a guest star in mine, and had been since The After. Some juicy scenes, sure. But mostly the background noise.

"So how did Queen Catherine look?"

"A hundred years old. And sad." Since describing the sadness was sad, I added, "She was dressed like a queen, though. You should have seen all the brocade!"

"And the king?"

"Fat." Then I sighed. "No, that's not fair. At this stage, he's still in his prime and he hadn't gone full-blown sociopath yet." Wait. I was mixing tenses. The Tudor Court was definitely past-tense, though I'd been there half an hour ago. "In fact..."

"Yes?"

"I kind of liked him." This in the tone of voice I'd use to admit I drank straight out of the milk jug. "He was so—you get the feeling you're the only person in the world for him in that moment. It was... it was really something." Ugh. I sounded like I was describing a satisfactory drive-thru experience. "And I have to say, he and the queen didn't stink. I thought everyone back there would be various degrees of rank, but I've been in airport bathrooms that smelled worse."

"Glad your olfactory senses weren't insulted."

"Me, too," I said fervently. "Nothing worse than an insulted olfactory sense."

"I'm sending Dr. Inning home." Dr. Holt, the head of the project, had rushed in and headed straight for the coffee. "She's quite shaken, poor thing, but otherwise unharmed."

"I'll bet she didn't like all that paperwork." Unspoken: *I didn't like all that paperwork.*

"Ah. Well, we're streamlining the process a bit. We've got it down to a couple of pages, yeah?"

"What? Boo. Dentists have all the luck." Then the impact of his words sank in. "It almost sounds as if you're anticipating this will keep happening and are doing what you can to make it easier and less time-consuming for everyone involved."

"We prefer to plan for the worst-case scenario," Dr. Holt replied, taking a sip of terrible coffee. I wasn't a coffee drinker, but even I could tell it was old and burned. And everyone still looked like fried hell. "Whenever possible."

"Uh-huh. At what point does the I.T.C.H. brigade give up?"

"Never," Warren said fiercely.

Adorable! "Or ask for help?"

Warren blinked at me. "Who would we ask?"

"Uh." A fine question. Googling "24/7 Same day time-travel repair" probably wouldn't yield much. "Other scientists? The government? The people funding you? Or maybe tip off the police department in charge of missing persons? Or the—" I couldn't think of the British iteration of the F.B.I. "—the law enforcement agency in charge of kidnapping?"

"Nobody's been kidnapped!" This from Karen, who had stuck her head in long enough to be horrible, then scampered off.

"Well, not technically," I began. "But—"

"Everyone on this is working round the clock," Dr. Holt cut in.

"Yes, you keep telling me that like I don't believe it. I *do* believe it." The coffee breath alone was ample proof nobody had time for trivial matters like hygiene. "But what if you don't figure it out? There's a Plan B, right?"

They both looked at me, and after a few seconds, Dr. Holt said, "We will, though, lass, no need to fret."

All the assurances that I shouldn't fret were making me fret.

Warren jumped in. "But if by chance we can't—"

"We *will.*"

"—then of course we'd have to notify the proper parties."

I wanted to ask who the proper parties were, but I didn't think they knew any better than I did. And how would they even go about it? Who would they reach out to? If they tried the local cops, they'd be laughed at. Even if you dragged a detective inspector to the lab and showed him or her the equipment, what could they do? Would they have to coax a cop up onto the launch pad and send him back five hundred years? Seemed extreme.

Or maybe a fed? "You know how people think so-and-so has been kidnapped? They actually fell through a time rift and are alive and well in the 16th century. Well, not really. They're centuries dead *now*, of course. But now their families will have closure, so … you know. Carry on, and all that."

Or: "Queen Elizabeth? Help! We accidentally invented time travel, lost control of the tech, and random people are disappearing. Send someone!"

"To that end, anything and everything you can tell us about your trip will be incredibly helpful." Warren was almost leaning into my tea again. "You said you entered the old world beside an enormous willow tree?"

The old world? Well, it was as good a name as any. "Yes, which was odd, because last time I appeared in Calais."

"Yes, we've been over that." Holt waved Calais away, which was appropriate given what a waste of time The Field Of Cloth Of Etcetera had been.

"Could someone go back further than 1520? Will one of these jumps plop me in the middle of the Wars of the Roses?" Christ, I hoped not. The only thing I had going for me in TudorTime is that I knew who the players were.

"We don't know," was the simple, terrifying response. "Now, as you explained—you followed the crowd, because you deduced that's what Dr. Inning would have done."

"Yes. Which was your advice."

"And then you brought her back to the willow."

"Also your advice."

"Yes, one of our theories is that a tear in the—never mind." Which should have been irritating, but really was more a time saver than anything else. I wasn't going to get it. They knew I wasn't going to get it. "And then you saw the transport window?"

"Yes."

"But Dr. Inning couldn't see it."

"Should I just read my report out loud to you? Would that be easier?" No response, and I reminded myself the sour-breathed geeks were exhausted. "That's correct, the dentist couldn't see it. I haven't had a chance to think about what that means—if it even means anything, that's your department—I just pulled her through. We got here just in time for us to *not* be noticed by any of you." Hmm. I clearly had some unresolved issues about that. Something else to think about later.

"And you did a great job!" This from the ever-enthusiastic Warren, who was like a nerdy Labrador. "When we finally solve this, I'd love to take you out for coffee."

"Not here, though."

"Ah. No." Warren barely restrained a shudder. "Not here."

"Somewhere wonderful. High tea at Patisserie Valerie wonderful." At his expression, I laughed. "I know. It's like going to New York and wanting to see the Statue of Liberty. You see it all the time, so it's not special to you. But that's what I want."

"Fair enough." He made a grand gesture like a pageant winner acknowledging the crowd. "All the tea shall be yours!"

"*Warren.*"

Whoa. The boss was not a fan of fraternizing in the workplace. "I didn't mean right this minute," I clarified. Although I wouldn't have said no. And I might have asked that he shower first. "Obviously."

"Yeah," Warren agreed. "Sorry, Ian."

"Hmph." Dr. Grumpypants sighed and rubbed his eyes. "Thank you again for your help, Ms. Howe. We'll all be going over your report in detail. And Dr. Innings'. As many times as we need to."

"You probably didn't intend for that to sound like a threat, but it sounded like a threat."

"It wasn't a threat." He sighed. "Is there anything else you can tell us at this time, lass?"

Aw. He looked and talked like someone's exhausted uncle. Not mine—I never had any. As to his question...

Funny you should ask. I might have tweaked one of the rules. Some of the rules. Most of the rules. And by 'tweaked', I mean 'disregarded'.

"I think that's everything!" *Argh. Tone down the bright-eyed enthusiasm.*

"Are you certain? Anything happen that you didn't expect?"

"Aside from the 'whoa, why am I in the 16th century?' angle? Well, Cromwell was a lot nicer than his rep suggested." And Henry Tudor almost choked to death but for my timely and shouty intervention, breaking rules one and four. And I predicted the failure of the Field of the Cloth of Gold to Wolsey's bastard years before it happened, breaking rules one and three. And I was planning on breaking rule number two when the opportunity presented itself, but that was more out of self-preservation than any desire to wreak havoc on I.T.C.H. and/or the timeline.

I know what you're thinking: I was making a classic bone-headed move, one we've seen in a thousand movies and TV shows, one doomed to come back and bite the heroine on the ass. And that's not inaccurate. But keeping some things to myself was worth the risk, especially given our unsatisfactory meeting. *All* our unsatisfactory meetings, in fact.

Believe it or not, I had given this some thought. Say I told them. Say I laid it all out. I'd already broken most of the rules. I was planning to break the last one on my very next trip. But never mind, say I'd come clean. I'd coughed up the whole truth and nothing but. At best, I.T.C.H. wouldn't send me back again, knowing I'd go rogue all over the Tudor Court, and that was problematic, because I had to go back.

Well. I didn't *have* to, but I would. They hadn't fixed the problem. They had no idea what was wrong or how long it would go on. The only preventive measure they had taken was to keep an eye on the news and any missing person reports. So it was a safe bet that more Losties were inevitable. And as absurd as it sounds, only I, Joan Howe, orphaned part-time medical transcriptionist, could save them. Probably.

And they were keeping things from me. Not just the science; I couldn't shake the impression there was something going on here they weren't telling me about. And I couldn't ask about it without setting off alarm bells.

So I didn't tell them. Instead, I started planning on how I'd break rule number four because I'm a flouter of regulations and a scofflaw, too.

"No, not that I can think of." I stood. "But if I think of something, I'll call right away."

"Please," Dr. Holt said fervently, giving me a handshake that made my hand throb, since it was still sore from the dentist's death-grip. Men built like fire hydrants were always so *strong*. Probably something to do with their low center of gravity. "And thank you again, lass."

"That's okay," I told Warren, who'd also gotten to his feet. "I know the way out."

"Sure? Okay. See ya next time," he said. "And high tea, very soon."

"Okay. Try to get a nap or something, I'm starting to worry you might die."

They both laughed, which was sad since I hadn't been joking. "We'll talk soon," Warren promised. "And I hope it's to tell you that all's well."

Well, we'd see about that. Either way, I planned to be ready.

CHAPTER TWENTY-ONE

"I'm so sorry."

"Nnnnnfff."

"Really very terribly sorry."

"Hnnnff?"

"We've sent a car for you."

"R'fills are free …"

"Again, terribly sorry about this."

"M'steak was overdone …"

"*Joan.*"

"Warren?" I sat up and shook my head to clear the sleep out of my brain. "What time is it?" Oh. Wait. The thing I was talking on could also tell time. I held my cell away from my face and squinted. "Three a.m.? Dammit!"

"Yeah, sorry to say there's been another one. The car'll be there in fifteen minutes."

"Just enough time to dress, brush, and question every life decision I have ever made. Got it." Warren laughed like I'd been joking and hung up.

As it happened, I only needed eleven minutes, which left time to leave a note. A paper note, stuck to the fridge. (We were *old* old school.) But *Dear Lisa* was as far as I got.

What could I say? *Dear Lisa: My new job is a time traveler who scoops up people who fall through a gate created by people who don't understand how it works and I get a five figure check every time I jump but please don't tell anyone because I signed a non-disclosure agreement with a bunch of mysterious think tank/tech techs the violation of which could mean imprisonment. Also I'll pick up milk on my way home.*

No. Too wordy and Lisa didn't care if we were out of milk. Besides, I was starting to wonder about the validity of those non-dis agreements. If I.T.C.H. hadn't called me on them yet, when would they? What were they waiting for? Or was it worse than that—they weren't waiting because they didn't know what I had done?

In the end, I went with *Running errands, will pick up milk.* And tried not to think about what would happen if I died over there. Back there. Whatever. Lisa would never know, because I.T.C.H. was unlikely to admit their involvement. From her perspective, I would have simply vanished one night, and my body never turned up. Or, if it *did* turn up, no one would connect a 500-year-old skeleton with a missing 21st century ex-pat.

But there was nothing I could do about that now. So I went off to handle a crisis I *could* do something about.

CHAPTER TWENTY-TWO

B ack to the willow tree.

A willow tree, not *the* willow tree. Because I wasn't on the outskirts of London. Not unless Windsor Castle had moved twenty miles west. I was in a small grove of trees just off the main path, which led to the bridge that led to the palace. From here, the world's largest and oldest occupied castle kept watch over the town.

So the willow tree outside London wasn't any kind of anchor point. Or, if it was, it was only an anchor point for London. Or it was just a tree. Or I was reading too much into the presence of trees, which were literally everywhere in the 16th century. And there was always the possibility that I'd gotten into the absinthe again and none of this was happening.

I couldn't wait for I.T.C.H. to get the gates under control; there had to be a more efficient way to rescue Losties. A way to track them, or at least me. But I couldn't worry about that now. I had to track down Amy Donovan, American tourist and *TGIFridays* manager who had vanished so completely, her family told the authorities she might as well have been abducted by aliens.

(They *wish*.)

I started walking briskly through Windsor Great Park, looking straight ahead and giving off what I hoped were 'I know where I'm going and even if I don't I am a very important person on pressing business' vibes.

There was no botanically beautiful Long Walk in the 16th century; the garden just led straight to the castle. If I *was* in the 16th century. Everyone's clothes looked much the way they had in 1529, which was encouraging, as was the fact that was another warm, sunny day. Which reminded me—not only was there no way to find out the year until the gate closed behind me, there was no way to know what the weather would be like. What if I jumped into a blizzard next time?

(Yes, "next time". I was resigned to more leaps.)

I was also anxious to find out how much time had passed; I'd gone nine days between jumps, and nine years had passed. This time less than 24 hours had passed; what year had I plopped into?

No time like the present to find out. And by now I was at one of the entrances. There were lots of people going to and fro, including soldiers, but no one was being stopped or asked for a secret password. I figured they were the 16th century's version of metal detectors: they know the majority of people who go in don't pose any threat. Or would they be the 16th century version of the TSA? I hoped not. A pat-down would be disastrous.

I swept past the guards, nose in the air, working so hard to appear unconcerned I was actually sweating, but at least I was pulling it off, because the last thing I needed was—

"Ow!"

—to draw attention to myself.

"A thousand apologies, my lady!"

"No, it was my fault," I said in my new seductive-yet-nasal voice, because ouch! I rubbed my nose and was relieved there wasn't any blood.

"Not at all, the fault lies entirely wi—oh! Lady Joan."

Dammit! "Hello again, Master Cromwell." *All right, not great, but it could have been worse. Right?*

"A thousand apologies!"

Accept his apology and run away? Or stay put and see if I could put him to use? He liked it when I was blunt before.

"I should hope so," I said, still sexily nasal. "If you weren't determined to lurk, you wouldn't have run into me. You would've seen me coming."

Cromwell grinned. "But I learn so *much* when I lurk. And, of course, I run into fascinating visitors, quite literally in this case. How nice to see you again; it has been years."

It has? Really? Eureka: time to put Cromwell's legendary memory to good use *and* stay on his good side. "Surely it hasn't been that long," I said with what I hoped was convincing (nasal) simpering.

"Alas, it has."

"No, no, can't have been." Simper. Bat eyelashes. Bat-bat-bat.

Cromwell was already shaking his head. "My lady, I last saw you on the 21st of June in 1529—"

"It feels like yesterday!" *Sorry, Cromwell. Time traveler humor.*

"—and here you are three years later, on the 30th of August. For which I am sure we are all fortunate." That last seemed more of a sop to my ego than anything else. But at least I knew when I was, and could figure out what was going on at this stage of the King's Great Crapfest. "May I ask your business here today?"

"I'm looking for a friend."

"Yes, I thought as much."

"Uh, why? Why would you think as much?" Someone would have told me if *Time-travelin' Lostie Wrangler* was written on my forehead, right?

"My late master's son, Thomas," he replied simply. "He said you have a gift for showing up when those who must be pitied need help. And given the regrettable state of the world, that we were sure to see you again."

"Well, that was..." Presumptuous. Clever. And most of all... "Accurate." Then I realized the import of his words. "I'm sorry about your patron. Cardinal Wolsey." *Poor Thomas. Not this one. The other Thomas. Wait, Cardinal Wolsey's first name was Thomas, too. Why was everyone named Catherine and Thomas? This is 7th grade with four Sophias and three Lucases all over again.*

Cromwell's smile had faded. "The finest master a man could have, no matter what they said about him. I have him to thank for my place here... despite what the Boleyns say."

"I don't doubt it." Tough luck about Wolsey, but the rest of it was lining up with what Cromwell had said: Wolsey was dead, so it was after the winter of 1530. Anne wasn't queen yet, so it was before the spring of 1533. "And it might not be politic to say so, but the king will regret his loss."

"Bringing the grand total of mourners to... two." Cromwell produced a thin smile. "But you did not come here to console me on my master's loss. You don't care for platitudes. And words don't change anything. Especially a stranger's words."

Okay. Creepy to hear him parrot my exact words back to me. "Wise words, Master Cromwell. Whoever told you that was so, so wise. Oh, stop laughing. And Thomas was right, someone here needs my help. Her name is Amy Donovan, and she's a little shorter than me..." I touched my shoulder, demonstrating. "She'll be confused and scared; she won't know where she is, like the dent—like my other friend. Amy has blonde hair and brown eyes and was last seen at the—" I stopped. Probably best not to finish that sentence.

Cromwell shook his head. "I am sorry, Lady Joan, but I know of no one who—"

"Master Cromwell?"

He turned and we both saw the slender, dark-haired man approach. He looked like he was in his mid-thirties and had what my mother would have politely described as a "heroic" nose, as well as a sharp widow's peak. He was dressed in what appeared to be a pile of colorful silks: gold for his legs, blue for his jerkin, and a brown hat which he doffed when he saw me and then dropped back on at an angle.

"Ah!" Cromwell smiled in real pleasure. "Good morning, Will."

"I shall be the one to decide if the morning is good or not, you impudent son of an oaf." This spoken with about as much venom as "nice to see you again, love your jacket".

Cromwell laughed, and I was reminded of what Thomas had said of the man with such a fearsome reputation: anyone who'd spent more than an hour at his home would see how friendly and low-key he was. It was almost enough to make me forget about all the people he would help Henry kill. And if I was ever tempted to do so, I needed to keep in mind that he'd met me once, *very* briefly, years ago, and remembered exactly what I said and the circumstances under which I said it.

Cromwell turned to me. "If it is not already patently obvious, my lady, this is the king's fool. Will, this is the lady Joan Howe, new-come to court."

He sketched me a shallow bow while I tried to think. The king's fool. I didn't know much about him—my mother was never very interested in the people *around* the Tudors, just the Tudors themselves, and read and watched accordingly. All I knew was that he served Henry for most of his reign, and didn't retire after the king's death, though I couldn't remember when he did retire, or the circumstances. He was one of the few people Henry had never turned on, which is why he lived *to* retire Will, the king's fool, Will...argh! I knew this. Will Winter? Will Springs?

"Sommers!" I yelped.

"Eh?"

"My lady?"

"Your name," I explained. Why was I still bad at this? "Will Sommers. Is what I meant."

"Your reputation precedes you, old hound," Cromwell teased.

"You're the last one to chide anyone for their reputation." (Zing!) Then, to me: "I believe you are the only woman who has been *that* enthusiastic to see me, and I count my dear mother among that lot. Your friend came close, though—I assume that is why you have come to call?"

"I—yes."

"You have the same accent," he explained. "When I heard your speech, I was curious."

First, we don't have the same accent—Amy was from Boston and dropped her Rs all over the place, while I'd never left the Midwest. Except to go to England. And time travel to France. Second... "Is she all right? My friend? She's...ill."

"How odd. She seems in good health to me. Exceptionally robust," he added, and then laughed, but I didn't get the joke. "I found her to be delightful. She has joined our troupe—temporarily, of course. *Quite* enthusiastic about all the goings-on and not afraid to show it; I think His Majesty will enjoy her."

I wasn't sure I liked the sound of that.

"And—even better—she was kind enough to pledge to remain until after the investiture, so we shall enjoy her company through Sunday."

I *definitely* didn't like the sound of that.

"See, then, how handy Will is? Whereas I failed you, he steps in to help. And not for the first time."

Will waved that away, but Cromwell wasn't having it. Pretending Will Sommers wasn't three feet away and hearing every word, he added, "Will is invaluable to me. Aside from being a good man and loyal servant to His Majesty—"

"Are you proposing, Cromwell? Because I can assure you, I am taken."

"—his jokes bring the king's attention to problems His Majesty may occasionally … ah … overlook."

"Or ignore," Will said cheerfully. "Or forget about. Or never care about in the first place." When I just blinked at him, he added, "No fear; I have a fool's prerogative."

Yes, yes, whatever. It was great that he and Cromwell were pals, but I had business to attend to. "I—could I see her, please? My friend?" See her. Grab her. Hustle her the hell away from Windsor and into the welcoming, polluted arms of the 21st century, all without drawing notice or, worse, suspicion.

"She's in rehearsal," was the bewildering answer. "But aside from that—"

"His Majesty comes: the king!"

Dammit!

CHAPTER TWENTY-THREE

A nd thence he came, Henry Tudor, Fattest of his Name, clip-clopping into the courtyard with a retinue of gaily dressed men and women, plus or minus a dozen guards. Except in 1532 he wasn't the obese monster immortalized forever in grease paint by Hans Holbein.

Everyone in the courtyard stopped what they were doing and bowed or curtsyed, but he barely noticed as he swung down from his big black horse. (Charger? Steed? I don't know from horses. It was big. And it was black. All over!) All his attention was on the dark-haired, dark-eyed woman he was helping down from a slightly less gigantic horse (hers was white). They both turned and saw me at the same moment, because I was the only one who didn't know how to bow/curtsy, and thus stuck out like a time-traveling dumbass.

His eyes widened; hers narrowed. His mouth fell open in a pleased smile; her eyebrows arched. "Why, 'tis the holy fool here with us again!" He rushed over, which I decided to take as a good sign, pulling the woman who could only be Anne Boleyn along with him.

"King Henry," I replied. To her: "My lady."

"Not for long," was the instant reply. "Tomorrow I'll be *Marquis de Pembroke*." She pronounced it just like that, with a French inflection, though she was pure English, then gave Henry's arm a squeeze.

And wasn't that interesting? Announcing to a stranger she just met that she was up for a promotion. And not just any promotion. A promotion to peerage. And not just eventually. Tomorrow. Oh no, there was nobody overcompensating for any insecurity in *this* courtyard.

"My love, this—"

Nope, she wasn't having it. "You do not bow to your king?"

"You interrupt yours?" She opened her mouth and to head off a possible command to have my head off, I added, "He's not my king."

This time, her eyebrows climbed so high they tried to disappear into her hairline. Meanwhile, people all over the courtyard had come up from their genuflecting and were working hard to give the impression of people who couldn't hear a thing while sidling closer and listening harder. "No? Queer. Your accent is... unusual." Which was ironic coming from the Englishwoman affecting a French *patois*. "But surely you learned simple courtesy wherever you hailed from, is it not so? To show respect to—to whomever it is you respect?"

"No, future *Marquis de Pembroke*." Stick with the truth until you had to lie, my new old motto. I should make that the family crest. "We don't have kings. Or queens. Nobody bows or curtsies. We just shake hands."

"Shake them? Together?"

Oh, come on! She was yanking my chain, right? She had to know what I was talking about; America didn't invent the handshake. No *way* America invented the handshake. "Uh..."

Several people broke into giggles, Henry included. "See, sweetheart? I told you she was different," he said to the woman he would legally murder in four years. "They have all sorts of odd and interesting customs—and thanks be to God, else I might not be here!"

No question: saving Henry's life was, in retrospect, a good idea.

"But I must speak with you," he said, the bright smile fading. "Privately." Anne squeezed his arm again—she must have a grip like a sloth to penetrate that thick jacket—and he added, "Just the three of us."

"But—" *Stop. Shut up.* Bad idea to play the 'angels don't want me to linger' card again so soon. Besides, I knew what he wanted to talk about. And it was interesting that he was fine with the future *Marquis de Pembroke* hearing about it. That could be useful in future trips. "—of course," I finished. "I am at your service, King Henry, and yours, future *Marquis de Pembroke*."

This time they both smiled, which was a relief. "You must remain through the investiture at least," Ann Boleyn told me. She had picked up Henry's habit of making requests that weren't requests. "So I can have the pleasure of hearing you call me by my proper title."

"You want me to drop the future," I guessed.

"Yes, exactly."

Oh, Anne, you poor idiot. Don't get me started on the future. Especially yours.

CHAPTER TWENTY-FOUR

Henry (or Anne) led us through the castle, where I had a blurred impression of large rooms, stone vaulting, fireplaces big enough to roast a Prius in, tapestries, stained glass windows, servants rushing up to Henry and Anne with goblets of wine and then scrambling out of the way, and lots of gold and silver gleaming everywhere. Anne must have noticed me trying and failing not to stare like a yokel, because she giggled—and it was a nice one, it gave the impression she was genuinely amused. "Your first visit to Windsor, Lady Joan?"

"Yes..." Had I killed the joke yet? Only one way to find out. "...future *Marquis de Pembroke.*"

Another giggle. "We shall have to give you the royal tour."

"I have every confidence you have better things to do with your time." Besides, I didn't need it. Although I'd never been, my mother had studied Windsor, the Tower of London, Westminster, etc., *ad nauseum.* Windsor was extra special to her, because Henry VIII was (would be?) interred here. Which meant Anne had just volunteered Henry to give me a tour of his tomb. Which is why *I* was the one giggling now. That, or nerves. Or both. Probably both.

Henry slammed the doors shut—I assumed this smaller, more intimate but still luxuriously furnished room was his privy chamber—and turned to me, put a hand on his chest as if he was going to start singing an aria (*please* don't let him sing an aria), and said, "My lady, I have kept the secret you entrusted to me all this time; I have never spoken of it, not to my confessor, not even to the Lady Anne, whom I love more than my own heart and soul."

(Side note: at least half of that declarative sentence was a total lie.)

"But as you are here now, do I have your leave to share your vision?"

I briefly toyed with the idea of refusing, then regained my sanity. "Of course."

I expected him to launch into a flowery speech, but all he did was turn to Anne and say, with no fuss and no drama, "She predicted Wolsey's death."

Anne blinked at that, then replied, "Why, my lord king, many people knew the Cardinal was—"

"She predicted it to the month." Anne seemed startled, but I wasn't sure if it was because the king had cut her off or if she thought I had superpowers. "As well as the circumstances, and the cause, and where he died, and why. And she did so a year and a half before it happened."

"Oh," was all the next queen of England had to say.

"And then she charged me not to tell anyone without her leave, a promise I kept."

"My lord king keeps all his promises," was the automatic reply, and for a horrible few seconds I thought I was going to laugh again. But Anne Boleyn fixed me with her black gaze and that dried up any impulse to laugh. Henry's regard made me feel as if I was the only person in the room. Anne's made me feel like a bug on a microscope slide. An interesting bug, but still, just a bug. Easily ignored, or squashed. "So it is true. One of my ladies told me, but I did not believe. You have the Sight."

I shook my head at once. "I don't know what I have, Lady Anne. I just do what the angels tell me."

"Your presence here today is no coincidence," she declared. "Do you not see it, my lord king? Today of all days? You had to send the Duke of Suffolk away, and good riddance I say, but the Lord has provided you a holy fool who sees true at the moment when we must show the legitimacy of our claim."

"Is it so, sweetheart?" Rhetorical, because I could see at once that Henry loved—*loved*—the idea of God sending him his own personal holy fool in the nick of what-have-you. She knew how to play him, no question. "It does seem providential. What are the odds that you would simply choose to visit at such a time?"

Damn good question. Not that I ever chose, per se, but Henry was on to something. Every jump landed me in chaos central. I had never showed up on a random Tuesday when everything was business as usual. Every time I came, it was during times of upheaval and unprecedented events. No one had ever seen anything like the treaty at Calais—but there I was. Ditto Queen Catherine's testimony at Blackfriars— but I was there for that, too. And now, the day before a king ennobles a commoner he'll toss his Catholic wife to marry—here I was again.

It could have been a coincidence, but I made a mental note to tell I.T.C.H. anyway.

"So you must have something for us," Anne finished. "Your angels must have sent you for a specific purpose."

"Indeed!" From Henry, enthusiastic as a teacher getting excited about a three-day weekend. "Else why would you be here?"

I know this will be tough for you to grasp, but this actually has nothing to do with either of you egotistical nitwits. Would it be satisfying to say? Yes indeed. Did I want to be beaten to death by Henry's guards? I did not.

So because I couldn't see any way around it, and at this stage of the game it really was a foregone conclusion, I broke the rule again: "You will be queen, future *Marquis de Pembroke.*"

You poor thing.

CHAPTER TWENTY-FIVE

I talk too much.

Except when I don't talk enough. Seems like I've spent years trying to find the middle ground. Which is why I was suffering a tour of Windsor as conducted by Henry VIII: I couldn't think of how to get out of it, and I didn't want to press my luck. And I had Amy to think of.

Anne had left us; one of her ladies—the brunette jerk who'd made fun of my hair at Blackfriars, appropriately dressed in poison green—came to fetch her away for a nap or a snack or whatever Anne needed to do at that particular moment.

Incredibly, Henry seemed to have no idea what to do with himself during her nap or snack, because the tour was Anne's suggestion. One he jumped on at once. You'd think he had better things to do, but you'd be wrong.

"Of course, sweetheart! And I will see you at dinner. You *are* staying," he said to me; it wasn't a question.

"Through Sunday," I said with what I hoped was credible enthusiasm. Unless I could figure out a way out of it without jeopardizing my safety or Amy's life. But sure. Put me down for a spot at the table tomorrow. I'll have the vegetarian alternative. You guys do gluten-free, right?

So: Windsor Castle. Built by William the Conqueror (he needed a new hobby after the conquest), improved by

Henry II (replaced wood with stone, built the King's Gate, shored up the foundation), improved further by Henry III (strengthened the defenses by rebuilding and put in a new gatehouse, then added the Curfew, Salisbury, and Garter towers), and extended by Edward III (built the Norman Gate, rebuilt much of the existing structure).

The place was mostly ignored during the Wars of the Roses, until Edward IV built St. George's Chapel to encourage pilgrimages (because between winning battles, Edward IV was apparently the kingdom's director of tourism). Richard III didn't have time to wreck anything or build anything, which brought us to Henry's father, Henry VII, who finished the roof of St. George's Chapel, rebuilt the Great Kitchen, and built a new tower.

Henry's contribution? "Behold, Lady Joan!" This, with a grand gesture, like he was showing me buried treasure.

He put in a tennis court.

I made impressed sounds with my mouth ("Oooh!"), and more sounds ("Unh?") when he showed me the wooden terrace that made his life easier *and* gave him a lovely view of the River Thames, but radically weakened the castle's defenses. Jesus wept.

"One of my favorites!" he announced, looking out over the Windsor gardens, "now that I have had the time to study and make the appropriate alterations."

"Wonderful!" For once, my enthusiasm was genuine, as it meant the tour was over. *Your son will hate this place, BTW. Oh, and die young. But again, because it bears repeating: Edward will hate this place and then die before he has kids.* "Thank you for showing me around."

He stopped walking, so I did, too. We were on one of the terraces overlooking the grounds, and there were people behind us in the room, but we had the illusion of privacy.

He lowered his voice and said, "I know the true reason you are here."

"You do?"

"You are a bringer of peace from chaos."

Don't laugh. Don't laugh.

"And so I must ask you to bring your message to she who was never my wife."

"Catherine of Aragon?"

He smiled, probably because I hadn't slipped up and said, "The rightful Queen of England you dumped so you can grind on someone younger and cuter?"

"Exactly so. She is at The More, and quite comfortably, I might add." This in a tone of some petulance. For a man who prided himself on subtle craftiness, he had an easy face to read. She has a nice roof over her head, he was thinking. Plenty to eat, wonderful clothes, plenty of servants. Just what was the woman's problem? "I have sent her there. She obeys... in most things."

Oh, did she draw the line at meekly standing by and letting you name her a whore and her daughter a bastard? Weird!

"I fear," he continued, staring down at the gardens, "that she means war."

There was a long silence, and to my horror I realized he was waiting for me to demur. Or say something comforting. Or something bitchy. "Well, a woman scorned," was all I could come up with.

Henry shook his head. "I am speaking of literal war. She is rallying troops. She broods. She plots. But I need proof, I cannot have her thrown into the Tower on supposition alone; I would have a rebellion on my hands."

He wasn't staring grimly at his gardens anymore. He was staring grimly at *me*. "You... want me..."

"I need proof."

"…to spy on…Catherine of Aragon?" Yes, it definitely sounded as insane out loud as it did in my head. "Find proof so you can arrest her? Catherine of Aragon? You want to put Catherine of Aragon in the Tower?" Was I saying 'Catherine of Aragon' too much? It felt like I was saying 'Catherine of Aragon' too much.

"Or if there is no proof to be found, talk to her. Tell her we know of her plots, tell her how you are divinely guided, by her God and her king. Tell her waging war will not help her cause."

I was too flabbergasted to come up with anything, so I just stood there.

"That is why you are here," he replied simply, so smug and certain that the angels had sent me to keep his wayward wife in line and God help me, I actually thought about booting him off the terrace. It would screw the timeline and result in my protracted death by torture, but it could be worth it just to see the look on his face as he went down.

And speaking of screwing the timeline, that wasn't right. None of this was right. Queen Catherine didn't—doesn't—do that. She never mustered troops, she never even *discussed* bringing an army to retain her place and put Princess Mary on the throne. In fact, she repeatedly *refused* the suggestion and trust me, she was tempted. By her ambassador, Edward or Edmund Chapuys (I could never remember), and her nephew, Emperor Charles, he of the gigantic jaw and genius I.Q. By her people, many of whom would have taken up arms against Henry. Not so much because they hated him (that would come later), but because they hated *her*: Anne Boleyn.

So I had to stay through the investiture, rescue Amy from Will Sommers' clutches, and pay a visit to the Queen of England to talk a woman smarter and more educated than I was out of war, knowing she had every justification to kick Henry's ass all over the battlefield because she was *in the right.*

I must have looked vaguely horrified, because Henry Tudor chose that moment to take my hand and lean in and *dammit.* Pinned by his gaze, now I wanted him to be pleased with me. Fuck you, Henry Tudor, and fuck your charisma. "I know it seems daunting," he said with almost painful earnestness, "but your angels will guide and protect you. You are doing God's will. And you won't be alone."

"You're coming with me?" There was simply no way to keep the horrified tone out of my voice. *No* way.

"No, of course not." He sniffed at the very effrontery of the question, because he was a massive dickhead. "I have had my fill of that woman and her stubborn stupidity." Oh. Right. I'd forgotten: by now, Henry would only send lackeys to try to "reason with" (bully) the Queen. The Duke of Suffolk. The Duke of Norfolk. Cardinal Campeggio. A medical transcriptionist from Wisconsin.

Be fair, I reminded myself. Your last jumps were easy, relatively speaking. I.T.C.H. isn't coughing up £££££for you to chit-chat with Cromwell and enjoy an uneventful trip back. Except when they are.

"Of course I'll go," I said, and was annoyed to see that Henry Tudor was pleased, but not surprised. "But I have no idea what the angels will tell me to do or say."

He literally shrugged that off; his big stiff jacket moved up and down as he replied, "The angels desire to see Anne on the throne of England. Why else would they have sent you to save me? And serve me? To warn me about Wolsey's betrayal and well-deserved death? And so I know they will guide you rightly in this. I have utter confidence in them." Big, charming Tudor grin. "And you."

Well. That makes one of us.

CHAPTER TWENTY-SIX

I don't like to travel. My New Year's Eve goal was to slowly transform myself into a shut-in. (I'm aware of the irony.)

Worse, I found out what Henry meant by 'you won't be alone': he'd saddled me with the Duke of Norfolk and Anne's main Mean Girl, Lady Eleanor Stanley. Tough call as to who was more aggravating.

"Your hair is not *so* bad. This time, at least. I could help you. But the dress is dreadful."

Never mind; Lady Eleanor was more aggravating.

When Henry and I came back down to the courtyard, Anne was once again surrounded by her ladies and a number of new people had shown up. Fifty or so men, all wearing the same livery and milling about with purpose. (You'd think those two things would contradict each other, but they didn't.) A sober-but-richly dressed old man—late seventies?—was just then swinging down from his horse, and he stumped over at once, stiff from the ride, and bowed. "Your Majesty."

"Your Grace. I fear I must send you off again, and you still dusty from my last task."

"My lot in life," the older man said with a thin smile. He'd nodded at Anne on his way past her to greet his sovereign, and though she was several feet away, I could see those big eyes of hers narrow.

As for myself, I was staring at the flags and the man's guards, because there was something familiar about the coat of arms they were all sporting: what looked like a big cat—or a lion designed by someone who'd never seen one?—with an arrow sticking out of its mouth, and three other cats against a yellow and blue checkerboard.

"Your Grace, may I introduce my friend, the Lady—"

Wait, *what*? Friend?

"—Joan? Joan, this is His Grace Thomas Howard—"

"The Duke of Norfolk." Now I had it. This was the older arrogant nobleman who'd had the dentist clapped in irons. Given what I knew about him, that wasn't surprising. "Nice to meet you."

He raised grizzled eyebrows at me. "Eh? What's that, lass? I cannot understand you."

The king was smiling fondly. "Her accent takes some getting used to. Joan hails from..." He cut himself off and turned to me. "I don't believe you ever told us where you hail from."

"Far *far* away, Your Majesty. The journey takes years." Well, that part was true at least. Hundreds of years. "Across the great wide sea, in a land known as, um, Merka." So don't mind my accent. Or my clothing. Or my cluelessness about current events. Or the way I don't know how to curtsy. And my general lack of deference. And my terrific teeth. Well, I had a cavity filled last year, but still—not bad.

"Uncle."

Norfolk turned. "Niece."

Anne had strolled up with one of her ladies, the pretty brunette in the dark green dress. On closer inspection, her kirtle was a dark green which brought out her eyes, underneath was a bright blue surcoat, which she'd topped off with a deep brown French hood. I was wearing one, too, and it was beyond irritating—it kept wanting to slip no matter how many pins I jammed into it. I was considering staples. Her entire ensemble reminded me of a peacock. But that may have been the way she liked to toss her head and stare down her nose/beak at me.

"Here is my lady-in-waiting, Lady Eleanor Stanley."

And here is me, not caring. "Hello again."

"Oh, have we met?"

Nice try. But if I had to take an unscheduled trip, I wasn't going to be the only one inconvenienced and annoyed and put on the spot. "Yes, you made fun of my hair at Blackfriars."

"Yes, well." Unruffled, she nodded at my wig. "Can you blame me?"

When Anne didn't titter along with her, she immediately checked herself. In fact, now that she suspected I might be Someone Important, her entire demeanor was changing even as I watched. Her voice, when she spoke again, was at least twenty degrees warmer. "The Lady Anne has honored me by asking that I accompany you to The More to see the Dowager Princess."

"Ah," Norfolk said. He'd been absently staring at Eleanor's cleavage, but now looked up. "My errand."

"Just so, Thomas." Oh. Right. Here was another Thomas, argh. "But you will hurry back. Neither the Lady Jane nor the Lady Eleanor can be allowed to miss the investiture."

"Yeah, perish the thought."

"I beg your pardon?"

"I said the idea of missing it makes me want to perish."

"Ah."

So just like that, we were on the road to The More. And by "just like that" I meant fortyfive minutes later, because in 1532, no one could just pick up and leave. And by the time everyone was ready, I was in full fret-mode about the oncoming nightmare *(this is nuts, I'm actually getting far-ther away from Amy-the-lost and what the hell am I going to say to Catherine of friggin' Aragon of all people?)* as well as trans-port to the oncoming nightmare until I saw the carriage Eleanor and I were meant to ride in. Since my horseback skills weren't anything to take pride in, that was a relief. Or it was until we got moving.

"How much further?" I groaned as the wheels went over several boulders because, for some reason, they had paved the road with boulders. They had to have. No other explanation.

"Nearly there." This from Eleanor, who hadn't dropped the smirk since the guards slammed the carriage closed and locked us up in this rolling, jouncing tomb.

"You keep saying that—ow!" Christ, my head almost made contact with the roof that time. "And it keeps not being true."

And this was First Class! *Delta, I owe you a profound apol-ogy. And to whomever invented shock absorbers, I'll never take your contribution to society for granted ever again.*

Desperate to distract myself from the misery, I asked, "So how do you know Anne and Henry?"

"Anne and Henry? My, such informality from a citizen of—where did you say, again?"

"Merka. We don't have kings there."

"Yes, so you said. Sounds rather uncivilized."

"Well. Yes."

"To answer, my family has long served the *crown*, going back to Bosworth."

"Okay." That was an odd emphasis. Wait. Bosworth—that was when Richard III got his head handed to him by Henry VII. "Oh." *That* Stanley.

"So. New-come as you are, you know my family's history." She sounded relaxed, but her mouth was a straight, neutral line and there was no way to tell what she was thinking. I made a mental note to never play poker with the woman. "My family's long, storied history."

"Yes, I get it, you guys are mean to everybody, so I shouldn't take it personally."

"Oh, stop that, you sound like a child." This from the granddaughter (or grand-niece or something like that) of the guy who promised to help Richard III, then stood back and watched Henry VII's men butcher him like a pig on pork chop day. "As I said, we serve the crown."

"Yes, you keep going out of your way to emphasize that. I get it, you've convinced yourself you're not traitors because it's not the individual you follow, it's the butt on the throne you follow. I'll bet you get along great with the Howard family."

"As a matter of fact." She pointed, and I realized she wasn't gesturing to me, but past me, to where the Duke of Norfolk—the head of the Howard family, the highest peer of the realm after Henry—was currently riding ahead as he escorted us to The More. "We get along *quite* well." Then she laughed, and for a second, she was almost likeable. "But wherever you hail from, I warn you, the Dowager Princess will brook no disrespect. So curb your cruder instincts, if you have that ability, which I doubt."

The second was over, so I went back to loathing her.

Finally, we slowed, and thank goodness, because if I had to guess, I'd say we'd been trapped inside the carriage for two thousand hours. So you can imagine my surprise, when the thing lurched to a stop and I booted the door open, to see it was still daylight. And summer.

"Oooooh, better, that's so much better, my back!" I'd gotten down with no help, by which I mean I'd almost fallen out onto my face in the dust, and now I was hobbling in a small circle trying not to groan. "And my legs. And my everything else. Yow-ow-ow!"

Our escort was staring at me like I'd spontaneously burst into flames and yelled how hot I was. "What ails the lass, Lady Eleanor?"

"I'm standing right here," I advised the Duke of Norfolk, who had swung down from his horse in a manner I could only envy. He might have been pushing eighty, but he was in better shape than I was, the lithe buzzard. "You could just ask me directly."

"Your Grace, I'm afraid the poor thing isn't used to the finer things." Then she let out that titter again. I was so relieved to be out, I didn't mind this time.

"I am not," I agreed. "At all."

"Your Grace is kind to escort us today," She Who Titters went on. "I know you have many pressing matters to attend to."

"I am not kind, Lady Eleanor." Whoa! He'd almost cracked a smile. His lips moved up at the corners and everything. "And nothing is more pressing than the king's pleasure." He'd emphasized the last word, so I assumed it was some sort of sly commentary on Anne Boleyn giving it up to Henry pretty soon, since he was making her a Marquess tomorrow.

"On that, Your Grace and I agree." She stretched out one of her hands, laid it lightly on the Duke's sleeve. "Shall we?" They swept onward as I stumbled (literally—still didn't have all the feeling back in my legs) in their wake.

I'd been so grateful to escape the hellish contraption, I needed a few seconds to take in The More. The place was impressive and fit for royalty, at least to my untrained commoner's eye. The main building was a long structure of red brick three stories high, with several chimneys and quite a few of stained glass windows. There were three low buildings set back—stables, I assumed, the Tudor equivalent of garages—and we were surrounded by beautifully tended long, rolling lawns. There were moated gardens, and knot gardens, and the sun had come out so the rays were bathing the ground and turning everything to gold. One thing about TudorTime, depending on where you were, the place looked gorgeous.

"All right, ladies," the Duke was mumble-grumbling as we came up the walk to the house. "Quickest in, quickest out."

I had to call on vast reservoirs of self-control to avoid adding "That's what your mom said."

All I'd known about Thomas Howard before today was that he was Anne Boleyn's uncle, as well as Catherine Howard's (wife number five, poor doomed teenager). He'd do everything in his power to put both women on the throne (twice), and when it turned bad (twice), he'd betray them (twice!) to stay in Henry's good graces. Here was a man who was so good at covering his ass and sucking up, he outlived almost all the players—including Henry VIII.

To that scant knowledge I could now add that he had eye-watering halitosis. If I had to guess, I'd say he enjoyed a diet of rotten meat, tobacco, and booze, with a chaser of horse manure and a sprinkling of flat beer.

All this to say I was glad Eleanor was touching him and walking close, not me.

"My lady Joan!"

Hey, I knew that voice! I could feel a big silly smile forming as I looked, and here came the first (and best) Thomas, Wolsey's bastard, loping toward us from the building on the west side of the property.

I waved, which probably wasn't done, but who cared? "Hi!"

His hat was already off as he ran up and bowed. "So your angels have sent you back to us! Will you permit me to say how very good it is to see you again, Lady Joan?"

"Yes, and how about we drop the lady?"

"What lady?"

"Sorry, I meant that you could call me Joan. Just Joan."

"That is a kindness indeed, Just Joan." He bowed again, then seemed to realize I wasn't alone. "Your Grace. Lady Eleanor."

"Eh, you again. Come along, then."

"Why, it's Wolsey's bastard! Soooo terribly sorry about your father. Though he was a traitor, it must have been difficult for your family. The shame of it."

First of all, use of 'Wolsey's bastard' was a privilege, not a right. Second: "Why do you have to constantly be a huge bitch?" Oh, hell. That one slipped out before I could swallow it back.

"What did she say?" Norfolk was shaking his head like a horse trying to get the mosquitos off. "God's teeth," he snapped. "I can barely understand her."

"Again, standing right here. Not even three feet away. Close enough to touch." Unfortunately. "And I said that although it's sad to lose a father, you are rich with the good memories he left you." Not my best ad lib. But Norfolk didn't care what I said anyway. Neither did Lady Eleanor.

"I thank you for your condolences, Lady Eleanor," Thomas said in a perfectly neutral tone. Then, to me, "I would have come out straight away when I heard you coming, but I was in the deer barn."

"There are deer barns? Domesticated for pulling sleighs, or what? Is there a petting zoo? I wouldn't mind seeing a petting zoo."

"Ladies, come *along*." This from the Duke of Dour, who wasn't slowing down. In fact, Thomas had to break into a jog to keep up.

I grabbed Thomas's arm and, over the noise of our announced arrival, murmured, "I really *am* sorry about your dad."

"And so I thank you, also." He took my hand, patted it. "Though I don't believe I ever called him 'Dad'." And he laughed.

"Why's that funny?"

"It's not," he assured me. "Well. Perhaps a little. I do enjoy listening to you talk, but to some ears, your accent sounds, ah, provincial." Pause. "In the very best of ways. Unsullied. So many at court are hopeless cynics."

"Provinc—oh. Like a country bumpkin." If some of the Tudor Townies thought I sounded like a poor woman's Dolly Parton, well, there were worse things. "And in keeping with the passive aggression also prevalent at court, I won't tell you that your accent sounds like you're talking through your nose and being strangled at the same time. Yours, too, Eleanor!" I added loudly, because I'd heard that damned titter again. "What brings you to the castle?"

"It is not a castle, Lady Joan." Unlike Lady Eleanor, Thomas could correct me without sneering his way through it. "It is a great house."

"What's the difference?"

"Castles are for royalty; great houses are for those with high status but who are not royal themselves."

"Like a cabin versus a cottage?"

"Beg pardon?"

"Never mind."

By now, we were inside, and I could see several household servants going about their business. There was a lot of subdued flurry and going back-and-forth, and I had the impression that the queen, banished to The More, wasn't getting many visitors these days. So on the increasingly rare occasion they showed up, the staff was caught off-guard.

And it would get worse. Bet on it: much, much worse. These poor people were going to be—well, poor people. They would spend the next three years moving to smaller, danker, damper houses, going longer and longer without visitors unless the king sent some to badger his wife, until Catherine of Aragon died in the dankest dampest prison of them all.

This is as good as it gets, gang. It is almost literally downhill from here.

Unfortunately, I didn't take my own advice. I had since found out The More is long gone in my own time, which is a real shame, because that sprawling palace—excuse me, great house—was exceptional. The worst part is, by now I had seen so *many* exceptional things, they were starting to blur together. So when I think of The More now, what stands out is all the magnificent dark wood furniture—not one piece had been barfed out by Ikea—the gorgeous rugs on the walls, the hushed reverence of the place, the snacks, and Thomas Howard's foul breath.

Oh, and Catherine of Aragon. And the Princess Mary, who we caught playing hooky. And María de Salinas, who helped her play hooky. Come to think of it, it was something of a miracle that we didn't end up spending the weekend in the Tower of London while various state employees used the rack to make us taller.

But again: mostly the handmade furniture and Howard's dog-breath.

CHAPTER TWENTY-SEVEN

"The Duke of Norfolk, the Lady Joan, and the Lady Eleanor to see Her Grace the queen."

"Now, now," Eleanor chided the announcer. "Even bastards are allowed a formal introduction. Well. It would depend on the bastard, I think."

"I am not slighted in the least, Lady Eleanor," Thomas replied, calm as a clam. "The queen already knew I was here. There was no need to announce me again."

"Yes, *Eleanor*, the queen already knew he was here. And you noticed how he said my name before yours, right?"

"As a courtesy," Eleanor said, and I actually heard her teeth grind together, which was glorious. "Not a promotion."

There was a polite throat-clearing, and I remembered the Queen of England was sitting five feet away.

"Your Grace," Catherine said as the Duke bowed over her hand.

"Your Grace," he replied.

"And Lady Eleanor, how nice to see you twice in the same month."

Twice in the same month? My God, was there no end to the sheer hell this poor woman must endure?

"The pleasure and honor are mine, Majesty."

"And Thomas Wynter, of course." She turned to me with a lovely smile. "And the king's holy fool."

"You're half right, ma'am."

She laughed, then said, "Ma'am?"

"Forgive her, Your Grace," Eleanor said, because she couldn't wait even half a second to butt in. "She's from a primitive place rather far from here."

"And the Lady Eleanor is also half right," I said. "But I meant no disrespect. Ma'am is a contraction for Madame where I come from." Right? That sounded right. I was positive America didn't invent "ma'am".

"What brings you to us?"

Silence. I peeked at Eleanor and the Duke out of the corner of my eye and saw them doing the same to me. Whoops. Missed my cue. "The king asked me to speak with you about—about your plans."

"My plans."

No upward inflection, so it wasn't a question. She knew why I was here. Well. She *thought* she knew why I was here. She was (probably) ignorant of the "Operation Rescue Amy" aspect of my plan.

"May we speak in private, ma'am?"

"Oh, why? Is that necessary?"

"I'm afraid so." I was about to elaborate when the Duke made a "hrehm-*hem!*" noise that sounded equal parts patient and put-upon.

"Will you stop?" I cried, turning on him. "You're in a hurry, you don't want to be here, *we get it.*"

A shocked silence followed my unbelievably ill-timed outburst, broken by—of all things—the Duke of Norfolk's rusty laughter. It was like listening to a gravel truck chuckle.

"Lady Joan." Queen Catherine spoke gently, but she was reproving me just the same and we all knew it. "You do wrong to speak to the Duke in such a manner. It is not for you to question his schedule or his priorities."

"Sorry, Your Grace."

"I am not the one to whom you should apologize."

"I'm sorry, Your Other Grace," I repeated, never looking away from the queen. For that I got a small smile, gone so quickly I wondered if I'd imagined it. But before she could keep gently ripping me a new one, Thomas jumped in.

"My lord Duke, I can make sure the Lady Joan returns safely to Windsor. We all understand you have pressing matters that demand your attention elsewhere." He gestured, indicating the room and/or The More in general. "Nothing is happening *here*."

"Quite so," Eleanor murmured, so low I don't think Catherine heard it.

Another short silence fell, this one significantly less awkward. I tried not to gawp at Wolsey's bastard. I failed.

The Duke made that rusty gravel truck noise again. "Kind of you, lad. And I know my niece does not enjoy being parted long from the Lady Eleanor. Nor do we. Heaven knows she is the only one who can manage Anne's temper these days." That last in an indiscreet mutter. Oooh, dish-dish-dish! On second thought, don't.

"Oh, I would dearly *love* to go back to my lady," Eleanor gushed, so breathy it put Marilyn Monroe to shame. "With Her Grace's most gracious leave to return, of course."

Catherine nodded, and while they said their fare-thee-wells, I grabbed Thomas's hand again. "Thanks, but—are you sure?" It was 1532; we couldn't just hop in a car and zoom up the interstate. If he was lucky, this would only take up the bulk of his afternoon. But it could take up more than that. *I* certainly hadn't planned on spending the long weekend in 1532, but guess what?

"Of course," he replied easily. "The purpose of my visit has long concluded. And it would be no trouble to escort you to Windsor. I'm certain the queen will provide you with one or two of her ladies as temporary companions; you need not fear being compromised."

He was a sweetie, all right, but on my list of fears, "being compromised" was nowhere near the top. Or the bottom. Or the middle. Technically I'd been compromised five hundred years from now, right after Prom.

"It is just as well," Eleanor snarked on her way out. "I simply could not bear the incessant complaints from our oh-so-charming country visitor every time the carriage took a bump."

"A *bump*? It was a lot more than—" I cut myself off as it hit me. Thomas Wynter, he of the glorious Cherry Coke hair, and his kind offer meant no carriage ride! I hadn't even thought of that! I reached out and grabbed him again, a little too hard going by the stifled yelp. "Thank you so much. I'd love to ride back with you." Absolutely. On a horse. Or a pony. Or a cow. Or a pig. Whatever. I was in.

But first I had to talk the rightful Queen of England out of war.

CHAPTER TWENTY-EIGHT

Catherine of Aragon gestured to a low chair just a couple of feet from hers, and I reminded myself it wasn't our living room couch and thus resisted gracelessly plopping down. Instead I sat so slowly and carefully she probably thought I had early onset arthritis.

Close-up, I could see how beautiful she'd been. But the red hair was faded and gray, the blue eyes lined and shadowed, the round face sinking into fat. But none of it mattered—or, if it did, only to her husband. She was a queen, no matter how many crow's feet she had.

"Wine, Lady Joan?"

Right out of the gate, a stumper. I'd already been here for hours and was thirsty, but I knew fresh water wasn't a primary or safe beverage here, unlike the 21st century, where we routinely traveled with our own clear fluids. On the other hand, alcohol wasn't going to quench my thirst. On the other other hand, the queen of England was waiting for me to stop dithering and take a glass of wine (or not).

"Yes, please, your—" And there was one of her ladies, bringing two glasses of wine and *(joy joy joy joy joy)* some plums, blackberries, what looked like small, pale green early pears, walnuts, and figs, spread out on a wide silver tray. I hadn't even taken a bite and I was drooling; they were so fresh and plump, I could already smell them.

"…and…but…king…holy fool…"

Is she talking? I think she's talking.

"…cannot…however…king…God…"

"This is the best fruit I've ever had!"

The queen stopped making noises at me and smiled. "You are kind to say so; my larder is lacking just now and this is a poor offering."

"It's a *wonderful* offering."

She made a *comme ci, comme ça* gesture. "I wish you had been here only last week; we had some wonderful porpoise."

Ye gods. The last thing I wanted was a Flipper filet. "That's all right, I had porpoise for lunch."

"It can be difficult getting delicacies…I am pleased you like it."

"They're so good!" Each bite popped the thumb-sized plump berry, flooding my mouth with dark, sweet juice that went down easy. The wine they made from these must be sublime, and I don't even like wine.

"Your people enjoy fresh fruit?"

"Oh, yes. Over in Merka, we have access to lots of it year-round." I decided not to elaborate, as I wasn't sure I could explain a supermarket to a medieval queen. Or triple coupon Tuesday. Or sample day, the most glorious shopping day of the week.

"I admit I have had something of a battle to encourage my people to eat fresh fruit. The English don't trust it that way. They prefer to stew it, or make pies from it."

"Don't knock pies, those are good, too." I was going through such pear rhapsodies, it took me a few seconds to get my focus back. "Your Majesty, speaking of a battle—"

"Ah. Were we?"

"We were trying to find a way to subtly lead up to it," I admitted. "Then you distracted me with a pile of wonderful fruit."

"And I shall distract you again, and ask you the secret you told the king my husband."

"Secret?" (This was me stalling so I could gulp down the last pear.)

"When you were here last."

"Oh." I swallowed. If my mother knew I was talking to a queen with my mouth full, she'd come back and give me *such* a smack. "That secret."

"You pulled him aside. You told him things." Catherine was leaning forward, her tired eyes bright with curiosity. "I can count on the fingers of both hands how often I have seen my husband so shaken these twenty years. And here you are, to speak to me of battles. But first: the secret. He said he could not tell me without your leave."

"I told him when Wolsey was going to die. And how. And under what circumstances. He didn't believe me." I sucked down the last blackberry, a juicy sweet thing that was one of the best snacks I ever had. "Then."

"*Madre de Dios.*" She crossed herself, then sat back. "And here you are again."

Here I am again. But not to help you. Or Henry. Or England. No, not any of them. I just wanted to grab my Lostie and get the hell gone. And maybe take a fruit plate with me.

"The thing is, nobody doubts you could do it. I mean, with Queen Isabella being your mother and all. She stomped on plenty of throats in her day."

"So she did. Though I have never heard it described quite like that."

"That's not the issue."

"Pray tell me what is, holy fool."

"You can't," I said simply. By which I meant *you don't.*
"That's not how you're supposed to fight this."

Her eyes—I know it's a cliché, but they really did seem
to light up. Or at least get a bit bigger and brighter. "But I
am to fight...?"

Right. Right! I was an idiot. Here was the perfect way
to present this. "Oh yes! And you will. Not all battles take
place in the field. You'll fight and you'll be unrelenting and
constant. And if you do this—if you don't use violence—
Princess Mary will be queen."

She was holding herself very still and watching me. "You
swear it," she ordered. "To your lord and mine, on pain of
your soul's everlasting torment should you lie."

I raised a hand, wiped the blackberry juice off, then
raised it again. "I swear that if you raise no armies against
Henry, your daughter, the Princess Mary of England, will
be queen and if I'm lying, may I burn for a billion years and
then starve to death and then have my head cut off fifty-five
times and then the whole thing will start all over again."

"I think," she said after what sounded suspiciously like a
snort, "that will be sufficient. And what of my daughter, the
Princess? Her long absence troubleth me, as it pleases the
king her father to separate us."

I was starting to notice Catherine slipped Henry's
résumé into the conversation (and wavered between formal
and not-so-formal) every chance she got. Reminding others, I guess. Or herself, when things looked bleak.

*Oh, did I forget to mention you'll never see your daughter
again? Guess it slipped my mind.* "It pains me to tell you—"
Literal pain, right in the middle of my stomach. Either that
or the fourth fistful of blackberries wasn't agreeing with

me. "I'm sorry to tell you that you will never see Princess Mary aga—what the hell?"

Queen Catherine, who had spotted the new arrivals without the slightest sign of surprise, now beckoned them forward with ringed fingers. "Attend us, please, ladies."

I stared.

"Princess Mary, Countess Willoughby, this is Lady Joan, the king my husband's holy fool, who comes to us on the king's business."

Gaping like a full-on yokel, that was my business. "This is completely screwed up! And for the record, I'm not the king's holy anything."

All three women looked puzzled, and when the princess spoke, I was surprised by the deep voice coming out of that frail frame. She was short—even for the times—and pale, with large blue-gray eyes, skinny little wrists barely an inch wide, and an adorable spray of freckles across her nose. So the harsh voice was startling. "I beg your pardon, Lady Joan, I am having trouble with your—"

"You can't be here!" No. *No.* Catherine never saw her after the king banished her in 1532. It was one of the sorrows of their lives and may have hastened Catherine's end. It was also a huge reason why the pretty girl before me was destined to become Bloody Mary. This was all wrong—again. "This is bad, this is very bad!"

The countess pulled herself up to her height of four foot ten and speared me with a dark glare. I'd never seen someone a head shorter look down her nose at me before.

(Authentic!)

"It's *not* bad, nor very bad. The queen has done no wrong. She is blameless in this, as I followed no instructions save those of my conscience."

"That's not what I meant. I mean you're—" I stuffed a fist in my mouth to stop the flood of profanity I wanted to cough out. "Nnngggnn mmmmsssffff." *Shit-fuck-shit! And dammit! And I'll throw a motherfucker in there, too! Because why the hell not!*

And above all of it, the constant drumbeat cycling through my brain: *I have to get my Lostie and get the holy hell out of here. I have to get my Lostie and get THE HOLY HELL OUT OF HERE.*

I sighed, mentally squared my shoulders, and set about doing what I do best. "Are there any more plums? Pears would also be fine."

CHAPTER TWENTY-NINE

Princess Mary Tudor had what my mother would have called "pinched prettiness". Beautiful, no question, but also...strained. My mom thought girls like that spent so much time worrying, it was ultimately stamped into their features.

In Princess Mary's case, she had plenty to be anxious about. If anything, she wasn't anxious *enough*. Not that I could—or would—tell her. And though the situation was rife with imprisonment/torture/burning potential for at least four of us (five, if the Duke of Norfolk was in on it), it was impossible to look at mother and daughter, reunited after so long, and not feel glad.

My mother used to say (usually after *The Tudors* credits rolled, especially seasons three and four) that Princess Mary Tudor was her mother's daughter, but I never thought that was true. She was the child of both parents, which meant she got a double dose of stubbornness but, unfortunately, none of the charisma. I think one of the reasons Anne Boleyn's daughter did so well was because she got her parents' brains *and* stubbornness *and* charisma.

With an effort I put my *Tudor 2.0: The Next Generation* musings aside, as we were at least getting ready to depart. Everyone said their goodbyes, politely laughed at me when I confessed I had no idea how to curtsy, rattled their rosaries, and then the Countess escorted me to the courtyard. When I saw Thomas Wolsey again, this time with horses fitted out for travel and a small escort, I realized what must have happened.

"Ah, Lady Joan, I see you've had the pleasure of meeting *ouch!*"

"That's why you didn't come out when we first got here," I hissed, and pinched him again for good measure. "You were stashing the princess and the Countess in the deer barn!"

This time he caught my fingers before I could give him another zap. "It grieves me to argue with a lady, but I had already 'stashed' them in—"

"You were up to no good in that deer barn and we both know it!" I tried to stomp on my temper. And lower my voice. "You know the king doesn't want them to see each other. He sent the Countess away from Catherine for the same reason! He doesn't want the queen to have *any* comfort, nothing that will help her stick this out! If you'd been caught, do you have any idea what he would have done?"

"No." Thomas was very calm, watching my face as he held my fingers in his. "What would he have done?"

I shut up. I couldn't tell him, and if I did he wouldn't believe it. Henry hadn't gone full-blown monster at this point; he was still loved more than he was feared. Plenty of Germans would have laughed in 1933 if you'd told them what Hitler would get up to in 1941.

"Your concern touches me," he said, and his breath tickled my fingers. "How very kind—"

"May I be of assistance, Lady Joan?" The tiny and terrible Countess Willoughby had glided over on her infinitesimal feet. One thing about TudorTime[TM1], eavesdropping was a

---

1   There. I trademarked it. Don't even think about stealing it.

popular pastime, but they were polite about it, always subtly intruding on private conversations with offers to assist.

"No, thank you. Wait. Yes." I shot Wolsey's son another glare and yanked my hand out of his grasp. "You, don't go anywhere. Ma'am, I need a word."

"As you wish."

"Ma'am? As you like." Her English was perfect, which was to be expected from someone who'd been speaking it for forty-plus years. "Such a helpful gentleman," she continued in that mystifying vein, because who cared? "A young man with a rare devotion to duty. His father's son, I think."

"Uh-huh." By now we were just inside one of the knot gardens off the courtyard. Time was my enemy (ironic, given my weird new part-time job), which meant I had to get back to Windsor pronto which meant I couldn't slip away, or at least not too far. The nearest garden, full of thyme and rosemary and smelling like a dream downwind, would have to do. "It's going to get worse before it gets better."

"I beg your pardon, Lady Joan?"

I squashed the irritation. People having trouble understanding me was saving me a *lot* of trouble, just as the holy fool gig did. Stupid to get annoyed; I clearly needed a nap. Or a massage. "Her. Queen Catherine. And this." I gestured to The More. "The situation." Now I was flapping my arms like a chicken trying to take flight. "A lot worse."

"I do not—"

"Keep an eye on the food. Cut back on waste. If you think you've got too much of something, set it aside, put it into storage, do *not* get rid of it." *This is a waste of time. At best she'll write you off as a lunatic, at worst you'll scare her into hysterics.* But I was never one for taking my own advice, which was probably why I was still talking. "Same for everyone's clothing and plate and furniture and jewelry and any other accessories you have. Hold on to whatever you can for as long as you can."

"I see, Lady Joan." The teeny Countess was peering at me. "Like that, is it?"

"Not yet." It was all I dared say. And I was gratified to see I had her attention. I should have known she wouldn't scare easily. In her petite ferocity, with the dark graying hair and dark eyes and reddish-brown gown, she reminded me of a kestrel. I pegged her at mid-fifties, with plenty of fight left. "I'm sure you think I'm being an alarmist."

"I beg your pardon, a what? Your accent confounds me."

"Someone who expects the worst." When she just looked at me, I plunged ahead. "I know how it seems like domestic disaster won't ever show up at your door or, worse, a budget you have to stick to, but—"

"Holy fool or no, do not presume to tell me what I think. And I hear and heed your warning. I will see to Her Grace Queen Catherine. *And* the Princess Mary."

"Thank you." I knew how Catherine's sad story ended, and Mary's. But what about the small, fierce woman in front of me?

I'd have to look her up when I got back (if I got back). I had the vague recollection the Countess lived a long and happy life, and I couldn't wait to check to see if it was true. It *must* be true. Who'd mess with the kestrel in silk? Nobody. Probably not even God.

"Farewell, Lady Joan. May your angels keep you safe."

"Amen," I said, and I'd never meant it more.

CHAPTER THIRTY

After what happened to my parents, I was too stressed to go out with anyone in high school.

So I didn't. And current events notwithstanding, I usually kept to myself and didn't date much in England, either.

So this trip back to Windsor on a lovely day with sunshine on our shoulders and spirited horses with their heads held high was the closest to a date I'd had in almost a year. Not that I was going to admit that to Thomas Wynter, since I was too busy yelling at him.

"Have you lost your mind? Big trouble, Thomas, that's what you were looking at, and not just for you but for the queen and Princess Mary and the tiny countess, too." And me, but he couldn't have known I'd be there, so I let that one go. "What were you thinking?"

"I was thinking my queen and my princess needed me," was the calm reply. "And so they did. And so do you."

"Just a roving Good Samaritan, huh?"

He laughed. "Does that not describe you as well, Lady Joan? Which lamb of God has gone astray this time?"

"Her name is Amy and Will Sommers maybe kidnapped her."

"Your pardon, Lady Joan?"

"Or hired her," I mused. "There wasn't time to get details before the king dispatched me to The More. Where, in case you're keeping a list, I had to endure a thousand-hour cart ride, squash Catherine's rebellion, talk the queen and the princess out of violence, talk to the Countess about something I can't tell you about, and try *not* to get arrested along with everyone else in the deer barn." Who knew deer barns were such hotbeds of rebellion?

"I would never have allowed such a thing," Thomas said quietly. "I would have taken full responsibility and seen to your safety."

"Tough to see to my safety from the Tower of London."

"Tough," he agreed, "but not impossible."

"Oh, listen to you." I had to shake my head. "So much confidence."

"Or faith in our ability to avoid serious trouble. We are, after all, on the side of the angels."

Damn. Thomas Wynter was slick.

"Ah!" He pointed, delighted. "A smile at last. I have labored hard to earn one. You were much more easily amused in Calais."

Only because I didn't know what I'd be putting up with. "Here are some tips to earn another one. First—"

"Do not foment rebellion?"

"See?" I pointed to my teeth. "Smile number two, just like that."

He laughed again and I couldn't help noticing that for a guy born hundreds of years before dental floss, he had a beautiful grin. But then, Thomas always looked good to me, and I'd like to think it wasn't (entirely) because I was shallow. He was always helpful and nice; the thick red hair, long strong limbs, beautifully cut and clean clothing, bright blue eyes, and delectable forearms were just a bonus. A yummy bonus.

And then, out of nowhere: "It is most agreeable to see you again."

I snorted. "I yelled at you and pinched you and then yelled some more."

"As I said. Most agreeable."

I rolled my eyes, but mostly for show. "Cut the flattery, please."

We talked all the way back to Windsor, passing more and more people the closer we got to the castle, our armed escort never more than twenty or thirty feet behind us and nobody bothering us. I could actually feel myself relaxing the closer we got to Windsor.

Thomas kept solicitously asking if I wanted a rest, some food, "a moment to myself", which I assumed was code for taking a pee break, if the sun was too warm, if the breeze was too cool, and I finally had to tell him that unless I advised him otherwise, he should assume the sun was just the right amount of hot, the breeze just the right amount of cool, a nap could wait, and I required zero moments to myself. This was taking too long as it was, and I preferred to use whatever passed for a public restroom in the castle to copping a squat in a muddy ditch while a gorgeous man politely pretends he can't hear me peeing.

Soon enough the castle emerged, seeming to appear suddenly in the middle of the woods. You could see how they picked a prime spot overlooking the Thames, cleared the forest to accommodate structures, and the town and castle sprouted and spread from there, like Coachella. The ride had taken hours, but—sorry about the trite phrasing—time flew. I'd be sore tomorrow, but the horse Thomas tossed me on (a true gentleman, he ignored my grunt as I tried to situate myself in the saddle without toppling over the other side) was a big brown mare with velvety brown ears and eyes, and a big belly like a barrel. I was riding, but she was in charge and knew where to go, so I just let her do her thing.

When I factored in the cart-less return ride, the lack of the Duke of Norfolk and the Lady Eleanor, Thomas' company, and the fruit plate, this was the best time I'd had in Tudorville. I was almost sorry to see it end as we trotted into the courtyard. Suddenly everyone was busy dismounting and helping with horses and greeting each other and it was a good few minutes of uncomplicated chaos which gave me time to think.

I'd been able to un-do the disastrous idea Queen Catherine had caught like a fever, then put into her daughter's head. I'd made it to Windsor, but had to stay to see the future *Marquis de Pembroke* become the actual *Marquis de Pembroke*, spring my Lostie, and get back to the 21st century.

And pee.

And I wouldn't say no to a sandwich, either.

"My Lord Wynter."

"Yes?" My redheaded escort had turned to the newcomer with a big smile. "Ah! Sir Henry, how nice to see you."

"And how nice to be seen."

"I well remember your kindness to my father during his lowest days."

Sir Henry's smile faded. "Courtesy to a guest is no kindness." He was a couple of inches taller than me, with brown hair, dark eyes, and a beard trimmed in such a way it made his face look like a triangle. He bowed to both of us. "Welcome to Windsor Castle, Lady Joan. I am Sir Henry Norris."

I knew the name. Vaguely. It made me uneasy. "Hello."

"The king wishes an audience with the Lady Joan to discuss your visit with Her Majesty the queen. The Lord Chamberlin has asked me to escort you to your chambers where you might freshen up before your audience with His Majesty."

"Lead on."

We followed Sir Henry through the castle, past various drawing rooms (or receiving rooms, or whatever they were called here), past servants and courtiers of all stripes, many of whom nodded or bowed or smiled greetings at Sir Henry, and made no secret of staring at me.

After several corridors and confusing stairs, we were in a wing that I would guess was set aside for visitors. I would have been happy to get a small room with a door that locked and some clean water to wash my face and maybe a bed to dramatically fall back onto, which is why I gasped in appreciation when he escorted us into a lovely suite overlooking the Thames.

Hardwood floors covered with rugs wrought in deep jewel tones and rush mats strewn with herbs. Heavy dark furniture that was simultaneously gorgeous and sturdy, a fireplace with the wood already laid in, lacking only a match (they had those now, right?) to get the blaze going, several cream-colored fat candles the width of my wrist set out everywhere for light, and a lovely yet oddly sized bed (TudorTime's version of a super single, maybe?) with gorgeous bedcovers.

I resisted the urge to bite one of the candleholders to see if it was real gold. "This is beautiful!"

Sir Henry smiled. He was, clearly, a busy man—I'd almost had to trot to keep up with him and he had no time for the people who kept hailing him. But on short acquaintance, he also seemed nice. And I wanted to get Thomas alone to find out just what kindness Sir Henry had offered Wolsey. "His Majesty will be pleased; he extends all courtesy to his honored guests."

"Does 'honored guests' encompass me as well, or only the two of you, Sir Henry?" Thomas teased.

Henry actually looked embarrassed. "Ah, Thomas. Though I am certain the king would have no objection were you to attend the spectacle tomorrow, you know the sight of you makes the king feel ... ah ..."

"Regretful?" the guy who probably majored in Tact suggested. "Melancholy?"

Guilty, I decided. And no wonder. Hank the Tank hounded to death the best servant he ever had: Cardinal Wolsey. And however I knew Norris' name, I also had the feeling it was associated with the late, mostly unlamented cardinal.

Two teenage girls—maids, going by their simple, uniform garb—had paused respectfully at the door, then came in when Sir Henry beckoned them forward. One of them had a loaded tray. The other was also carrying something I didn't care about because of the loaded tray.

"This is Mistress Gwyn and Mistress Parker. The Lord Chamberlin has assigned them to help you attend to your toilet after which, if you'll be so kind to permit me, I shall take you to your audience with His Majesty."

"Uh-huh, sure, sounds fine, um—cherries?" I was sniffing over the various goodies on the tray: a small dish of cherries that smelled as if they were swimming in some kind of cinnamon sugar syrup, plump prunes in some sort of wine–syrup hybrid, a small pile of what looked like fat lumpy grains of rice, some things that looked like white postage stamps but weren't, and a cute loaf of bread not much bigger around than my hand. The crust crackled just a bit when I squeezed (yes, I already had my grimy paws all over the tray), and I got a whiff of rose water along with the wonderful yeasty smell of freshly baked bread.

All this, presented alongside a small carafe of wine, what I thought was a linen bath towel (which turned out to be a huge napkin), and a bowl of water for washing, which I belatedly noticed Mistress Gwyn was carrying.

"This…this is all…I can't…"

"Lady Joan!" Sir Henry sounded astounded while Thomas laughed. "Are you…weeping?"

"No! Well, a little. I have something in my eye. Both eyes. The dust."

"Do you enjoy such things in Merka?"

I almost giggled (was the Merka thing my greatest triumph or my most profound moment of idiocy?), briefly considered telling them about Panera Bread's bread bowls, then recovered my sanity even as I bit into the tender white loaf. "Yes, but it's just I'm very hungry." *Stop talking with your mouth full.* I gulped the bite down and tried to decide if I would chase it with the cherries or some of the bumpy grains of rice. "And it's so good! But I don't recognize some of these delicacies." I pointed at the bumpy rice.

"Muscadines."

Does not compute. "I'm sorry?"

"Pearled comfits," Thomas explained. "Tiny pieces of cinnamon—you know cinnamon, Lady Joan?" At my nod, he continued. "They're made by coating the small pieces of the bark in sugar syrup; the longer in the syrup, the more layers build up and the bumpier they get."

"Yum! And these?"

"Prunes in syrup."

"And these?"

"Conserved cherries."

"Ohhhhh." I picked up one of the stiff postage stamps. "What about these?"

"Kissing comfits." I must have looked dimmer than usual, because he elaborated. "Pressed sugar plates."

I popped it into my mouth. Mmmm...sugary post-age stamps...clever snacks paired with a luxurious suite! Windsor was even better than the Marriott.

"Thank you so much," I told the maids, who seemed equal parts pleased and amused. "This is all perfect. I don't need any help on the toilet. I mean with my toilet. So, good-bye." I was shooing them away as politely as I could. Their presence, meant to be helpful, was actually problematic, since I couldn't risk them getting a look at what was under my wig and gown. And when possible, I preferred to make an utter pig of myself in private. To their credit, they curt-syed, murmured polite things, and took themselves away.

Where to start? The cherries looked incredible, but my face was streaked with dust and I could use a wash. The rest of the bread was begging to go into my belly, but I had to pee. Argh, time travel dilemmas!

"I am so glad you are pleased," he replied, giving Thomas a poke in the hopes that the man would stop giggling. Ha! Good luck with that, Sir Henry.

"Well, I'm glad you're glad, Sir. Give me ten minutes to freshen up, and we can go see the king."

"I shall be waiting," he replied, and bowed.

"I shall, as well," Thomas added.

"Lucky, lucky me," I replied sweetly, and closed the door in their faces.

CHAPTER THIRTY-ONE

Side note: 16th century water closets were surprisingly not awful. I've been in gas station bathrooms that were worse. Hand to God.

CHAPTER THIRTY-TWO

And who should show up to escort me to the king but Thomas Cromwell? Did none of the major players of this regime have actual work to do? Surely there was a monastery Cromwell could be foreclosing on?

Not that I was complaining. Well, I was, but my heart wasn't in it. Because although I knew Cromwell was dangerous, I also knew that history had skipped over some of his nicer qualities. Case in point, his courteous yet gratifying greeting: "The angels have brought you back to us, and once again set you to work for the good of the kingdom."

Plus, I needed him. Or someone who knew the castle. My other escorts were doing a fade and there was no way, *no* way, I could find the king's apartment on my own. I'd slip up and arouse suspicion in all kinds of ways or I'd get lost or both.

Sir Henry Norris politely-yet-firmly bid us farewell, and Thomas Wynter, mindful of how the king felt vaguely guilty at the sight of those he'd orphaned, wasn't far behind.

"Until we meet again," he said, breathing on my fingers. It shouldn't have been exciting—I had no idea until this moment that someone breathing on my fingers was a kink—but it was. The fact that he was no longer a gangly teenager was also exciting. "And we will, I am sure, as I will be on my knees tonight and all nights thereafter until I see you again."

"Try to get some work done in the meantime," I sug-gested. "And thank you again. For everything. Again."

"I remain your good servant, my Lady Joan. God grant you safe journey."

"Thank you, Thomas. Take care of yourself."

Cromwell and I watched him go, and then I put my hand out. I'd found that half the time the guide in question would absently take my hand and place it palm-down on their sleeve, giving me one less thing to worry about getting wrong.

"Lady Joan, I hope you will forgive an impertinence—"

"I usually do."

"—but am I correct in assuming your holy work has kept you from marrying and raising a family these many years?"

Many—? Oh. I was an old maid in TudorTime, a withered infertile worthless hag. Well, TudorTime and Hollywood. "That's correct, Master Cromwell."

"Your—ah—family is not—they have not made an arrangement... if they do such things in Merka?"

"I just have my work," I replied shortly.

"Ah." A couple of seconds went by, and then: "Thomas Wynter is a fine young man."

"So people keep telling me. I've known him..." Less than a month. "Since Calais." Perfect! The truth wrapped in a lie—my ethical sweet spot. "But how do you know him? Through his dad?"

Cromwell nodded. "Yes, as you know, the late Cardinal was my lord. Though his bastard was careful never to embar-rass his father. It is the reason young Thomas Wynter is so fond of Sir Henry."

"Can you elaborate?"

"My late master was often the target of the Lady Anne's spite. Never more so than when she arranged for the

Cardinal to join the court, but neglected to provide him chambers."

Ding! The penny dropped. "And Sir Henry offered Wolsey the use of *his* rooms." If memory served, it won him no friends on Team Boleyn, though Team Wolsey appreciated it. They *still* appreciated it. "He walks the walk with that 'courtesy is no kindness' spiel, doesn't he?"

"Er... Lady Joan, I am having difficulty..."

"Never mind. So Henry Norris gave Wolsey shelter, but not for long, obviously. And then..." The fall. Decades to get where he was, less than two years to hit bottom. Henry VIII was a disaster to so many people's resumés.

Cromwell shrugged. "The Cardinal was a good man, but easily tempted."

"So you stayed in touch after Wolsey—"

"Cardinal Wolsey, if it pleases my lady."

"Sorry, I meant no offense, titles are a bit of an afterthought in Merka."

"Astonishing."

"So after Cardinal Wolsey died, you kept in touch with his son?"

"Yes, and even now Wynter is kind enough to run an occasional errand for me."

"Out of the purest impulses of the heart, no doubt."

Cromwell grinned. "We do each other favors. Now and again."

I'll bet. "I wasn't here when it happ—when Cardinal Wolsey died. If you don't mind my asking, how did Thomas take it?"

"He took it as the king did. Outwardly indifferent, inwardly sorrowful."

"Yes, that sounds about right." I peeped at him with my peripheral vision. Cromwell was leading me through multiple corridors and past several rooms, gaze fixed and straight ahead. People either nodded at him or deliberately looked away; no one was indifferent. "I'm sure you miss the Cardinal—"

"A kinder and more generous master there never was, save for His Majesty."

"—but you have to admit his downfall was a pretty big career boost for you."

"I beg your—"

"It's just nice to see you doing so well." Especially since it wouldn't last. "And I appreciate the escort, since I'll bet you have five thousand more pressing matters to attend to."

"Nothing is more pressing than my duty to His Majesty. Though it *is* terribly kind of me to assist you," he said cheerfully.

"Ha! I see you, Thomas Cromwell."

"Of course you—"

"You want to help me, but you want me in your debt even more. You're on board with the first because you're secretly nice, and you're in for the second because you're not-so-secretly ambitious."

It took him a minute to translate that into TudorTalk, but his reply was mild. "Hush. I will destroy you in an instant if you dare tell anyone I am secretly nice."

We had to be near the king's apartment, because the furniture and wall-hangings had gotten progressively nicer, and we didn't have to so much as touch the door—"Master Cromwell and the Lady Joan to see His Majesty the king!"— since it was instantly thrown open. Much less efficient than doorbells, to be frank. Noisier, too. And how did the Royal Yellers know who I was?

And there he was, Henry Tudor, in his Presence chamber with arms outstretched, looking like a big bundle of gold chains and silver brocade. And curled up like a cat in the window (but unfolding herself to join us across the room) was Anne Boleyn.

"Your Grace." Cromwell bowed.

I nodded. "Hello again, Your Majesty."

Anne greeted me with, "Ah, yes, they do not know how to curtsy where you're from."

"We know how," I lied pleasantly. "We just don't bother." I got a smirk for that one, but no lightning. Anne Boleyn, I think, liked a little fight.

"Now, beloved," Henry said, gently chiding. "We are not come to our holy station because people show reverence, but by God's will." To me: "Welcome back to court. We greet you with joy, Lady Joan."

"And lots more joy when I tell you Catherine won't move against you. Not that she ever said in so many words that she was raising an army. Because she would never do that. But if she did—and she did *not*—she has decided it's God's will that the Emperor and his troops keep out of it. As well as any private armies here in England."

"Just so! I knew the angels would guide you rightly in this!"

"She should have been seized and imprisoned in the tower," Anne snapped.

"Which would have improved your situation how, exactly?" Cromwell interjected smoothly.

Cue an awkward silence (if jukeboxes had been around, there would have been a jarring record scratch), which I broke because I despise awkward silences. "Anyway, everything has been taken care of. So if you could point me toward Amy—"

"Oh, but you cannot leave us so soon!"

So soon? It already felt like decades. "Just to see her," I clarified. "I said I'd stay until your fiancé—uh, betrothed?— was the *Marquis de Pembroke* and I will." Mostly because I couldn't weasel my way out of it. "But I need to see her. She's my responsibility."

"Your devotion to your holy cause is most commendable, and of course you may see your friend. Cromwell, make sure she finds Will."

A shallow bow. "Majesty." And, again: what did this guy actually do all day?

"Are your chambers to your liking, Lady Joan?" Anne asked. She had changed into a different outfit from this morning, this time a wine-red gown. The color would have dominated a paleface like me—they'd look at the dress, not the person wearing it—but it warmed her complexion and made her eyes seem bigger and blacker.

She was also wearing her famous Boleyn necklace, a large gold B with three dangling teardrop pearls, with two more strings of pearls that twined around her famously slender neck. She stretched her hands out to me in warm greeting, and I wasn't sure if I was supposed to clasp them or bow over them or what. (The Wisconsin public school system is perfectly adequate, but there were a few things they didn't cover.)

Then I realized she was showing off her pale perfect hands and long fingers, which was equal parts adorable (*"Look at me!"*) and vain (*"Look at me!"*). Not that I blamed her—she could have modeled Tiffany watches with those gorgeous mitts.

"My what?" I asked, because I'd been so distracted by the shiny B and unnecessary hand-waving that I'd forgotten the question.

"Your chambers. I had a word with the Lord Chamberlin on your behalf."

"Oh, yes! One of the nicest rooms I've ever seen. We don't have anything like that where I'm from." It was true! Wisconsin was a privy-free zone.

Henry predictably swelled (with pride, this time), and I got a condescending, "Well, of course," from Anne.

"My new queen is pleased to tend to all household matters large and small," he bragged. "Her elegant touch is most appreciated, don't you think?"

"Your queen," Anne snapped. "Not your *new* queen, your only queen. Your *first* queen. Catherine of Aragon was never your wife."

To my surprise—I knew he catered to her, but I didn't know how much was history and how much was hyperbole—Henry folded like origami. If he'd been a dog, he'd have flopped over and exposed his belly for scratching. "Yes-yes-yes, of course, beloved, you are my first queen. My only queen, and the keeper of my heart."

(There were at least two lies in those two sentences.)

Mollified, Anne turned back to me. "Have your angels told you anything new? Are there more holy signs that ours will be a true union, that I will be the true queen of England?"

I shook my head. "You don't need them. You will be queen; nothing can stop it now." Hmm. That came out sounding more dire than I intended.

There was a rattling crash—I flinched hard enough to elicit smiles from the others—and then the Royal Yeller was informing everyone in the room (and the next room, and the next floor, and probably the next castle) about the imminent arrival of...

"The Duke of Norfolk and the Lady Mary Carey!"

Oh, joy, the *other* Boleyn girl. Someone else to pop up out of nowhere and slow everything down. It was official: I was going to die here, but not by fire. Of old age.

CHAPTER THIRTY-THREE

The Boleyn trope is that Mary was the pretty one, and Anne was the smart one. (And their brother George was maybe the gay-or-bi one.)

This was true, as far as it went. (About the ladies. I had no idea about George.) But it didn't mean that Mary wasn't even a bit smart, or that Anne was ugly.

Though there was no denying Mary Boleyn Carey (eventually Stafford) was gorgeous, pretty as a Botticelli beauty with creamy skin (set off to superb effect by her sapphire-colored gown) an Irish milkmaid would envy. I could see a stripe of dark reddish-blonde hair peeking from beneath her French hood, which offset her big brown eyes, lush mouth, and the long Boleyn nose.

As she entered with the sentient piece of gristle known as the Duke of Norfolk, I saw her gaze go to the king, then me, then Cromwell, then Anne, and you could almost hear the click-click-click as she put it all together. "Your Majesty," she said in a low, pleasant voice, curtsying. "*Madame La Marquis.*"

"Not quite yet, dear sister," Anne replied. "But soon enough."

"Master Cromwell. Lady Joan."

"It's nice to meet you," I replied as Cromwell bowed over her hand.

Mary looked around the room again and added, "It's all settled with Queen Cath—with the Princess Dowager, then? She will not bring war to our doorstep?"

Anne's smirk fell away at Mary's slip, which I suspected wasn't a slip. It would be an asinine blunder for a noted idiot, never mind the future queen's sister, who was also the king's former mistress. A courtier from a family of courtiers who knew the value of proper titles, probably from the cradle, wouldn't make such a bone-headed move. And when I saw Anne shrug off Mary's gaffe with an eye roll, I realized Mary Boleyn was taking full advantage of her "dumb but pretty" reputation.

Which was wonderful.

"Indeed, yes. We thank you, Norfolk, for your assistance in seeing Lady Joan about her holy business for the realm."

"Howards serve the crown," was the *faux* modest reply.

"As do Boleyns," Anne said dryly. "Occasionally."

Mary nodded. "No one could say we Boleyns failed to service the king."

"Now we lack only the Duke of Suffolk," Henry said, his mouth disappearing as he pursed his lips. He looked like a toddler trying to decide whether a tantrum was going to be worth the energy.

Norfolk cackled. "Still in disgrace, eh? Charles Brandon was never clever."

"We don't require 'clever'," Henry snapped, and Anne didn't bother hiding her grin. "Only loyalty. So let him stew and fume down there in Southwark until he remembers his duty to his king, and to his future queen. As the Lady Joan has said, nothing can stop us now."

Uh, could you maybe keep me out of it? All of it? Everything? Just keep me out of everything. That's all I ask.

Henry was still fretting, and I guess the plan was to stay quiet and let him, since no one was changing the subject or leaving. A pity I wanted to do both. "Still. As much as he tries us, sweetheart, he is my oldest and dearest friend. If he would spend more time in your presence, surely he would grow to love you as I have."

"The Duke of Suffolk has had seven years," Mary pointed out. "Either he cannot love my sister or she is simply unlovable. I am sure it is the former."

Damn. Anyone else would have been devoured on the spot, but the only thing coming Mary's way was Anne's sarcastic, "Oh, look who finally learned to count!"

Mary Boleyn: veritable ninja of shade. But I wasn't able to fully appreciate her skills, because something had started poking at my brain (figurative poking, thank goodness). Something about the Duke and *La Marquis*. Something wasn't right. Or was off.

Enh, I'd think of it later. In the meantime: "May I go? Master Cromwell was going to take me to Will Sommers." Where we'd probably run into Jane Seymour, George Boleyn, Bishop Gardiner, and my great-great-great-great grandfather, all of whom would no doubt slow me down another six hours. "Please?"

"Of course. We shall see you later, dear *dear* Lady Joan," Henry promised, and he probably thought that sounded warm and affectionate.

There were murmured goodbyes and Cromwell and I were almost to the door when it happened. I was so relieved to have jumped through all the hoops, happy the king was happy, and glad I'd finally get to comfort Amy and promise her we would be going home tomorrow. (Poor thing must be losing her mind.)

So my relief swamped my good sense, and I laughed and babbled without thinking, "I actually feel sorry for the Duke of Suffolk!"

"*What?*"

Remember the awkward pause earlier that was worthy of a record scratch? This one was worse.

CHAPTER THIRTY-FOUR

*O*h, *shit.*

I turned back *(so close to a clean getaway!)* and beheld a pissy monarch. "Is there a problem, King Henry?"

"I should say so! You take the side of a traitor, Lady Joan? It is difficult for us to believe your angels would countenance such an immoral act."

I'll bet. My angels only arrange things to your *satisfaction, isn't that right?*

To distract myself from calling him out on his ongoing hypocrisy, I considered my options. I was reluctant to pull the "angels told me to say that!" ruse again. One, anything loses its effectiveness when it's overused, and two, I preferred to save it for when I was in a corner (one worse than this), or one of my Losties was.

Given that the guy who could have me imprisoned (or worse) without a warrant was angry with me, I was surprisingly calm. I figured it was like worrying about falling versus *actually* falling: the thing you were scared of is happening, so there's nothing to be scared of anymore.

Except the landing.

"Taking his wife's side over the future *Marquis de Pembroke's* isn't treason. It's being married. He has to live with her." I was pretty sure—what the hell did I know about treason *or* marriage? "And yes, I feel sorry for him. Anyone who has spent more than five minutes with a Tudor would feel sorry for him." So, even as I was figuring out what to do, I'd apparently decided: Plan Double-Down was going into effect. A glance around the room showed expressions ranging from anger to horror to blank incomprehension (nice try, Mary Boleyn, not buying it). "It's not obvious?"

"It is not, and you had best explain yourself! For angels or no angels, Lady Joan, I'll not countenance traitors, nor those who sympathize with such unnatural creatures."

Gosh, and everything was all smiles and sunshine thirty seconds ago, Henry, you raging piece of shit. If I talked myself out of this one, it would be a lesson I wouldn't forget in a hurry: Henry Tudor was a mercurial fellow.

Anne had put a placating hand on Henry's arm but aside from that, didn't make a move or a sound. She just watched me; I felt like a mouse a few inches from her hole— safety was so close! But the cat was *right there.*

"What happens when a Tudor wants something?" I ignored the stifled gasps and, in Cromwell's case, the muffled groan. I also ignored the Duke of Norfolk's smirk. *Keep smiling, pal. Your day is coming. You'll see everything you did wrong, but not in time to save your son and heir.* "Like when a Tudor wants, say, the love of a queen, despite being a humble steward, like Owen Tudor? Or the hand of the greatest heiress in England, like Edmund Tudor? How about when a Tudor— your royal father—decides the throne of England is his for the taking, despite the longest odds anyone has ever seen?"

No reaction. But at least he wasn't shouting.

"How about when a Tudor decides to take a French town just because he can? What happens?"

For that, I got a reluctant chuckle from Henry, and I could almost feel everyone else unclench.

"Or when a Tudor reasserts his God-given supremacy over a corrupt church to better shepherd his people?" If I was speaking to anyone but Henry VIII, I might've worried I was laying it on too thick. However. "Or when he chooses to expose mass fraudulence, no matter the cost to the church? Or when a Tudor took B—" Ack! *Careful. That hasn't happened yet.*

"My point—my point is that Tudors get what they set their gaze on. And that's why I was laughing. And that's why I feel sorry for Charles Brandon. Because that poor loyal idiot never had a chance, not once Mary Tudor made up her mind to have him, and you know it."

A quiet chuckle from Cromwell, who kept his gaze on the floor. Henry kept staring me down, but his mouth didn't look *quite* so tiny, and after a few seconds he made an offhand gesture: keep going, you.

"Charles Brandon didn't have a chance. He didn't have one this month or last month or last year or five years ago." When did Suffolk marry the dowager Queen of France, anyway? My mom would know. "Or ten years ago." There. Best to hedge my bets.

"He ought to have reckoned the cost," Henry said sullenly, but the Smiling Sociopath was settling down. "His head, to begin."

"Don't you think he did? This man has been your best friend since you were boys. He has been constantly at your side. For decades. He loves you, he knows your mercy and he knows what happens to people who cross you." Mmm, that could be construed as Henry being petty when thwarted. Can't have that. "He knows what happens to traitors," I amended.

"He's done a bit more than 'cross' me in the past," the king reminded me. (I also noticed he was having no trouble understanding me, nor me him. Either we were all getting used to each other's temporal and cultural accents, or Henry paid more attention when he was pissed. Or both.) "As everyone knows. As even you, a foreigner, know."

Oh, now I was 'a foreigner', no longer a holy fool guided by angels to help him work God's will. (Which in Henry's mind was synonymous with *his* will.) On the whole, I preferred being a foreigner, though it was manifestly more dangerous.

"He has," I agreed. Marrying the king's sister had, technically, been treason. "But again—Suffolk knows that. He knew his marriage could cost him everything and he *still* couldn't say no to the Tudor who needed him. Just like he couldn't say no to her last month. Even though he knew how important it was.

"And here's something else: it's easy to love a king. Practically everyone does, and even if they don't, they'll never admit it to your face." That brought some uneasy murmuring from the studio audience. I made a shushing motion at them and turned back to Henry. "People *want* to do things for kings. They'll fall over themselves to do the littlest thing because you wear a crown, and they'll try to tell you the crown had nothing to do with it. But the crown has everything to do with it. You know this, you saw how people treated your father and you see how they treat you.

"But here's the thing: everyone wants to be best friends with a crown, but Charles Brandon would have been your best friend if you'd been the cook's son. And you know that."

"Are we sure he wasn't?" Norfolk asked, and cackled. An honest-to-God cackle, like the witch from Snow White. If he offered me an apple, I'd probably start screaming.

But at least the king had calmed down, was (almost) smiling while I prettied up the story of his family, a pack of selfish, greedy, grasping assholes who brought trouble everywhere they went, sometimes years of it. Who killed to get their way, and killed to keep their way. A band of sociopathic thieves with charisma to spare: behold, the house of Tudor.

I fought a wave of dizziness and realized I'd been holding my breath. I forced a deep calming inhale and said, "King Henry, I'm not trying to talk you into anything. Or out of anything."

"Oh no?" Anne murmured.

I shrugged. "Whatever I say, you'll do what you'll do, and why not? You're the king. I can't stop you. No one can. You wanted to know why I laughed. You wanted to know why I felt sorry for the Duke of Suffolk. I told you why." Hmm. Should probably throw some humility in there. "I didn't mean to offend you, especially after you've been so gracious." I almost choked on 'gracious'. "If you're not still angry with me—or even if you are—may I go?"

Yes. Go. Now. Right now. Because one way or the other, I had no desire to see what happened next. Not because I thought the Duke of Suffolk was going to stay away in disgrace. But because I knew he *wasn't*. And I had finally figured out why.

As it turned out, after he shook his head and let out a disbelieving snort, like a bull dazzled by sunshine, Henry did let me go. And I'd either made a few friends in that room, or a few enemies. Certainly Cromwell, the Boleyn girls, and the Duke were all looking at me with expressions I'd never seen before. Whether that was good or bad, I had no idea.

Either way, Cromwell was again instructed to take me to Will Sommers, and thank goodness, and *finally*. So we took our leave and walked in silence for a minute, until he said in a tone of almost indecent satisfaction, "You and I are going to be great friends, Lady Joan."

"Don't threaten me, Cromwell."

He laughed, so I decided I'd been joking and laughed, too.

CHAPTER THIRTY-FIVE

I hate throwing up.

Obvious, right? Goes without saying, because who enjoys it? I've never once run across someone who led with, "You know what I love? Puking."

I hate it because I view it as my body going rogue, because I associate throwing up with my migraines, and because just the sight or sound of someone else vomiting often pushes *my* vomit button.

That said...

"I think I'm done," I managed weakly, backing away from the bowl. No toilets in TudorTime; just basins. I groped blindly and Will Sommers put a handkerchief in my hand. "Thanks. Sorry for what I'm about to do to it."

Sommers was a cool customer, though. "I am grateful to have lived long enough to see a holy fool scrub her tongue with my personal linen."

"Mumgladuations," I mumbled around the handkerchief. Then, to the rest of my audience, "Sorry. It's been a stressful day."

"Small wonder!" Mary Boleyn squealed. "She provoked the king—"

"Not on purpose! I wasn't thinking."

"Yes," Will snickered, "that would be how it happens."

"Then she faced him down and got the Duke of Suffolk invited back to court and all my sister and uncle could do was stare at her. *Never* apologize, Lady Joan."

Cromwell and I hadn't gotten far when we were overtaken by Mary, who had picked up her skirts and trotted after us the second she'd been excused.

"Wonderful," she gasped when she caught up to us. She pressed a hand to her heaving bosom and smiled up at me. It was such a winning, warm grin that I couldn't help smiling back. "That was wonderful. Please say you'll stay past tomorrow. I very much wish to see what you do next."

"As do we all," Cromwell said.

"I can't." *Though it's nice to be wanted.* "I'm sorry."

"Oh, too bad," she replied, blinking her big dark eyes at me. I guessed it was a reflex, some sort of Bambi Effect. "Who knew the Lord was such a demanding master?"

"Anyone who has read the Bible or heard a sermon," was Cromwell's dry reply.

"Oh. Yes. How stupid of me." Bambi look. "What you must think of me, Lady Joan." What I thought was that she was stupid like a fox. "Master Secretary, will you permit me to relieve you of her company? And bring her to Will's menagerie? Surely you have more important work to do? Like taking the rolls or counting the Crown Jewels or changing long-term fiscal policy or whatever it is you do?" she Bambi'd. "I want to help. Everyone is so busy getting ready for Anne's, um, elevation. Oh, Master Secretary, I don't want to be left out!"

Cromwell melted like a sugar cube in hot coffee. "Of course, my lady, no one could doubt your generosity of spirit. It's not your fault your sister was blessed w—ah. A topic for another time. With Lady Joan's leave, of course you may be her escort." At my shrug (what was another delay? I imagined Amy had died of old age by now), he handed me off like the baton in a relay race. "Very well, allow me to take my leave of two most charming ladies." Which he did, and very graciously, and then Mary Boleyn seized my arm— "Yow!"—and away we went.

"Finally," she muttered.

"You are *terrifying*," I said, with no small amount of admiration. She was hauling me along at such a good clip, it felt like my feet were barely touching the floor.

"And *you* know I am not the feeble-minded slut many take me for. I must ask—did your angels tell you this?"

"No. But you didn't give yourself away or anything," I assured her, because who knew what this woman was capable of? Besides physically overpowering me and dragging me through a castle? "Where I come from, it's generally accepted that women are as smart as men."

For that, I got a most unladylike guffaw. Then she saw my face and checked at once. "Ah. Hmm. I apologize, I was certain you were jesting. Your home … er …?"

"Merka."

"It sounds lovely."

"Yes, and I'd love to get back there." *Hint. HINT. HINTHINTHINT.*

"Oh, you will." Mary Boleyn, I could see, was much more popular than Cromwell. Virtually everyone she was hauling me past had a smile or a friendly greeting for her, and she smiled back and apologized for not stopping while keeping us moving. She was like a harried cheerleader trying to get to class on time while everyone else wanted to talk about Homecoming. "The king so promised."

"Uh-huh. Please don't take this the wrong way—"

"Shall I now expect to hear something offensive? Because that invariably follows 'don't take this the wrong way'."

Damn! She even nailed my accent. Hearing my Midwestern twang come out of Lady Carey's mouth was beyond hilarious.

"All right, that was terrific, but didn't the king also promise to love you forever and ever?"

"Not once," she replied cheerfully, "not even as he thrashed in the throes." She was remarkably angst-free for someone who was used by a narcissist, forced to birth to at least one bastard, then was chucked for her sister. "He only wanted what the king of France had. Rather like a child who has no interest in a toy unless another child touches it. *Le roi a un amour: lui-même.*[2]"

"Oh." In a sudden fit of insecurity, I didn't want Mary Boleyn, secret genius, to realize I had no idea what she just said. "I see."

"I am not sure you do, Lady Joan, but your angels see, and they surely know that the king, though a great man, is not a perfect one."

"Well, that's true."

"And I say this with all respect due my sovereign lord: Henry has proved intractable and capricious in the past, which is rather a good trick, don't you find? I pray nightly he has outgrown those most unfortunate traits. Surely he has?"

When I said nothing despite her hard stare—what *could* I say?—she added, "I note you are not contradicting me. My poor sister."

"I can't—"

"And here we are!" We'd passed through several more halls and were now on the far end of the castle, where a

---

2   The king has one love: himself.

number of people were bustling about in what looked like a gigantic dining room minus the table. "Halloooo, Will! Look who I've brought you!"

Wow! Smart *and* efficient. It took Cromwell twice as long to cover the same distance. From now on, I wanted Mary Tudor to be my escort wherever I was. Windsor. The Tower. Various malls. The post office.

"Very well: I am presaged. One more thing," she muttered, the dazzling smile never wavering as she beckoned and Will wandered over. "I've no love for His Grace my uncle, and so this warning: he very much liked being the only Duke at court with Henry's ear. Of course, there is also Richmond, but he hardly counts, for all he insists he is a man grown. My uncle will not thank you for getting Suffolk back."

I looked at her. "That's kind of you."

"Not really." An elegant shrug. "You don't strike me as the type to hold your tongue; I am certain you shall find trouble again. I only wish to point out where it is most likely to originate."

She was right. Hell, I was lucky I'd made it out of Henry's chambers of my own free will (more or less). He could have had me locked up, and then poor Amy! And me. Poor, poor me.

I actually swayed a little on my feet as the adrenaline rush at last began to fade. And Will Sommers didn't like the look of me at all, judging from the way he lunged for a basin (no table in the dining room, but chairs and at least one basin for some reason?). Three seconds later, I was throwing up, but at least I wasn't barfing all over the court jester.

As far as victories went, it was a small one.

CHAPTER THIRTY-SIX

Amy Donovan, as it turned out, was a high-functioning alcoholic.

Thank *God*.

"Aw, don't feel bad. I throw up in public alla time. I threw up twice just today! An' it's, what? Like, not even noon?" She shared this with me while I was scrubbing my tongue with Will Sommers' handkerchief. "That ale they got here, that's got some real kick to it but they keep tryin' ta water it down, which—yuck! Okay? Does that help?"

"Oddly, yes."

Amy Donovan, audacious T.G.I.F. manager, was another blonde with brown eyes, bouncy and energetic and drunk off her ass. Unlike other Losties, she was neither confused nor frightened. Well, she was a *little* confused, but she was putting it down to stumbling across a Renaissance Fair crammed with staff who committed to their art.

"I shouldn't a snuck away from the tour, but Jesus, I can only look at so many churches in one morning, y'know?"

"I understand."

"And look how great it worked out!"

"Uh-huh. Great. Yes."

And the best part, according to her? "Everything's free!" she exclaimed, swinging her mug to emphasize her point. From obvious practice, Will ducked and avoided the splash.

"You don't have to pay for anything and everyone's so nice and we're gonna be in a play tomorrow for some reason and the guy playing the king is gonna love it and then after it's done summa the girls and I are gonna play skittles, whatever that is. Are ya staying?"

"Yes."

"You gotta stay."

"*Yes.* I'm aware." And more than that—I saw now what Will meant when he had described Amy: delightful and *quite* enthusiastic. I hadn't realized that was TudorTime code for "friendly and relaxed drunk up for anything".

I was so relieved she was intact and unburnt, I figured the best thing was to leave it to the I.T.C.H. gang to disabuse her of her RenFair fantasy once we were safe. No telling how she'd react if I explained the vast amount of danger we were in. By pure luck, her choice of church-viewing attire was outlandish to Tudor eyes but not indecent: Amy was a fan of long cotton skirts, long-sleeved blouses, no jewelry, and her shoulder-length hair was pulled back in a braid. It could have been worse; she could have chosen shorts, sandals, and a *Rolling Stones* t-shirt cut above the midriff.

"If anything, her accent is harder to fathom than yours, Lady Joan," Will snarked. "But we can accommodate."

"What are you planning for us, Will?" Mary asked. She seemed terribly amused by Amy and/or by Will's bitchiness, and her bright gaze missed nothing. "Something that will please my sister, I trust."

"Doubtful; her plays have a streak of cruelty I find off-putting and blunt. Especially ironic when you consider she fancies herself a most subtle player."

From around us, a chorus of muffled gasps and whispers of, "Will!" and "Take care, for the sake of God…and your head!"

"Fool's prerogative," he retorted to the muttering few. "And how is it none of you can hear me when I'm critiquing your performance, but you follow every word out of my mouth in a private conversation?"

"The Cardinal Goes To Hell," I remembered out loud. That had won Anne few friends when word got around. Except for her inner circle, most people found a play celebrating Wolsey's fall and descent into Hell to be in poor taste (go figure!), even those who had been fine with Wolsey's death.

"Further proof that women have no sense of humor." Will shrugged. "I am certain by comparison my modest effort will seem quite dull," he added with touching modesty.

"We're all quite dull when compared to Anne," Mary said with touching loyalty. "But it was kind of you to offer to write something new, the better for her to rest. You could have fobbed it off on John Heywood."

"An hour of nothing followed by yet more nothing? I should die first."

"I thought you liked John."

"When have I said otherwise? Thomas More's nephew by marriage," he told me. "But his plays run too long and they have nothing to say. About anything. Which many people choose to believe is bold, but in actuality? Simply tedious."

Mental note: Seinfeld didn't invent a show about nothing. The things I learn while time-traveling!

"Still, it was kind of you to take on the task. Anne has enough to fret about."

"No kindness. Merely the proper order of things. I refrain from telling her how to be queen; she need not tell me how to fool," Will sniffed.

Mary laughed. "Now, Will…"

Jesus, who cares about any of this? "Where are you sleeping tonight?" I asked Amy, who was topping off her mug again. "Did they tell you? Do you want to stay in my rooms?" My adorable, beautiful rooms which would, I hoped, be filled with snacks upon my return, and perhaps some turkey legs.

"That will not do, Lady Joan," Mary said firmly. "I mean no offense, but you are gentle, while your companion..."

"For today at least, she is one of our own and we shall see to her needs. The troupe has ample quarters near the kitchens, and Amy will have her own bed."

"And my own drink, right, Sommers?" Amy gave him an elbow in the ribs that nearly knocked the slender man over. "Don't sweat it, Joanie." Ugh. That nickname had better not catch on here; I barely tolerated it when Lisa used it. "I'll be fine. Won't be worse than camping in parks."

I almost giggled at the Bostonism ("pahks"), but restrained myself. And I wanted to ask Mary how she had come to insist I was a lady and Amy wasn't—the clothing? The fact that I wasn't drunk? Surely it wasn't Amy's accent. To Tudor ears, we sounded equally awful. But there was a fine line between playing dumb and appearing suspiciously stupid, so I left it alone.

"I guess I'll leave you to it," I said, and I realized just then how tired I was. The day wasn't just catching up with me, it was ganging up on me, and I turned to Mary. "Would you mind taking me to my rooms? This place is a maze and I'd love a nap."

"Not at all. Lovely to meet you, Amy. Will, I know it's a cliché, but it really is always a pleasure to see you."

"Of course it is," he agreed.

"Thanks for looking after Amy for me, Will. It was nice seeing you again."

"Lady Joan. Lady Carey."

We left, and there weren't words for the extent of my relief. The end was finally in sight, we were (relatively) safe, and I had a guaranteed roof over my head for the next several hours. Nothing frightened me more as a child than wondering where I would sleep after The After.

It's not like being a Tudor hanger-on was akin to checking into a Marriott. Someone had to tell me or, better, show me where I'd sleep, when and what I'd be allowed to eat, and where, and at what times, and when bathroom breaks were appropriate, and when I could wander around by myself and when I had to have an escort...and that was just off the top of my head. There were a thousand unwritten rules and I didn't know any of them. But there was one advantage, as Amy pointed out: money wasn't an issue.

Which was good, because TudorTime didn't take Visa.

CHAPTER THIRTY-SEVEN

I will give the Tudors praise for one thing and only one thing: they invented breakfast. Don't ask me why breakfast didn't officially happen earlier than the 16th century; I have no idea. Leave it to the House of Tudor to take the "two meals a day? naw, we want three, and if you don't like it, say goodbye to your head" road.

All that to say this was a wonderful breakfast, partly because it was ceremonial and thus fancy, but mostly because of the blancmange quivering on a serving platter. It wasn't the dessert you're thinking of, either; in fact, I'd never had anything like it. It was a sort-of stew with fish and flour mixed with rosewater, cinnamon and some other spices (saffron?), then pressed into a mold and cooked. I know the combo sounds odd, but after my first startled mouthful I got a taste for it. The bland fish contrasted nicely with the cinnamon, the flour gave it heft, and the rosewater somehow made it all work.

There was also almond milk to drink, which I found out when I took a gulp and sputtered, "This is almond milk!"

"Have you never had such a thing?" Cromwell asked indulgently. He, Henry, Anne, Mary, Cromwell, and various servants were all glancing at me with various expressions of "aw, isn't that cute?" which, while annoying, was vastly preferable to "off with her head!", so I shut up about it. I considered, and rejected, telling Cromwell that almond milk was so trendy in the 21st century I'd had to go out of my way to avoid the stuff. *Milk* is milk. Almond milk is not. Soy milk is not. Nor is cashew milk. And don't talk to me about lupin milk.

But I was happy to slurp it down, since there was only so much ale and wine I could handle before 8:00 a.m. Small wonder Amy Donovan was thriving here. She probably didn't even have a hangover. I was beginning to suspect metabolizing alcohol with no ill effects was her superpower.

There were more than half a dozen offerings on the sprawling table, including a bowl of oranges and early apples that perfumed the air, but Mary Boleyn *and* Cromwell both apologized for the "meagre offering". My new motto: bring on more meagre! Because among other things, I was enjoying some sort of savory pie with buttery lumps of seafood swimming in leeks, parsnips, and a creamy gravy, and all of it tucked under a flaky crust with so many layers it shattered on my tongue.

There was also more of that tender manchet bread served with butter and sage, and a tray of cold leftovers I was told were peacock and lark. (Before you ask, peacocks don't taste like chicken. Larks might. I didn't try them because they reminded me of a blue crab: lots of work for very little reward. Like artichokes.)

Then there was a custard tart that had been baked so gently, the pudding shivered in its crust and the smell of nutmeg and sugar made me think of Christmas. A *good* Christmas, one before The After.

Add to this wine, ale, and plates of smoked herring and hazelnuts, and I didn't even care that forks hadn't been invented yet. Spoons and knives and bare hands were more than acceptable, even when breaking the fast with a king and a future *Marquis de Pembroke*. Plus, Mary Boleyn was kind enough to procure a knife for me (everyone else carried theirs around with them, because you never knew when you might have to slice up a peacock).

This might sound out of character, but despite my satisfying culinary experience the day before, I initially hesitated before plowing into the food. Not from indifference, either; I'd woken up positively raging for a meal.

Wait.

I'll back up.

After Mary brought me back to my rooms, she summoned my maids *pro tem*, whose names I had forgotten because there wasn't a Tudor TV show or book about them, and left me to their tender care. Which mostly consisted of them pleading with me to change my clothes for tomorrow's ceremony, and me gently telling them to buzz off. They (finally) left, threatening—er, promising—to return in the morning to help me get ready.

Possibly the most unexpected thing about that long, long day: the bed was surprisingly comfortable and I slept so soundly I didn't remember my dreams. That's always a good thing.

In the morning, the maids returned with fresh water for a quick-and-dirty sponge bath. Not to worry: I'd brushed out my hair, stuffed it back under the cap, and had the wig in place before I let them in. They came in with a basin full of fresh water in which sage, rosemary, and orange peels floated, and there was a separate, smaller bowl to rinse my teeth and spit into. Since my mouth tasted like I'd been sucking on dirty cotton, the latter was particularly welcome, as was the clean cloth they gave me to scrub my teeth, the mint they encouraged me to use as chaw, the clean towel, and the olive oil soap to scrub my hands and face.

I was careful with my morning ablutions, not just for my own sake, but because I knew Henry famously loathed bad smells and filth in general. For the times, he was practically a fanatic. I'd avoid him if I could, but if I had to be around him, I'd rather he got pissed at what I said than what I smelled like.

The girls tried yet again to talk me into a new outfit, employing the But What About The Mean Girls argument, which fell on deaf/indifferent ears.

"The Lady prefers those about her to be—to be most stylish," Gwyn began. "In the French fashion. Your gown is—is very nice, but it is somewhat, er, out of style. More like what Queen Catherine wears. Which is also very nice. But the Lady Anne…"

Parker picked up the ball. "And her friend Lady Eleanor can be—can, at times—"

"Ladies, thank you, but I don't care about Lady Eleanor's opinion on anything, especially clothing. I'm wearing what I'm wearing. Trust me, this is Anne Boleyn's big day; nobody's going to care about what's on my back. And even if they did…" I shrugged. "Who cares? It's clothing."

They looked at each other, then at me. I had a brief moment of panic, which Parker alleviated with, "You do us too much honor, Lady Joan. We are not gentle."

Argh, archaic class systems! "You're helping a stranger and being nice to me. It could be argued that the first part is your job, but the second isn't. You're also trying to help me fit in, which is over and above. As far as I'm concerned, you're ladies. Did everybody follow that? My accent's not in the way? Great. Now point me in the direction of wherever it is I'm supposed to be and stand back. Unless you think I need an escort. In which case, go get my escort, please."

Thus, twenty minutes later I was staring down the blanc-mange-that-wasn't-dessert and recalling a few home truths.

They don't have the FDA here. Or pasteurization. There's no Department of Health and Human Services. No Food Standards Agency. This could be Grade E beef. Or Grade A rat.

Yes, but... you have to eat.

So I took a bite, and damn! That's good Grade A rat! (I found out later it was whitefish.) And later, when I had time to think about it, I realized I shouldn't have been so surprised. Food couldn't be transported any great distance in TudorTime, or frozen, so by necessity we were eating pesticide-free fresh food. If the consequence of an extra slice of custard tart and bonus blancmange was a tapeworm or E. coli, I'd deal with it then.

Anne rose to excuse herself as I restrained myself from licking the crumbs off my plate, so everyone else stood, too. (Though that may have been because as soon as Anne's butt was off the chair by a bare inch, Henry had leaped to his feet. Even I knew that when the king stands, everyone stands.)

"I shall see you soon, my own sweetheart," he promised, kissing her hand. His beard must have tickled her knuckles, because she smiled. "My darling Marquess."

She nodded, then looked at me. "No more future *Marquis de Pembroke*, eh, holy fool?"

"I guess not. And please call me Joan. And I'll call you Marquess. But not for long."

She beamed, and it transformed her. Here was a woman who had made ambition her watchword, and to see her closing in on her years-long goal was to see her come alive. Which was all the more awful when I remembered where her bred-in-the-bone ambition would take her.

Luckily I didn't have to think about it any longer, because Anne left with a casual "Come, Mary," and headed for the door without bothering to glance back to see if she was being followed. Mary—the luckiest of the Boleyns, and wouldn't she be surprised to know it!—forced a demure smile and joined her sister.

"My lady Joan, I trust you and your angels found the fare acceptable?"

"Oh, yes! Thank you so much for a very fine meal, King Henry," I replied, and for once I was being sincere. He was, after all, my host. And the custard was, after all, exquisite. "Everything I ate was better than the last thing I ate!"

He threw his head back and guffawed at the ceiling, which put broad smiles on everyone else's face. Henry Tudor was someone who, when he let loose with a belly laugh, you couldn't help laughing yourself, or at least grinning like a dolt. I knew this because my mouth was sore from grinning like a dolt.

"Lady Joan," he said, still chuckling, "you are the best of guests: a holy maid who serves my kingdom and is grateful for the simplest things."

"Thanks. Could I maybe wrap some simple things in a napkin for later? Like a medieval doggy bag?"

"I beg your pardon, my lady?"

"Never mind."

"His Grace the Duke of Suffolk!"

I nearly dropped my cup. *How are they so loud without megaphones? It's got to be sorcery.*

"Too late to break the fast, Charles!" was Henry's boisterous greeting when a man almost as big and broad entered the room and bowed. "And Lady Joan has finished the custard tart."

I looked up from where I definitely wasn't chasing crumbs to pop in my mouth. "Is that my cue to apologize, King Henry? Because I won't apologize."

"Unrepentant wretch," he said, blue eyes twinkling. My, someone was in a good mood. Was he thinking he'd get laid once the future *Marquis de Pembroke* was a current *Marquis de Pembroke*? Because that was hilarious. Anne wouldn't give it up until Calais, and that was weeks from now. Ha!

"Majesty," the Duke said to his toes, still in a reverential bow.

"A fine morning to you, Charles," Henry replied, and the Duke looked up at the friendly greeting with a tentative smile.

Charles Brandon, as I'd noticed when he entered, was almost Henry's equal in size, with brown eyes, a full beard, a fleshy nose, and a small, red mouth. He was so broad he probably had trouble walking through normal-sized doorways, and was dressed in rich robes trimmed with fur and gold. They were peers, close to the same age. They'd grown up together, as I'd reminded Henry.

"Welcome back to court, Charles."

"A great pleasure to return. Your Majesty is generous."

Henry let out a regal snort (if there was such a thing). "Your thanks are due to the Lady Joan, my holy fool…"

No. No. No. I wasn't 'your' anything, Hank.

"…who was good enough to refresh my memory on certain points."

"Your reputation as a good woman guided by God precedes you, my lady, and you have my gratitude," he replied, and I got a bow, too.

"Your Grace, I was happy to help," I replied, trying not to preen the way Henry did when someone gave him a compliment. I have to admit, although my (laughable) plan was originally to avoid history's major players if at all possible, Brandon was someone I didn't mind running into. "Modesty forces me to point out it was the king's decision."

"The lady is too kind," Henry said, and ugh, he looked like a red-headed frog when he puffed up like that. "How does my sister, the Dowager Queen of France?"

At once, Brandon's smile fell away. "Alas, she was too ill to make the trip. She sends her warmest good wishes to Your Majesty."

There was a short silence, and I realized Henry was looking at me. Waiting, actually. Then I got it. "I'm sorry your wife is sick," I told the Duke, because she was. But I knew why Henry thought she might be shamming to get out of showing up for Anne's big day. Mary Tudor had been a loyal ally of Queen Catherine and would be until the end, one of the few who wasn't afraid to get in Henry's face and tell him he was making a fool of himself. But she was starting to die, probably from tuberculosis. "And I'm sorry to say it'll get worse before it gets better." A *lot* worse. And by "better" I meant she'd die, and be out of her pain, and wouldn't have to live in a world where a Dowager Queen of France had to give precedent to the diplomat's daughter who had shoved her sister-in-law off the throne of England.

"Ah, that grieves me," Henry said, and to his credit, he sounded genuinely sorrowful. "Charles, I shall send my best physician to see to her; you could both leave on the morrow and be at Westhorpe by sundown."

"Ours is very fine, Harry, and frequently attends Her Grace my wife," the Duke replied gently. "And I believe it is no longer a matter for physicians."

"Perhaps not, but you will not leave us without some of my special medicines," he ordered. "I have used them myself; they will do her much good."

"Thank you, Harry."

"That's really nice of you," I added, because it was.

"…my beautiful baby sister." Then the king seemed to come back to himself with a curt nod. "And now if you will excuse me, I need to see to the last of the preparations. Crum, with me, if you please." And he was off in a swirl of robes and jewelry, probably to micro-manage the florist or threaten to behead the caterer. No time for sick sisters; he had a *Marquis* to make! And Thomas Cromwell was right behind him, ready to do everything except tuck Anne into bed with the king. And maybe that, too, depending on how things went today.

I was idly glancing around and wondering where I should go until the ceremony started when I realized Charles Brandon was standing beside me, though I'd never heard him move. Large men who move quietly are uniquely frightening; I always want to hang bells on them.

"Lady Joan, I heard about what you said," the stealthy giant told me in a low voice.

"Well, I already told the king I wouldn't apologize. I'm sure the cook would make another custard tart if you asked."

"Ah. No." He cocked his head and studied me for a few seconds. "They told me you were different." Who the hell was *they*? Cromwell? Thomas Wynter? How long had the Duke been in the building? "I explained myself poorly. I meant to say I heard about what you told Harry yesterday. That I would have been his best friend even if he was a ken-nelman's get."

"Yessss," I replied cautiously, though I believe I said cook's boy. Was this a trap? Or just a friendly conversation?

"You had it *exactly* right," he said with peculiar emphasis, like he couldn't believe someone understood this basic fact of his life. "I always liked Harry for himself, even when he—ah—never mind. But you do not hail from our shores, and we have never met. I would have remembered," he added with (it must be said) a roguish smile.

Given that Charles Brandon had a reputation for 1) genial stupidity and 2) inveterate womanizing, I doubted that was true. He had a great grin, though.

"No, Your Grace. We've never met. I just—I just knew things about you." Also, Henry Cavill played you in *The Tudors* and what to say to that except *yum-yum-yum?* "I hope that doesn't make you uncomfortable."

"Indeed, no." He'd been leaning in, speaking in a low, intimate voice, but now he straightened to his full height and beamed down at me. "In point of fact, I am in your debt. If not for your kind intervention, I may have gone many more months outside Henry's regard. The king is...I know he wished me back at court, but...outside influences...ah..."

"But you're back now," I said brightly. "So no need to dwell. Right?"

He caught on a little quicker this time, nodding before I'd finished my sentence. "Just so, Lady Joan. The past is the past, and best left there, don't you find?"

For a moment I thought I was going to burst out laughing, but I reminded myself the custard tart was gone and retained my sober mien. The Duke was still talking, so he likely hadn't noticed my brief internal wrestling match. "I only wished to convey my gratitude. And...to ask...are your angels—is there anything else you wish to convey?"

Be nice to your wife. She'll be dead within the year. "Just cherish your loved ones. But that's good advice for all of us, don't you think?"

"Just so," he agreed, and smiled again, and *damn.* Charisma was like porn: it was hard to quantify, but you knew it when you saw it. Brandon had buckets of it.

"Your Grace, welcome back to court," someone snapped, and we both looked up. Mary Boleyn had swept back into the room, eyes narrow and mouth tight. There was a handprint on the side of her face that got redder while we watched. I decided against telling her she sounded exactly like her sister when she raised her voice. "I know the king is overjoyed you have returned to us."

"Thank you, Lady Carey." The Duke shifted his weight from one foot to the other and looked everywhere but Mary's face. "How go the, uh, preparations?"

"Well in hand." She touched her cheek and grimaced, and I had to bite my lip so I wouldn't smirk at the pun that sailed over the Duke's head. "As it turns out, my sister does not require my assistance so I thought I would see to the Lady Joan."

What? Don't drag me (further) into this!

"Yes, well. I am glad you are, ah, well. Both of you, I mean. Well, both of you and Henry. The king. So all three of you. Are well. Which is very fine." Charles Brandon, who didn't hesitate to lay waste to the north of France back in the day, was literally backing away from the aftermath of a cat fight. "I must see to my, um. And so farewell, ladies."

"Coward," I muttered as the doors slammed shut behind him, and Mary Boleyn giggled.

CHAPTER THIRTY-EIGHT

"Wow. That looks nasty. C'mere." Mary trudged over to me while I rooted through the detritus on the table and found clean water and a clean(ish) towel. I dipped the towel, then tipped her chin up and pressed the damp cloth to her face. She hissed and closed her eyes in relief at the same time. "Stings like crazy, I know. A slap actually hurts more than a fist. The surface area of contact is larger, and it's just as disorienting as a punch."

"I beg your pardon, Lady Joan, I cannot understand what you are saying."

"Your sister's a bitch."

She snorted against my palm. "They have such creatures where you come from?"

"Bitches be everywhere," I promised. "And most of them are bullies, also like your sister."

"Born and bred," she agreed. "My earliest memory is of baby Anne ripping up one of my dolls. When I complained, Mother told me I was too old for such things anyway." She sighed. "And all these years later, it seems I am fated to carry her train for the rest of my life."

No, you aren't.

"And her sons will lord it over mine, and so the tiresome acrimony will perpetuate for another generation."

No.

"If you can do it without drawing attention to yourself, you should keep that on your face at least half an hour. It'll help with the sting and keep the swelling down."

"Or," she replied, pulling the towel away, "I can let everyone see what a vindictive witch my sister is."

"You think they don't already know?"

"A good point." She put the towel back on her cheek with a wet smack. "I wish to be more like you."

"Uh. What?"

"Above the petty, too focused on the Lord Our Father's divine will to care about superficial idiocy."

"Yes, that's me all right," I lied. "Also, where did you get that idea? We've met twice."

"Do serving maids not gossip in Merka? Your refusal to don a fine gown for the ceremony is all over the court. How you insisted clothing was as nothing compared to the Lord's work—"

"That's not exactly what I insisted."

"—and that though such things are superficial, you were gracious in your refusal."

"Well, I was raised to be polite. But so were lots of people."

"Yes. About that. Your family...?"

"You guys really have that whole 'tactful pause' thing down, don't you?"

"I beg your—"

"Gone," I said shortly. Dead, five hundred years from now. "When I was younger. I've been on my own for a while."

Mary nodded. "Just so. And you were called to the Lord and go where you will. Where *He* wills." She looked at me with a steady dark gaze and added, "You are one of the freest women I know. Some days you know not where you will lay your head, but..."

"I don't have to carry anyone's train?" I guessed.

"Just so."

"The job has its perks." No one seemed surprised that a holy fool randomly wandered the country with no escort. I assumed they filed that under "the Lord works in mysterious ways" and didn't give it another thought. Why did that reassure me *and* piss me off?

Before I could give that any more thought, Mary gasped. Since I hadn't slapped her other cheek, I assume she could see something I couldn't, and turned. The attendants/guards had left with the maids when the food was cleared, probably because random nobodies didn't need to be announced, or maybe for shift change. The result: I had no idea who the man hesitating in the doorway was.

"Hello," I said, and he bowed.

"He is William Stafford," Mary hissed in my ear. "One of the king's soldiers."

"Why are you whispering? Is it a secret?"

"No, of course not." And was she ...? She was! Mary Boleyn, mistress to kings, mother of bastards, player of her family (and almost everyone else) was blushing. Adorable!

"Mister Stafford," she said as he approached.

"Lady Carey. And you are the Lady Joan."

That's what's written on my underpants. Except not really. "It's nice to meet you, Mr. Stafford." I knew that name. And as I watched them watch each other, I had it. The unassuming soldier with the Caesar haircut was Mary Boleyn's next husband.

"And it is nice to meet you, Lady Joan," which was nice, except he said it to Mary. In fact, after a cursory glance, he wasn't looking at anything *but* Mary. And she was looking back.

He was as unassuming in appearance as history had painted him: a distant relative of the Duke of Buckingham (which meant the blood of traitors flowed, however weakly, in his veins), a dark-haired man of medium height, with a square-ish face and hardly any chin, wearing practical clothing in practical shades: brown, mustard, darker brown, all of it topped with a cream-colored ruff, a competent and uncomplicated man. The most daring thing he would ever do would be to marry the queen's sister without permission.

But that was years from now.

"I have been told I will have the honor of accompanying you to Calais, Lady Carey."

"Me?" she gasped, her heaving bosom back in play.

"And the king and your sister, of course," he added, lest we think it was just him and Mary Boleyn on a pleasure trip to England's last toehold on French territory.

"I know I shall be safe in your company," she breathed. "And the king and my sister, of course."

Then they just stared at each other.

Which got awkward after about ten seconds, but only for me.

"Well," I said. *Ahem.* "I think I'll go find the kitchens and chat with the cooks. I have some questions about those sugar postage stamps and the blancmange. Don't worry. I'll just follow my nose." Nope. Nothing. "So I'll see you la—"

"Mary!"

All three of us jumped, which was a surprise—I didn't think a tornado would have gotten their attention. A short, slender woman with dark blonde hair, a broad forehead, and wide-set blue eyes was standing in the doorway radiating impatience. She was pale, even her lips, which made her eyes seem bluer and the rest of her almost bloodless by comparison. She hadn't touched me but I had the impression that she would radiate cold. Which was ridiculous—what, I was coming up with character judgments based on how a stranger said one word?

"What is it, Rochford?" Mary asked, clearly not pleased to be interrupted. Given the dislike in her tone and the casual use of Rochford instead of Lady or a first name, I deduced this was her sister-in-law, Jane Boleyn, a treacherous snake I needed to avoid at all costs.

"Anne wants you."

"Ha! I have the mark to prove she does not."

"Tell her so yourself." Then, lower, "*I'm* not going back in there."

"Oh, very well." She gave Stafford one last long look, hurried to the doorway, and turned back at the last second. "Mr. Stafford!"

He straightened at once, like a hound on point. "Yes, Lady Carey?"

"Will you please see to it that Lady Joan makes it to the ceremony? The king is adamant she be in attendance. And—and I shall be there, too. If anyone were to wonder."

He bowed low, like he'd been given the Holy Grail to tote around as opposed to a random American intent on grilling a chef about the merits of custard versus syllabub. "I should be pleased to do whatever you command, Lady Carey."

"Oh, thank you. Thank you so much, Mr. Stafford. Thank you very, very much." She paused as if she was going to say something else (thank you?), then walked out. Rochford rolled her eyes so hard she was probably glaring at her own brain, then followed.

Stafford let out a breath like he'd been punched. "I—I shall be pleased to take you to the kitchens first, if that is your wish. There is time."

"Oh, you heard that? I had the impression neither of you was listening to me."

He laughed, which made his Caesar haircut seem slightly less silly. "I would be a poor soldier if I could not focus on more than one thing at one time."

"An original multi-tasker, good for you. And thank you. I'd love to visit the kitchens. That probably sounds odd."

"'Tis not for me to question the whims of angels, or their messengers. Please, this way."

We walked for a few seconds in companionable silence, which I broke because I am an idiot who talks far more often than is wise. "Lady Carey likes you." *Ugh. Why not get really juvenile and say she LIKES–likes him?* "I'm new, but I could tell right away." Yes, it wasn't subtle.

"Lady Carey is one of the kindest and most beautiful and charming ladies at court. She is kind to everyone."

"I didn't say she was kind to you, I said she liked you." *Liked–liked.*

"She has the sweetest nature. She likes everyone."

"No, she doesn't," I insisted, because I knew of at least two people she despised, and, again, I'd only been here a day and a half.

"Even—even if that were true, Lady Carey will be sister-in-law to His Grace the king. She is a Howard by birth and will be royalty by marriage. She could be with anyone. Anyone in the world." He sounded positively awed just thinking about it.

"Exactly. She could be with anyone—but she likes you."

He brightened, but his tone stayed even and non-committal. "She has known kings."

"Well. Yes." To his credit, it didn't sound like slut-shaming. More like he thought it was more proof she was out of his league. "Think about that: she's known kings, and she likes *you*." Goofy haircut and all.

"Oh," was all I got for a response, and then he changed the subject, and then we were meeting the cook and I forgot all about Mary's future as a Stafford bride because the cook let me taste anything I wanted and I started with the gilded marzipan cake.

CHAPTER THIRTY-NINE

Anne Boleyn reminded me of one of the greatest books in literature, specifically, the opening of *Gone With The Wind:* "Scarlett O'Hara was not beautiful, but men seldom realized it when caught by her charm as the Tarleton twins were."

Anne's nose was too narrow. Her mouth was too wide. Her face was too long. Her skin was too sallow. Her boobs were too small. Her fingers were too long.

But she made it work. And there were the eyes, of course, those justly famous black pools that seemed like a welcoming darkness or a bottomless pit, depending on whether you were Team Anne or Team Catherine, besotted king or exiled queen.

That was something else. I noticed Team Catherine stuck with less flashy clothing and the gable hood, a hat that made them look like they were wearing roofs. (Who? Who designs a tiny roof and plops it on a woman's head and says, "There! Exactly what I was going for.")

Team Ann was flashier, brighter, and preferred the hood shaped like a half moon. Still annoying but slightly less cumbersome. Anne wasn't conventionally gorgeous, but she was sexy. Even I, straight as a ruler per the Kinsey scale, could feel it.

As for those "six fingers, large wen" rumors (what *was* a wen? a mole? a skin tag? benign tumor? whaaaat?), they were, in a word, nonsense. She couldn't hide a wen/birthmark/third nipple on her neck in any of the gowns I'd seen her wear. Everyone could see her throat was long and flawless. And if memory served (my mom would know for sure), the people who described her as having such "deformities" had never met her.

"He has to give her status," Mary whispered as Anne was escorted to Henry by the Garter King-at-Arms. "He cannot crown a nobody."

"At least you're not stuck with her train," I murmured, and she smirked. (That honor had gone to the Duke of Norfolk's daughter, another Mary, and a couple of random countesses.)

As for the Duke of Grump, he was front-and-center by Henry's side, with the Duke of Suffolk on Henry's left. They both had identical expressions of *I can't believe this is happening*, which went nicely with everyone else's. It was a packed house, and stifling, and I was very aware of the fact that antiperspirant had yet to be invented.

Anne was serene, though, and why not? She was a gold medal social climber who made Cinderella look like a hack. Her black hair flowed past her shoulders, a stunning contrast to her red velvet mantle, and she wore so many jewels she glittered. Henry, who had been fidgeting during Anne's "look ye upon me and despair" glide, all but sprang forward and plopped a gold coronet on her small bent head, and followed it with still more furs, until she was more ermine than Marquis. The room was hushed and you could feel the weight of it all, the import of what was happening right in front of us: the dress rehearsal for her inevitable coronation.

Anne ascendant was a freight train: you could hop on or not but either way, she was getting to her destination, and if you got run over, that was your own fault.

Then the bishop—Gardiner, if I had to guess—read aloud the patent that transformed her from random courtier to a peer(ess) of the realm.

And then, cake!

CHAPTER FORTY

B ut first another audience.

"Say it."

"Congratulations, former-future *Marquis de Pembroke*."

A short laugh that was almost a bark. "You are impossible."

"And *you* are a peer, and soon to be queen. So there's that."

"Just so." She nodded, smiling. "But do not think I will not box your ears for insolence."

"And don't think I won't smack you back." She snorted, doubtless assuming I was joking, how adorable. Smacking back in self-defense fell under the fool's prerogative, right? And what was involved with boxing ears? Was it like when you clapped your palms over someone's ears and they got disoriented, or just grabbing a random earlobe and yanking? I had no idea.

We were in Anne's presence chamber, where she'd retreated to rest or plot or whatever she was up to when she wasn't dragging out my time travel to-do list. She'd discarded her attendants, a fawning Henry, Mary Boleyn, and the ermine. (I could see why—the mantle was heavy and it smelled, um, old.)

"Your stubborn nonsense aside—"

"Hello, pot. Behold, for I am kettle."

"—I am grateful for your attendance today. It means much to me. And the king," she added as an afterthought.

"You'll recall I didn't have much choice." Then I realized the import of her words. "Is that why you both insisted I stay? Do you think my presence in your presence means God's on board with what you're doing?"

"God is—what?"

"That God sanctions this?"

"How *else* would I interpret it?"

Wow, the ego. She and Henry were made for each other.

"Your angels whisper our future," she pointed out. "You knew when the cardinal would die. You went to Catherine and dissuaded her from bringing war. You told me I would be queen. Of course God countenances my upcoming marriage. We have always known this. But now, everyone who saw me enter the king's presence as a knight's daughter and leave as a Marquess knows as well. I have to be safe."

"Look, I don't—what?" She'd practically whispered the last part, and I was so busy getting annoyed I'd almost missed it.

She just looked at me. "What happens when a Tudor wants something?"

"Wh—oh."

Because that's how obtuse I am. Because until that moment I hadn't realized a stark truth: the whole time I was telling Henry the Duke of Suffolk's story, I was also telling Anne Boleyn's story. Anne wasn't driving this slow car crash, she was a passenger.

"They get their way," I replied. "One way or another."

"Just so. And the king is…"

"Intractable and capricious?"

She sniffed. "You have been listening to my sister."

"You shouldn't have hit her."

"And she shouldn't be an idiot. But alas, we do not reside in a perfect world." And then, mimicking: "So there's that."

"What is it with Boleyns and accents?" They were the Rich Littles of TudorTime! Then I laughed, because everything was strange and slightly funny. She joined me, and we both pretended a lone tear hadn't tracked down her face to be impatiently dashed away.

After that, I liked her more than I felt sorry for her, when before it had been the other way around. I couldn't even tell you why, really. She was still a vindictive bully who wouldn't hesitate to stomp anyone in her way. Maybe I had a soft spot for self-aware asshats?

I clumsily changed the subject to satisfy my curiosity and give her a few seconds to compose herself, and asked to see the Letter Patent proclaiming Anne a peer. In my time, it had long crumbled into dust (or, if it existed, I had no idea where) but today the ink was practically wet. Not for the first time, I thought how much my mother would adore this.

She indulged me, but the first sentence ("Creacion of lady Anne, doughter to therle of Wilteshier …") was almost enough to trigger a migraine: difficult to read, so many curliqued letters, and argh, no universal standardized spelling! They didn't even have dictionaries yet. So if one person wrote "creation" and another wrote "creacion", they were both right. Which was wrong.

"Shall we command your return for my trip to Calais?"

"I don't think it works like that." A lie: I was positive it didn't. "And who is 'we'? Are you doing the Royal We thing already?"

She made an impatient gesture. "I need the practice, don't you think? Will you come? Even if you have no warnings to divulge? I understand you have to ensure, ah, her—your companion's safety …"

"Her name is Amy," I sniffed, and hopefully she didn't notice the short pause while I frantically (*Amanda? Abigail? Ava?*) tried to remember.

"Yes, yes." She waved Amy away with long-fingered hands. "Do you think your angels will send you back to us in time for Calais?"

"I have no idea," I replied, relishing the rare chance to tell a Tudor the truth.

"It makes no difference."

"That's the spirit."

"First this, then Calais to meet Francis as a near equal," Anne said with relish—you could practically see her scratching off her Road To Queenship list. "Then coronation. Then consummation. Then a prince."

"Yes, well, it sounds like you've got it all fig—*then* consummation?"

She tossed her head. "Oh, tiresome. Don't tell me you're one of those unimaginative scandal mongers who whisper the king and I have been lovers for years."

"No, I know you haven't been lovers. In the clinical sense, I mean."

"Oh!" She smiled. "So God knows I have been pure."

"Uh, no, God knows you've been with Henry Percy. And I'm not even going to bring up Thomas Wyatt." Risky, but I had to reinforce her belief that I was otherworldly guided. Because it was happening again. And I didn't know why. Nor did I know for sure about Wyatt—there were rumors of an affair, but it had never been confirmed for the historical record, which is why I didn't dare get into specifics.

What I *did* know? I had something to fix. Again.

When she spoke, I had to listen closely as she forced each word out through gritted teeth. "Do. Not. Repeat. That. To anyone."

"Do I look like the Spanish Ambassador to you? I'm no gossip." This was also true, but not because I was morally opposed. There was a time when gossip would have finished me. Literally destroyed life as I knew it. So I rarely indulged. "I've had plenty of time to spread that word, and you know I haven't. You think I care what you did back in the day? I absolutely don't."

She'd smiled—well, bared her teeth—at my mention of Eustace Chapuys, Spanish ambassador and inveterate gossip and tale-teller. His bitchy letters to Emperor Charles were one of the reasons why we knew so much about what happened in TudorTime. "And so?"

"And so you need to give in to Henry during the Calais trip."

She was already shaking her head. "No and no and no."

"I think one 'no' would have—"

"All I have is my honor, poor thing though it is, and the knowledge that no matter what they say of me, I was never a whore like my sister."

"Wow."

"Even if they never believe it, I will know, and His Majesty and my family will know, I will not give myself to the king until I am the queen."

I opened my mouth again but she cut me off. "*Seven years*, Joan. The better part of a decade. Only to—what? Toss it all out the window? Risk everything with an illegitimate son?"

"No and no and no?" I guessed.

I got a grim nod for that one. "I can wait a few more months. Archbishop Warham is a frail ancient; when he dies, and I pray it will be soon—do not look shocked, I am not the only one who prays for such a thing—Henry will appoint Cranmer as his new Archbishop and we shall be married. I can wait. And Henry, though he would say otherwise, can wait, too."

I saw it, then. The way to convince her—she was a harder sell than Henry, so I needed that edge. She wouldn't immediately bend just because I told her what she wanted to hear.

"Warham's dead," I said flatly. "A few days ago."

She sat. Hard. Thank goodness there was a chair there! "That is not yet public knowledge," she managed, trying—and failing—to hide how I had taken her by surprise. I was also trying to hide my reaction—my relief—that the gamble worked. I only had a vague idea that Warham died in August; I couldn't remember when. "Less than a dozen people know; the official announcement will not come until we are prepared."

"He's dead," I said again. "I know that like I know you need to give it up in Calais. The future of the greatest monarch England has ever seen depends on it."

"Ah." She straightened in her chair. She smiled. She glowed. And I felt like an utter shit. Because she would make assumptions I wouldn't correct. Because she was a woman ahead of her time, but even she wouldn't assume England's greatest monarch could be a woman. (Fun fact: England's other greatest monarch was *also* a woman. Ditto its longest-lived monarch.) "I see it now. This changes things."

"Besides, you've already made preparations."

"Have I, all-seeing fool?"

"Occasional-seeing fool." I picked up the Letter Patent and waved it at her. "'Heirs male of your body.' That's how it reads." I was pretty sure. The thing looked like the Sunday jumble to my modern eyes. "Not 'legitimate heirs male'. Even if you have a bastard, he'll be a peer. Even if the king doesn't marry you, you're set for life and so are your children. And I *know* the wording of this thing wasn't Henry's idea. He wouldn't dare put down in writing anything that even *suggests* he won't marry you." I waved it again. It made a great prop. "You're hedging your bets because it's been seven years and you're still not queen. Give in to him, Anne. Because either way, you're covered. *You* saw to that."

"Hand that back at once." She snatched the letter away, carefully set it aside. "Fine. You are correct, I need to look after my own interests, and that of my children's, and so I took appropriate steps. Some would call that mercenary."

"Some would call it smart."

"But I shall do as you say." She sighed. "But not so much because you say it. In truth, I tire of waiting. It feels like a hundred years."

"I can't imagine."

"Fortunately, we do not require your imagination. Shall we?" She stood, running her hands all over herself and patting her hair in case anything was out of place. Nothing was. "That is an awful sound your stomach is making. It's a wonder you can hear your angels with all that internal rumbling."

"I'm hoping for more custard."

Eye roll. "I am sure we can accommodate. Come along. And if you find yourself back with us in time for Calais, I pray you join us."

Pass. Really didn't need to be on the trip where two of the most egotistical people I'd ever met got sweaty and coital for the first time.

"I guess we'll see what happens."

"Why must you be either unnervingly precise or maddeningly vague, and nothing in-between?"

"It's part of my mystique?" I guessed, and she laughed at me.

CHAPTER FORTY-ONE

Banquets, by definition, are exhausting. It takes hours, you eat, you drink, you get sleepy, you eat and drink more. It's inevitable.

Not this one, though.

For one thing, this banquet wasn't divvied up into courses. The servants didn't start with appetizers and work their way to dessert. Instead they were bringing in roasts and pies and cheese and fish and candied fruit, so you never knew what you were going to get. What was next, saffron meatballs or marzipan? Mallard or scones? Who could get sleepy with that set-up? The next course could be the TudorTime version of French Silk Pie! Or turkey legs!

Guests were seated on one side of the table, which at first struck me as wasteful, but after a few minutes I realized the servers needed the extra room to bring in and take away all the platters of food. I had the, um, honor of being at the king's table with Anne, Henry, Cromwell, the Duke of Norfolk, the Duke of Suffolk, and a couple of others I didn't know.

And one I did.

"Oh, darling, that gown? Again?"

"Nice to see you, too, Eleanor."

"*Lady* Eleanor."

"I don't care."

"So there's that," Anne mimicked, and she and Mary Boleyn giggled, locking eyes and behaving like sisters for the first time.

Eleanor, who had doubtless been preparing some verbal evisceration, took another look at the Boleyn girls and switched tactics. "I do wish you would allow me to assist you, my dear, *dear* Lady Joan. One of my maids is a wonder with hair, and I have some old gowns I should be happy to lend."

"I don't care about that, either." Hmm. Better not push my luck. "Though it's kind of you to offer."

"Yes. It is."

"Take care, fool," Anne warned. "Your country may well suffer customs that differ from ours, but surely they understand the concept of courtesy."

"They understand the concept," I admitted. "It's the execution that needs work."

Eleanor laughed at that—a genuine laugh, I think—and we both silently agreed to back off each other. Which was perfect from a timing standpoint, as the next course was being carried in.

"Do you find—"

"Turkey legs, turkey legs, they're bringing out turkey legs *turkey legs!*"

"It is of no use, Master Cromwell," Anne explained while Henry started laughing. "She is deeply enamored of food."

"I like what I like," I replied, wondering if it was uncouth to wave the servers over. If it was socially acceptable, I'd be guiding them to me like a ground crewman waving in a 747. "Let me guess—you're one of those people who only eat for sustenance."

"It *is* only sustenance." She sniffed and tossed her small, sleek head. "Hardly important in the larger scheme."

"Tell me that when you've had to go to bed without supper a few times, with no idea if there'll be breakfast when you wake up."

I was so busy forking a turkey leg onto my platter (after furtive glances revealed people only helped themselves to one at a time, *dammit*) I didn't realize everyone had gone quiet. I looked up and saw something astonishing: Anne Boleyn and Henry VIII looking at me with clear sympathy.

"God's regard can be a burden, Lady Joan, as Job himself would attest," Anne pointed out kindly. "But he only asks much of those whom He values, *n'est-ce pas?*"

"I suppose that's true." I wasn't going to get into The After with any of these people. Irrelevant, and ancient history centuries from now. "But I think even someone who never missed a meal would love this banquet, Anne."

(I hadn't realized my slip, but later Mary Boleyn told me everyone at the table had been shocked when Anne didn't loudly and violently correct my use of her first name. Which was good to know, but jeez! Who could worry about niceties when the capon with lemon sauce was being served? And fried oranges? *Fried oranges!* I didn't know oranges were a thing you could fry!)

While the devouring went on, Will Sommers and his troupe were performing some kind of skit I had trouble following. It was a little like *Robin Hood* if the titular character had a limp and yelled at the king about the futility and folly of the Trojan War. Or maybe he was praising the king about the Trojan War? No idea, and it didn't matter. What did matter was that I could see Amy having a wonderful time and getting her fair share of laughs, so the end was *finally* in sight.

Which was 1) fine and 2) dandy for all sorts of reasons. One, we'd been here too long. Hours and hours and hours too long. Even if we made it back without a scratch, my luck wasn't going to hold every time.

Two, I'd had to fix history again, twice in one trip. Without my time travel blundering, Henry would have choked to death last year. Or, if he hadn't, Catherine would have brought the Emperor's soldiers into the King's Private Bullshit this year. Or, if she hadn't, Elizabeth I would not have been conceived next month.

Madness, all of it, and I refused to believe my role in society was to put Elizabeth Tudor on the throne after saving her wretch of a dad from choking to death. Something else was going on, which meant I needed to solve the mystery or come clean to I.T.C.H. Neither sounded a bit palatable (unlike the turkey leg). And speaking of I.T.C.H., they had to be worried. I'd never been gone this long. And I didn't want to think about what my roommate was going through.

For God's sake, was I going to eventually find myself in the historical record, a paragraph somewhere about a random holy fool with a terrible wig and worse fashion sense who saved Henry's life?

No. And check it—the skit was over, everyone was taking their bows, Anne and Henry were gazing into each other's eyes for some reason, servants were running to and fro, Mary Boleyn was flirting with a fellow wearing a *lot* of shiny things on his jacket, Lady Eleanor had done a fade, and the delightful chaos was the perfect time to leave.

"Oh, hey!" Amy was happy to see me—and when I thought about it, the one nice thing about TudorTime (aside from the food) is that most people seemed delighted when I turned up. "Hey, it's you, Foolio!"

"My name is not Foolio. I'm Henry's holy fool." Oh my God, *what the hell did I just say?* "Forget that. Forget I said that. And never speak of it. Ever. To anyone. Please?"

"Didja see me up there?" She gestured with her mug to the front of the room; ale flew like rain. "Ha, and they let me wear my regular clothes so I'd look crazy!"

"Brilliant. You're the next Olivier. Time to go." I gently seized her by the elbow and started plowing through the chaos. "I have to say, Amy, you've been a hell of a good sport about all of this."

"Nuh-uh ... it's fun! But prob'ly I should get back to my family. They don't like the, y'know, my drinking, but the headaches c'n get really—I should get back."

"We are on the same page one hundred percent." We were clear of the hall by now, headed for the exit and sweet, sweet freedom (and, eventually, sweet, sweet 21st century air pollution). I spared a brief moment of mourning for the stash of sugar postage stamps I'd left in my rooms. "And I'm taking the fact that our departure caused no notice as a very good *ow jeez!*"

I'd seized Amy, and then someone had seized me while I was babbling.

"Not so fast, lass." For a guy nearing his 90th birthday, the Duke of Norfolk had a grip like a python. "I need a word."

Aaaaarrrrrrrrrrrrrrrrrrrrggggggggghhhhhhh!

CHAPTER FORTY-TWO

"Hello, Your Grace."

"Fool, I cannot fathom what it is you think you're playing at—"

"This is Amy, by the way."

"—but the king needs to keep his feet on the ground—"

"She's pleased to meet you."

"—and bend an ear to long-time loyal servants of the Crown—"

"And I'm sure you're pleased to meet her."

"—which necessitates spending less time listening to whey-faced fools, whether they be holy or not!"

"And now that the pleasantries are over, Your Grace, what can I do for you?"

"Halt!"

"Halt? Seriously?"

He'd hollered that last because we were still headed for the exit. The only difference was, now I was dragging two people. Norfolk was strong, but not heavy, probably because he was 95% gristle.

And something else... I noticed there wasn't anyone around. No guards, no servants, no musicians, no loiterers. He'd either sent everyone away or chosen his moment carefully. Neither boded well for Amy or me.

"Are you deaf, fool? Stop!"

I stopped and glared. If I was a gauge, the needle would be edging into the red. "I don't have time for this." Good God, the exit was right there. *Right there.* "We have to go."

I turned and he tightened his grip on my wrist. "Do not turn your back on a peer of the realm!"

"Shhhh," Amy whispered. She'd gone pale and was rubbing her forehead. "You guys. C'mon. M'gettin' headache."

"Small wonder. We call those hangovers in Merka."

"Yeah, it's not a hang—hey, are you trying to pronounce Ameri—"

"We are leaving, Your Grace. Amy's not well and we're overdue. Have a nice day."

At this, the Duke of Disaster not only tightened his scrawny hold, he twisted my wrist, proving Americans didn't invent the Indian Burn. "Now, girl, lend an attentive ear," he snarled, and oh my God, the halitosis. "In future, you— what are you doing? God's breath, that *hurts!*"

CHAPTER FORTY-THREE

My father held a black belt *dan* in *aikido* and got me started when I was six. I quit when I hit middle school, but took it up again after The After. It's remarkably simple to learn, though it takes practice and I always get hungry after a class.

Chapter Forty-Four

"Take your hands off me, fool!"

"Yes, I don't like being grabbed, either. It's disrespectful, right? And cheap bullying, when you strip away the niceties."

"I'll have my guards skin you screaming!" Which would have been a lot more intimidating if his face wasn't mashed into the table.

"I'll be screaming or your guards will be screaming? I think that's an important distinction." I tightened my wrist lock and, because I'm a rotten bitch, smiled when he yelped. I had him face down on some sort of side table just to the left of the main entrance. Freedom: so near, so far. "And what will you say? 'Help, help, guards! Come save me from this fool, a lone woman who has me at her mercy even though I'm a war hero!' Yes, you should definitely summon them. They'll drink on that story for a year."

"I—you—I—nnf—gggnnnn—"

"If I let you up, will you behave?"

No answer but the grinding of his teeth. Or he was unhinging his jaw. But he wasn't hollering for his guards, and that was good enough.

I let him out of the wrist lock, seized him by the (now sore) shoulder, yanked him back up. His face was so red he resembled a peeved tomato, his hooked nose was full of burst capillaries and I could see a vein throbbing at his temple. His blocky hands were balled into fists. He was still grinding his teeth.

"In the future, Norfolk, do not touch me without permission. In the future, keep out of my way. In the future, brush your fucking teeth. All of those are equally important."

"I will see you in the Tower for this!"

"Shut. Up." I was about medium height for a 21st century American, and Norfolk was tall for a 16th century jerkass. He wasn't used to being glared at by a woman at eye level, which was probably why he hadn't stabbed me yet: pure astonishment at the goings-on. Or he was worried there'd be divine retribution for striking a holy fool. I wouldn't get this lucky again, so I had to make it count. "If you don't respect my, um, holy visions, at least respect the fact that your king and your future queen enjoy having me around and wouldn't think much of your bullying. If you do that much, we can keep it civil. If you do that much, we can keep this between us. Provided you mind your manners in the future."

"You dare to lecture me on courtesy, you, a common—"

"Yes, me. A common. Think about that. A nobody who isn't from around here had to teach the Duke of Norfolk a lesson in common courtesy. *That's* what you should be upset about, not the fact that I could have broken your arm in two places. Now stay. Away. From me." Each pause was punctuated by a jab to his chest. "Amy, it's time to go. Again."

We left him staring with his mouth open and, as if on cue, the room started filling with servants and courtiers as we took our leave. I don't think he noticed.

"So that geezer's kinda your bitch now?"

"Doubtful," I replied, but hey. Never say never. Or sometimes say never. I didn't know; it had been a loooong weekend. "Look, we need to get clear of the castle, and then we need to head for the big willow tree just off the bridge and then—" And then hopefully a magical science-portal no one understood would somehow know we were there and what we wanted and would open up for us and hurl us five centuries into the future where Amy would sign many non-dis agreements and I'd get another £10,000 which as of two days ago converted to $14,515 American.

The whole thing sounded ludicrous, *I* could barely believe it, and I'd seen I.T.C.H.'s tech in action. Amy's good nature was going to be put to the test. Again. Which was a shame, because the poor thing was white to the lips and having trouble keeping her balance.

And then. Like a miracle. We were outside, we were moving past people intent on their own lives and attracting no serious attention (other than some puzzled looks) and I could see the wavy gold shimmer that meant the gate was opening and when I looked to my left there was another one! And another on my right! And in front of us, and I glanced back and there was one behind us and *oh shit* they weren't gates *oh shit* they were visual auras and we weren't saved at all because I was getting a migraine.

I wanted to cry.

I wanted to throw up.

I did both.

CHAPTER FORTY-FIVE

A s we staggered past the bridge and headed for the trees, we were taken for scandalous, badly dressed drunken prostitutes and mocked, but nobody tried to impede our progress. Everyone was busy being busy, thank goodness.

I had two of Lisa's experimental pills in the fanny pack under my skirt, so I hiked it up, unzipped the pack, dry swallowed, and let my skirt drop back into place in the time it took to walk three steps. But I was in no shape to make a note of the start time and what could I write? "Migraine started just after Anne Boleyn's elevation to peerage, Windsor Castle, 1532"?

"Christ, my head. You have too much ale for breakfast, too?"

"Nish. Jush grain." Dammit! Along with the aura, aphasia sometimes kicked in. I tried again: "It's jush—*just* a migraine. This is—the leasht marfan piece. Of the post office." *GODDAMMIT!* There was nothing more frustrating than aphasia (unless I was trying to buy a Shamrock Shake in the summertime). I knew what I wanted to say but I couldn't get what was in my brain to match up with what came out of my mouth.

Pull it together. It's not as bad as the immediate aftermath of The After.

Right. My go-to "it could be worse!" psych-up. I had to keep us moving until something happened. An arrest for drunk and disorderly. A gate. An aneurysm. Something.

And then we were there: the willow! While I watched, a new aura was forming right in front of the trunk, or the gate was opening. Or both? I guess it could be both.

Please be a gate. I'll do anything if it's a gate. I'll give up meat! Well, not all meat. I'll give up fish. Okay, not sushi or fish n'chips or grouper or tuna or—cod! I'll give up cod.

It was a gate, glory be to the highest! (Also, no more cod for me, because a deal was a deal.) I felt the familiar tingling as I groped for the wavering, shining thing. Watching my arm disappear up to the elbow into the glow was as exciting as it was disturbing.

"What are you *doing*? Why are you groping the trunk?"

"Hey, itsh science." At least the aphasia was losing its grip. I was slurring but coherent, the way I was when I was two-and-a-half daiquiris in. "Man, they are going to be so impressed to see ush! Especially me! Againsht all odds I brought you back and shtopped a war and got Anne knocked up with Queen Elizabeth. No wonder I need a nap."

We took the plunge, and then we were standing on the platform.

The dark platform. The dark, quiet platform.

"What *is* this?"

"It—it's I.T.C.H.," I stammered. "But it looksh like ..."

No. I must have had it wrong. Because it looked like I.T.C.H. had closed for the day. It looked like the lights were out. It looked like no one was waiting for us. A few of the machines were glowing, but there was no one in the cavernous room, and all the overheads were off. The equipment beyond the platform was dark. Everything had gone dark.

No. I didn't have it wrong. Sometime in the last five hundred years, I.T.C.H. had been shut down.

"Ooooh, I don't feel good," Amy groaned, then bent forward and threw up on the platform. This seemed an entirely appropriate reaction, so I did, too.

(A good hostess never lets her guest feel self-conscious.)

CHAPTER FORTY-SIX

"Jesus Christ!" I couldn't see the speaker, but he sounded as appalled as I felt. It was a month for new experiences: time travel, employing the Heimlich five hundred years before it was invented, putting the Duke of Norfolk in a wristlock, and barfing in tandem with a fellow American after teleporting back to the 21st century.

The overhead lights started flickering on and I realized it was Warren, dressed in jeans and a long-sleeved black t-shirt (the sleeves were regrettably unrolled), hair damp from a recent shower, holding a cup of what I assumed was terrible coffee while he stood in the doorway and gawped.

"Jesus Christ!" he yelped (again). "You came back!"

"What the hell, Warren? Where ish everybody?"

He was staring up at us like we were apparitions. Violently ill apparitions. "I can't believe it. You did it!"

"Again," I reminded him. "I did it again. This is Amy. Amy, this is Dr. Warren, and he's going to have an enormous pile of paper for you to sign. *After* he cuts me a check. Don't jusht stand there," I commanded. "Help us down. Or find a mop. Maybe both. Where's everybody else?"

"We—you've been gone for a couple of days."

"Yes, you wouldn't *believe* how often I got hung up. Not to toot my own horn, but I was incredible in my perseverance and frankly, you got me at a bargain rate."

"We—I—we assumed you had—had failed."

While Warren was stammering, I was helping Amy down while skirting the edge of the puke puddle. (The platform wasn't especially high—it reminded me of the transporter room in a J.J. Abrams *Star Trek* movie.) But Warren's comment made me jerk my head up and glare. "So you *closed*?"

"You left on Friday. It's Sunday."

"So. You. *Closed*?"

"Yes." His face was starting to flush, which unfortunately only improved his looks. "Everyone was exhausted. No one knew what to do. As you know, we've been at this for weeks. And then a day went by … and then another … it was a miracle you made it back once, never mind—"

"Yesh, definitely don't factor my return rate of one hundred percent into your calculations," I snapped.

"And—well—it costs an enormous amount of money to keep this place running—the cooling units alone are—"

"So why are you here, Warren? If Dr. Holt told you all to go home?"

"I did go home. Had a real meal, took a shower. But." He actually had gone to a closet and grabbed one of those Swiffer mops, which was kind of cute, but now he stopped his mop prep and looked straight at me. "I wasn't ready to give up on you. So I came back."

Perhaps it was the migraine, but I nearly fell on his neck and wept. But *one* person coming back didn't make it right. Especially when I considered other factors. "I rishked my life, Warren!"

"What's wrong with your speech?"

"Migraine! Which I got risking my life! Repeatedly! Because *you begged me to*. So I went back—again. And I—" *Fixed history—again.* But this wasn't the best time to bring that up, though the conversation was inevitable. "And—and

I found Amy and brought her back and yes, I was gone for a couple of days. Can you figure out why?"

"Um—"

"Because sometimes it takes more than ninety minutes to go back in time, track a Lostie, find them, free them, get clear of any observers, and find a return gate, you shexy moron!" *Oh shit. I called him sexy. To his face. Which I'm going to put down to the migraine if he ever mentions it.*

"Huh. Is that what you've been doing?" From Amy, who had found a discarded lab coat—I hoped it was Karen's—and was wiping her mouth with it. "The last half hour is starting to make sense now. And now that I'm—ugh—sober, I have some questions..."

"Not now, Amy!" I turned back to Warren. "I did all that for you—for I.T.C.H., I mean—and you guysh couldn't give me until Monday before giving me up for dead and having your mail forwarded to your next mad scientist project?"

"Well—"

"I mean, Jesus!"

"Careful," Amy warned. "She knows karate."

"I do not! It's *aikido.*"

"I—I don't know what to say." Warren was just standing there, mop in hand and paralyzed by my rage. "There's nothing I *can* say, you're right to be pissed. There's no excuse. We—I have no excuse." He kept looking at me steadily, and under any other circumstance I'd be thrilled to be the focus of his regard.

But I had puke on my shoes and was going on day three in the same underpants and these people didn't give a shit about me and the headache was coming. I was in the sweet spot: the aura was gone, the aphasia was going, but the pain was about half an hour off.

"Joan, what can I say? We screwed up."

"Again. Screwed up *again.*"

"Yes."

"You know that old saying, fool me once, shame on you, fool me by sending me time traveling and then giving me up for dead, shame on me? I'm done. Cut me a check, call me a cab, explain things to Amy and call *her* a cab. And *don't* call me anymore. Parse your own problems, I am *out.*"

"But we need the details of your—"

"No. You don't get to debrief me this time. Nobody gets to debrief me, I'm going to debrief myself!" *Wait. What?* "The highlights: I was terrific, I.T.C.H. owes me, and apparently however long I'm gone in the past, the same amount of time passes here. And that's all you're getting."

"Joan, forgive me." The cup he was holding was trembling just a bit, but I steeled myself against it. "I am so incredibly sorry."

I stuck a finger under his nose. "Shut up. And call a cab."

"I'm confused," Amy confessed as Warren scurried off (still holding the mop—heh).

"Yeah? Be resigned, it'll only get worse," I warned her.

Chapter Forty-Seven

"Where in the name of ever-loving fuck have you been, you absent shithead?"

"Doing scads of drugs and having so much unprotected sex I lost track of time?"

"Nice try, you terrible liar." Lisa took a break from pacing to glare. "Jesus, Joan, I've been going out of my mind!"

"Migraine."

"Oh. I know they suck, and you know I'm trying to help, but they don't prevent you from telling me what's up so I don't yank my hair thinking you're in a botulism-induced coma."

(That's one of six ways Lisa has predicted I'll die: food poisoning so severe it kills me.)

"No, I mean I've got one now. Yes, I took a pill, and it started exactly two hours ago. But it's a baby, so it's not all bad."

"Silent migraine, okay, that's good, I'll put that in the data. Although these meds aren't supposed to lessen a migraine, they're supposed to eliminate it."

"Yes, but I'm not complaining."

"And that still doesn't explain where you've been all weekend."

"At work."

"No, you weren't, because I went to the Information Technology for Culture and History and you weren't there.

Also, what raging marketing fuckhead thought up a name with the acronym I.T.C.H.?"

"You—what?"

"Don't make this about invading your privacy," she snapped, "although I invaded your privacy. I was *scared*, Joan. And I fucking hate being scared so I checked the GPS and went to the lab I had no idea you worked for because you're keeping secrets for some reason."

"Um..."

"Joan. I thought we were done with that shit."

This was tricky territory for several reasons, the most problematic being that I'd spent my adolescence being secretive and she'd spent hers being hyper-vigilant.

I took a breath. Let it out slowly. And lied. "I'm not an official employee, so there'd be no record of me there." Wait. That wasn't a lie. "I'm an off-the-books intern working in their R&D department." That wasn't, either. "And I can't tell you about their work because I signed a non-disclosure agreement." Huh. What do you know? It's all true! (Don't tell me about lies by omission. I know all about lies by omission.)

"Okay, first? Literally no one calls them non-disclosures; they're NDAs and I can't believe I have to tell you this again. But that bullshit aside, you fucking hate paperwork of any kind." Lisa could not have been more amazed if I told her I'd taken up lap-dancing to make friends. "You almost didn't come to England *and* threw a shit-fit because the State Department requires a three-page form for ex-pats!"

"That's how important I think their work is. And I still think a two-page form would have been sufficient."

That made an impression. She stared at me. After a long moment, she said, "Can you at least tell me what kind of work you're doing?"

"No."

"Is it dangerous?"

"Yes."

"Can I help?" There was *no* pause before that question, because Lisa was as brave and loyal as she was profane and grumpy. (She would also write me a doctor's note whenever I wanted to get out of work. Money cannot buy such loyalty and good fellowship.)

"No. Besides, it's moot. I literally just quit. I might go back for—for some paperwork, but that's it. I'm done."

Again with the unblinking regard, then. "You'd tell me if you were in trouble, right?"

"Yes."

"Do you promise?"

"Yes."

"Okay. The important thing is you're back. I mean, that's what I cared about the most. The minutiae, not so much."

"I know."

"So. Since you're back. And you quit. Then ... I guess ..." I think Lisa had anticipated the argument would last longer, because she seemed a bit unmoored as she groped for a new subject. "Are you hungry? I went to the Café and got an extra steak sandwich to go. D'you want it?"

"No, I'm not hungry."

"Oh shit, are you dying?"

I snorted at her histrionics. "Stop it. You know there are times when I'm not hungry."

"Yeah, and I can count 'em on both hands even though we've known each other over a decade."

"I just want a shower," I said, my truest statement that day so far. "And a nap. And then maybe another shower." Although I'd left the gown at I.T.C.H. and changed back into my street clothes before the cab picked me up, I was still in the same underwear. And my hair, after being squashed under a wig, was atrocious, staticky and wild like it was happy to be free at last and anxious to escape my skull. "And a brush. Maybe several brushes." And not just my hair. My teeth needed a Crest caress in the worst way.

"Yeah, about that, and don't get pissy and take this the wrong way—"

"I'm not getting it cut!" I snapped. "I'm growing it out." Partly because I have hair ADD (I grow out bangs, then cut my bangs, then decide I don't want bangs anymore and grow them out, a vicious circle I'll never escape), but also so I could eventually ditch the wigs.

Oh. But I wasn't doing that anymore.

But still: my drab mane was at that awkward stage of too long to be considered short and too short to be considered long. If I kept ignoring it, eventually it'd be long.

"Fine, starve yourself *and* keep your cute hair looking awful, see if I care. Tea?"

"Tea would be great. And. Um." I cleared my throat. "I'm sorry I scared you."

"I'm just glad you're back, fucking hideous hair and all. And I'm a little bummed you weren't actually doing drugs and getting laid. Chai or jasmine?"

"Jasmine, please." Something delicate to look forward to sipping while I counted the blessings afforded by 21st century plumbing and shaved my legs. No more time-travel for me, which was just as well—I'd live longer, probably.

Thomas Wynter is long dead. He's a pile of bones by now.

Now where had *that* come from?

I shrugged it off and went to shower.

CHAPTER FORTY-EIGHT

An hour later, I was in my favorite spot: sprawled on our couch in front of a fire while the latest *Game of Thrones* spinoff streamed and Lisa sat on the floor muttering at her tablet.

I felt unappreciated but clean. I had flossed so much I sounded as if I was twanging a harp strung with dental floss, and my clean hair gleamed like a mud puddle after a heavy rain.

And my bank account looked great. Warren had given me a check, which wasn't the brightest move because now I had no incentive to go back. I would, because they should know what I'd been up to while in the grip of their tech, and maybe my info could help them solve some of the problems, but I didn't *have* to. That made all the difference.

I was also catching up on my Tudor history. Not the pop culture stuff—I'd had all that memorized for years—but the actual history. Which was hilarious on its own merits; I hadn't willingly opened a non-fic Tudor tome since my training bra days.

And as I read up on Cromwell, Henry, Catherine, Norfolk and the rest of their wacky gang, I realized I was guessing everyone's ages wrong. *Argh, stop using the present tense!*

Let's try again: it occurred to me that I had guessed everyone's ages wrong. And not by a little. Norfolk, whom

I'd pegged as in his eighties, was barely out of his fifties. Catherine's fierce advocate, Countess Willoughby, was only in her early forties when I met her. Henry and Catherine were both younger than they appeared to me. Living in the Tudor era must be stressful as hell. Remember those before-and-after the Civil War pictures of Lincoln? Like that.

And speaking of the Countess, she'd hit my expectations and then some, which made me laugh out loud.

"It freaks me out when you huddle up on the couch and giggle," Lisa said. "What are you even holding?"

"Stop that. You know what a book made from trees looks like." Lisa embraced modernity in all things, which was hilarious given how much she liked wood-burning stoves. I think it was her way of confirming that old-fashioned = bad. Beloved mothers don't O.D. on meth in the paperless and addiction-free world Lisa was determined to make. The only dead-tree book she owned was *Gray's Anatomy.* "Just some history."

"Why the fuck are you reading about the Tudors?"

"I lost a bet."

"Yeah, figures." She shook her head. "You don't know you're doing it, do you?" I must have looked blanker than usual, because she added, "You're picking up the accent."

Lisa had made this observation while reading. And when I say "reading", I mean she had a newspaper out (the old-fashioned kind, but only because she was about to burn it), had unfolded her phone into tablet mode, and had her all-time favorite storybook, *Gray's Anatomy,* open to one of the penis pages.

Since she didn't make a habit of *quiet* observation, that got my attention.

"I am? It doesn't sound forced, does it? Like I'm faking it?" Was this something to fret over? Perhaps I should fret.

"No. That's my point. We've only lived here a few months and you're starting to sound like a native. And you're not aware of it. At all. It's... it's just what you do."

"And?" If it didn't sound like a pretentious affect, big deal, right?

"You don't have to camouflage." Now she was speaking quietly *and* gently as I tried not to be terrified. Lisa didn't do quiet or gentle. "You don't have to hide. No one's coming in the middle of the night to take you. The things you did to survive your childhood... you don't have to do them anymore."

Abort. Abort! "I. Know. That."

"I thought if I got you out of Wisconsin, away from where it all happened, you wouldn't work so hard to camouflage yourself. That you'd be free to..." She trailed off and frowned. "Well. It hasn't even been a year. Give it time."

"Give what time? Scratch that, I don't want to know. I don't need to be fixed," I warned.

"Sure you do," she replied cheerfully. "But don't feel bad. Most people do. I do."

Got *that* right. But because I wasn't as brave as she was, I didn't say it out loud.

So I was picking up the accent. What, blending in was a bad thing? Ha! Shows what Dr. Destructo knew; blending in would keep me from getting killed when I went back to TudorTime except I just remembered I quit so I'll never go back to TudorTime.

And that's fine.

It's totally fine.

Really. It's all fine.

CHAPTER FORTY-NINE

I was transcribing the clinic notes for Mr. Stollen's chronic obstructive pulmonary disease when my phone clicked at me. I.T.C.H. was calling, either looking for a debriefing or because we—they—had a new Lostie.

I let it go to voicemail.

All three times.

And then I went to bed.

"You want me to talk to them?" Lisa asked. She had a vase-sized glass of chocolate milk in one hand and was holding a Pop Tart with tongs in the other. This despite several discussions about how the toaster was a better option than her Bunsen burner.

"No."

"Because I'll be glad to have a chat with them."

I smirked down at Suzannah Lipscomb's *A Journey Through Tudor England*. Lisa's chats—with a sexually harassing prof, the dumbass who tried to steal her identity, the utilities company, a meth dealer—were mild forms of 'I am become Death, the destroyer of worlds'. "No, things haven't gotten that bad."

"What is going on?" she demanded, and I jumped, because she'd crossed the room and was reading over my shoulder.

"Writing!" It was the first thing to leap into my brain, then out my mouth. "I've taken up writing things down. Well, first reading and then writing things down."

"What kind—"

"Tudor period."

I braced myself for the fallout. But I lucked out—she just blinked, *sans* comment. A perfect time to bring up my agenda.

"And I wanted to ask you some stuff. For starters, I wondered if you knew any old-timey cures for migraines."

"Well, death is technically a cure in that it results in the total abatement of symptoms."

"And also the total abatement of a pulse. Next."

"Why do you need to know? And, again: what's with the Tudor reading? You hate that shit."

"No, I was bored by that shit. For years. But lately it's gotten interesting to me again. Possibly because I'm maturing into a sophisticated, well-read woman who—stop laughing, jerk."

"So you're picking up the accent *and* turning into a Tudor-phile before my eyes. Goddamn unending horror, that's what I'm in for."

"But you always knew that. Also I need to talk to you about drugs."

"You..." She took a gulp of milk and sputtered. "What?"

I put the book aside and followed her back into the kitchen. "I'm writing a book about time travel back to the Tudor era. Well. Thinking about it."

"Why? Lose another bet?"

I shrugged.

"I smell the Information Technology for Culture and History all over this."

"You're literally the only person who doesn't use the acronym. And you're right, but I can't go into it."

"NDAs suck a dead donkey's balls."

"The restriction can be annoying, but a deal's a deal. And nobody made me sign it."

"I'm still astonished you *did* sign it. Now I'm gonna haveta get you drunk and get the whole story out of you."

"You might not have to get me drunk. There might be a way around it, but I have to do some more research first. But I can't pretend I didn't get anything out of it." Twenty-nine thousand thirty dollars and eighteen cents, to be specific. And a lifetime of yummy historical food memories. And some memorable afternoons with the yummy Thomas Wynter. And a crush on Warren's forearms. And profound disillusionment.

I shoved it all to the back of my brain. "Let's say a modern heroine knows she'll end up in the mid-sixteenth century."

"Hey, I'm just glad to see you're engaged in something. Anything."

"Don't start," I warned. "I engage all over the place. Now. My heroine can't bring much, maybe a backpack's worth. What medications should she have on hand?"

"How long is she stuck there?"

"It could be a couple of hours to several days."

"But she can expect to return?"

Please God, yes. I nodded.

There was a 'fwoosh!' as Lisa fired up the burner and started caramelizing the Pop Tart. "Well, antibiotics, to start. If she gets even a splinter, she's gonna want something to kill any infection, especially if she's stuck there a while. I wouldn't set a sole fucking toe in the 16th century without a couple of cycles of Keflex. And some opioids. Hydro, maybe. Or Oxy."

I was putting it all into my phone. "What else?"

"Well, the water back then was essentially sludge. And the diet was less than varied."

"Right, but on the upside—no MSG, no artificial growth hormones, no pesticides."

"Fair point. But still—water purification tabs and vitamins. OTC laxatives and antacids would be good. Maybe some antihistamines. A *really* good First Aid kit. Is she gonna fuck?"

"God, no! I mean—I don't think so. She's not there long enough and even if she wanted to there can be no happily ever after so she'd never have sex with anybody." I let out the breath I hadn't realized I was holding. "At least, that's my take on it."

"All right, calm down. If she's on the Pill she'll need to bring some, that's all I was saying. Modern condoms would be tough to explain."

"Just a bit." I almost laughed at the idea of waving a Magnum condom at Thomas Wynter, to use an example of something that wouldn't happen because I was done with all of it.

"If she has time before she goes, immunizations would be good. With time for boosters, ideally. MMR, diphtheria-tetanus-pertussis. Varicella, polio, hepatitis, typhoid. A flu shot."

Before long, we were off meds and onto other practicalities ("Tampons. And hand sanitizer. A fucking oil drum of hand sanitizer. And a good pocket knife."). Lisa got caught up in the challenge in spite of herself, which led to speculation about whether or not smuggling a .38 to the past was brilliant or suicidal.

I know, I know: what did I think I was doing? I was done with I.T.C.H. and they were done with me. They had been done with me before I even returned on their last danger-fraught escapade. It wasn't my job and it had never been my responsibility.

But I still had to go in for the debriefing, and maybe my notes would be helpful to whomever they got to be their new Lostie wrangler. And who knew? Maybe I *would* write a book about my adventures, non-disclosure agreement be damned.

After we were done brainstorming, Lisa demanded I try a caramelized chocolate Pop Tart. So I bit. Chewed. Swallowed. "Dammit."

"Right? They're so much better this way! That's it, I'm throwin' away the toaster."

"I am lost without you."

I crumpled the card in my fist and watched the floral truck drive away. "Lost? Oh, very funny, Warren." Though I had to admit, the two dozen peachy-pink roses were gorgeous.

"Oh you manipulative pricks." I.T.C.H. had texted me a picture of a lovely dark-skinned woman with cheekbones you could cut yourself on. Teresa Lupez, visiting from Washington D.C., missing thirty hours, last seen at The Tower of London. Family and friends very concerned, any-one with information, please call the Missing Persons hot-line or the police, etc.

"Concerned, but not enough to risk an I.T.C.H. tech," I snapped at my phone. "Concerned, but not enough to tell the authorities what really happened." I'd always known I was dispensable, but I.T.C.H. was really rubbing it in.

And why wasn't I going to the police, non-dis be damned?

Because they won't believe me. And once they decide I'm deluded or a pathological liar, which they'll decide pretty quickly, they'll look into me, not I.T.C.H., which will lead to inevitable questions about The After and big trouble when they find my gun.

I deleted the text. I didn't owe them anything, and *them* included Teresa Lupez. Besides, I had a number of errands to run. Not that I had to explain myself. Because I didn't. And I wouldn't! Over and done, all of it.

Yep.

CHAPTER FIFTY

"All right, you pack of amoral Igors, fine, I'm here, fine, *Jesus*, you win."

I'd stormed past the non-existent receptionist (coffee break? sick day? laid off?), blew past all the stupid corporate retreat photos, and made my way to the warehouse-sized lab.

"Did you hear? I'll go. I'll go. All right? I'm here. I'll go."

Silence except for the humming and whirring of various machines. Dr. Holt stretched out a hand to Karen, who grimaced, pulled out her wallet, and slapped a bill in his palm.

"Really, Karen? *Really?*"

"Thank you, Joan." This in a tone of deep relief as Dr. Holt rushed over to me. He, like Warren and Karen, had showered and eaten recently. He was much less hollow-eyed and rank. "Thank you so much. And I'd like to apologize—"

"Save it. If you get me thinking about Project Abandon Joan To A Nasty Fate, I'll change my mind. I might anyway. Are you any closer to figuring out why this keeps happening?"

"Ah. Well." He cleared his throat and looked at the floor. "About that…"

"Sorry, I'll rephrase. Are you any closer to clueing me in on what you're really up to?"

That got his attention. "What? What makes you think—"

"Please." I folded my arms across my chest and leveled a Lisa-like glare. Tried, anyway. I couldn't see my face. Maybe I just looked tired and constipated. "You guys have been squirrely from Day One. First off, there aren't enough of you. I've only ever seen you three and one or two others. Pretty light staff for a lab this size. Second, you're not reading any of the non-disclosure agreements you've gotten us to sign. Third, there doesn't appear to be any long-term plan in place—you're only concerned with the little fires, not the bonfire that might burn everything down—and fourth, you haven't reached out to any of the Losties once you've got their paperwork."

(My errands? Were informative.)

"There's no way you—"

"I called them all, Dr. Holt." I resisted the urge to grab him and give a tooth-rattling shake. Holt was blocky and sturdy, but I had adrenaline and irritation on my side. "What, you think I'd go to the trouble of risking my life bringing them back and then never think of them again? That they'd never think of me and have questions once the shock wore off? Just 'See ya!' and that would be that? Of course we exchanged contact info."

"Which was strictly forbidden in our agreement," Holt said sharply. Which was fine; I *wanted* him to get pissy.

"I signed and initialed all the paperwork as Martha Washington."

"You—what?"

"And dated it all 1776."

"*What?*"

"Which you didn't notice because you didn't bother reading any of it. Or, at best, you skimmed for details but didn't bother with any of the signature pages. You're not looking closely at the paperwork because you don't actually care about it, it's just a way to intimidate your victims, keep us out of your face, and discourage us from contacting the authorities."

"Who would you even contact?"

"Exactly—*that's* where your focus is: keeping secrets. The only reason you're worried about Losties is because you can't afford *any* scrutiny—good or bad."

Total silence.

"None of you are even supposed to be here, are you?"

"Oh, hell." From Karen. "How'd you figure it out?"

"The real question is why it took me so long." I decided to ignore the urge to indulge the trope, 'I didn't. *You* just told me.' "You guys are not slick."

I.T.C.H. didn't ask many questions, that had been one tip-off. For cutting-edge scientists with a supposed seven-figure budget who were devoted to culture and history and who had the godlike power of time travel at their fingertips, they were remarkably incurious. Other than Warren's inter-est (and not to blast my own trumpet, but I think that had more to do with me personally than any love of Tudor lore), there was never any of the "tell me about the past I can't believe you time-traveled what's Anne of Cleves really like *wow!*" attitude I'd expected.

No, it was always more like, "Huh? Oh. You're back. Hooray?"

At the time, I reasoned that they were focused on the bigger problem: how to stop random gates from opening and grabbing the unsuspecting.

But here's what it really was: a total lack of interest because none of them cared about time travel, or Losties. I just couldn't figure out what they *did* care about.

And when they did ask questions, they were the wrong ones. "Don't tell anyone, okay?" "You understand our arbitrary rules, right?" "You don't have family? Great! But you're not going to divulge to your roommate, either, got it?"

"Tell me what happened."

So it all came out. I think they were glad of it. They were all interrupting each other to explain the details behind the unfolding crapfest. How Warren and Holt were practically the only original team members left. How they'd worked on information teleportation right up until they blew through their funding. How the entire project was shutting down, their lease was up in sixty days, most of the group had transferred out, and the ones left got Senioritis and started goofing around with the tech and accidentally exposed wormholes.

"You accidentally exposed wormholes," I parroted, because *for God's sake.* This was insane, they were insane, we were all deeply, incurably insane.

"There was some kind of power surge that coincided with what we were doing." This from Karen, who added, "I don't think we could recreate the accident, to be honest."

"No, of course not. Power surge? So, what, a Frankenstein's monster effect? The 'a lightning storm happened during the experiment so now there are wormholes' excuse? Seriously?"

"Well, it sounds stupid when you put it like—"

"*It's stupid, Karen!* It's not about the phrasing!" Jesus. These people. "So a bunch of—what? Science temps? A bunch of you were dicking around with equipment you didn't understand and the resulting power surge made wormholes."

"Exposed," Holt was careful to differentiate. "Not invented."

"The gates," I guessed.

"Correct."

"So after you dolts did whatever-it-was, suddenly people within—what? seventy, eighty miles of your facility?—could see wormholes, and they either fell or blundered into them by mistake. But usually the wormholes aren't...uh..."

"Traversable."

"That's it." I gritted my teeth over the irritation of a careless moron knowing a word I didn't. "They aren't traversable all the time, and even when they *are*, not everyone can see them." Otherwise half the population would have gone missing, not half a dozen in a month. "And none of you have been able to figure out why." Not that I could blame them for that last one. As far as I could tell, other than accidental time-travel, the Losties, myself included, had nothing in common. Different nationalities, races, races, religions, creeds, genders, political leanings, education, upbringing, blood type, etcetera.

"Say, gang, do you know what might have provided you some valuable clues? *Reading the paperwork you made us sign.*" My God. That's how much trouble poor Teresa Lupez was in: I had more common sense than the scientists responsible for her plight. "So I.T.C.H. was government-funded, but is now officially shut down. And you guys decided to keep the lights on how? Private funds?"

"Yes."

"And were inspired to play with unregulated tech."

"Yes."

"With no fucking idea what to do next."

"Well. Uh. Yes."

(I tend to be liberal with the F bombs when I'm beyond aggravated, unlike Lisa, who treats them like everyday adjectives.)

"Which is why you shut everything down and went on your merry way last weekend. You gave me up for lost or dead so..."

"...so we figured shutting everything down for a few hours was worth a try. Experiments often yield negative results which in turn lead us to—"

"Shut up, Karen. It was a pathetically desperate attempt to fix something you weren't sure would work and if that meant stranding me, oh well, bigger picture and all that. Right?"

"I have the feeling that if I answer you're going to hit me."

"Excellent instincts, Karen. Cripes, you're wearing a lab coat that isn't even yours!"

"I like the extra room," she whined, flapping her arms.

"Warren even needled you about your background when I came back from Calais! He asked if they mailed your diploma or sent an e-card."

Warren cleared his throat. "That was more because I don't like her as opposed to thinking her credentials suck."

"Understandable." To Ian Holt: "You can't get the authorities involved because not only did you inadvertently kidnap several people, you're basically running a fraudulent operation and breaking about twenty laws, from misdemeanors all the way up to felony. And maybe murder, if I can't save Teresa. Or myself."

"Why are you narrating?" Warren asked.

"It helps me think!" I snapped. "And not a single one of you was a decent enough human being to risk getting into trouble for strangers. Jesus! No wonder you were so amazed when I came back from Calais."

"It was miraculous," Warren said quietly. "Appearing out of nowhere, the only one to make it back. You were a goddamned miracle."

"Don't you dare try to be nice to me now. So how'd you pay me? How are you keeping the lights on? If you're out of funding? Is that why the receptionist is gone? And the parking lot's always empty?"

Warren cleared his throat. "Yeah. And that was me. I paid you with my own money." When I just looked at him he added, "I thought you were worth it. And then some."

I remained unmoved. (Right? Yes. Unmoved.) If he hadn't technically lied, he'd withheld a lot of necessary information. The fact that he was the only one of the lot who had any faith in me was irrelevant. Right? Yes. Because I historically didn't have a soft spot for the one person in a group (Lisa, Warren, Mary Boleyn) who valued me. Not at all.

"And I'm happy you came back," he continued, "but in the interest of full disclosure—"

"Why? Is that a new thing you're trying?"

"—my funds are nearly depleted. I can't pay you this time."

"Not a factor." I couldn't take it even if he had the money. I was now officially an accessory to their bullshit. I wasn't going to make it worse by taking more money. And when these complicit shitheads got caught—and they would—I might have to give the $29,030 back. "I don't care about the money. And poor Teresa has been kept waiting long enough, so I need to get moving. Now: what is your plan if it takes me more than an hour and a half to find Teresa?"

"Um ... to *not* shut everything down and leave?"

"Very good, Karen!" I clapped. Hey, she deserved it. She'd just taken a huge step. My applause was only 80% mockery. "But just in case you forgetful idiots get forgetful, believe that I've left some contingencies in place, *none* of which will rain down on your lives provided you do the right thing."

Karen's eyes practically bulged. "But—my God, you can't—what if you get killed over there?"

"That is literally the most upset I've seen you get at the prospect of my death—when it's going to screw up *your* weekend plans. Hope I don't die, Karen! Obviously!"

"Risky," Holt said. He wasn't as visibly upset as Karen, he just seemed dourly resigned.

"Yes, Dr. Holt—wait, are you even a doctor?"

"Of course I'm a doctor, I got my doctorate after—"

"Shut up now. Yes, it's risky—just like every single trip I've taken for you duplicitous dillholes has been risky. And yes, it could end badly. Just like every single—"

"We get it," Holt snapped.

"Really? Are you sure? Because for scientists, you guys aren't bright. You're the 'book smart but no common sense' trope come to life."

"But you admit we're book smart?"

"*Shut. Up.*" I took a breath so I wouldn't kill someone while simultaneously suffering a fatal heart attack. "Give me ten minutes, and then do whatever it is you do to summon a gate. Try not to shatter the space–time continuum while you're at it."

"And then what?"

"Pray I come back. Obviously."

CHAPTER FIFTY-ONE

Dear Lisa,

*D*on't *freak out. But if I'm not back in 24 hours, it's because I'm a time traveler who scoops up people who fall through a wormhole accidentally created by imposter scientists who don't understand how any of it works and they cut me a five figure check every time I jump. Well, they used to. Not anymore, because now I'm an accessory to fraud. And time travel, I guess?*

I'm not crazy.

This is why I couldn't tell you what I've been doing for I.T.C.H., because your first instinct after screaming "What the fucking fuck are you even talking about?" would be to slap a seventy-two hour psych hold on me. I don't have time for a ten-hour psych hold, never mind one that lasts for three days. Also the food would be terrible. Don't try to tell me different.

Anyway, if I'm not back, DO NOT GO TO I.T.C.H. I'm serious, Lisa. Do not behave like one of those silly horror movie heroines and seek out danger by yourself. KEEP CLEAR. You'll never be able to convince the cops that I.T.C.H. had anything to do with my disappearance, or that time travel is real, and if you show the cops this letter, they'll wonder why you didn't place a psych hold on me when you had the chance. The only thing storming

I.T.C.H. will do is bring trouble on your head—perhaps a lethal amount. STAY AWAY.

For a while. But when things have quieted down and they think they've gotten away with everything, you can use the stuff I left you in my strongbox to wreak fiscally ruinous and violent revenge upon them. There's simply no one in the world who would rain havoc on their lives like you, which is one of many reasons I adore you.

When I return (because I'm actually getting a handle on this and am pretty confident I'll be back and yes, I'm aware that sounds as insane as thinking I'm a time traveler), I'll tell you everything, full disclosure, NDAs be damned.

If I don't return, I've made arrangements for you to take possession of my money (not that you need it) and my stuff (not that you want it).

You know where the key to my strongbox is.

I've loved you from the minute you helped me out of the ice cube pile I made when I got sick that first time.

I hope to see you soon.

Love,
Joan

CHAPTER FIFTY-TWO

The willow outside London again. And soon enough, since I had founded Horse Hertz, I was riding into the city on a good-natured bay gelding who had a back so broad I felt like I was doing the splits. And yes, I was attracting attention, and it would get worse the closer to the city I got, but I could handle—

"Lady Joan!"

"Thomas Wynter." I pulled up, smiling when I saw him lope out of one of the buildings on my right. "What in the world are you doing out here?"

He gestured at The Gray Horse with his hat, which he'd plucked off when he saw me. "I took a room at the inn so I could better focus on my studies of the—"

"Great! Listen, Thomas, I'm on the trail of one of my Losties."

"Yes, I assumed when I saw you." His smile was a little crooked. "One of these days I hope to catch you at your leisure. Your devotion to your wayward lambs is commendable, but you seem to take no time for your own pleasure."

"I do, just not, um, around here. But listen: I'm looking for a woman named Teresa Lupez. She's about this tall..." I had no idea what 5'9" was in centimeters, so I held my hand up to my eyebrows. "...with brown skin and short black hair and brown eyes and she's thin."

"A long, dark lass?"

"If that helps you. She would have gotten here about two days ago and her clothing probably attracted a lot of attention and why are you looking at me like that?"

Thomas was gazing at me with not a little sympathy. "A woman matching that description did come through, but it grieves me to tell you she has been taken to the Tower."

Dammit. "Because they think she's insane," I sighed, resigned that my errand had gotten exponentially more dangerous.

He shook his head. "No, Lady Joan. They do not think she is mad."

Oh. Oh, *shit*. What could be worse than the locals thinking you're insane? Thinking you're a traitor or a witch. And I doubt they'd assume she was a traitor. I was about to dig my heels into the horse's side for a madcap ride to the when I felt Thomas' hand close around my ankle.

"Wait."

I did, because I had an inkling what he was up to. He came back not three minutes later in a riding cloak atop a black mare, and hit the road with me right behind him.

(Inkling confirmed.)

An hour later, we were pulling up to the Tower of London, which looked odd as it wasn't surrounded by souvenir shops. That was a money-making venture Henry VIII was missing out on.

We both swung down, and I almost fell while my knees convened for a few seconds to determine if they were going to hold me up. I will never dismiss dressage events as purely ornamental ever again, and the next time Lisa does, I will scold the hell out of her.

"Ooof! Sorry, I'm out of practice. And color me crazy—"

"I beg your pardon?"

"—but it's really hot." I needed to know the date, and there was no time to be subtle. "So so so hot. Unseasonably hot?"

"Yes, about that." Thomas lowered his voice as he tied up the horses, though no one was paying attention to us. "There are some who claim the heat is God's punishment for Cardinal Fisher's execution. They warn the crops will fail again and fear many will starve come winter."

"Oh." Okay, that put us at 1535. Elizabeth I has been born, to her parents' disappointment, and there is definitely trouble in paradise. "That sounds bad." And inadequate. Plus I was distracted by the urge I had to run my fingers through Thomas' mop of hair. Which was nuts: if I was going to go for anyone, it would be Warren, the only member of I.T.C.H. who valued my contribution to their dysfunctional team of science imposters. Plus he got bonus points for living in the same century I did.

Thomas was looking down, as if someone had just slung a weight across his shoulders. "And as you doubtless heard, More was beheaded this morning."

I nodded. *Oh, sure, you betcha. I knew all about it! You'd have to be from a different time period not to know all about it!*

July 1535, then. Anne Boleyn has less than a year to live, and once again, a wormhole had spit me out on a significant date in British history. When Henry killed Thomas More, he rocked his country as well as the continent. The repercussions would be severe and ongoing, and if so many innocents wouldn't also suffer, I'd say the megalomaniacal jackass deserved all the trouble coming his way.

"Is that why everyone is so subdued?" I'd been worried about attracting unwanted attention, but the closer to the Tower we got, the quieter people became. Everyone looked exhausted and uneasy, everyone seemed to be waiting for the next terrible thing.

"Oh yes," Thomas murmured back. "No one thought he would execute Fisher … and then he did. But More was one of the king's oldest friends. He's known him since he was a lad. And all the world admires Thomas More."

"Sure. The *Utopia* fellow."

"Just so. There's not a prince on the continent who would not move the heavens to have More's singular skills at their disposal. So it was unthinkable the king would execute an old friend who had one of the finest minds in the world … over *this* … but …"

Worse: this was only the start. Henry Tudor, Waste of his Name, was realizing no one—not the Pope, not other monarchs, not his Privy Council, not Parliament, not public opinion—could thwart his murderous impulses.

"But there's nothing we can do about it," I said, heartless yet practical. "So let's focus on what we *can* do." I eyed the Tower looming before us. It wasn't a tourist attraction in 1535, which wasn't a problem. It was a residence, a fortress, and a prison in 1535; *that* was the problem. The Tower was built to keep people out. Or in.

So it wasn't a matter of simply strolling in whistling "God Save the Queen." Which I shouldn't whistle, not least because I had no idea when the song was written.

"Thomas, will the guards let us in?"

"No," a voice said from behind us. "But I will."

We turned and Thomas bowed. "My Lord Cromwell. You remember the Lady Joan."

"My Lord, huh?" Cromwell looked almost exactly the way he did the last time I saw him, except he was wearing more velvet and jewelry. I couldn't imagine having to wear velvet in this heat, so I felt sorry for him. "You're coming up in the world."

Cromwell inclined his head and showed a thin smile. "It is my good fortune to serve a generous master in the king.

What brings you to the Tower on such a..." He paused and I could practically see him groping for *le mot juste*. "...reha-bilitating day?"

"The Lady Joan's angels have once again sent her to fetch a wayward lamb," Thomas explained on my behalf, which was annoying, but this was neither the time nor place for a chat about feminism.

"Is it so?" Then, to me: "Dark skin and eyes? Bizarre clothing and speech?"

"That's her. Is she here?"

"Yes, I regret to tell you that yon wayward lass was, ah, pursued by a group of concerned citizens—"

"Chased by a mob," I said flatly.

"—and fell into the Thames in her attempt to flee. My men plucked her from the river not long ago and brought her here."

I could have swooned with relief. One of these days I *would* swoon, just to see what it was like to do it when it was socially acceptable. "May I see her?"

"Of course."

"Great! Thank you so much. Before we go in, though— I've been on a horse for a while. Is there somewhere I could freshen up just a bit?" Blink-blink-blinketey-blink.

"Are you all right, Lady Joan? Do you have something in your eye?"

Dammit! Mary Boleyn makes it look easy.

Doubtless worried I was coming down with chronic pinkeye, the Thomases escorted me to the Beauchamp Tower, where I was shown a room just off the entrance. It was small, gloomy, and sparsely furnished (a table, two chairs, not much else), but suited my purpose. With about as much delicacy as you might imagine, I hiked my skirt up, grabbed my fanny pack, yanked my phone out, and looked up the first week in July, 1535. After my "what should my hypothetical book heroine who definitely isn't me bring to the 16th century" chat with Lisa, I downloaded several libraries' worth of 16th century history (specifically Tudor England). In a minute I had an idea of what would happen this week (or, at least, events that made enough of an impact to be noted by historians) and felt better prepared to chitchat with the Thomases and spring Teresa. With luck, I'd be back before Lisa even read my note.

I emerged refreshed (but not really), thanked the Thomases and followed them past several guards into the tower.

I vaguely remembered Beauchamp's fame for distinguished prisoners like Jane Boleyn, Catherine Howard, and Lady Jane Grey, which boded ill for Teresa. The Tower didn't even reek that badly; there was an overall fishy, muddy smell—doubtless the proximity to the Thames—and the smell of rotting vegetation underneath that, and everything was damp and chill, but I'd been to fish markets that had been more unpleasant.

Yes, it was fair to say that my confident mood held right up until I saw Teresa Lupez's corpse.

CHAPTER FIFTY-THREE

Call me sheltered, but I had only ever seen one dead body—my mother. (My dad had been cremated; I saw him dying in the hospital, and then in an urn four days later.) And like everything about The After, I tried not to dwell on it.

So it was fair to say I was taken by surprise.

"Oh my God!"

"Your lamb," Cromwell said with no ceremony, because he was a heartless prick.

"I thought—you said—she—you said—"

"I said she fell into the Thames, and she did. I said my men fished her out, and they did."

I whirled on Cromwell, who was as calm as a clam. Not a hair out of place. By contrast, I felt like a sweaty hysterical wreck. "You inferred she was okay!"

"No. *You* inferred she was 'okay'. Nor did I imply; that was simply your conclusion." Because on top of everything else, Thomas Cromwell was a fucking grammar Nazi.

"Lord Cromwell, I must protest." I'd never seen Thomas so angry: tight jaw, narrow eyes, hands into fists. He was, I realized, one of those people who got quieter when he was angry. (I was more the shouty type.) "You should have prepared the lady."

"There we disagree, Master Wynter."

"Oh-ho," he replied slowly, fists relaxing. "No longer 'Thomas'?"

"That depends on you, sir."

I tuned out the TudorTime verbal bitch-slapping; I couldn't stop staring at Teresa. She was wearing the shorts and t-shirt her folks had described to the police, but her clothing was torn, she was barefoot, and there were cuts on her face and long deep scratches on her arms. You didn't have to be Kay Scarpetta to deduce she'd torn free of a mob and had been running for her life when she fell into the Thames. Or jumped. Or was thrown.

It suddenly occurred to me that the vaguely muddy, fishy, rotting vegetation smell was Teresa, and I had to grit my teeth to keep the barf back. When I was (kinda) sure I had my gorge under control, I turned to Cromwell. "You sneaky *prick*," I marveled. "You set me up and marched me in. Why did you bring me here? Why not just tell me what happened?"

"She bears several witch's marks." He pointed to an immunization scar, and her belly button ring. "We should like you to explain them."

"You don't know what a piercing is?" I refused to believe that Thomas Cromwell, sneaky hatchet man and world traveler, had never seen a piercing before.

"I do not know why any lady would have such a thing *there*. To what purpose? No one would ever see it. Why punch a hole in your belly only to cover it up? Why would she make a mark, then hide a mark?"

"For the same reason sailors get tattoos! It's something private for them and *they* decide who sees it. And what makes you think I know anything? I've never even met Teresa."

Cromwell didn't bother answering. "To that end, you are under arrest by order of the king."

"Why?" I knew, but I wanted him to say it.

"Suspicion of witchcraft."

Suspicion of bullshit, I managed not to say. "Oh, sure. When I make predictions the king *likes*, it's God's will. But he changed his mind about me when Elizabeth was born, didn't he?"

"It is not for me to know the workings of the king's mind."

"Ha!"

Angry as he was, Cromwell smiled at that. Meanwhile, he was still self-righteously explaining himself. "Suffice it to say when I told him about your drowned lamb he ordered me to keep watch for you."

"Lady Joan is not the king's subject," Thomas pointed out. "And is not subject to his—or your—jurisdiction."

"How so? We only have her word for that."

"Rude! And Thomas is right, I'm not from around here. Surely that's obvious."

"So then," Cromwell continued, ignoring the interruption, "I am certain that her country of origin can be easily proved." To me: "Surely you have papers or some such to prove your Merka citizenship. We should like to see them."

As a matter of fact I did. But it wouldn't help my case at all.

"I've done nothing wrong, and I think you know it, Cromwell."

It was like I hadn't spoken. Like I wasn't in the room at all. "The king is preparing to go on progress with Queen Anne, but I have sent a page to inform him I have you in custody. I daresay he shall command an audience with you before he departs. For now, you are my guest."

"Is that supposed to be funny?"

"No. Merely courteous."

"To think I felt sorry for you! I'm *glad* you're broiling in velvet!"

Nothing. It was like yelling at a paperweight. No matter what you said, the thing just sat there wrapped in velvet and did its job.

Cromwell turned and left the room, except it wasn't a room at all. It was a cell, and I realized three seconds too late that he was going to lock me in with Teresa's corpse, which was as clever as it was heartless. However long I had to wait for the king, I'd be stuck staring at a dead body and wondering what Henry was going to do to me. It would rattle anybody.

"Fear not, Lady Jane. I shall remain with—hey!"

I'd seized Thomas by the arm and shoved him out into the corridor—the adrenaline surge had helped me pull a Hulk, because under ordinary circumstances I doubt I could have budged him. Then I grabbed the door and yanked it closed before Thomas could come back in with me.

"Bad enough I'm in here," I told his shocked face. "I won't have you in here, too. Especially when all you're guilty of is being nice to me. Go home, Thomas."

He'd seized the bars and I saw his knuckles whiten. "The hell I will!"

"Shut up. Don't get yourself arrested for disturbing the peace of the Tower or whatever." I put my hands over his. "There's not one thing you can do for me and you know it. I'll either convince Henry I'm not a witch, or I won't. Anything else—any*one* else—won't be a factor. You know this."

"I'm not leaving you," he said, forehead already grooved in stubborn lines.

"Please *please* go. You don't know—" How bad this could get. What Henry's becoming. "Just go. Okay? Please."

"I will not leave you."

"Idiot." No, it was safe to say Thomas Wynter didn't know anything about the monster his king was becoming and I couldn't enlighten him. All I could do was give him the advice I gave Lisa: "Keep clear."

But he wouldn't. When he saw Cromwell didn't care either way, he settled on the chilly stone floor, got as comfortable as possible under the circumstance, and stuck his hand through the bars.

After a few seconds, I took it, and he held my hand and talked about growing up in Calais, his studies, and all the good food we were going to eat once I was back in Henry's good graces. His tone never wavered from warm confidence, and his voice seemed to beat back the dark and gave me something to focus on besides Teresa's corpse, until the guards came for me.

CHAPTER FIFTY-FOUR

Hampton Court Palace is one of many Tudor palaces I didn't bother visiting five hundred years from now.

So I didn't expect to see it for the first time as a prisoner of the Crown while in the company of Thomas Cromwell, Cardinal Wolsey's illegitimate son, and three guards, one of whom smelled like someone set a pound of garlic on fire.

Also, Thomas Wynter had the tenacity of a lamprey, because I could *not* shake him.

"If you will attend, please," Cromwell said, pausing before the closed double doors to Henry's chamber, and it was downright adorable how he couched compulsory commands as polite requests. No. Wait. It was irritating. Very, very irritating.

"Sure. Just me, though," I said. "Other Thomas can go home, right, Other Thomas? Right. Okay, bye!"

"I will not leave you." This was the only thing he'd said since Cromwell's guards came for me. And a good thing, because he was a little hoarse from gabbing half the afternoon away.

"Listen, you." I grabbed his earlobe, tugged him down so I could hiss in his ear. "This is the nicest, dumbest thing anyone's ever done for me but you are painting a target on your back, now go away, you gorgeous dolt!"

The presence of said target was, of course, entirely my fault, which is why I was still reeling over my stupidity. *Gosh, if only Cromwell had a historical reputation for being a behind-the-scenes genius who employed treachery as needed and saw any number of innocents legally murdered OH WAIT.* (I know, the 'oh wait' thing is dead and dated, but it fits here.)

And to think I'd felt prepared, felt in control just because I had the Tudor Version of the Farmer's Almanac in my phone and ran into men who had been nice to me before. *Idiot.*

The doors were flung open and we walked in with the guards shrieking "Lord Cromwell! Master Wynter! The Lady Joan!" in the background, which I figured was the TudorTime equivalent of elevator music.

And there he was, Henry Tudor, wooer of women, slayer of elderly priests, abandoner of wives, de-legitimizer of children, devourer of pudding. He was seated on a short dais, the better to glare down at us, and his clothing was so ornate and puffed and slashed, I was willing to bet any blade under four inches wouldn't penetrate his flesh. And speaking of his flesh, I was meanly glad to note he'd gained several pounds since I saw him last.

"Your Majesty." From Cromwell. "May I present Thomas Wynter and the Lady Joan?"

Thomas bowed, and I knew they were both looking at me out of the corner of their eye.

(Do you even have to ask? Of course I didn't bow.)

It was odd how calm I was. The thing I'd fretted about most—an accusation of witchcraft, the prospect of torture and an agonizing death—was happening. I didn't have to be nervous about it now, I just had to survive it.

So it was good to remember that Henry Tudor, Waste of His Name, was used to gold medal ass-kissing. When unlucky citizens were hauled before him, they were, at best, tense. At worst, they were gibbering in terror while simultaneously giving up bladder control. Begging and pleading were no guarantee of leniency. Neither were pleas for forgiveness.

So.

"Hello, King Henry. How's Princess Elizabeth? Congratulations, by the way."

His beady blue eyes, already narrowed in pique, almost disappeared. I heard Thomas Wynter stifle a pained groan. Cromwell, of course, was a rock. A velvet-swathed rock. "We shall ask the questions, Lady Joan. What have you to say for yourself?"

"About what?" *The weather? Your youngest daughter? Your queen pro tem?* Speaking of, where *was* Anne?

Oh. Right. Dumb question...Henry wanted to know why I hadn't warned him of one of the biggest disappointments of his life. With Anne in the room? Awkward.

"About the witch Cromwell's men pulled from the Thames. What say you about *that?*"

"I say it's disgusting she was beaten and pursued and murdered by a lawless mob. Is that how you do things here, King Henry? If you're afraid of someone, if you don't like how they look or what they're wearing, you can kill her on sight? A woman alone, without protection?"

"Lady Joan! *We* will ask the questions." Ugh, the royal we. The definition of pretentious. Though the way he squirmed was a good sign—he didn't want to think of his people as a mob, or himself as a bad man. "You are here under suspicion of witchcraft."

"Yes, but why now?"

"Furthermore, you—what?"

"Why didn't you have me tossed in the Tower the last time you saw me? Or the time before that? And yes, I know—you're asking the questions. So I'll answer this one for you: you had no problem with 'witchcraft' when it benefited you." Oh, hell. I just used air quotes in 1535. "Or did you forget I saved your life?"

"We have forgotten nothing."

"Good to know. The only reason I'm in the Tower now is because you think I should have warned you about Elizabeth. If Anne had given you a son, you'd have given me a feast."

"That is definitely untrue," he declared, and I noticed he didn't seem to have trouble understanding me. Either Lisa had a point about me picking up the accent or he just paid better attention when he was pissed. "But if it was so, why would you not warn me?"

"Why are you assuming I knew?"

"Because—because you—"

"What? Because I got it right twice, that must mean I know every single thing there is to know about anything? Every possible permutation of every moment of your life, and Catherine of Aragon's, and Queen Anne's?" *Here's hoping he doesn't notice I didn't deny knowing about the future Virgin Queen.* "Is that how you think it works?"

"We know not how it works," he said with more than a hint of petulance. "Which is why we sent for you."

"*Sent* for me." I laughed. "Is that what you call it?"

"Lady Joan," Cromwell began. "Do not think to—"

"Shut up, Other Thomas." I turned back to Henry, who had lifted a hand to stifle his snicker. I made a note to remember that he liked playing his advisers against each other, and didn't mind (sometimes) when someone else got snippy with them. "I am sent here with tasks from which I am not allowed to deviate unless I want to bring down God's wrath." Or worse, confused pseudo-scientists. "When that task is done, I go home. That's it." I shrugged, holding my hands out palm-up. "That's the beginning, the middle, and the end of what I do. You understood that in the past. You even appreciated it."

I realized I'd taken a few steps forward, so I was standing right at the foot of the dais glaring up at him. "And what if I had? What if I told you last August that Anne was carrying a girl? What would you have done? Believed me? Cancelled all your plans? Scaled down the celebration? How would you have told your queen? 'Sorry, sweetheart, but Joan Howe says it's a girl. Don't even bother planning the celebratory jousts.'"

Henry-the-henpecked literally shivered in his chair at the prospect. I let him picture the ball-busting scene for a couple of horrifying seconds, then finished with, "Or would you have tossed me in The Tower the way you did The Nun of Kent?"

"The Nun of Kent—"

"Made predictions you didn't like."

"—was a traitor!"

"For predicting your death. You'll notice I did no such thing. In fact, I *saved* you from death. And yet." I made a gesture encompassing his luxe chambers. "Here we are."

Cromwell smoothly stepped into the silence. "Your friend—"

"She isn't my friend. I never met her. And thanks to the mob mentality fostered in London, I never will."

Unlike Henry, who was as red as an overripe tomato—if Lisa saw his face, she'd take his blood pressure—Cromwell remained emotionally aloof. "Your friend was taken into custody—"

"Is that what fishing a battered corpse out of the Thames is? Custody?"

"—yesterday. And yet you arrived only this afternoon. Why the delay?"

Ouch. Tough one.

Henry seemed to realize that Cromwell had touched upon something I didn't want to discuss, because he snapped, "You will answer My Lord Cromwell."

I stared at the floor. "Because when I found out they— when the angels gave me a new task, I didn't want to come. So I ignored my instructions." Gah, my sinuses were filling like a clogged sink. Bad enough I had to explain myself to an asshat, but I might cry in front of him, too. "And Teresa paid for it. I should have come straight away."

Henry leaned back. "Ah. You turned your face away from God like any heretic."

"Don't call me that!" Though it was accurate, as I was an atheist, but he shouldn't make assumptions, dammit! "Do you think I'm the only person who ever struggled with bending to someone else's will? Don't you think I feel bad enough?" Angry. Angry was good. Anger was loads better than tears. I was no Boleyn; I couldn't compel men to pity and shelter me. All I could do was harangue them into sheltering me. "And why are you talking like I have any control over any of this? Do you think I want to be here? Away from my home? Do you think I enjoy roaming a strange land? Do you think it's *fun* to have to figure out the customs and courtesy as I go, knowing at any moment if I say the wrong thing to the wrong person I could get hurt or arrested? Or chased into the river by a mob? Where I'm always afraid? And then I make it back, but sooner or later I have to come back and it starts all over again?

"So yes. I hid from my duty, and the unthinkable happened. And now I have to explain myself, so here it is: I am doing the best I can with what I have. If you don't like it, too bad."

And then, to my mortification, I burst into tears.

This was awkward for everyone in the room. It got worse when Henry rose and came toward me, patting my back with his huge paw. "Now then, Lady Joan. We had not considered your age, nor the difficulty of your calling. We shall overlook your impertinence this once."

"S'not impertinence," I wept.

"Your Majesty, I must protest." I started a little; I'd almost forgotten the Thomases were there, they'd been so quiet. Wynter had raised his hand like he wanted to pat me, too, then let it drop to his side. "This treatment ill befits a lady and a guest. See her distress!"

"I am," I said tearfully. "I *am* distressed."

"Not only is the Lady Joan blameless, Cromwell locked her in with the corpse for hours. It was a singular cruelty."

"Ah. Yes. Well." Henry's complexion, which had been calming down in the face of my hysterics, flushed again, and I realized that bit of mind-fuckery must have been his idea. "That is most unacceptable. Yes. Truly. And to a guest. Cromwell! Apologize to the lady."

Yeah, Cromwell. Apologize to the—me. I was starting to see why Mary Boleyn got off on playing dim and helpless.

"My most sincere apologies, Lady Joan." He bowed. "I ask your forgiveness."

"I just don't understand why you would be so mean to someone who saved your life." I thought pitiful thoughts and ostentatiously sniffled, hoping I looked woebegone, not constipated.

"We had heard worrisome things about you from a dear friend and wished to see for ourselves," Henry admitted. "You must understand, I have a responsibility to my kingdom and to my God, no matter how fond of a comely visitor I might personally be."

"Oh, well. Comely." I patted my terrible wig and heavy hood. "I don't know about that…" *Ugh. I'm already sick of this. How does Boleyn do this with a straight face?* I made a note to keep in mind that Henry was better at treating women like crap at a distance. Face to face, he chickened out every time.

"But I will tell my friend she need not fear you any longer."

"I would be happy to speak with the lady," I said at once. "To set her mind at ease."

Henry waved that away. "That will not be necessary. I will tend to that myself."

"As you wish," I replied. "But Anne's got nothing to fear from me." Wasn't *that* the truth. Anne should be watching over her shoulder for her husband and uncle, poor doomed lady.

"It is not—" Henry cut himself off at the same moment Cromwell stifled a tiny cough.

Oh.

"Anne isn't the one pouring poison in your ear?" Like a dolt, I finally put it together. "Oh, for heaven's sake. You're cheating on the new wife already and letting some random wench talk crap about me? But *I'm* the one who has to explain myself?"

"Lady Joan—" the Thomases began in union, but I was too irked to heed them.

"Does Anne even know that you don't take your marriage vows seriously? Of course she does, because you cheated on Catherine, too." I was doing the slow you-have-disappointed-me head shake. "What if the angels told me to tell you to keep it in your codpiece? Would you?"

"*That is enough!* You overreach, even with a fool's prerogative!"

And here I thought he'd been red-faced before. "Did you ever think that God isn't punishing you for marrying your brother's widow, but for constantly breaking your promises?"

I know, I know. Total insanity. The worst thing I could have done. I was almost out. I had him on my side again. But something rose in me that I couldn't squash, and it wasn't just Teresa's stupid sad death. It was the situation, the environment, it was *him*. He'd go on and on while innocents died, while he legally murdered his wives, while he disinherited and reinstated his children, all of whom would go on to wreak their own havoc with worldwide consequences. He'd make the rules and break the rules and hold everyone accountable while avoiding all responsibility himself and I was so fucking sick of it I couldn't keep it back one second longer.

"You're the biggest hypocrite I've ever met," I told him, because I had a previously undiagnosed death wish. "Literally. Who's the lucky lady?" It was too early for Jane Seymour—she didn't emerge as a player until 1536. So who knew me, was afraid of me and/or didn't like me, and was in a position to whisper poison in Henry's ear *oh shit* I knew who it was. "It's Lady Eleanor. The one who loves to talk about what a good friend she is to Anne."

"She has been a good friend to us—"

I laughed. "Friend!"

"We need not explain ourselves to you!"

"Then why are you?"

"Joan, shut up." This from Wynter, who'd gone so pale his eyes almost appeared to burn. "Right now."

"Pass." To Henry: "Please tell Lady Eleanor that though she slandered me and is betraying a friend, I'm going to do her a good turn. Tell her it's going to hail tomorrow."

"I certainly will n—what?"

"Hard. It'll start before dawn and it'll go on for hours. I imagine people will find it upsetting. I mean … hail? In July? Maybe London will worry the world is coming to an end. Maybe they'll think God is punishing them. Or maybe they'll think God is punishing you for breaking your word again. Or maybe they'll just gather up the hailstones and make ice cream."

"What?"

Too early for ice cream. Noted. "Either way, if you decide to go out early tomorrow morning, you should probably buckle on a helmet."

"My Lord Cromwell." Speaking of ice cream, Henry's voice was cold enough to make some. "Escort the Lady Joan back to the Tower. When she remembers how to comport herself like a trueborn lady—"

"A lady like Eleanor?"

"—and apologizes to us for making up spiteful stories—"

"What's spiteful about a weather report?"

"—perhaps she can be allowed to return home."

"Someone's going to apologize," I predicted, "but it won't be me."

"We shall see."

"I suppose we will."

So there it was. In five minutes, I had talked myself out of the Tower and then right back into it. My tenth grade Civics teacher, Mr. Polk, said I'd never do anything of note, so the joke was on him.

"I know, I know," I told Thomas, who looked stricken as Cromwell signaled the guards and I was escorted to the double doors. "You don't have to say it." Then, over my shoulder as they hauled me away, "Go home this time!"

The worst part? Now I wanted ice cream.

CHAPTER FIFTY-FIVE

I mentioned earlier that I don't make friends easily.

So I was surprised when Mary Boleyn stopped by.

"Tell me *everything*," she begged, and I had to laugh. Actually I'd been giggling on and off for the last hour, mostly at my own stupidity and the absurdity of my situation. The man in charge of the Tower, whose name I kept forgetting, kept poking his head in, looking fretful, then leaving, only to return a short while later and peek in again. He seemed more unnerved each time I waved cheerfully at him and called "S'up, dawg?" (I know. Nobody says 's'up, dawg' anymore, but *he* didn't know that.)

"There's not much to tell," I said as The Other Boleyn Girl bustled around the cell. It was a nice room, but the windows were high, the sturdy door was locked, and I didn't have a key, so: luxurious prison cell. "I yelled at the king for breaking his marriage vows—again—and suggested that a coming hailstorm might be punishment for him being such a hound."

"And he took offense?"

"Yes, and I think he revoked my fool's prerogative."

"How terribly unlike him."

I snickered from my vantage point at the writing desk. Last time (or, to put it another way, 'earlier in the day') I'd been a prisoner of the state, I'd been too focused on finding

Teresa to pay much mind to the Tower's many differences between now and five hundred years from now. But now I realized it was almost like a tiny town. It had its own armory and treasury and chapel and zoo. (Because sometimes visitors eyeballing the Tower would think, "You know what this fortress needs? Lions.") It also had a mansion, which is where I was currently detained, and taken as a whole, the Tower of London sprawled over a dozen acres.

So my comfortable cell didn't need many 16th century upgrades. But Mary Boleyn was here anyway, and she'd brought me two heavy quilts and something called a bolster, which looked like a giant Tootsie Roll if giant Tootsie Rolls were deep green and you could sleep on them. This was extra adorable because the bed was on a platform, and she was a little thing who almost needed a stepladder to clamber up on top of the bed to spread out the quilts.

Then she turned to the bundle she'd set on the table and started taking out all sorts of delicious-looking things: a soft loaf of manchet bread, a small pot of jam, a dish of fly balls, which were pork meatballs studded with raisins (so they looked like flies on balls—get it?), and something called prymerose, which was rice pudding with honey and almonds. Which was amazing not just because it looked very fine, but because I had no idea the Boleyns had access to rice. I had a vague idea that China and Japan had all the rice until it magically turned up in America in the 20th century.

There were also several small cubes called leeches, which I found out were confections made from milk, sugar, and rosewater, all cooked together and then pressed into square wafers and used to make edible chess boards. Yes! *Edible chess boards.* How could TudorTime be so horrible and glorious at once? If they had those when I went to school, they would have needed a court order to stop me from joining the chess team.

"This is so nice of you," I said, "but it's been a difficult day and I'm just not that *oh my God*, these leeches are wonderful!"

"Yes, I noted you had a sweet tooth."

"Several." I set the remaining leeches aside for later, then nibbled bread and washed it down with the flask of wine she'd also brought. "Mary Boleyn, never think I'm not happy to see you, but why are you here?"

"Partly because you *are* happy to see me. But foremost to show my gratitude." She held out her small hand and I saw a dull gold band on her left ring finger. "I am no longer a Boleyn. You must call me Mary Stafford now." She had been watching me carefully, and when I smiled she added, "You are not surprised."

"Well. No. But he's a good man, and you love him, don't you?"

"I do indeed. I wrote Lord Cromwell—"

"You were in bondage and glad you were to be set at liberty. You would rather beg bread with your husband than be the greatest queen in Christendom."

"My God, that's off-putting." She crossed herself. "I mean no disrespect."

"None taken." Mary's letter was famous, almost as well-known as Catherine of Aragon's "where have I offended you" speech at Blackfriars. I re-read it a few days ago to refresh my memory. And now that I knew her a little better, I saw it as another example of Mary Boleyn Carey Stafford saying exactly what she pleased—that her life in obscurity was better than her sister's life in the public eye—and people dismissing it as her being too dim to understand when she was being tactless. "That 'greatest queen' line didn't help your cause, y'know."

She smirked. "I do know." The smile dropped away. "I came because I do not forget how kind you were. And how you nudged me toward Stafford. And after, when I found out about the baby—you know about the baby?—he told me you had nudged him toward me. We were two, now we are three, and so we remain in your debt."

Her life had to have been pretty bleak if she attached such import to a casual conversation with a stranger a year ago. So when I answered I told the full truth: "I was happy to help in my own small way—and it *was* small, Mary. You two would have gotten together without my help." This was, of course, cold historical fact, not modesty.

"Well." She shrugged. "The letter to Cromwell is part of the reason I am here. Although the Queen's Grace forgave me the sin of my private happiness, Cromwell knew he had made no headway with Anne on my behalf, so he took pity and wrote me a pass to see you."

I snapped my fingers. "That's right, you weren't just quietly rusticating in the country, you were formally banished."

"Yes, the queen my sister sits high on her dignity. She felt—feels—my marriage was a mésalliance. She never would have granted permission for the match." She smiled. Well. Bared her teeth. "If Anne Boleyn is unhappy, all must be unhappy."

"Which is why you didn't ask. There's a saying where I come from: better to beg forgiveness than ask permission."

"Yes, we have something much like that saying, too. But as I said, she has relented. Though I will be heading home tomorrow, and glad I will be to be gone." She patted her flat stomach, and I realized yet another Stafford was on the way.

"That's great, but why'd she change her mind? From her perspective, nothing's changed. You're still married beneath your station. And it can't be easy for her to see how happy and, um, fertile you are."

"Indeed." This time, when Mary Boleyn smiled, she looked exactly like her sister. "But that aside, it is your habit to suddenly disappear for several months or years afterward, but should you choose to remain this once, please keep my most happy news to yourself."

"Is that my habit?" Leave it to Mary Boleyn to notice *and* bluntly lay it out there. "No worries, I won't say anything about your new baby. But if Anne doesn't know about your pregnancy, why did she change her mind?"

"Not from any charitable impulse you may be sure. She is lonely," Mary said frankly, "and as poisonous a viper as she can be, I pity her. She is afraid."

Not as afraid as she should be. "Well, you're a good sister." I was scraping the bowl to get the last tasty remnants of the prymerose. God *damn* but that was good rice pudding.

"I am no such thing, but that is irrelevant. I wanted to see you and lighten your confinement, and so I have, and so I must take my leave. Ah! I nearly forgot." She extracted a book from the bag and handed it to me. "To pass the time."

"Thank you." *Utopia.* By Thomas More. I looked up. "Did you think Henry would do it? Kill him?"

"Yes."

"Really? Because my understanding is that everyone else is pretty shocked." Certainly my guards couldn't shut up about it.

"It has become Henry's pattern; one need only take note of his escalation. And he is never more deadly than when he fears the loss of power. Even power that had heretofore never been his. His Grace the Duke of Buckingham told Henry he could not have a son to inherit the crown; His Grace is dead. Fisher told Henry he could not be master of men's souls. Fisher is dead. More told Henry he could not have something. More is dead."

"Escalation". What an incredibly polite way to put it.

At my expression, Mary got brisk. "As to the book, I do like the concept of men and women doing the same work, but I found More's views about the incompatibility of politics and philosophy to be utterly nonsensical."

"…okay."

"You may wish to keep that," she added. "I suspect the value will only increase."

"No doubt." Not for the first time I was glad she was on my side. "And thanks again."

"Before I take my leave, do you have a message for Thomas Wynter?"

I blinked. "Why would you—oh, hell, he's outside, isn't he? He's skulking around out there like some comely weirdo!"

"What is 'weirdo'?"

"I told him to go home! Again."

"He did not heed; I passed him on my way in." She was smiling as she packed up the empty dishes. "He begged me to tell you that he will hold a vigil as long as necessary and he is fully prepared for hail, whatever on earth that means."

"It means it's going to hail. It also means I'm going to give him a smack when I see him again." *Thomas, you beautiful dumbass, where is your sense of self-preservation?*

Then I realized my cheeks hurt, which raised another question: *if you're pissed at him, why are you grinning, idiot?*

"Ah, well. Like to like, and the two of you seem, er, strong-willed when the mood strikes you. Or so I have observed."

"Oh, listen to you, 'strong-willed'. I've got to take that from a Boleyn?"

"Touché," she giggled. "I must take my leave of you, Lady Joan. I would wish you good luck, but I believe you make yours." She paused and sobered. "Is there—do you have any, er, information for me before I depart?"

She's looking for a prediction. A warning. And here's the thing to ponder—would she and Stafford have hooked up if I'd never come back in time?

I had no idea. At all. Mary must have taken my silence for 'nope, nothing on this end' because she turned to go, and I stepped forward and caught her by the arm. "Keep clear next spring, d'you understand? Stay home with your babies. No matter what you hear."

She searched my face with her wide brown eyes, then nodded, extricated herself from my grip, tapped the door, and was out of there in a matter of seconds, leaving me content—and not just because of the food. Mary, I knew, would get the happy ending.

My ending remained to be seen, but I put some leeches under my pillow in case I wanted a midnight snack but didn't want to get out of bed. My incarceration, my rules.

CHAPTER FIFTY-SIX

I came awake just before dawn, wondering where the hell I was and why I'd woken up. After a few bleary seconds, I realized I'd been awakened by hail hammering on the roof, which helped me remember why my bedroom was chilly and why my bed felt weird and smelled weirder.

I chortled like a hyena and munched on leeches while I listened to the storm in the dark. I'd give up sugar for a month just to be a fly on the wall of Henry's privy chamber this morning.

Well. Maybe a week.

If you're a holy fool arrested in Henry Tudor's England, they don't frisk you. They politely escort you to your room/cell and leave you be.

To that I say: whew!

Since I couldn't be 100% sure when—or if—I returned to a horrified Lisa (who, since I.T.C.H. time travel ran on San Dimas time, had surely read my note by now), I opened my pomander and ate a Flintstones chewable. Mmmm...iron.

Oh, sorry—a pomander was ball-shaped (like an orange—sometimes they were actual oranges) and was studded with things like cloves. You hung it from your waist so when you walked past a hip-high pile of shit, you could sniff your pomander and smell shit *and* oranges.

Mine was filled with items other than cloves.

Likewise, the lack of pat-down and/or cavity search meant the things in my fanny pack and up my sleeves hadn't been discovered. It made for lumpy sleeping since I didn't dare pile it all on a nearby table—who knew when someone might barge in?—but thanks to Mary's extra quilts and giant green Tootsie Roll, I was more comfortable than I thought I'd be.

In fact, the average person who came in and eyeballed me would probably assume I'd had an uneventful evening and was sitting at the writing desk without a care in the world while (pretending to be) reading *Utopia*.

"Make way for His Majesty!"

My door was unlocked and thrown open, and there he was: King Bloat. And staring at me over his shoulder: Thomas Cromwell. And staring over *his* shoulder, the lieutenant of the Tower. There was probably someone behind him, too. They were like TudorTime nesting dolls.

"Lady Joan," Henry began, and I could have cheered at how vastly uncomfortable he looked. "We have—"

"COULD YOU SPEAK UP PLEASE? IT'S HARD TO HEAR YOU OVER ALL THE HAIL."

The king cocked his head to one side. "The hail stopped an hour ago."

"OH." I coughed and lowered my voice. "Oh. Sorry. It was so loud, I guess I thought I was still hearing it. Also, good morning, King Henry. And Thomas. And man-behind-Thomas whose name I forget."

"Sir Edmund, if you will excuse us." But we would never know if Sir Edmund would excuse us, because Cromwell closed the door in his face.

"So!" Henry began briskly, but almost immediately petered out. "Erm…"

"My goodness," I said, and he perked up. "This weather! Very out of season. I can tell you it never hails in July in Merka."

"Ah. Yes. Most unseasonable."

"Aren't you glad I warned you?" I asked sweetly. "About the unseasonableness?"

"Yes." The king cleared his throat. "As dawn broke, no one was allowed to leave without 'buckling a helmet'." He chuckled, which made me smile because ugh, charisma. "And glad I am to see you looking so well."

"Well, my room was very comfortable. And I had ways to pass the time." I tapped *Utopia*, making the recently beheaded Thomas More the official elephant in the room. "Remarkable, don't you think? His vision?" Not that I could get through much of it. Or any of it. Luckily there were other ways to pass the time. I hoped they wouldn't notice where I'd carved HENRY SUX.

"A vision that shone in only one direction," the king replied darkly.

"Not anymore."

"No." More's murderer had the gall to look *sad* if you can believe it. "Not anymore."

I rose to my feet. "May I go?"

"You should have stood when the king was announced." This from Cromwell, who had finally found his tongue. "And curtsied."

"I should have done a lot of things." Like getting my ass in gear on poor Teresa's behalf. Which reminded me. "Thank you for not locking me up with Teresa's dead body overnight, by the way. But where *is* her body? I need to let her family know." What I would tell them, and under what circumstances, remained to be seen.

At Henry's questioning look, Cromwell replied, "She was interred at Cross Bones."

I made a mental note to look that up if and when I got back. "And what should I tell her family?" I asked sweetly. "Regarding the manner of her death? A mob?"

Henry cleared his throat. "A misunderstanding."

I just looked at them. After a looong uncomfortable moment, I said, "Really."

"A regrettable one." Henry spread his hands in the universal gesture for "eh, what are ya gonna do?" This was alarming, as were his tone and body language, which were all wrong. I figured he'd be furious or terrified or a combo. Instead he was ... regretfully pained? "But misfortunes, alas, happen every day, to the best of us as well as the least." Now he was walking toward me and ... extending his arm? I gingerly put out my hand and he took it, placed it onto his padded sleeve, patted it, and started walking me out the door, out of the Tower, into sweet sweet freedom and the smell of too many unwashed bodies.

"We grieve to see you leaving us, Lady Joan, but I hope that if your angels bid you come again, you will seek us out straight away. We are best placed to help you with God's work."

"Okay," I managed.

"And as you so kindly reminded me last evening, you have been a friend to the Crown," he added with smug pomposity. "And will be in the future, we trust."

"Yes."

Now he made a concerned 'hmmm' noise and squinted at me. "Are you well, Lady Joan? You are uncharacteristically withdrawn. Perhaps you should consult with my physician before you take your leave of us?"

"I'm well," I said. "I'm still recovering from yesterday. It was an eventful day."

Henry laughed, because he thought executing an old friend and/or putting a guest who'd broken no laws into custody was hilarious. "Most definitely! But I trust Mary Stafford's visit was beneficial." At my confused blinking, he added, "Did you think Cromwell could give a subject permission to visit my holy fool and I would not know?"

"I ... guess not. That was nice of you."

Henry waved that away. "Nonsense. A trifle for an honored guest."

"A trifle." I thought about that for a couple of seconds. "No, I don't think it was that."

Before my eyes I was seeing Henry's fabled talent for self-delusion unfold. Teresa's death was a misunderstanding because what else could it be? Not a mob—that might indicate the populace was beyond his control. Not something a holy fool could have prevented—that might indicate the Lord's agenda differed from Henry's.

As for me? I hadn't spent the night as a prisoner of the Crown, oh, heavens no! I was an honored guest. Wasn't I housed in a beautiful room? Didn't the queen's own sister come to check on me and bring delicious treats? Weren't the sovereign of the realm and his Number One goon here first thing in the morning to courteously see me on my way?

The worst part: Cromwell's total lack of surprise.

The Lieutenant of the Tower bowed as we passed him, as did all the servants. They all look much less confused than I felt.

"Now that your work here is finished," Guess Who was jabbering, "we shall see you on your way. Cromwell will arrange for any transportation you need."

"Thank you." What else could I say? You're freaking me out? You're as dangerous as you are delusional, and you're really fucking delusional? "I am always happy to serve the

Crown." And how I got *that* lie past my teeth I will never, ever know.

"But before we bid you farewell, do you have anything to impart to us? Some … knowledge you wish to share?"

A guard had his hand on the outer door, but paused. Everyone paused. And Henry's smile had vanished as he watched me carefully.

I stared into those beady blue eyes and thought, *your queen will die next year. Your illegitimate son will die next year. Your heir will die young. Your daughter will hand the country back to the Pope. Your other daughter will doom your dynasty.*

And there's nothing you can do to prevent any of it.

"No. Nothing's coming to mind."

"That is very well." Open door, exit Henry and fool (and Cromwell). Now that the formalities were over, Henry was all brisk courtesy. "We hope to see you soon, Lady Joan."

"Your Majesty! My lady!"

Thomas Wynter looked terrible. To be specific, he looked as if he'd slept outside all night and woken up in a hailstorm which, for some unfathomable reason, he didn't get out of.

"You're still *here*?" The poor dumbass had a welt on his forehead from what I estimated was a golf-ball-sized hail-stone. "It's official, Thomas, you've lost your mind."

"Master Wynter!" Henry said, looking as surprised as I felt.

"Your Grace," he replied, and bowed, and nearly fell. "It is a pleasure to see you God's beard I'm c-cold I might needtositdown."

Cromwell had stepped forward to steady Thomas, which made me loathe him a tiny bit less. "There are easier ways to show devotion," he muttered, and Other Thomas shrugged. Then, to King Henry, "Your Grace, I will tend to these matters for you. I believe you are to leave on progress later today?"

"Indeed," the king replied, and then said some things I didn't pay attention to, kissed my hand, and got lost. *Finally.*

"He has a room at the The Gray Horse Inn," I said. "Will you take us there?" *And then fuck off?*

As it happened, Cromwell did both.

CHAPTER FIFTY-SEVEN

The Gray Horse Inn was the Sheraton of TudorTime; it existed in the netherworld between TudorTime Marriott and TudorTime Super 8.

To give him credit, Cromwell had gotten us there in less than an hour with an escort as well as a litter for Thomas, who bitched non-stop ("I can ride, dammit! Stop coddling me!") while I had a quick chat with Other Thomas.

"We have this thing in Merka called spin," I began. "It's a person's individual interpretation of an event."

"This is an interesting salvo," Cromwell commented, looking straight ahead.

Since I didn't know what a salvo was, I ignored the (rude!) interruption. "For example, my spin on recent events would be that the king got angry and had me locked up for the night, only releasing me when he was reminded that the angels were on my side."

Nothing from Cromwell. He was just a lump of velvet on a big white gelding.

"But it seems to me that the king's spin is that nobody was angry, nobody was detained, and everyone had a nice evening and a pleasant morning and, oh yes, it hailed in July which was of no consequence whatsoever."

"I cannot speak for the king, but *I* had a pleasant morning."

I had to shake my head. Had I thought I could rattle him? Or coax a confidence? That alone was proof I was indeed a fool.

"Just like the king's spin for twenty years was that Catherine of Aragon was the love of his life and the queen of his heart and their daughter Mary was the heir to the throne. And then suddenly she was the Princess Dowager and they'd never been married and Mary's a bastard. He *believes* that. That's what I find frightening. He's not lying. He doesn't ever lie."

"I am gratified you stop short of calling my king a liar," Cromwell said, nodding to the occasional citizen on the street who recognized him and waved or hailed him. They all appeared to be merchants of one kind or another; interesting that none of the aristocrats at court would lower themselves to acknowledge Thomas Cromwell, fist of the king, but the man on the street wouldn't hesitate. "I enjoy your company but some things I cannot abide."

"But you know the truth. You *know* it. So ..."

"Yes, Lady Joan?"

I lowered my voice. "How can you stand it?"

Cromwell just looked at me. "I come from nothing," he replied steadily. "And he is everything."

I shook my head. "I don't even know why I'm having this conversation. I don't like you anymore; why should I care about your motivations?"

"Yes, you declared I should broil in velvet." He smiled, a genuine grin that took years off his face. "I have been called many things, and had many ills wished upon me, but yours had the virtue of being original."

"You must know he's going to turn on you." This wasn't me breaking an I.T.C.H. rule. Cromwell was brilliant and he'd been around the block a few times. He saw what happened to Wolsey. If Mary Boleyn knew the pattern; no way this guy hadn't spotted it. Nor did I think Cromwell would make the mistake of hubris, indulging the "but that couldn't happen to *me*" mindset. "You must *see* that."

Nothing.

"So why stay?" I persisted. He just looked at me and I sighed and answered my own question, something only a fool would ask. "Because he's everything."

"The sun," Cromwell agreed.

So that was it. It wasn't about money, or even recognition. It was the thrill of finally being an insider, not just one of the cool kids but *the* cool kid, indispensable and, after the king, the ultimate authority. Having worked so hard to get here, Cromwell would rather risk a fatal loss of favor than retire to safe, wealthy, dull obscurity far from the sun.

"I don't know how you can do it," I confessed. "I hate being where everyone can see me. If I could, I'd stay home all the time."

"Then you are in a most curious line of work."

"You bet I am."

"Perhaps," Cromwell said gently, and his dark eyes were unnervingly kind, "God wants you in the light as well."

"I can't imagine," I replied, because I really couldn't. But I could see now how Cromwell was so feared at court but, as Thomas Wynter had confided, adored by his family. Work Cromwell and Family Cromwell might as well be two different people.

I hated that. It was just another way to lie.

But at least we'd reached the Inn, which was great timing because Other Thomas was snoring in the litter he'd insisted he didn't need.

With Cromwell's help we got him on his feet and inside, and the locals recognized him at once. The innkeeper, a short, stout redhead with a thousand freckles and faded green eyes, came forward and introduced herself as Eileen O'Bannon, but we could call her Lee and was there anything she could do for His Lordship or Master Wynter or the Lady Joan?

"I've got it in hand," I told Cromwell, which was the truth for a change. Thomas was standing; his brief snooze during our return to The Gray Horse had perked him right up. "Thanks."

"Thomas. My Lady." Cromwell bowed and came up grinning. "I look forward to your next visit."

"Uh-huh." I'd had about enough of Henry and his head goon, and there was Other Thomas to think about. "Can you just imagine I said something appropriately polite and then made a graceful exit?"

"I have an excellent imagination," he replied, and (obligingly) departed.

The innkeeper immediately gave us a tour, bringing us through the dining area and parlor and then up the front stairs. She took great pride in her twelve feather beds ("We only need two.") and the inn's ability to stable twenty-four horses ("We only nee—never mind.") and their house wine. ("I could use quite a bit of that, come to think of it.")

"A pity, my lady, but we'll have no cockfight tonight."

"That's okay. If you've seen one, you've seen them all. The bird wins."

At the end of the passage she produced a key and unlocked the door to Thomas' chamber, two good-sized rooms stuffed with dark furniture with windows overlooking the courtyard.

"I'll have your meal sent up in a wee, Lady Joan," she promised.

Does she mean small? Or a week? Please be the former. "Thank you so much, that sounds—wait. That's the second time. How do you know my name?"

Like many TudorTime tenants, she had to pay attention to decipher my accent. "How do—ah! How could I not? Thomas talks about you all the time, doesn't he? Waits for you, doesn't he?"

"Weird. I mean, thank you. I'll just stay here with him and get him settled and I'm really looking forward to the food you're going to bring us. I mean, he is. It's his food. And they're his rooms." It belatedly occurred to me that I was a single woman about to be alone with a man *sans* chaperone and had no idea how that was going to go over with the management *circa* 1535.

It was going to go over fine, because Lee didn't give a shit. Which was refreshing. She just dropped a quick curtsy and let herself out.

"There you go—oof!" I straightened from where I'd eased Thomas down on the bed which, it must be said, wasn't as nice as the one I'd had last night, though it *was* fat with feathers. "I still can't believe you stayed outside all night. Are you *trying* to catch pneumonia?"

"Of course not," he grumbled, trying to sit up. He pushed a hank of auburn hair out of his face and scowled. "Why would anyone try to catch that? That makes—argh."

"Lie down, I'll do that." With some judicious tugging his boots came off. Although he was pale and damp, I have to give him credit, he wasn't rank.

But he *was* apparently a mind-reader, because he said, "It's the linen."

"Sorry?" I'd been rummaging through the chest looking for dry clothes for him but looked up at the linen remark.

"My mother taught me to always wear clean linen. She would make me change it twice a day if necessary. She couldn't abide noxious odors."

"Well, she was a smart lady. My mom had a thing about liners in the garbage can." Thomas' mother had a point, though; it sounded deeply nuts, but I was discovering that in TudorTime, clean linen was (almost) an acceptable substitute for a shower. And of course the more money you had, the more linen long underwear you had. "Anyway, just lie there and the innkeeper will be up with food. Your blood sugar's probably in the sub-basement."

"My what?"

"When did you eat last?"

"Uh...what day is it?" He squinted up at the ceiling, then yelped when I smacked his foot.

"What were you thinking, courting pneumonia *and* malnourishment?"

"I was thinking that you were imprisoned through no fault of your own and with no one to speak for you."

"Aw."

"And I was burdened with the knowledge that without someone to look out for you, my favorite fool would end up in ever deeper trouble."

"Ugh."

"Not least because you have made an enemy of the Duke of Norfolk."

"You're the second person to tell me that," I admitted. "And Lady Eleanor! Apparently she spent the last year seducing the king and talking crap about me. I can't imagine Anne doesn't know. Henry's not subtle."

"The queen knows," was the short reply.

"Oh. She'd rather Henry was cheating on her with a 'friend' who will promote Boleyn interests." I shook my head at the sheer cold-bloodedness of it all. "Look, for what it's worth, I try to avoid the major players. But sometimes I can't. Sometimes I've just got to be in the middle of it all to get the job done."

His brow knitted while he tried to follow my babble. Talking with Thomas was so easy. I was (almost) myself around him. After a bit, he replied, "Thus my presence at the Tower."

Before I could comment, there was a rap on the door, and in came a couple of maids with pitchers, linen, and food oh the food my God *look at the food.*

"Wow!"

"Our thanks," Thomas said, sitting up and swinging his legs over the edge of the bed. "Please leave ..." He looked at me and smiled. "Well. All of it."

"Of course all of it! What, only leaving part of it was on the table? The theoretical table, not the literal table they're putting the food on?" It fairly groaned under the weight of the tray and pitchers. "Ohhhhh, where to start? Thomas! Sit your butt back down!"

"I beg your pardon?"

"I mean it. I'll fix you a plate. Sit on the bed before you fall over again. What do you want? There's bread here, two different kinds. And ..." I sniffed one of the pitchers. "Some beer. Well, it's 9:00 a.m. somewhere, right?"

"You care not for ale?"

"I'm not used to it. The water is perfectly drinkable in Merka. Only really dedicated drinkers need beer in the morning, or one of my friend Lisa's professors. Hey! Milk!"

I poured myself a small cup, then hesitated. It hadn't been pasteurized. Hell, it was still warm. Raw milk, straight from an un-inoculated bovine on a diet of who-knew-what, whose milk could be teeming with any number of things. Listeria. Salmonella. E. coli. Rabies?

Sure, but consider what the milk isn't teeming with: artificial growth hormones or additives. It can't be that dangerous, or cows would have wiped us out 1,000 years ago.

I took a breath and took a sip. Then another. Then a gulp, because raw milk was delicious, creamy and frothy and warm, and so rich it was more like a dessert than a drink.

Thomas had been watching me, smiling. "They do not have such things in your world?"

"Not like this." I topped off the cup and handed it to him. "Here, have some, it'll perk you right up. Okay, what else?"

"What else" was ravel, a nut-brown chewy bread, and another small loaf of spice bread, a dense dark bread with lots of spices, studded with dried fruit and served with fresh butter.

And a venison pasty, which was especially delicious as I hadn't had deer meat since before The After. They didn't have legal hunting seasons yet, which is why venison was even available, and the cook had baked the meat with spices and bacon fat, because the cook was a masterful genius.

There was also something called spermys cheese, in which curds had been mixed with liquid extracted from fresh thyme sprigs, which sounded like it took forever but tasted like glory.

And finally, a tart filled with "yellow tart stuff". They actually called it "yellow tart stuff", because "apricot" was too much trouble, I guess. And a cheesecake (I had no idea they'd been around that long) with cinnamon, mace, and ground almonds.

"Ohhhhhhh. Oh, that was good. So so good. Um. Is there any venison pasty left?"

"Only the crumbs that fell into your lap."

I flapped my napkin, sending crumbs flying. "Everything was so good. Even the super creamy raw milk was so good!"

"You should not be so quick to abandon us for your home shore, then, as the cream eating festivals will soon be upon us."

"There are ... there are *cream eating festivals?*"

"Oh yes, beginning on Twelfth Night."

"And the purpose of these festivals is ... to eat cream?"

"Yes."

"You guys built an entire festival around doing something terrific?"

"So it would seem."

"I love TudorTime," I said with fervent, cream-craving sincerity. "I really do. I love it when I don't hate it and right now I don't hate it."

Then I remembered Tereza Lupez had hated it, and why, and burst into tears. I was as startled as Thomas—I could count on one hand how often I'd wept in the last three years. Now I was two for two days.

"I'm tired," I managed by way of explanation, scrubbing my cheeks with my palms. "I *never* do this."

"Please. Lady Joan." I'd gone and sat on his bed once I'd consumed the last of the yellow tart stuff, so all he had to do was sit up and lean over until he had an arm around my shoulders. "You've nothing to apologize for."

"I think," I blubbered, "after what we've been through, you should call me Joan."

"Joan. Whom the angels send."

"Not really," I replied, and cried harder.

CHAPTER FIFTY-EIGHT

Somehow we ended up lying down on the featherbed, facing each other while I sobbed and Thomas made soothing noises. After a minute I said, "This will look odd but don't worry about it," then took off my hood and several strands of hair that came with the pins. Then the wig so I could let my hair roam free on my scalp. "Ever try sleeping in one of these? Yuck."

Thomas slowly reached up like he thought I might flee (possibly while screaming), and when I didn't move he ran his fingers through my hair, smoothing over the little dents left by the pins. I groaned and tipped my head forward to give him more access. "When were you ill?"

"Huh? I almost never get sick. Except for headaches."

"Those afflicted with a fever often have their hair shorn. Do they not do that in Merka?"

"Of course they do. What I meant was I never get sick except for that bad fever a year or so ago when I was sick. And also one way back, when I was just a kid. It was so high it literally burned some of my brain!" (I have to stop telling that story like it's a positive.)

"I like this," he said, holding up a strand of my hair like a jeweler eyeballing a diamond. "It suits you better than the rest of it."

"At least the wig had some nice auburn highlights. My natural hair is an exotic hue known as Boring Brown. It's my fault she's dead." *Huh. I didn't know I was going to come out with that until I came out with that.*

"Joan…"

"It *is*. I should have set out straight away. But I was tired of it, and I didn't trust—I didn't want to come and because I was a self-absorbed brat, Teresa was run down by a mob. She must have been terrified. And I was—I was home feeling sorry for myself."

"You are being too hard on yourself," he said to my temple, still massaging my scalp. "And while I do not know how long your journey takes, I do know that Teresa died—"

"Was murdered. Was run down like a dog in the street and murdered by savages."

"—almost immediately upon her arrival."

"What?" I sniffed and sat up. "How d'you know?"

"I spoke with the Tower guards." At my raised eyebrows, he shrugged. "It helped pass the time. Apparently your friend appeared in a flash of light—an exaggeration, but this is what the guard claimed to have seen—and citizens set upon her almost immediately."

I winced. "It makes no difference. I still shouldn't have waited."

"Perhaps you should pray for guidance," he suggested.

"Okay. I'll do that while you rub my head some more?"

He smiled at my hopeful tone. "Of course."

"Not that I think of you as particularly maternal—"

"I should hope not."

"—but it's a little like when my mother would rub my head when I'd get a migraine. That's what we call a really, really bad headache where I come from. Like, monstrously bad."

"Ah. I have suffered one or two monsters myself. Come here."

So I did. Lay back down with him, I mean. I didn't pray. And after a suitable period of time—I assumed three or four minutes was long enough for a nice prayer—I said. "Amen."

Then I grabbed him by the ears and kissed him. Because praying makes me horny, apparently.

CHAPTER FIFTY-NINE

Remember earlier when I said I didn't date much? Needless to say, my go-to seductive moves aren't especially subtle. Or seductive.

"Oh God, I'm so sorry!" I let go of Thomas' ears like they were hot pot handles. "This has been the strangest few days, I shouldn't have done th—what are you—oh."

Thomas' technique, by contrast, was first rate. He didn't even *touch* my ears. Smooooth. Instead his mouth slotted over mine in a gentle press of lips, while one hand cupped the nape of my neck to keep me steady. After a few wondrous seconds, he broke off. And I definitely didn't whimper just a bit at the loss.

"Have you gone mad, Joan?" His blue eyes were the world as he smiled and brought our foreheads together. "I have been fighting to keep my hands off you from the moment you told me my accent was awful."

"I did?" *Doesn't sound like me.*

"The day we met. You said 'your accent is awful, by the way', which is laughable when one considers your unique *patois*. Ow! Don't pinch; you know it's true. And then you *reminded* me you had just disparaged my accent. All within two minutes of meeting me."

Sounds exactly like me. "Got it. Carry on."

So we did, kissing and sighing and moaning a little for a lovely long time. Thomas kissed like he did everything else, with unconscious skill. I finally had a chance to run my fingers through those auburn locks, thick and dark and wavy, and then I *really* indulged my kink and went to town on his forearms, caressing them while gently prodding at his mouth with my tongue until he opened with a happy sigh and I tasted milk and apricots and Thomas.

When his hands moved from my waist to my skirt and he started inching the material up, I had to put a stop to it. Bad enough I'd let him see my natural hair; I wasn't going to try to explain my Wonder Woman underpants.

"You are not being waved in," I murmured against his mouth. "Sorry."

"What? Oh. My apologies," he replied, letting go of my skirt at once. Our make-out session (sounds juvenile, but that's what it was) had put color in his cheeks, and his pupils were so dilated I could only see a thin sliver of blue around the iris. (Unconscious physiological signs of arousal are *so* hot.)

I groaned and rested my head on his chest. "Believe me, I wish I could. That *we* could." Hey, how about that, I accidentally told the truth again! Because I did want him, and not just because he always dropped everything to help me, and not just because he risked prison for me, and not just because of his forearms, although those were all huge pluses. "I can't." Major regret, though. *What do you mean there isn't any more French Silk Pie?* levels of regret.

"I would never dream of dishonoring you, Joan," he said earnestly. "Truly. I would take a blade to my own throat before ever doing such a thing. Ever *contemplating* such a thing."

"That's really not necessary." (Though, no lie, I loved hearing it.)

"I decided some time ago that I would take whatever you could give and call myself the most fortunate of men."

"It's not that I don't want to…"

"You do not have to explain. About this or anything."

I leaned back so I could look at him, because I knew he had questions; he was one of the most curious people I'd ever met. His literal job as a scholar was to learn new things, but he'd been content to let me keep my secrets. Until this moment I hadn't realized what a gift that was.

But he was also wonderful about going with the flow. He wasn't laid-back, exactly, but he was open-minded and had been able to handle everything I'd thrown at him. That was a valuable trait in every century.

"Thank you, Thomas." I took his hand in mine, squeezed gently. "This will sound inadequate, but I'm so happy to know you."

"On the contrary, that is one of the kindest things anyone has ever told me. Certainly no one with hair as short as yours has ever seemed so fond of me."

"Shut up now. Over the years, I've come to realize, the best things in my life are the things I find by accident." Thomas, Lisa, butter chicken (I'd actually ordered Tandoori chicken), I.T.C.H … the list was long and not-so-distinguished.

Wait. Did I just put I.T.C.H. on my list of best things?

"Joan, I understand the limitations you were quite right to put on our intimacy, but may I hold you?"

Later. I'd think about my list and I.T.C.H.'s place on it later. "Oh, sure. You can do that all you want. I like it. Here, be a spoon."

"What?"

I pushed and prodded until we were both on our sides and he was tucked up behind me, his knees behind mine and his arms holding me around my middle. He nuzzled the back of my neck, which tickled and surprised a giggle out of me. "I am now a spoon, it would seem."

"Among other things," I teased.

"We call this bundling."

"That's cute."

"I will spend every night on Tower Green if it means that afterward you'll eat half my lunch and then let me hold you like this."

"So romantic. And I ate barely a third of your lunch." Or two-thirds. Again: math was not a specialty of mine. I wasn't sure what my specialty was, just that it wasn't math. "Go to sleep, Thomas. I know you're exhausted."

"I leap to obey my lady's command."

I snorted, and ended up dozing a little myself, because the next thing I knew I was wide awake and the shadows in the room had all moved around. Late afternoon? Early evening?

Thomas was still down for the count, his snores occasionally riffling the hair on the back of my neck. Small wonder—he probably hadn't gotten any sleep the night before.

I eased out of his embrace until I was standing over him like Katie over Micah in *Paranormal Activity*. (Classic horror!) I watched him snore for a minute (that's how tired I'd been—I hadn't heard it until I was awake) and thought about my next move. Stay and have another meal? Followed by more cuddling? Possibly topless cuddling? And then a nice long sleep followed by a wonderful breakfast?

Tempting. But it was just another way for me to hide. Teresa was dead, and I had to go back and say so, would have to admit I had failed her in the worst of ways. Understanding that I.T.C.H. was staffed with incompetent frauds didn't make that task any easier.

And Lisa deserved an explanation as well. I had promised to tell her everything, and despite my longtime habit of rampant dishonesty, I kept my promises.

And even if none of those things were true, I still couldn't stay. The food was sublime, as was Thomas Wynter, but I was too fond of the 21st century, its drinking water and healthcare and transportation options and technology, to turn my back on it to bundle with Thomas and travel the world looking for cream eating festivals.

So I kissed him on the forehead and when he didn't stir, I took the coward's way out and crept away like a thief, leaving Thomas without an explanation or even a note.

I mean, come on. What did you think I had done?

CHAPTER SIXTY

"I'm back, you pack of fraudulent shitheads."

The pack of fraudulent shitheads looked delighted and relieved to see me, though I was glad to see most of them had chucked the lab coats and were in street clothes.

"Alone," Karen noted.

"But at least no one bet on you to die this time," Warren put in, because he was cluelessly adorable. I knew I should be just as irked with him as the others, but he, at least, never treated me as a glorified temp (laughable, given that most of them were glorified temps). And he cared enough about what I was doing to put up significant amounts of his own money, which was more than I could say about the rest of them. "We thought you might appreciate it."

"Oh, I do, Warren. I really really appreciate you guys not betting on me to die. Did anyone bet on Teresa Lupez to die?"

Silence, broken by Ian Holt's, "Oh, shit."

"The eloquence of a scientist, the lifestyle of a grifter. Yeah, 'oh, shit'." I stepped down from the pad. "Things went sideways, to put it very *very* mildly. But at least I know where they buried her. What?" I asked before anyone could object. "It's hard enough getting back without trying to unobtrusively time travel with a corpse."

"Literally no one's arguing with you." At my glare, Warren threw up his hands like he was being arrested. "We swear!"

"Mmmm. I assume I was gone about a day and a half?"

Nods all around. One of them even glanced at the clock on the wall, as if mentally confirming I had, indeed, been in the 16th century for thirty-six hours. San Dimas time travel confirmed.

"And can I also assume you have made zero progress, can't stop the wormholes from gobbling people up, are in too deep so you can't simply abandon ship and flee to create false identities and new lives, and have no idea what to tell Teresa Lupez' family?"

"That's…a fair assumption." This from Holt, who was playing with his pad and probably thought he looked terribly busy and important when really, he looked as if he was losing at Solitaire. "Though we did make some progress—we can now see you through the gate just before you come back. It's about a thirty second window."

"So if there's a howling mob on my ass, you can see it?"

"Part of it," Holt admitted. "It's a small window. So if you'd had a corpse, we would have briefly seen you both. And I have to admit I'm surprised you came back solo. We thought you'd pull it off."

My expression must have been eloquent and pissy, because Karen chimed in with, "So you get mad when we think you'll fail and get yourself killed—"

"Get *myself* killed?"

"—and you get mad when we think you won't?" Insult to injury: she was playing with her phone while she said it.

"Well, now you can think about what you're going to tell the Lupez family. 'Terribly sorry, but your loved one's remains are in Cross Bones cemetery. If you have her exhumed, her skeleton will be about 500 years old. But at least she died in fear and terror, so it's not all bad.'"

The glum silence that followed actually had me feeling sorry for the merry band of morons. I sighed and rubbed my forehead and tried to think.

"Okay, so—again, can't believe the layman is suggesting this, but have you guys considered just shutting it all down? Not the half-assed 'Joan's probably dead so everybody take a half day' shutdown you did before. I mean these things. This thing." I gestured to the pad, the gate, the computer monitors, all of it. "Just cut power to everything. Go full dark. Like you were *supposed* to before you started frigging around with equipment you didn't understand."

"Well. That might work." Karen stopped talking (and texting) and looked at her colleagues for help, so I was suddenly terrified. What could be terrible enough to make her hesitate? Had they started a nuclear war while I was gone? Did they take a figurative dump on the space-time continuum?

"That's the problem with going dark," Holt said bluntly, putting his pad aside. "It might work."

By now I had marched to the break room for terrible coffee, so I thought about what he'd just said. It might work, which meant no one would take a five hundred year fall. But it also meant…

"Dammit, you guys!" I felt an urge to dramatically smack myself in the forehead, but didn't want to spill the creamer. So I just waved it around irritably while Warren prepped my awful coffee. "Who's the V.I.P. you need back? What did you selectively forget to mention this time?"

"It's just that if we do shut everything down, there's no guarantee we could recreate the accident, or even get running at all," Holt explained. "It's like when your computer isn't working but you don't know what the trouble is. Sometimes a reboot works and the problem is solved. But sometimes the problem isn't solved, or, worse, sometimes you can't get the computer back up. And you still don't know why, and you've made things worse."

This was rich from the poster child for Team Making Things Worse. "So you're saying shutting it down might be permanent." Nods all around. "Which, incomprehensibly, you think is a bad thing." Don't get me wrong. I didn't feel right about stranding anyone in TudorTime. But the alternative was more victims. The alternative was another Teresa.

So we drank coffee and yelled at each other, which was as productive as you might imagine, and I changed back into street clothes and came back and yelled more, and I had just made up my mind (as I had in truth before I came back) that I would go to the authorities (whoever they would prove to be) and make them believe me regardless of what I.T.C.H. did. I'd start with whomever was working Teresa's case. The props I'd smuggled back would be helpful.

But before I could make my getaway: "What in the fucking fuck is going on here?"

I nearly dropped my awful coffee. "Lisa?"

My thoroughly enraged roommate was standing in the doorway of the break room and behind her were two burly fellows in dark suits. Feds? Her car pool buddies? Two random guys in suits she'd met in the lobby? Future patients? Past patients? Pharmacy reps?

And strangest of all: "Hey!" I pointed at her head. "You colored your hair!"

In retrospect, I had probably focused on the wrong thing.

CHAPTER SIXTY-ONE

"**D**on't move."

"I know."

"I mean it, Joan. Don't move one goddamn centimeter."

"I *know.*" And I wasn't sulking from inside the magnetic resonance imaging scanner, if you were wondering. "Stop acting like this is my first MRI."

"Moving your lips is fucking moving, Joan!"

I know you are, I thought. *But what am I?* Enh, not my best. At least this wouldn't take as long as the CT scan.

Things had been, um, tense since she and her chums from Bodyguards, Inc. yanked me ("Wait! My time-travel tote bag! And can we get a candy bar out of the vending machine before we go?") from the bowels of I.T.C.H. to the bowels of Oxford University Hospital.

Once I'd gotten over her radical hair color change— Easter Egg Pink to Jet Black—I asked the most pertinent question: "Do you not know what 'keep clear' means? Because this is the opposite. Literally the polar opposite. What the hell are you doing here?"

"I texted her."

I turned and stared at Karen. "How? Why? How do you even know her?"

"I don't." Karen had set her phone aside to re-roll up her sleeves because the coat was too big because, again, *it wasn't her lab coat.* "She and my brother work at the same clinic and they've been fucking each other."

I blinked. Had I really only been gone a day and a half? Maybe it had been a year and a half. "Lisa has a boyfriend?"

"No. They're fucking each other."

"Oh. *Oh!* That's why you didn't bet on me to die this time!" I said triumphantly. "You're terrified of Lisa!" I lowered my voice. "Good call, by the way. And however scared you are? You're not scared enough. Honest to God. And I wouldn't recommend doing that thing where we talk about her like she isn't here, either. She hates that."

"After I read your delusional note," Lisa announced, "I reached out to your new bosses."

"They are not my bosses, just like I am not Henry VIII's holy fool and I have told them both that exact thing!" Argh. I don't think I could have yelled something that sounded crazier.

"So I told *this* bitch …" Pointing to a cowed Karen. "… to text the moment you turned up, and explained how I'd express my displeasure if she didn't comply. It would involve her ass, my fist, and quick-drying concrete."

"Yikes."

"Then I put these guys on retainer…" Jerking her thumb at the men.

"Right, who are they again?"

"…and here we are and you're coming with me right fucking now and Jesus Christ, I don't even know where to start with you."

I took a closer look at Lisa who, though normally very pretty, looked exhausted. The circles under her eyes looked like bruises; she'd bitten all her nails back—and this was a woman who breezed through med school on four hours of sleep a night. Although threats of death and mutilation (or death by mutilation) were her normal, she was so frazzled there was a chance she might carry them out.

"Look, I'm fine. I'm sorry you were worried, thus the note."

"That fucking piece of paper did not set my mind at ease at all."

"Okay, I can see how that could be true. I'm not crazy. Back me up, I.T.C.H." But even as I said it, I knew they were going to burn me. "Tell her about trying to invent teleportation but accidentally inventing time travel and then being too dumb to undo it and needing me to find the Losties while you worked on your cover story." Yes: they were definitely going to burn me. *I* might have burned me.

"Do you hear yourself?" I could count on one hand how often Lisa had looked so horrified. She whirled on the I.T.C.H. gang and hissed, "I swear. I *swear* to fucking *Christ* in his *cradle,* if you've exposed her to *anything* that made her sick, if you fuckfarts are screwing around with something *toxic* here—"

"They are! Only it's not a drug. And I'm not sick. I'm not sick!" (Not sure why I felt I needed to say it twice. Probably should squash that urge next time.)

"—I will tie each of you up and run you through an automated carwash until the brushes scrub away your epidermis and/or you drown in soap and/or are dried to death."

(I've always loved Lisa's weirdly specific and profane threats. Also points to Warren, who was the only one who looked intrigued and not angry or terrified.)

Dr. Holt cleared his throat. "Nothing like that. While it's true we've managed to make progress with quantum teleportation, it's also true that our funding has dried up and subsequent experimentation has been shelved. But Joan has been tremendously helpful in—"

"Yeah, we're going now." Lisa made a curt motion and suddenly all four of us were on our way out.

"Wait! He's explaining, sort of! Okay, he's leaving out critical information because that's what he does but he's backing most of my story and what is the *rush?*" Because we were practically jogging to the parking lot. "You're not even gonna hear him out?"

"Joan! Fuck's sake! He is not gonna tell me you're his time traveling errand girl!"

"Well, that's true, he won't, but not for the reason you think."

"I need to run tests *immediately*. We need to find out what's wrong right the fuck *now*. We're already way behind; I should have done this weeks ago, we're not waiting another minute."

"There's nothing wrong with me! Physiologically, I mean." I looked up at one of her rent-a-guards, whose fingers were curled around my biceps as I was hustled to the waiting car. "You're very good at this, by the way. Much better than Henry VIII's guards."

Lisa groaned.

"Maybe that's what I'm meant to do: analyze and write about the dragging techniques of various guards through the ages."

"Jesus Christ!"

I could guess what she was worried about. She was a neuro-in-training; her first fear was going to be a tumor or something equally terrible lurking in my brain and driving me insane. And since I hadn't been insane a month ago (as far as she knew), that meant she was worried it was something fast-acting. I was just a layman, but even I knew fast-acting brain tumors = get your affairs in order.

And let's not forget I was on experimental medication. She had to be worried about that, too.

"Don't worry," I assured her as we piled into the car, a sleek black sedan I'd never seen before. "I have proof I'm not clinically insane. Y'know, about this."

Except I didn't. I just didn't realize it at the time.

CHAPTER SIXTY-TWO

L isa is very good at her job.

But even an efficient and ruthless genius can be thwarted by hospital bureaucracy.

"A full *day*?" she snarled into her phone, then paused to listen. "But this *is* an emergency! What? Yeah, I'm looking at her confused-ass face right now. She's staring at me like a big dummy."

"Thanks for that," I said. "And I'm not staring. I'm glaring."

"Obviously she's fine right now, but that doesn't mean—no, wait, you can't—hello?" She slammed the phone down. "That wiener-slurping jackoff!"

"I'm not sure homophobia is the way to handle this."

"It's literal! He's straight! And he microwaves hot dogs and then licks them before eating them and he doesn't use a bun!"

"That's a weird way to eat hot dogs," I admitted.

Have I mentioned Lisa used to get into fist fights with meth dealers? Until you've seen a bruised and bloody meth dealer running away from a 10th grade girl, you haven't really lived.

"Apparently since you aren't bleeding out, unconscious, or otherwise fucked sideways, your scans are low-pri." Lisa booted the stool so hard it shot across the lab and bounced off the far wall. "Fascist dingbats!"

"As it should be," I pointed out. "Come on, Lisa. Some poor kid knocked out in a car crash needs his results back a lot faster than I do."

"We have no way of knowing if that's true. *No fucking way.* But do you know how we could definitively find out?"

"Does it have something to do with prioritizing my tests?"

"By prioritizing your tests!" She scrubbed her face with her palms, then glared at me with puffy eyes. "I should get you to an ER. I should put a Psych hold on you."

"The ER won't do anything to me since I'm not a danger to myself or others, and you don't have Psych privileges." Right? That seemed like it would be correct. Could any random M.D. put any random person on a Psych hold? In truth, I had no idea, since I spent The After avoiding check-ups and health care of any kind.

But I knew what would put Lisa's big fat brain at ease. "Look, see?"

"What am I looking at?"

I'd brought my tote bag in with us and had upended it all over the table. Now I grabbed the bundle of blue and green fabric and held it up. "See this dress? It's my special time-traveling dress. It's rigged, it only *looks* like an impractical pile of clothing that would hinder and stifle anyone who put it on. See the zipper? And the Velcro? I started with something authentic and modified it."

She just looked at me.

"And see these?" I showed her the gorgeous knife and spoon I'd kept after Anne's Marquis banquet. "This is from Henry VIII's court! Windsor, specifically. I picked it up in 1532." I wasn't bragging, just imparting information. Okay, I was bragging a little. At her prolonged stare (if she didn't blink soon, her eyeballs were going to shrivel like raisins),

I got defensive. "I had to steal it. Bringing your own spoon and knife is just basic good manners back there. It would have looked weird if I didn't have those on me, and believe me, you do not want to stand out in Tudor England."

"No," Lisa said quietly. "*You* don't want to stand out. Anywhere."

"Not that again."

"Very fucking much that again."

I ignored her attempted foray into irrelevancy. "C'mon, look at it." The knife was sharp and gleaming, with a scrolled silver blade and an even more scrolled gold handle topped with a tiny crown. It was solid from end to end, about seven inches long with a comfortable weight in the palm that was perfect for skewering meat off the group trencher. The spoon was from the same set, only heavier, with a nice deep bowl. "They don't use forks yet," I explained. "Or I would have grabbed one of those, too. And I'm sorry to say the spoons are shared around a little, but everyone catching the same cold is a small price to pay for the astonishing food. But look at this set… it's five hundred years old and it looks brand new!"

"Yeah. It looks brand new."

I sighed. "My point is, it shouldn't, because I used it last week. In 1535."

Lisa took a breath before answering. If it had been anyone else, I would have assumed they were trying to figure out how to spare my feelings. "This is England, Joan. Everybody has a pile of ancient junk in their attic dating back to William the Conqueror."

"Yes, and it all looks *old*. This doesn't! And where did I get it? I mean, you can tell it's the real deal. So now I'm some kind of high end flatware thief? And look here! This is my pomander, which is like a portable Glade air freshener. But

I've put other stuff in it—remember that talk we had about the book I lied about writing so you wouldn't find out I was time traveling and think I was insane?"

"Jesus Christ." She'd twisted it open and was staring in disbelief. "You've stuffed it with Flintstones Chewables and Tootsie Rolls."

"I'm saving those for later!" I snatched both halves back and put them back together. "And hydrocodone. And anti-inflammatories. That was all I had time to pull from our medicine cabinet before I had to go rescue Teresa Lupez who's been dead and buried in Crossed Bones for five centuries. Which reminds me." I pulled out my phone and started to look up the cemetery.

"Joan. Listen to yourself."

"Also I could really use your advice on how to break the news to the Lupez family. If I'm even the one to tell them— maybe the cops should do that? I don't know the protocol. You've told people when a family member died—do you just say it right out loud or do you lead up to it a little?"

"Joan. Don't you think if people were randomly being sucked into—into time portals or whatever—"

"Gates." I sniffed. "Nobody calls them portals, Lisa, learn the lingo."

"What*ever* the goddamned things are," she continued, exasperated, "don't you think there'd be more of a ruckus?"

"No, because less than a dozen people have disappeared in the last six weeks or so. Over a quarter of a million people disappear every year *without* time travel, and there are eight million people in London." I glanced up from my phone. "Don't look so surprised. I did some research. That's why there hasn't been a fuss. And I.T.C.H. doesn't know why only a fraction of a fraction of the population falls through these gates. Which I could also use your help with—none of the Losties, including me, have anything in common. But you're brilliant and terrible so I think you—oh, this is unacceptable bullshit!"

"Exactly what I was thinking."

I was clenching my phone so hard my fingers ached. "They dumped poor Teresa in a graveyard for prostitutes!"

"Who are 'they'?"

"Henry VIII and Thomas Cromwell. Not cool, Cromwell!" I showed Lisa the entry for Cross Bones cemetery, which was so stuffed with dead sex workers they had to quit using it in 1853. *Oh, that velvet-clad prick!* "I can't tell Teresa's family to dig her out of a pile of prostitutes! No one should have to do that!"

"Joan, will you *stop* it?"

I set my phone down so I wouldn't throw it. Possibly at Lisa. "I promised you I'd tell you everything if I got back. But I never promised you'd like what you heard. So stop pretending like you can't handle it when we both know you've handled far worse."

"Christ, you don't think much of me, do you? Or yourself. My best friend is either very sick or mentally unbalanced; 'far worse' pretty much covers it." She rubbed her forehead and said, "All right. So you take these trips back to—"

"TudorTime. I'm trademarking that, by the way. Don't steal it."

"Yeah, because that's where my focus is right now."

"Just sayin'," I mumbled.

"I caught some of it in the car, but I was more worried about booking time in the scanners than taking notes. So you had to go back for this—Teresa? Whose family reported her missing a couple of days ago?"

"Yes. But by the time I stopped feeling sorry for myself and jumped, she was dead. Then I yelled at King Henry VIII and got thrown in the Tower."

"Right, and Anne Boleyn brought you Tootsie Rolls and leeches."

"No, *Mary* Boleyn brought me a bolster, which looked like a giant Tootsie Roll. The leeches part is correct. But not the kind of leeches you're thinking. No wonder you think I'm lying. You weren't paying attention so you're only getting half the story. And since *I* only know half the story, that's bad. You know, math-wise."

"Please don't misunderstand," she said gently, which was terrifying. "I don't think you're lying at all."

"Just batshit crazy."

"I would never use that word to describe you. You know I fucking hate bats. So after King Henry let you go …"

"Thomas Cromwell and Cardinal Wolsey's bastard and I went to The Gray Horse Inn where I had venison pie and raw milk and then took a nap but first Other Thomas tried to talk me into hanging around for a cream-eating festival."

She was rubbing her forehead again like she was trying to fend off a migraine. Which was—huh. Why did that suddenly feel important? Lisa had never had a migraine in her life. She *gave* migraines; she'd never take one.

But it wasn't important. It was just my brain trying to distract me from the fact that I was doing a piss-poor job convincing my friend I wasn't clinically insane.

"Cream-eating festivals. Uh-huh. And how'd you get back to I.T.C.H.?"

"The Gray Horse Inn is only half a mile down the road from the gate, so when nobody was watching I went to the willow." It had been a five minute wait, and I'd been less anxious about it than usual. The innkeeper's husband had shared an interesting tidbit: locals think the willow is haunted and keep clear. Can't imagine why. "I only had to wait a couple of minutes."

"For a gate to open."

"Yes."

"One just eventually opens for you?"

"Yes."

"But not for any of the others. They're stuck unless you come along and rescue them."

"That's right."

"And it's always on a significant date in Tudor history. Like Anne Boleyn's execution."

"That hasn't happened yet!" I protested. "Um. You know what I mean. But yes. I never seem to show up on a random Tuesday for poker night. Come to think of it, I've never showed up at night at all. Or in the winter. Huh … don't ask me to explain."

"Well, who *should* I ask?"

"I don't know, okay? The I.T.C.H. scientists? They explained it to me and now I'm explaining it to you. Of course it doesn't make any sense—it's goddamned time travel as accidentally invented by frauds!"

"All right, calm down. So this morning you were in the past. And this afternoon you made it back to the—what? Transporter pad?"

I rolled my eyes at 'transporter pad'. It was almost as if she was deliberately trying to make it sound like I'd seen too many sci-fi movies, which was impossible, because you can never see too many sci-fi movies. "Yes. And the first thing I did when I got back was yell at I.T.C.H. because they're duplicitous jerks and sentenced Teresa to death with their tomfuckery, and then you came with your rental guards. Which was kind of awesome now that I think about it. Nice of them to drop us off at the hospital, by the way. And then they vanished into the night. Which reminds me. Where'd you find them? *Why'd* you find them?"

"Your note. When you didn't come back last night—"

"I couldn't—I was in the Tower by then, in the custody of the Crown. On San Dimas time."

She sucked in a long breath and let it slowly out her nose, which is what she sometimes did when she was trying to restraining herself from felony assault. "Right, you said that earlier. Bill and Ted, right? However long you're in the past, that's how long you're gone in the present? So you were in 1532—"

"No, that was two trips ago. This time I was in 1535."

"Uh-huh. You were in 1535." I didn't care for the borderline-indulgent tone she was using at all. "When you didn't immediately return, I took steps. To tell you the truth, I already knew something was up."

"Reading all the Tudor non-fiction of my own free will," I guessed. "And telling you I was going to write a book when you know—"

"When I know you'd never do anything that would call that kind of attention to yourself. Yes. Exactly. Weird as shit. So I was never going to keep clear—you were a moron to think otherwise."

"Nice."

"But that didn't mean I wasn't going to take precautions."

"So you can just rent personal security guards on less than a day's notice?" How had I reached my twenties without knowing this?

"You can rent just about anything on short notice if you have the money," the 17th winner of the Online Poker Series reminded me.

"Okay, so you got my note—but why didn't—"

"I never looked in your lockbox. There wasn't time. But I imagine you had stashed trinkets in there you 'found' in Tudor England that you smuggled back."

"Jesus. I can actually hear the air quotes. And they're hardly trinkets, though with that attitude, it's probably just as well you didn't look. Besides, there's proof all around you." I gestured to the silverware and gown. "Even if you think this incredibly authentic and heavy and impractical silverware which should literally be in a museum is a case of 'ho-hum, doesn't everyone in England have a set in their basement?', the dress proves I'm telling the truth!"

"Again: I believe you really think this. I never called you a liar and I never would. But Joanie..." She reached out, touched the fabric. "This dress doesn't prove you went back in time, it only proves you *think* you went back in time."

Joanie. Wow. She almost never called me that. Not since we were kids, or when she was really worried about me.

"I.T.C.H.! They can prove me right even if they didn't actually get around to proving me right but why would I pick a random tech company doing work in an area so far from my field it's laughable and then fixate on them and convince myself they discovered time travel?" I gasped for breath. Run-on sentences were hard.

"I don't know," Lisa admitted.

"If I'm not running temporal errands for them, what *am* I doing for them?"

"I have no idea."

"Ah-*ha*!" Oh. Wait. That didn't actually prove anything.

"I would assume that when you were there, you heard about their research—quantum teleportation, wasn't it?—and conflated it into actual teleportation."

"But why was I there at all?"

"I don't know."

"The money!" I gasped. "They paid me twenty thousand pounds. It's just sitting in my account but it's there, I can prove it."

Lisa didn't say anything.

"Right," I sighed. "It only proves that I've got twenty thousand pounds, not that I'm a time traveler. And I'm sure you've got an explanation for the non-dis agreements I.T.C.H. got me to sign."

"Again, stop calling them that, and yeah. My assumption is that you were paid for whatever the NDAs are for. And I'll bet if I tried to read them, they'd be full of jargon laymen couldn't understand."

"Well, if you'd *opened my lockbox* you'd have seen them, and yeah, they're hundreds of pages of Quantum something-something and temporal something-something in teeny type. And if I'm breaking into museums or attics to steal fancy cutlery, maybe I also stole or scammed the twenty grand. So, what?" I began stuffing my loot back into my tote. It was hard to look at her. She looked like she would burst into tears if I said one more crazy thing. "I'm making it up in a pathetic bid for attention? If I wanted attention—"

"You do want attention. But you're also fucking terrified of attention, which is the great dichotomy of your nature."

"Do not psychoanalyze me. If it was just about getting noticed, don't you think I could have come up with a more plausible lie than 'part-time time traveler'?"

"Part-time time traveler to *Tudor England*."

"Don't start."

"Not the Wild West. Or the future. Or the Civil War. Or the British Civil War. Not the Victorian age or World War I or the French Revolution."

"Don't make this about my mother," I warned, "or The After."

"You know why I wanted you to move here with me, right?"

"Because you're a shit cook?"

"Yeah, but that was a lesser consideration. I wanted to jolt you out of your complacency."

We were leaving the scanners and other miscellaneous machinery behind as we headed outside, which was a shame because I'd have preferred to hide inside the MRI for a few days rather than have this conversation. But not only was Lisa still talking, I had the impression she wasn't exactly relishing the conversation, either. We were discussing a topic so bad and unpleasant, *Lisa Harris* was reluctant to bring it up.

"I wanted you to be an active participant in your own life."

I snorted. "That sounds like something you'd read on the back of a box of power bars."

"But it didn't work. Or it worked too well."

"Are you *sure* you're a genius?"

"For fuck's sake!" she practically screamed, stopping so quickly I almost walked into her (it was a narrow hallway, but at least we were almost to the lobby). "Are you ever going to get tired of being a spectator in your own life?"

"How am I supposed to answer that?"

"Look, I get it…"

(People always say "I get it" just before coming out with something that proves that they do *not*, in fact, get it.)

"…you had to keep a low profile when you were a kid. But that's done now, it's been done for years, you're not fifteen anymore. You don't have to keep it up."

(See? Doesn't get it.)

"Look, Joanie, I love you and I'm glad we live together, but you're a coaster. You got Bs and Cs because you couldn't be bothered to work for As. And when—"

"Couldn't be *bothered*? I had bills to pay, groceries to buy, a house to run *on my own*…"

"And Child Services to avoid," she added quietly.

"Well, yes." That was the whole point. It was how I dealt with The After. Lisa *knew* that.

"So you coasted in college because you prefer drifting to living. You went to college so you wouldn't stand out because by then, you were in the habit of avoiding notice at all costs. But you didn't really participate. Partly because you live your life in camouflage, but also because you couldn't be bothered to give a fuck."

"We don't all have genius I.Q.s and an obsession to cure addiction because our parents were meth heads who ignored their only child's gambling addiction."

"Jesus, *finally*." She stopped walking and squared off to face me, almost like a boxer lining up a shot. "That's the bitchiest thing you've said to me all year, and look at what I had to say to get you to do it! I mean, Christ, I call you up out of nowhere, tell you we're moving to England—"

"Great Britain," I corrected.

"—and you were all, 'okey-dokey, guess I'll start packing, let me know what my new address is when you get a chance'. I was glad, I even knew you'd come, but...who *does* that?"

"I does that, apparently."

By now we were outside, and I was grateful that it was after clinic hours, so hardly anyone was around to see this...this *mess*. "Your fear of being noticed has hardened into something almost pathological. Except scratch 'almost' because you've convinced yourself that you have an impossible, sexy, straight-out-of-science-fiction job—"

"Sexy? There's shit on all the streets! Actual shit!"

"—where you're always the heroine who saves the day—"

"That's demonstrably untrue."

"—where you're the only one who can go back and forth between centuries, a job even scientists can't do. A fantastical dream job—"

"Spend some time locked up with a drowned corpse, then tell me about dream jobs."

"—where you can swoop in out of nowhere, do something incredible, then go back into your own life to hide."

Nothing. I had nothing to say to that. I just glared at her. And I wasn't going to yell. And I wasn't going to cry.

"Where's the rest of it?" she asked quietly.

"What?"

"The bulk of your clothes. Your furniture. Your lifetime of *stuff.*"

I blinked. When that didn't help, I blinked more. After about a thousand blinks, I managed an answer. "You know where. It's—it's mostly in storage. You know I don't need every single scrap of clothing, every chair and plate." So what if I only had about a week or so of outfits at any given time? I liked to rotate. I also liked keeping an eye on the bulk of my things, safely locked up where no one can take them away from me. *It's called thriftiness, Lisa!*

"It's like living with someone who is constantly on vacation. Or on the run. You keep the bulk of your possessions where you *aren't*. Most people put *things* in storage. You put your life in storage."

"I'll bet you think that's profound."

"No. Just the truth"

I opened my mouth to say—I had no idea. But in a feat of magnificent timing, my phone rang and that was a call I would be taking. Survey? Bill collector? Death threat? It mattered not. And even better, a quick glance told me it was Warren.

"Sorry, gotta take this. The fake scientist who helped me with my fake job needs me to fake something else that's fake because you're always right and I never am." Huh. Kind of lost it at the end there ... well, she was smart. She'd know she was being savagely dissed. "Hello?"

"Joan. I'm so sorry to bug you, I just wanted to—"

"Yes."

"—ask if—you will? That's wonderful! I didn't—jeez, thanks! I'll text the address."

"Great." Dinner? Another Lostie? An audit? My murder? It mattered not. Wherever he wanted me was better than here.

"Joan—"

"No. We're done. I didn't expect you to believe me, and I appreciate you showing up with guards in case you had to rescue me, but you could have saved the bullshit psychoanalysis."

"Joanie—"

"Now I'm going with Warren, who not only doesn't think I'm crazy, but who *actually* cares and *actually* understands what I'm going through and understands what I've accomplished in the face of, yes, I'll say it, incredible odds. Not 'incredible odds' that I made up because I'm a pathetic introvert who yearns to be an extrovert, but actual and factual incredible odds. In fact, he's the only one who understands." Even as I said it, I knew it was true. Lisa—well. Enough said. Other Thomas? He was great, but he thought I was just robotically following orders from a heavenly choir so I'd get into heaven, not undertaking dangerous tasks of my own free will with no hope of everlasting grace. *"Don't* call me an ambulance. And don't try to put a Psych hold on me, either."

"Joanie—"

"And don't wait up, either."

Then I realized I had no way of getting to Warren, because the guards had dropped us off at the hospital and I had no idea where Lisa's car was. So we had to wait on the sidewalk for separate cabs while simultaneously fuming and avoiding eye contact. Probably should have saved my dramatic blistering exit speech for when I could have followed it with a dramatic exit.

CHAPTER SIXTY-THREE

I'm not so shallow that the way to my heart is through my stomach.

But a seven-course meal doesn't hurt your chances. Especially one at *Le Manoir aux Quat' Saisons*, the mega-posh hotel restaurant in Great Milton where an overnight stay started at £800 and dinner could set you back...well, I had no idea. They also had cooking classes. Which, again, were so expensive it hardly bore inquiry, much less consideration.

"Please don't worry about it," Warren said after I opened the menu and gasped in horror. "Have whatever you like. It still won't even come close to what we owe you."

Ahhhhh. (You'll excuse me while I bask in some praise.)

"This isn't necessary," I said, because I was the epitome of modesty. "I only did what—ooooh, confit of sea trout! I love trout...I haven't had it since before The Af—never mind." Yes, never mind. Lisa was not in my head. The After was a logical response to the untimely deaths of my caregivers. I was having an exquisite dinner with a man with lovely forearms. All was (temporarily) well. "Hey! Fillet of Cornish Turbot. What is a Cornish Turbot?"

"It's a flatfish." Warren puffed his dark, messy bangs out of his eyes—he was still overdue for that haircut, though he cleaned up nicely and looked wonderful in his understated dark suit. "Please, have whatever you like."

"Be careful," I warned. "Most people say that to be polite. I'm not one of them. I *will* have whatever I like, because eating here is a once-in-a-timeline chance I won't squander. You'd better make sure there's room on your Visa."

"Of course. I have."

"How are you rich?"

"I—I'm sorry?"

"I know that's a rude question. But you didn't sign on with I.T.C.H. to get rich—they get government funding, right? That's the problem—that you could get in trouble for fraud?"

He laughed. "Damn right! And no, I didn't sign on to get rich. It's family money. And a lot of it is tied up in trusts and such. What I could get my hands on to help you, I did."

"Thank you for that."

"I wish I could have given you more."

He clearly had pull, not least because though I was in jeans and a long-sleeved t-shirt (a nice navy blue one that was almost new, but still a t-shirt), no one was acting like I was woefully underdressed. No one was acting like I was woefully anything.

So I ordered the turbot. And the Aberdeen Angus beef with alliums. And the Cullen skink. And the braised Jacob's Ladder. And the risotto of wild mushrooms. And Warren never so much as blinked, just listened while I reeled off my order to the waiter and, when I was finished, smiled at me.

"I want to hear all about your latest jump—are you sure you don't want any wine?"

"The perfect question—you'd think I'd want a barrel of booze after all that, right? No, all wine tastes like bad grape juice to me. I'll stick with milk. And my latest jump was a clusterfuck, pardon my French, though that's not French." I glanced around and lowered my voice. "Are you certain it's okay to talk here?"

"Here" was a cozy alcove in the far corner of the restaurant, overlooking the gardens but set apart from most of the other tables. There was a living tree behind me which, while impressive, wasn't big enough to hide an eavesdropper. During the day, the room was probably splashed with sunshine. Now, in the evening, we could see all the fairy lights strung through the trees outside, making the grounds glow and giving fireflies a run for their money. It was as magical a setting as possible without actual magic.

"Please—I wouldn't take you somewhere you couldn't be yourself. And I'm done keeping I.T.C.H.'s secrets—besides, what if someone did overhear? They wouldn't believe us."

"Fair point." Our efficient waiter, clad head to toe in spotless white, returned with drinks, then unobtrusively glided away. "I never thanked you for the flowers."

He inclined his head. "You deserve flowers. You deserve a greenhouse. A dozen greenhouses."

"Maybe, but where would I put them?"

So Warren drank his wine and I guzzled my milk and told him how a med student from Washington D.C. ended up interred five hundred years ago in a London cemetery full of sex workers.

"That's terrible, Joan, and my heart breaks for her family. But you said yourself—you couldn't have saved her. Even if you'd left as soon as we sent you the report."

"Doesn't make me feel any better." I could barely do justice to the smoky Cullen skink, in which creamy potatoes did wonderful things with smoked haddock and parsley. "What are we going to tell the Lupez family? Or the cops who will tell the Lupez family?"

"That poor woman. I don't know." Warren shook his head. "Thank God you made it back at least." He reached out and touched the hand I wasn't using to scoop skink. "We were all relieved, and not just because we had very real concerns that your roommate would have us tortured and killed."

I had to smile. "Isn't she the best? And don't worry, she saved the torture for me. Dragged me to the hospital and had me scanned up, down, and all around. It took forever and you can't bring snacks into those scanners, you know."

He laughed. "No, you can't. She's just looking out for you. And I'm sure she'll be relieved when she gets the test results and they show you're perfectly normal."

"They'll show nothing of the kind, because I'm not 'perfectly' anything, but you're sweet to say it. And she won't be relieved, either; if there's no physiological damage she'll have to assume I'm crazy. If it was a tumor, she could at least come up with a treatment plan. That's where she shines. She's a formidable maker-of-plans."

"But she doesn't have a baseline."

By now I was noshing my way through the Aberdeen Angus beef with alliums, which managed to be meaty and delicate at the same time, with the reduced red wine sauce brightening the dish and giving it a pleasant tang. "She does, though. I'm in a drug protocol for a new migraine med, and we needed a baseline for me to get into the study. Which I listed in the paperwork you didn't bother to read."

Warren groaned so loudly, he puffed his bangs out of his face. "God, that was embarrassing. I don't know what Ian Holt was thinking. He added a completely unnecessary step that ultimately helped you figure out we didn't know what the hell we were doing. I was against it from the beginning."

"Probably figured I would have thought it weirder if I didn't have to sign one," I suggested. Which was true. If they'd been all 'hey, glad you're back, run along now, nothing to see here and have a great life and we don't care who you tell about this', that would have set off every alarm bell in my brain. "But the sneakiness made it worse. There are so few of you left, it makes the potential for errors a lot bigger. Your little group always seemed—don't take this the wrong way—dangerously fragile. So not only did I have to wonder what you were keeping from me, I had to wonder when you guys were going to shatter under pressure, possibly while I was on the wrong side of a gate."

"Shattering under pressure did seem inevitable," he admitted. "Who wouldn't, eventually?"

Well. Thomas Wynter, for example. He seemed to thrive on the chaos I brought with me. And why was I thinking of Thomas while on an outing with Warren? Time to get back to it. "When did you decide to officially give up?"

"About ten minutes after you and your friend left, that's when. It's ridiculous that we allowed it to go on for this long."

"Ridiculous, insane, self-serving..."

"Yes and yes and yes. Ian's reached out to a few colleagues at the Oxford Research Institute, he wants to bring in some outsiders, show 'em what we've done. And go from there."

I shrugged. "Boot a few up on the platform and open a gate, they'll get the picture."

"Let's call that Plan B," he suggested, which made me laugh.

"Are you worried? About getting in trouble?"

He'd been about to take another sip of wine, and paused. "I...a little. Ian thinks once people see what we accidentally accomplished, they'll be sore amazed and niceties such as using property and equipment we didn't understand might be overlooked."

"Could be. Listen, if you want me to testify or whatever, I'd be glad to tell them that you took the disappearances seriously. Don't take this the wrong way, but none of you went near a shower once you realized what was wrong." Or a toothbrush. "I'll tell them you used your own money to keep things going, that you tried to save the people who fell through the gates."

"That would be very kind, Joan, but I'd never ask you to defend our crimes."

Well. I wouldn't defend everyone. Holt and Karen could suck eggs. But Dr. Forearms' heart was in the right place, at least. I wouldn't want to see him imprisoned. I loathe long-distance relationships.

"It is what it is," Warren continued. "Everything goes dark tomorrow, and we'll face whatever consequences there are. To tell you the truth, I'm almost looking forward to it."

"Weird that 'everything goes dark' sounds like a positive. Y'know, 'woo-hoo, everything's going dark! Finally!'"

In truth, I was a little giddy. One way or another, this was going to be over. Maybe the government would crack down and we'd all have to sign non-dis agreements for real and no one would ever speak of this ever again. Or maybe everything would change overnight, and different (and, it must be said, smarter) scientists would figure out the kinks. Maybe time travel would eventually be the new self-driving car. Who knew? Either way, I was well out of it.

"Are you sorry to be saying goodbye to Tudor England?"

I opened my mouth to answer in the resounding affirmative, then hesitated.

I'd never eat leeches again. I'd never go to a cream tasting festival. I'd never save a monarch, console a queen, or meet some of the most notorious figures from history. I'd never use a gold and silver-scrolled spoon to gobble apple mousse, or smell Other Thomas' hair and stroke his forearms. And I'd never be the world's only time-traveling wrangler of Losties. I'd go back to being ordinary.

Dammit! Was Lisa right? Not about me being crazy, but about me getting off on being a vital cog in I.T.C.H.'s machinery of scientific douchebaggery? Because that was a sobering thought. That was a *horrible* thought.

When a certified genius physician who has known you for over a decade points out certain fundamental facts of your personality, she's probably right.

"I won't miss Henry VIII," I said at last, and Warren jumped a little. Maybe the question had been rhetorical. "Or Anne. I'll be sorry to never see Mary Boleyn again—she was great." What can I say? I have a real fondness for sly geniuses. "Or Thomas Wynter." I also have a fondness for men who see the best in me, despite constant clues that I am, in fact, the worst.

Christ, my eyes were starting to water! And I knew why. I would have liked to have seen Mary Boleyn, happy in her country house with her fat babies and a besotted William Stafford, who probably walked around with the expression of a man who couldn't believe his good luck. I would have liked to have hit the cream eating festival circuit with Wolsey's bastard when we weren't making out like teenagers or taking long naps together on feather beds.

I decided to put my almost-tearfulness down to a stressful week. "Yes, some parts I'll miss. Sure. But the upside— no more doomed queens and no more Lady Eleanor."

"Yes, you mentioned her—one of Anne Boleyn's ladies?"

"Yes, she managed to get Henry all turned around on the issue of holy fools predicting the future, which could have really screwed me over. And speaking of screwing over…" Now for the hard part. But I'd made up my mind the minute I realized Warren was calling to ask me out: I had to tell him. "I have to tell you something. It's overdue."

"That sounds dire." He tried to smile.

"If I don't do this, I'm no better than I.T.C.H. Uh. That came out wrong."

"I'm in no position to take offense," he pointed out.

"True." This time I waited until the waiter had set down my pear Almondine with caramel croustillant and sorbet and left. "I broke your time traveling rules."

"Which?"

"All."

"When?"

"A lot."

Warren, who had started on his chocolate sorbet, dropped his spoon. "What are you saying?"

"I used the Heimlich to save Henry VIII from choking to death. I talked Catherine of Aragon out of war. I got Henry to invite the Duke of Suffolk back to court after his banishment. I got Anne to let Henry bone her at Calais instead of waiting for her wedding night. And I might have set Mary Boleyn up with her second husband—that one's still up in the air."

He stared at me, then stammered, "You—you changed history?"

"No, no! I fixed history. Maybe. Warren, what was I supposed to do? Let Henry VIII die years before Elizabeth I was born? The Heimlich wasn't me jumping the gun—he was *purple*, for God's sake. He was dying in front of everyone."

Warren looked utterly staggered. "But why wouldn't you tell us this?"

"Really, Warren? You're going to get pissy about me keeping *you* out of the loop?"

"This is a little more than 'out of the loop'. This has profound and world-wide consequences!"

"And losing control of time travel tech isn't? Why do you think I didn't want to say anything?" Hmm. I really *was* no better than I.T.C.H., which was unpleasant to think about. "Something weird was going on back there. I know the word's overused, but I mean weird like the diction-ary defines it: uncanny and/or supernatural. Abnormal. Mysterious. I could never figure it out so I just did the best I could and kept my head down."

"Okay. Okay." Warren was taking deep breaths while he clutched the table. He'd gone so pale, his brown eyes were so wide, I considered ordering him a brandy. "Okay. Well. It's not like you changed anything—you just—"

"Strove to put right what once went wrong."

"Yes. Er. Yes."

"Uncharted territory, Warren," I reminded him. "Territory *you* shoved me into."

"Yes." He was starting to calm a little, possibly because he'd drained his red wine in two monster gulps, then motioned for a refill. "Yeah, you're right. I get it. And as you pointed out, I don't have the moral high ground here."

"And it's not like I came back to a nuclear hellscape. Right?" I glanced around the restaurant. "Everything's the same as far as I can tell. The king is still the king, the presi-dent is still the president, velvet scrunchies were making a comeback when I left, and they still are—see? That girl over there has a red one. Although if anything had changed, would we even know? What if that girl had a velvet head-band? What would that mean?"

"Above my pay grade," Warren said shortly. "Both of ours."

"Tell me about it. Just thinking about it's enough to bring on a migraine. Look, it's obvious you're upset, and I'm sorry for that, but I—"

I cut myself off because there it was again—that niggle. That ticklish feeling that I was missing something so big, it might as well have been digging into my chest like the world's worst underwire bra. Warren's phone beeped at him and he snatched it up, but it didn't matter because ...

Because why? It wasn't like migraines were rare—millions of people had them every year. All over the world.

Millions.

Out of billions.

And like that—I had it.

CHAPTER SIXTY-FOUR

It took all night, and a lot of reading, and time wasted cursing the god of tiny fonts, and too many phone calls, but by morning I had it.

My first jump: I saw the squiggly, shining lines I assumed were migraine aphasia, popped an experimental Maxipan, and opened my eyes in Calais, France, 1520. *Sans* my icy cold Coke, which had arguably been the worst part.

The dentist. Dr. Inning. I'd warned her the font on the paperwork I.T.C.H. wanted her to sign was so small it would give her a headache. Her response: *I get enough headaches. Bad ones, the kind that make me throw up.*

Amy, who was drunk when she fell through the gate. I was so relieved to find her whole and unscathed I didn't think about *why* she'd been drinking. She even hinted that her family didn't approve of self-medicating her migraines: *But prob'ly I should get back to my family. They don't like the, y'know, my drinking, but the headaches c'n get really—I should get back.*

And, later: *You guys. C'mon. M'gettin' headache.* I'd even teased her about a hangover and she corrected me: *it's not a hangover.*

Teresa Lupez's missing person report: *visiting from Washington D.C., missing thirty hours, last seen leaving The Tower of London.* I called her family, apologized for disturbing them, then lied and said I was investigating her case (I was, but not for the reason they thought). They confirmed she suffered one or two migraines a month and her Imitrix prescription had run out. She'd left the Tower to go to Urgent Care for a shot.

The reason the whole of London hadn't fallen through gates was because the whole of London didn't suffer migraines. Very specific migraines: the kind preceded by a visual aura, which only hit 15% of migraine sufferers. The few who did have that particular migraine had to be in the London area *and* right on top of a gate *and* inadvertently walk into it.

But none of them could see the gates, which is why they needed help to get back. I could, but not, as Lisa suggested, because I was making something up to feel special.

No, I could see the gates because I was the only one who got migraines preceded by aura *and* was taking an experimental drug.

Which meant that this was all *Lisa's* fault! Yessssss! Vindication!

The stupid thing? It was in everyone's paperwork, including mine. I might not have signed the right name (or year), but I was pretty open about my headaches. Most migraine sufferers were—it's just easier if it's out there. And while solving the mystery made me feel good, I also understood how ridiculous it was that a layperson had been the one to see the pattern. Because it was *right there*. All I.T.C.H. had to do was read their own paperwork.

And speaking of I.T.C.H., I had to tell them. Especially Karen. Ooooh, I couldn't wait to rub everyone's chronic migraines in her face!

As if to punctuate this gleeful thought, I heard Lisa's car pull in, which was startling. I assumed she'd been deeply unconscious given that she was running on slow sleep rations. It was only eight a.m., where had she been?

But that was great! I couldn't wait to tell her, either. Then I—

Couldn't. The Losties getting migraines didn't prove I had gone back in time any more than my rigged gown or fancy flatware had. It just proved other people shared my delusion. If they would even back me up—Dr. Inning and Amy had both seemed in a rush to forget the whole thing; neither of them had been even a little pleased to hear from me.

Well. By now Lisa probably felt bad about our fight. She was volatile, but she wasn't too proud to admit when she got it wrong. I'd hear her out and we could go from there.

And just in time, because the kitchen door was delicately kicked open and Lisa, more wild-eyed than usual, rushed in laden with any number of file folders, X-rays, and lab reports. "Joan! Thank fuck."

"I accept your apology and I'm willing to—"

"We have to go see those itchy fuckers right now!"

"Okay, first, I love how you butchered the acronym, and second—hey!"

"Right now, right now, Joan, right the hell now!" She was herding me outside like a bewildered milk cow; I had to claw for my purse on the way out. "Come on! Before this gets any worse!"

"Worse? Oh. Shot in the dark: you did not like the results of my MRI and/or my CAT scan?"

"I'll kill them all," she swore, all but shoving me into the passenger seat before throwing my charts at me. Ack! Blizzard of paper! "I'll set those bastards on fire. Then I'll drown them. Then I'll shoot them in their dumb fucking faces. Then set them on fire again. Then more drowning."

"Aw. You love me."

"Buckle up, dumbass."

See?

CHAPTER SIXTY-FIVE

"*Brain damage*, you sociopaths! And you never warned her!"

"I.T.C.H., you remember my roommate, Dr. Harris. Dr. Harris, you remember the itchy fuckers."

"What are you talking about?" Karen asked. She, Warren, and Dr. Holt were all cornered in the break room. There'd been no receptionist, no security guards, nothing to stop Lisa from storming the place and taking hostages.

Lisa slapped my charts on the break room table: *FWHAP!* "Microscopic brain damage, *significant fucking changes*, that's what I'm talking about. Whatever chemical shit you exposed her to, whatever tech you had her using, is fucking up her brain."

"Now tell Dr. Harris that you're sorry," I prompted, "and that you won't do it again."

"Oh, Christ, that's all we need." Ian Holt, the guy with the build of a fire hydrant and the soul of a carpetbagger, was rubbing his eyes. "Brain damage."

"It's moot anyway," Karen huffed, setting the coffee pot down with a decisive thump. "We're shut down. Look around. Everybody packed their stuff and left. The lobby's been cleaned out, the pictures are off the walls. We agreed yesterday it was all over."

"Moot?" Lisa asked, and I pushed the coffee pot out of her reach. Also the mugs. And the microwave. I didn't worry so much about the refrigerator. If it was too heavy for me, it was too heavy for her. "What the fuck did you just say?"

"Just that, uh, nobodyelsewillbeexposedcuzwe'reshutd own."

Lisa stuck a finger in her face. "I am filing a complaint with EU-OSHA. I am reporting you to HSE. And that's just the warm-up. I'm going to lie awake nights plotting your professional and personal downfall. And I warn you, when I'm low on sleep? I'm a real bitch. You think *this* is bad? These are my Sunday school manners by comparison. You willfully incompetent fucks better have good lawyers, because I do, and we're gonna fuck you up."

Willfully incompetent! Excellent phrasing. Meanwhile, Warren had sidled over and handed me a cup of disgusting coffee. "Are you okay?" he murmured.

"I feel fine," I whispered back. "Honestly. I can't tell any difference. But it's like we were talking about last night— if something was radically changed, would we know? And I'm sorry about running out right after finishing my second dessert and your port." The tawny liquid had been the color of old blond wood and tasted like honey and raisins. Mmmm...liquid raisins...

"Oh, hell, that's okay, I'm just happy you made it home all right. If you're up to it, I wondered if I could take you to brunch today."

"Are you fucking kidding me?" With a start, I realized Lisa had finished terrorizing Karen and was now focused on Warren and me. I couldn't see Holt; he was either cowering in the alcove behind me or she had killed and devoured him. "You're going out with *him*?"

"I have to eat," I pointed out. "Do you want me to starve and die, Lisa? Because if I don't eat, I'll starve and *die*. Is that what you want? Huh? For me to starve? Huh? Lisa?"

She shrugged off my lingering death by malnutrition. "Are you seriously thinking about fucking one of the people who gave you brain damage?"

"Not…immediately." To Warren. "Right around date number five is when I'd most likely wave you in." To Lisa: "Can I have a word?" And when we were in the hallway, I continued, "Not that I have to explain—"

"Wrong."

"—but he's actually a good guy. He just got caught up in this disaster and he's trying to help me fix it."

"And does that generous interpretation of his actions have anything to do with the fact that he looks like a sexy Dr. Who?"

"First, you leave Time Lords out of this. Besides—don't you want at least one I.T.C.H. member on our side? Especially if things turn nasty? If you terrorize and alienate all of them, things will get a lot harder, especially if we're looking at eventual litigation." And what I didn't say, but what she must have been thinking, was that it wasn't just I.T.C.H. who had damaged me. Maxipan had a hand in this mess, too.

"Fuck 'eventual'." She ran her fingers through her hair, making the black strands stick out all over—she looked like a grumpy porcupine. "But—and I hate to admit this—that's a good point. Whistleblowers need allies."

"I'm not sure I qualify as a whistleblower."

"So you're shutting down?" Lisa had turned back to Karen and Holt, who had just crept in.

"Yes, we were going to get a last data drop and then—"

Lisa stepped into Holt who, to his credit, didn't back up. "Brain damage," she hissed at his neck.

"Yes, we—"

"Why the hell do you think we're here? It wasn't just to bitch slap the lot of you. It was to clue you in to the overly obvious fact that effective fucking *yesterday,* you can't let *anyone* use this equipment in this space under *any* circumstances. Not until the regulators have been over the place with STEHM microscopes!"

"Yes. All right." Holt had his hands up like Lisa was arresting him. He might want to get used to that pose. "I agree, we've all agreed. Come along."

We followed him to the lab, and with no hesitation, what was left of I.T.C.H. shut down every machine, every bank, everything that clicked or glowed or beeped, until the only thing still on were the overhead lights.

We all stood in the quiet gloom.

"Huh." Lisa glanced at me. "Kind of an anti-climax."

"Agreed." To Warren, "Brunch?"

CHAPTER SIXTY-SIX

Brunch! At the Queen's Lane Coffee House, est. 1654. As they tell it, "the oldest continually working coffee house in Europe". Not to sound like a tourist—I am in actuality an ex-pat—but this is what I liked about living here: someone's been serving coffee in this building going on four hundred years. I get off on stability.

I also got off on their fish and chips. The whitefish had been battered, then fried crisp and steamed as I bit into it, the tartar sauce was tangy, and a squeeze of lemon brightened everything. The chips were crispy and mealy and salty and almost too hot to hold and I was washing it all down with an ice-cold ginger beer and blotting grease with napkins. Outstanding.

The company wasn't bad, either. Warren and I were tucked into a cozy corner at a table so small our knees were touching. The wooden floors were gleaming, which was a good trick given all the foot traffic and the fact that they'd been open for hours. I had moved the lit candle off to the side and Warren laughed to see my frown.

"What? I can't stand candles on restaurant tables. The light they add is minimal and unnecessary. All it does is take up valuable space meant for better things." Better *edible* things.

"You don't find it romantic?" he teased.

I looked up with a mouth full of chips. "Momantikk?" Swallowed. "No." Was I blowing it? Was this killing the mood?

What *was* the mood? Did he get off when his date talked with her mouth full? Hope so. "Do you want me to move it back?"

"No, you don't want to waste valuable chip-eating time."

"Finally, someone gets it. And this is delicious, but you've got to let me pick up the check this time. Not that that evens us out—I shudder to imagine last night's dinner bill."

"It's not about evening anything out." Warren leaned forward despite our tiny table, and as a result, he was almost looming. But he'd rolled his sleeves up, so I didn't mind. "I told you before—I'm in your debt. I think it's remarkable that we lost only Teresa."

"Teresa and whoever went before my Calais jump," I pointed out. "You guys thought there'd been one or two others, right? I never saw them over there. Or would it be back there?"

"Maybe the guys who take over the project will have some ideas on how to get 'em back," he suggested.

"You think that's likely? That I.T.C.H. won't just stay permanently shut down?"

"I think you can't un-ring a bell."

"Point," I conceded. "You know, if they want to try to rescue them, I'd—I could help. I mean, obviously I can't take any more jumps, but maybe I could be a consultant or whatever."

What are you doing? Good question. I felt like John Cusack in *1408*: "I was out. I was ouuuuut!" Besides, if they wanted a consultant, they wouldn't call the American who watched *The Tudors* with her mom. They'd get an expert like Starkey or Weir.

"Listen, Joan—maybe we can't help them, but I think I can help your friend Lisa."

"That is literally the only time anyone has said that to me."

He shrugged. "Well, she's terrifying. Anyway, the building's locked down, but I still have my keys. I could bring her in and she could document whatever she liked before EU-OSHA or HUMINT get involved and prevent anyone else from coming and going."

"Helping her beat the rush, huh?"

"It might help your case."

"I have a case?"

"Brain damage," he reminded me.

Why did I keep forgetting that? And don't say 'brain damage'. "That's a great idea. Are you sure? You might get in more trouble if it comes out later."

"I don't give a damn," was the crisp reply, which I loved. A lot.

I pulled my phone and sent Lisa a text, which took a couple of tries because...because...because it was hard...couldn't see because...

"Shit," I managed. I could see the squiggles writhing across my field of vision, harbingers of pain (or, in the last few weeks, a temporal gate). "M'getting a migraine."

"You—oh. Joan, be careful!" He caught my phone as it fell from my hand which was deft or daft or something, I dunno, it was hard to think. "Oh, hell. You're in no shape to go to I.T.C.H. right now."

"Huh?"

"Could I take you to my place? It's within walking distance. You can rest as long as you need to and then we'll meet up with Lisa."

"Reshting don't count to five dates."

"Er...okay."

"Don't worry," I slurred. "I'll just get the Peking pie to go."

"Sorry?"

"'Scuse me, I have to go barf."

And I did, because I'm a woman of my worm.

Chapter Sixty-Seven

Sleeping during a migraine is like being a dog: you have no concept of how much time has passed. Or even what time *is*. Have I been here for half an hour? Or five days? Is it nighttime or are the blinds closed? Did I kick the migraine or are we in half-time? And, because my life has gotten progressively stranger: what century is this?

I sat up in Warren's (!!) bed, fumbled for the bedside light, and glanced around the room. The place looked like it had been decorated by a hurricane. Half empty boxes everywhere, clothes draped over the half-open closet doors, and I could see into the small *en suite* bathroom, which had a half-filled box on the floor and travel-sized toiletries on the sink.

I blinked, thought about what I was seeing, then carefully got out of bed and ... excellent, the migraine had gone to wherever they go when they aren't fucking me up. Now I just felt hollow and tired, despite napping for six hours. Or ten minutes.

"Warren?"

I left the bedroom and realized Warren lived in one of those extended stay hotels that accommodate people who don't live in the area, but will be in town longer than a couple of weeks. It was a perfectly adequate suite: double bed, small living room on the other side of the wall with a couch, dining room table for four, a television. The kitchen was also small and adequate: stove, microwave, sink, cupboards, tiny dishwasher. There was an open closet in the hall which revealed (not that I was snooping) a miniature washing machine stacked on top of a miniature dryer. Nothing on the walls but what the hotel had put there, and boxes all over.

No, there was nothing wrong with the place, but it made me uneasy. Warren was wealthy; I had the bank balance to prove it. I.T.C.H. was able to keep running without funding because of him. So why was he living rough in what was clearly a temp set-up? And where was he?

For that matter, where was my phone? And my purse? I stepped over to the dining room table, which was covered with files and boxes, and looked out the window. The view was nice: old brick buildings, a few cars, bikers and pedestrians. Still daylight, so I couldn't have been out that long. Unless it was the next day, which had been known to happen.

I told myself I was looking for my phone as I opened one of the boxes. It was stuffed with framed photos and diplomas and where was Warren and why was he living here?

I examined the first picture and recognized one of the photos from I.T.C.H.'s lobby. There were at least forty people in the pic and they were outside; you could see snow on the ground. And here was a diploma for Warren: Master of Computer Science. Here was another I.T.C.H. outing; someone was having a party judging by the booze and cake (my kind of party!), because I recognized the breakroom. I also recognized the woman sitting on Warren's lap.

I dug into the box again, pulled out another diploma. Tucked into the corner of the frame was a casual shot of that same woman.

And because my life had become a time travel/adventure/horror movie directed by M. Night (But not a good one, like *The Sixth Sense*; a silly one you couldn't take seriously, like *The Happening*), I heard the door open behind me and asked, without turning around, "Warren? Why is Lady Eleanor wearing a breast cancer awareness t-shirt in front of McDonalds?"

CHAPTER SIXTY-EIGHT

Warren shut the door and just stood there.

"And before you insist you barely know each other, I'm holding her diploma, which is how I know Lady Eleanor Stanley is actually Eleanor Warren and she has a degree in Mathematics and Philosophy, which is a good trick for a 16th century lady-in-waiting." I dropped the diploma face-down on the table—crunch. Oopsie. Then I waved the other picture, the one from the party. "She worked with you. She works for I.T.C.H.! And since there would be no reason for you to keep that from me if she was your sister, I'm assuming you're married."

Nothing. He just blinked at me with his big, stupid blinky eyes.

"So before I beat you to death with the contents of this box, I'd like you to explain what the hell is going on. And *don't* say it's complicated."

"Well." He spread his hands. "It is."

"You're married to Lady Eleanor!" That was the part I couldn't get over. Well, there was a lot I couldn't get over, but that one really jabbed me. Thank God his shirt sleeves were hiding his forearms so there was nothing to distract from my incredulous hurt rage. "This isn't a time travel movie, this is *Inception*! You had a crazy ex-wife running around you knew was trying to hurt me and you didn't say shit!"

"She's not my ex-wife."

I ignored the irrelevancy. "You've known all this time, you *know* she's been causing problems for me, and you never said! Worse—you had the gall to call *me* out for keeping things from *you*! And to think, I thought you were the stable, methodical one!"

"Compared to who?"

"Never mind! You get over here and you sit down and tell me the whole story, starting with 'I married the devil' and ending with 'then you beat me to death with the devil's diploma'."

"I need a drink," was his response, and ducked into the teeny kitchen. "Want one?"

"I don't drink on migraine days. Or when I'm planning to commit felony assault."

"Migraine days." He pulled a bottle of scotch from the cupboard and poured himself a shot. He probably thought it looked suave, but as he was using a juice glass, it just looked silly, like he was trying to soothe his jangled nerves with apple juice. "Yeah, that was inconvenient."

"Oh no! Did I inconvenience you with my chronic medical condition? I'm so sorry, Warren, how will I ever make it up to you?"

"My wife," Warren began, pouring himself a second drink—yikes. I hadn't seen him suck down the first one. "Has always hated my job. We both worked for I.T.C.H., but in different departments. At first it was great. I got to spend the day with my best friend and go home with her every night. I felt blessed. But then it went wrong."

"You know I'm not a marriage counselor, right? And that you're speaking cliché?"

"I got promoted to the QT project, which meant a big raise but a lot more lab time. She was supportive at first, but as we made more progress, my hours got longer. So we fought. And then I'd spend more time in the lab to avoid arguing, which made her angrier, so we fought more."

"Yes, yes, your love union was being shredded in a vicious circle of mutual recrimination, get to the part where she hangs out in the 16th century."

"We were working around the clock and it was just— we knew we were running out of funding, knew we were getting shut down. But we weren't ready to give up. We got more and more desperate and took stupid short cuts, and one night Eleanor showed up—I hadn't been home in a few nights and she'd—she'd had enough. So we fought. I was trying to get her to go, she wanted me to leave, everyone was exhausted, the fight got heated, Ian and Karen were trying to pull us apart and nobody noticed the phenomenon was unstable and then—she was gone."

"Jesus Christ."

"It's bad, huh? A tragedy."

"That is the *dumbest* thing I've ever heard. This is why I don't sweat not having a college degree yet. The two of you have how many years of schooling between you, but still channeled the Three Stooges in a secret lab with unstable tech? *Jesus.*"

"It was my fault. She was trying to get me to come home with her, trying to make our marriage work. She was fighting for us! She wanted to bring the romance back into our lives."

I nearly did a spit-take, which would have been disgusting as I wasn't drinking anything. "Then book a night in one of those silly fantasy suite hotels! Or go skinny-dipping! Or play with sexy dice! Don't have an impromptu wrestling match beside a wormhole!"

"We're trying to work it out," he whined.

"How? How? Howwwwwww? Screwing with the time-line? Trying to get me killed?" Even as I said it, I realized that was exactly what that rotten bitch had been doing. "She thought *you* would come looking for her," I groaned. "She caused problems that could potentially screw history and waited for you to show up ... was she leaving clues? Like temporal breadcrumbs?"

"I really feel like I let her down."

"*That's* your takeaway from this?" I rubbed my eyes, vaguely hoping I'd wake up and realize this was a weirder-than-usual migraine-induced hallucination. But alas, I opened my eyes and Warren was standing not two feet away, slurping his whiskey, Eleanor was his missing wife, I had (more) brain damage, and this was all really happening. "So Eleanor fell, which is why you didn't dare shut it down—you couldn't risk stranding her there. But after the accident, the gates kept opening and other people disappeared. It was never about Losties. It wasn't even about your work. It was just about getting Eleanor back so you could cover your blunders." I shook my head, remembering how the first thing Warren said to me was "who did you see?" Right out of the gate, he was dying to know if I'd run into his wife.

"Hey! I *need* Eleanor. Is that so hard to understand?"

I took another look around the small suite, in which the most expensive thing was the bottle of Scotch. I thought about our expensive dinner the night before. He said, *I didn't sign on to get rich.* He said, *it's family money. And a lot of it is tied up in trusts and such.*

"No," I said slowly. "It's not hard to understand."

My funds are nearly depleted. I can't pay you this time.

"It's Eleanor's money, isn't it? She's the wealthy one. She probably sensed your vast reserves of sociopathy and made you sign a pre-nup." His gaze dropped and shifted to the window. "You can't access most of the money without her. Which is why you're baching it up here. It's not even about getting her back, it's about getting her money back." Warren was like a diabolical onion: each layer peeled back exposed a darker motive. Had I thought this guy was stable and methodical and safe? Had I *really*?

"Aw, c'mon. I know what they say about a woman scorned, so you'll forgive me if I didn't let you in on every little detail of my life."

"You said..." My voice actually wobbled so I swallowed and tried again. "You said you paid me because I was worth it."

"Well. You weren't," he said kindly. "But Eleanor is. Literally. So if we could just owwww, *Jesus!*"

"Sorry, I meant to tell you I was going to smack you upside the head with your framed diploma but I didn't want to let you in on every little detail."

"That glass could have cut me!"

"Yes, and my knee could have smashed your balls."

"What's that suppooooooo..." Then he trailed off like a slowly leaking balloon and flopped to the floor, spilling his whiskey. The juice glass held up, though. *Good for you, juice glass.*

I stood over him. "Not to victim-blame, but how do you say all those things to someone and *not* expect them to go for your testicles? Also, your ex is quite the agent of chaos."

"We're only separated," he wheezed. "Nobody's signed any paperwork yet."

I stifled the urge to bury my foot in his ribcage. "Where's my phone and purse, Warren? The quicker I get them, the quicker you can go ice your balls."

"My wife," he gasped.

"Yes? So? What about the late Mrs. Warren, dead now for five hundred years?"

"No!"

"Yes. Simple fact. She's not here, so she's back there. If she's back there, she's dead. But she *might* have died of old age—Teresa didn't get that much, not that you cared. All you have to do is produce a pile of bones to prove you're a widower and then you can get your beautiful forearms on her money."

"My beautiful what?" He was slowly staggering to his feet, like he was rock climbing with a storm on the way. "Never mind. You listen. You have to go back and bring her out."

"Y'know, I thought you were working your way up to that, but even so, I couldn't quite believe it until the words came out of your mouth just now. You really are a reprehensible coward. I'll bet Eleanor lost her mind—well, more of her mind—when she realized you were never going to come for her, you were just going to keep talking me into it."

"I couldn't risk myself."

"Yeah, yeah, I've heard this speech from Holt. You fuck-ups are too smart and indispensable to jump. See that? See how I said that with a straight face?" I shook my head, thinking about Eleanor scheming from five centuries away. "She was supposed to identify as a Lostie and come back with me. That was your plan, right? But she wouldn't. Why wouldn't she tell me who she was? Why wouldn't she ask for help?"

"She'd never," he said with misplaced pride. "She's far too proud to ask for help."

"Is she far too proud to ask me to pass on a message? You get that there's pride, and there's pathological narcissism, right? And even now, knowing each jump builds up microscopic brain damage, you think you can talk me into going. Cripes, the ego." I turned to leave. "Keep my phone.

And the purse." The phone was stuffed with pictures of food (I followed a lot of pie accounts) and my contacts were mostly restaurants. He was also welcome to the ten pounds I had in my wallet. I'd regret losing the Tootsie Rolls, though. "And enjoy widowhood." Or would that be widowerhood?

"If my wife died five hundred years ago . . ." He was steadying himself with a hand on the back of the chair, wincing and adjusting his trousers. "Then so did your friend. Lisa."

I was halfway to the door and stopped dead, then turned and came back. "No you didn't."

"Yeah, I did. Why do you think I had the idea for her to get in and document everything before the feds shut us down? I got her over there, let her think I was helping her take stills and vids of the machinery, and shoved her through. I knew it was the only way you'd go."

"You were wrong." I turned to leave again. "Lisa would rather die in TudorTime then have me risk myself. I know that's incomprehensible to a sociopathic ding-dong like yourself so just take my word for it: she wouldn't want me to go so I won't. Have a nice life, you repellant shitstain."

"Wait!" He staggered forward a few clumsy steps and grabbed my elbow. "No, please—you have to!"

"I know. Of course I'm going. I just needed you to drop your guard."

CHAPTER SIXTY-NINE

"No, seriously," I said, standing over him for the second time in less than a minute. "How do you say those things and *not* expect another shot to the bean bag? These aren't rhetorical questions."

CHAPTER SEVENTY

"**I** can't emphasize how much I appreciate this. And you may find this hard to believe, but I think you and Eleanor would've gotten along in different circumstances."

"Shut up."

"I truly believe that once we put I.T.C.H. behind us, Eleanor and I can get a fresh start. Think of it: you'll be saving our marriage!"

"Do you see this?" I held up my coffee mug. The I.T.C.H. logo on the side meant nothing; it was mine now. "I'm going to hit you and hit you and hit you with it until there's nothing left but a piece of the handle if you don't. Shut. Up."

While I struggled into my gown, I kept up the interrogation. "What are you going to tell the others? That you're tossing bystanders into wormholes since your health insurance doesn't cover marriage counseling?"

"They won't know. They saw the writing on the wall. They're in the wind."

"In the wind, huh?" He really didn't hear it. It was amazing how he'd throw clichés around like they were original thoughts. He probably thought it made him sound like a real person, one with a conscience and everything. How had I not noticed this earlier?

"Yeah. They're long gone. They took one look at your friend and knew it was over."

"Yes, well. Lisa has that effect."

He went on as if he hadn't heard me. "We knew discovery—always inevitable—was now simply a matter of days. Perhaps hours, so we have to hurry...your migraine put us behind."

"Aw. Super-duper sorry about that, Warren. And the others ran off like terrified geese? Well, nothing Karen did would surprise me. Holt, though..." I snapped my fingers. "That's why he shut you down when you asked me out! He knew your ulterior motive." And since Holt was a card-carrying coward, he didn't have the courage to tell me what Warren was doing, so he settled for vague disapproval. Ugh.

Things were starting to make sense at last. "When I came back and you had shut down, you weren't upset about something happening to me." As I talked I was taking Thomas' advice and jamming my hair under the hood. Screw the wig; if anyone asked, I'd had a fever and was shorn to let the evil spirits out of my hair follicles or whatever. "You were hoping for Eleanor. All that 'I ran home to shower but felt sad about you being abandoned and came back', what bullshit."

"You know what, Warren?" I continued. "I almost hope this will kill me. Living in a world where I was outwitted by Eleanor's P.O.S. estranged husband is too embarrassing. What? I said estranged, not ex. God, you worry about the dumbest things."

"I don't expect you to understand what we have."

"I understand perfectly. A spiteful narcissist found a passive aggressive narcissist and they got married and nearly destroyed humanity. As far as love stories goes, it's not great."

"We're running out of time."

"Finally some truth out of you. So I'll find Lisa and Eleanor—"

"No." He looked up from his equipment. "My wife first. Return her and I'll let you go back. Remember, we can see you through the gate for a few seconds." At my silence, he elaborated. "We *did* learn a few things while you were gallivanting in the 16th century."

"Gallivanting." I clenched my teeth. "Fine. What if I can't find Eleanor? Or get her to come back with me?"

"When you see her, tell her 'the tennis balls were yellow, not green'. That's a private joke from our honeymoon. It's really a charming story. We had just—"

"No." I stepped up to the pad. My gown was on, my fanny pack was on, my pomander was full, my sleeves concealed all sorts of devilry, and my heart was filled with hatred and anxiety. Lisa, God love her, had brought my time travel tote bag to I.T.C.H., probably to do comparative readings or something; I had no idea, not my field. Her methodical mind might be the saving of us. "Don't care. And if Eleanor still won't come?"

"She'll come," Dr. Narcissist predicted.

"And when you're reunited with your she-Minotaur, you'll send me back to get Lisa?"

"Yes. You'll just have to trust me." When I gagged on my hysterical laughter, he continued. "No? Well, how about this—it's better for me if you two *don't* disappear from I.T.C.H.. Especially since the feds might be landing any minute."

"Hmm. Point."

"Bad enough there are those—those—what did you call them?"

"Innocent bystanders you didn't care about hurting because you're a selfish chickenshit bastard?" (Also Losties.)

"They're out there and they know what happened, which is bad enough, but add to that a local doctor's sudden mysterious disappearance *and* her roommate? When it can all be traced back here if the wrong person asks the right questions? Too much heat."

"You talk like a TV show. Not a good one."

"Ready, Cupid?"

"Please die while screaming and on fire, Warren."

I jumped.

CHAPTER SEVENTY-ONE

It's not the best version of King Arthur, but one line from *King Arthur: Legend of the Sword* has always stuck with me: "Why have enemies when you can have friends?" (Ooh, the forearms on that man!)

Case in point: TudorTime Hertz was delighted to see me. So was my nice new friend at The Gray Horse, Lee O'Bannon, she of the venison pasty and spermys cheese. From the former, a horse. From the latter, invaluable gossip, my orders, and a raspberry tart.

She greeted me with, "Yon sweet lad was right, here you are again!"

Despite my urgency, I had to smile. "If you called Thomas that to his face, he'd laugh."

"Oh, aye," she agreed cheerfully. It was baking day, if her flour-dusted dress and apron and hands were any indication. "Come with me, my lady, Tom will tend your horse."

Great, another Thomas in the mix. "I can't stay. I'm just wondering if you saw someone who looked out of place." *Way* out of place. I started to describe Lisa when Lee stopped me.

"Master Thomas scooped up your lamb, poor thing, she was so upset and feverish, too…"

"Feverish?"

"Oh, the raving! And the language! Poor thing's brains must be on fire; I never heard half so many words and my Fa loved his drink. When she fell ill her folk must have cut her hair off, but they weren't watching her close enough." Lee lowered her voice. "I think she must have run away in a daze, poor girl. Still so sick! And in her linen! In public!"

"Yes, that's her. Thomas, er, scooped her?"

"He had to take her to the Tower because of the Lady." At my confused blinking, she elaborated. "It's right horrid. That Anne Boleyn, they're going to chop her head off! And they're saying she did…unnatural things. With a host of men. And her brother. Lord Rochford."

That put me at May 1536. "Yes, that sounds very wicked, but what does it have to do with Thomas and my friend?"

"The Lady wants to see a holy fool before she…" Lee dragged her finger across her throat, but couldn't hide her distress. "Goes to He who made us. Poor thing. She was wrong to push the old queen off her throne, but it seems to me that she's being punished for doing just what the king liked about her in the first place."

"That's exactly why she's being punished," I said bluntly. "So Thomas took her?"

"To the Tower," Lee confirmed, and my heart definitely didn't drop into my stomach. "They'll be expecting you—he was sure you'd be along directly, and there you be, so here." From somewhere in her apron she produced a small bundle of cloth, which had been wrapped around a fruit tart.

"It's still warm!" I gasped, sniffing it. "Oh, thank you!"

"God bless you, Lady Joan. And give whatever peace you can to the queen, poor lady."

"No promises."

"Think of her baby! Orphaned by the end of the month, or as good as, poor lass. The king declares her a bastard before the world." Lee sighed. "They're saying baby Elizabeth isn't even the king's get. Her, with that red hair! There's nothing harder than love turned to hate."

I thought of Eleanor's poison, and Warren's desperation. "You're right about that," I replied, and went to work. On the tart, but also the road to the Tower.

CHAPTER SEVENTY-TWO

(It's easier to have Lisa tell this next part. I wasn't there for half the swearing and I missed the larceny altogether. So here you go, straight from her blog which for some reason she calls her frog.)

From the frog of Lisa Harris, M.D., F.U.

Holy crap, where do I even start with this shit? Minding my own business and it's my own fault for taking my eyes off George fucking Warren for half a second. Blah-blah, you should take a look at this particular piece of equipment let me help you up and then buh-bye.

The fucker buh-byed me!

Then I'm standing under this big-ass willow tree and my phone won't work and there aren't any power lines or highways. And there aren't any cars or bikes. And the buildings all look wrong. And everyone's dressed wrong. And sounds wrong.

And my friend isn't crazy.

I didn't want to show myself to this wrong-ass world but I didn't want to keep cowering under a tree either. So in a minute I start walking. I'm on the edge of a town where there were few houses but just over the hill, a two-story tavern called The Gray Horse because people in the past don't have any imagination I guess.

Then here comes this guy, big redheaded guy who'd been out in front doing whatever, and he takes one look at me and says, "No fear, lass, God's errand girl will be along directly."

He was being nice so I didn't tell him to fuck off. But when I kept walking (I mean, jeez, total stranger, what, I should linger and hope he asks me out?) he says, "My Lady Joan has made helping lost travelers her vocation. May I escort you somewhere safe to wait ere she comes?"

My teeth almost fall out. What are the chances that we both know the same Joan? So I stop and go, "Tell me what Joan looks like. Please."

He listens close and says she's about medium height with pale skin and 'eyes the color of the Mediterranean Sea' and 'hair like sable', I shit you not. Fucking sable. And the sea.

"That's my roommate!" Which I yelled because I was so excited and relieved, which was dumb because I shouldn't draw curious eyes. I take a closer look at the guy: yep. Just Joanie's type, dark reddish hair and light eyes—blue in his case—lean but not scrawny, tall, nice forearms. (It's a whole thing with her and hilarious as fuck.) And it sounded like Joan was his type, given the sappy look on his face. "How d'you know her?"

"It has been my honor to assist her in her godly vocation."

Oh yeah. This guy totally wants to fuck my roommate.

So in under five minutes I go from 20th century I.T.C.H. platform to a 16th century inn and meet a guy who's really into my roommate and she not only isn't crazy but, if anything, downplayed her activities over the past few days. I'm embarrassed to say 'days' because I don't know when the shit-show started and didn't bother getting a good timeline because I suck.

I hate apologizing. And I was gonna have to make it a good one. I never thought she was lying, but I did wonder if she'd inherited her family's genetic tendency toward substance abuse and obsession.

"If you will allow me to arrange more appropriate attire for you, I will then take you to where she will shortly be."

"You know that, don't you? You *know* she'll be along."

"It is her calling," he said simply.

"There's not a doubt in your mind, huh?" I guess I kept asking him because it made me feel better to hear that yeah, there was a rescue plan.

He smiled and inclined his head. Good teeth, so scratch that 16th century truism. "Nor is there a doubt in yours, my lady…?"

"Lisa." What harm, right? I decided not to mention my physician bona fides. That was probably a burning offense around here. "Just Lisa. I'm not a lady."

"I thought perhaps you were not gentle, but that takes away none of your charm," he said, just sooooooo fuckin' smooth. "It seems we both have the honor of knowing Lady Joan."

Yeah. Corny as hell, but sure. Joan would come for me, the big beautiful dumbass, but that worked, 'cause I'd have come for her, too. "Guess so."

"Allow me to introduce myself; my name is Thomas Wynter." And he honest-to-God bows. Bet he holds doors open like a champ motherfucker.

"Are you getting my enunciation?"

"I beg your pardon?"

"My accent." Because I wasn't having much trouble understanding him. And he didn't seem to be having trouble understanding me. Which I couldn't figure out.

"Ah! I hope I won't offend if I say you and my lady have the same charming *patois*."

"We sound like aggravated hillbillies with head colds." Especially to ancient English ears. "It's fine, I'm not offended."

"That, ah, may be, but if you were to meet people who did not also know Lady Joan, they would have some trouble at first."

"Got it. Say no more." Literally, because I had to think. Joan was one of the most gifted natural mimics I'd ever met. So good she didn't know she was doing it half the time. Which meant she was picking up modern London dialogue *and* English Renaissance dialogue while going about her daily life as an American part-time medical transcriptionist. All of which I damned well should have noticed weeks ago.

I'm the dumbest genius alive. In any century.

So we go inside and meet this nice pile of flour who goes by Lee, and this Thomas Wynter guy talks one of the maids out of her clothes, which are as gross as you'd imagine in a land without Tide pods. But I kept my gripe-hole shut; blending was good. And then I kinda had to laugh; wouldn't Joan bust a gut to hear *that* coming out of my mouth?

They also thought I'd had a fever because short hair or something? So Thomas explains that a common treatment for patients presenting with febrile symptoms is to cut their hair.

"You know that has no basis in medical science, right?"

"Eh?"

"Thank God I dyed it dark this week!" If it was still green, would they have thought I was a leprechaun? These are the questions.

Gotta say I like how Lee was confused but didn't treat me like a freak. Just smiled and nodded and tried to make us eat. No FDA? No government regs? Hard pass. This is no time to pick up an intestinal parasite. And Thomas is in a hurry, too, which makes me nervous.

Then I have to strap into this hellish contraption called a pillion saddle, which is basically a tiny chair attached to the back of a saddle because I was trapped in the fucking Dark Ages.

So Thomas hops on and I clamber up onto this stump and then onto the horse with a little help and before I got myself settled I'd shown half the yard my crotch but I gotta say, everyone was super classy about it.

So away we go! And I have to ask, because my God, a haircut? What other pure friggin' insanity is out there masquerading as medical treatment? "What else d'you guys do for fevers?"

Thomas rattles off any number of fucking horrifying or hilarious "cures", and then we moved on to epilepsy (the cure being licorice, roses, and cormorant blood!), sciatica (red ox gall bladder and the patient's urine!), and burns (grab a live snail and rub it on your patient! okay, that last one I wanted to try...).

"What if you're out of snails? And now that I think about it...maybe snail slime has properties similar to the aloe plant. Anti-inflammatory, maybe, and...collagen? Worth looking into." I poked him in the back. "What else? Tell me something else that's hilariously bad."

Apparently if you're afflicted with gout, the prescription is a dead owl you pluck, clean, salt, bake 'til burnt, rub boar grease all over, and then rub it on your afflicted limbs. For strep throat? A cat, and not just any cat, a *fat* cat. And not just any fat cat, one you flay, gut, and then stuff with hedgehog grease, sage, and wax. Then you roast the fucker and rub it on your throat.

I shit you not: half the cures were killing an animal, stuffing it with another animal, and then rubbing it all over your patient. Malpractice insurance coverage here must be a bitch.

"You have a lovely laugh," Thomas commented, and I had to give him props, since 1) I don't, and 2) he *had* to think I was right off my fucking rocker. Or he put it down to the fever he thought I was getting over. But he's not freaking out, which is cool.

Then he tells me the cure for smallpox: hang red curtains around the patient's bed. Apparently the red light that comes through them will cure them.

"You know why most of you guys don't live past forty? Stuff like that. Man, I wish we could swing by the local surgeon's office. I know we can't. Got a schedule to keep." But fuck me, I sure wanted to. Unprecedented opp!

So Thomas twists around in the saddle to smile at me and says, "Lady Lisa, are you studying to be a surgeon in your land of Merka?"

So that raises about a dozen questions. Big number one being, am I gonna be able to stop myself from laughing my ass off? *Merka?* Is that how the introverted extrovert I live with explained away her accent, her ignorance of local customs, and anything else that could have gotten her in big, big trouble? Fucking *genius*.

"You bet!" Because what the hell else am I gonna say? "Merka's...different." Wow. Billions of words to choose from and I come up with 'different'. Left half my brain in the I.T.C.H. lab, clearly. "And a long way away from here."

Part of the problem was these borrowed clothes are driving me nuts. I keep scratching at my forearms and wriggling against Thomas and if he thought I was coming onto him, he was gonna get disabused of that notion very fucking quickly. "Itchy, why am I so itchy? Don't answer that!" I commanded. Best case scenario: psychosomatic lice. Worst case? Actual lice. To distract myself, I cast about for something to say about, heh, Merka. "Yes, it's a strange land far from here. But we like it. Y'know, most of the time."

"So the Lady Joan has said. Not to impugn your birthplace, but a land without kings sounds strange indeed."

"Yeah, almost as dumb as giving absolute power to someone based solely on what vagina they came out of." Then I got hold of myself. "Sorry. That wasn't nice."

Fortunately Thomas was laughing too hard to take offense. Hanging out with Joan clearly set him up to tolerate me. Which got me wondering. "When'd you meet her?"

"Several years ago, when I was yet a lad. Calais."

"You met in *France?*" Holy shit, Joanie was time traveling all over Europe! Which she told me! Which I dismissed! Son of a bitch!

So while I'm beating the shit out of myself he's talking about how she basically came out of nowhere and at first he thought she was a mummy—mummer?—and they got to talking and then he had to hide from a bird I guess? And later when he looked for her she'd vanished but he never forgot her and then he saw her years later but in England this time and ever since then he's been mad crushin' on her and keeps an eye out to help her with her 'holiest of vocations'.

And all the while we're clip-clopping through London, which smells exactly like you'd expect a burg without a proper plumbing system to smell, and fucking *everyone* needs a shower and a dentist and a round of amoxicillin and a case of Ensure.

"Y'know, I met her in kind of a funny way, too."

And he's all over that: "Do tell, I pray you!"

So I tell him. All of it, a story I've never once said out loud. But who was *this* guy gonna tell? "Her parents died when she was still a girl. And her mom had been a ward—you know ward?" At his nod, I go on. "Well, she was a ward of the state, and they did a shit job of taking care of her. So then Joan's father dies of canc—of a growth in his lungs. And then, a year later, her mom dies. Accidental asphyxiation. By which I mean carbon monoxide pois—uh, there was a deadly odor in their house and it killed her mom. Joan got home from a slumber party and found the body."

"Oh, my poor lady," Thomas says, all mournful.

"Save your tears for the end, cuz it gets worse. So she sees her mom's body and knows she's alone and every terrible thing her mother said about the system is rushing through her mind, so Joan cleans out their freez—their storage space and keeps the body there. And goes to school the next day like nothing happened. Her dad's insurance paid off their house the year before, her folks had savings, and her mom even had a cash stash, but Joan still had to come up with a budget, pay bills, keep herself fed, go to school, and keep up the charade that she's not an orphan on her own. And this started when she was twelve. And went on until she was eighteen.

"And the only reason I know about any of it was, I met her at the market while she was sick with the flu, high fever, vomiting, dehydration, seriously screwed electrolyte balance, girl was a mess. She'd been too scared to go to the doctor."

"Oh yes! She told me about the fever and how it brought you together."

"She did?" So I file that away, because Joan never talks about her childhood. With anybody and it doesn't matter how sexy their forearms are. "Okay, so there she is, pouring ice cubes all over the floor, she basically makes a bed of ice and lies down in it and it was the cutest and silliest thing ever. So I calm down the store manager." Actually I told him to go fuck himself and said I'd pay for the ice if he didn't call the cops like a whiney little bitch, which he didn't, which is irrelevant to the story.

"And I get her home and she basically babbles out the whole story and I didn't believe her until I saw her mom's body in the freezer."

So I tell him about how exhausted she was back then, how scared. How lonely, and how she'd been living with this unthinkable burden for over a year. How she had to reconcile her mother's wishes with her responsibility for that same mother's body and estate. How even something as simple as going to the clinic for a check-up was terrifying, because at the first slip, any mandated reporter could bring it all down. How many times can you use the "my mom's sick but it's okay that I'm here alone" excuse? How she was breaking any number of laws, starting with abuse of a corpse. And how she still had years to go.

So I helped her. I treated her flu—I was used to taking care of my mom anyway. And speaking of Mom, I got her to pose as Joan's mom now and again—my mother felt so guilty about never getting clean, she'd do anything *else* I asked, which came in handy when I wanted booze or to help my friend commit fraud and improper storage of a corpse. I helped Joan get a part-time job since her parents' savings were almost used up by then. I even helped her get rid of the body. (God, that was the *weirdest* Labor Day weekend.)

"This explains much," Thomas said, and to his credit, he was more sympathetic than horrified. "I have noted the dichotomy of her traits."

"Nailed it." Joan was brave, but always behind the scenes. She liked positive attention—don't we all?—but it made her nervous. She loved exploring but didn't like being seen. She hated living alone but didn't mind solitude. I always knew she'd follow me to the United Kingdom. Never a doubt in my mind. Too bad I was too busy patting myself on the back to realize it wasn't timidity, it was loyalty.

"She divides her life into two phases: Before—when her folks were alive, when she had a normal life—and The After. Twice now she's told me something wild and I didn't believe her." Stupid fucking dust on this stupid fucking road aggravating my stupid fucking allergies.

"So then, make amends."

"No shit, Thomas. Sorry."

"You honor me with your confidence," he said simply. "If not your profanity. And my Lady Joan is fortunate in her choice of friends."

"Did you just compliment yourself?"

"Not *just* myself. And we need not speak of it further if it distresses you."

"Thanks." I rubbed my eyes and sniffed and told myself to get the fuck over myself. "When are we gonna get where we're going?"

"Nearly there," he said, pointing. And there it was, looming large, stupid that I hadn't noticed it 'til now, the thing I saw a couple times a week: the Tower of London, circa whenever-the-fuck-we-were. Only it wasn't a pathetic tourist trap now. It was a pathetic prison and torture chamber. And because everything was screwed, I was headed there with a random 16th century guy who had a crush on my room-mate, who was risking more brain damage to come for me because I.T.C.H. panicked when they ran out of funding.

Fuck.

I'd been here before; Joan and I both took the tour about a month after we moved. It was okay—history wasn't my bag, baby. And I didn't say anything about how the day she randomly picked happened to be the anniversary of her mother's death. What would've been the point?

So this isn't entirely new to me, though seeing it without gaggles of annoying tourists but with a working staff and multiple guards was intimidating. I keep my gaze down and try not to crowd Thomas, though I stick close and the urge to wring my hands is *very* fucking strong. And I'm doubly grateful to Thomas for arranging my access to socially and culturally appropriate clothing. Even if it meant I smelled like a sweaty ball of bacon grease.

Thomas was a townie for sure; most people seemed to know him and even the ones who didn't were polite. Even better, I don't get so much as a first glance never mind a second one because of their stupid-ass class system; being a scullery maid or whatever was as good as an invisibility cloak. And it takes me a few minutes to relax enough to notice that *everyone's* keeping their head down. Nobody was kidding around, hardly anyone was even smiling.

He brings me in through the south side of the White Tower, past the king's jewel house, crammed with gobs of shiny things I can't linger to examine. We end up cooling our heels in the great hall, where the staff's quiet scurrying is even more noticeable.

And 'great hall' barely begins to describe it. Like using 'big river' to describe the Mississippi. It's like an indoor stadium, all echoey and fancy, with the beams up on the ceiling looking like exposed ribs, and because the room's so big and the air circulation's better, it doesn't smell completely shitty.

"This is where they feasted her for the queen's coronation," Thomas says because I guess he's a tour guide now? Yeah, I get it, like sands in the fucking hourglass these are the days of our lives. Everything ends, pal. No exceptions to that one.

At first I'm plenty occupied just looking around, like I'd been doing since we got here—Thomas takes me through a number of corridors and galleries that don't exist anymore in my time. I see at least three people who could use a trip to the optometrist, another one who needed a buttload of Vitamin C, and a few candidates for a hypertension study. But after a while the tension gets to me.

"What's wrong?" I murmur, rubbing my arms in a futile attempt to soothe the goose bumps. We're bio creatures, we've kept some pack instincts. And right now my thalamus was yelling at me that everyone was very fucking tense and it might be time to book.

"The queen has been found guilty of treason," Thomas murmured back. "She is to be executed. The swordsman has been delayed."

I let out a breath. It could only be Anne Boleyn. "That's why we're here," I realize. "She wants to talk to the holy jester. Joan. Before they kill her. Anne."

Just then I hear a ruckus outside and I instantly tense up like a dog on point because I can't imagine this is a good thing. Thomas doesn't like it, either, because he puts his hand on his hip and I realize he's reaching for a sword. But he told me earlier he didn't bring one because 16th century London wasn't a fan of open carry or whatever.

But then I hear perfectly clear like she's standing right next to me. "My name is Lady Joan Howe. I am a holy fool here on His Grace the king's business, now *step back*."

Which naturally blows me away because back home? Somebody jostles Joan in line and *she* apologizes. (Makes me nuts.) Now here she comes into the hall, sort of sweeping in and her dark blue gown fits in all the right places and her hair's all sleek and pulled back under her hat—hood?—and her head's held high and her long sleeves are sort of majestically flapping as she strides and only I know her pomander is jammed with goddamned children's chewable vitamins and she just looks legit as fuck.

Which I ruin by bursting into tears and running to her like a toddler who's lost her mommy I mean god*dammit*, so fucking embarrassing. I haven't cried since my Bio professor died before I could tell him he was a waste of skin who didn't know mitosis from halitosis.

"Thank God you're here, I'm sorry, I'm so sorry I didn't believe you."

"Oh, Lisa, you're okay!" she says, and squeezes me back so hard all the breath whooshes out of my lungs so I can't talk, which was actually a win because I was already sick of apologizing. She loosens up to let me breathe and looks at me and she's all concerned which makes me cry harder because *she's* worrying about *me* when it should be the other way 'round, it should always be the other way 'round.

"Are you hurt? You never cry, Lisa. Were you thinking about how Dr. Binderman died before you could yell at him?"

I laughed and wiped my eyes. "Mostly I was thinking how glad I was to see you. And what an idiot I am. And that I can't believe you're risking further goddamned brain damage to help me. But yeah, he had a lot of nerve, succumbing to pneumonia before I could tell him to get fucked."

Then she looks past me and I shit you not, her face? Lights *right* up. Like somebody turned a little spotlight on it, right in the middle of the Tower. "Thomas!" she cries, and rushes to him, and the big lanky dork just opens up his arms without a word and she runs right into them and now she's the one who's getting all the air squeezed out of her lungs.

I sidle over and wait a few seconds, because I'm not completely bereft of tender emotions, and then a few more, and then I clear my throat, and now they're whispering to each other, stuff like "I'm sorry I left you" and "I was so terribly worried, thank God in His mercy you are safe" and yak-yak-yak, and you can't fit so much as a Kleenex between them and they're doing that dorky gazing-into-each-other's-eyes like they're in a Nicholas Sparks novel and finally I can't take it one more second.

"You *guys*. C'mon."

Then it's like they suddenly remember we're in jail, in the 16th century, and guards are staring, and somewhere in this maze of buildings Anne Boleyn is waiting to leave the scaffold in pieces and Joan has to figure out a way for us to get home and even if we *get* home there's a shitstorm waiting for us on the I.T.C.H. platform.

Also, Thomas Wynter *really* wants to fuck my roommate. Which is okay, because my roommate really wants to fuck him, too.

CHAPTER SEVENTY-THREE

Lisa's aggravated throat-clearing finally penetrated and I pulled back from Thomas with no small amount of reluctance. "Thank you for keeping her safe," I told him. And to her, "I'm delighted to find you unburnt!"

"Makes two of us, Joanie. What's the plan?"

Huh. I didn't think Lisa had ever asked me that when it wasn't food-related. "I have to talk to Anne."

"Time is short, my lady," Thomas reminded me.

"I know. They're building the scaffold. I walked right past it." I shook my head, trying to imagine. "She'll be able to hear the hammering from her rooms, my God."

"Creepy *and* demoralizing," Lisa said. "Poor silly bi—lady."

I cocked my head. "Silly?" (Bitch was accurate.)

Lisa shrugged. "She tried to upset the natural order of things, and hey—good for her. But it doesn't often end well for the individual who stirred the shit. Check any history book. And sorry if this is a dumb question, but why do you *have* to see the queen? Why can't we just try to get home now?"

Note to self: never tell Lisa how scared she sounded when she asked me that. "Because, trust me, it'll be more about filling a last request. Queen Anne will be contemplating doing something totally counter to the historical record and I'll have to talk her out of it which will take hours but I might get a nice snack out of it before we're done. I know that sounds a little self-involved, like I'm the only one who can fix the—"

"Stop." And she held up a hand, traffic cop style. "That was stupid. I was stupid. You *are* the only one. I wouldn't let myself see it. So get going. And if I was talking to anyone else I wouldn't have to throw this out there, but please prioritize our safety over your appetite."

"I can do both. And I have to find Lady Eleanor and talk her into coming home with us. And believe it or not, those two seemingly unrelated tasks are related."

Thomas coughed. "That reminds me. It pains me to speak of such things to ladies—"

"Let 'er rip, Tommy-Boy."

"What Lisa said. Let's hear it."

"Very well. I have heard some gossip which is not to anyone's credit. Apparently the king's mistress is pregnant."

I could actually feel the ligaments in my jaw creak as my mouth fell open. "*Jane Seymour* is pregnant?"

"No, no. Lady Jane is in seclusion to protect her reputation as a good and virtuous lady. One of the queen's other ladies is pregnant. Lady Eleanor."

"That doesn't happen!"

"I beg your pardon?"

"I—that—" No. No and no. Jane Seymour was very much on the scene at this point, the gleam in Henry's beady blue eye, but she's not pregnant. They aren't having sex, they aren't even married yet. She won't get pregnant for over a year.

No, this was Lady Eleanor's latest attempt to lure Warren in. Which was ridiculous *and* risky, because Warren would have no way of knowing she was *enceinte*. The definition of insanity is to repeatedly mess with history until your husband time travels to rescue you.

She befriended Anne, got close to Henry, then pounced when his eye wandered, as it always did when his queens were pregnant (and when they weren't). Now a woman born in the 21st century was pregnant with Henry VIII's baby which she did solely to screw the timeline because she had no faith in the therapy process.

"I hate that bitch," I managed through gritted teeth. "Is she here? In the city?"

"I believe so. And although the king wishes to make Lady Jane Seymour his wife—"

"Because of course he does."

"—he has not yet put Eleanor aside."

"Because of course he hasn't. He's got too few heirs as it is; he'll want to keep his options open."

"Um, Joan, you remember we're in a big hall with lots of other people, right? Talking at a volume that can be overheard?"

"It's fine." I waved off Lisa's concern. "Hardly anyone can understand us at first, plus, everyone's more invested in keeping their head down until the Henry storm passes than they are in what we're up to. Which reminds me, the reason I have to find Lady Eleanor is because she's from the same place we are." I was staring Lisa down, willing her to get it. I was falling for Thomas, but I wasn't ready to reveal all just yet. Subtlety must be my watchword. (I'll try anything once.) "And she needs to come back with us. To the place we're all from."

"A native Merkan!" she replied, then giggled. Not really—Eleanor was British. But this wasn't the time to haggle over details. Lisa stopped laughing long enough to add, "Yeah, I follow. But I'm putting two and two together and getting seventeen, so you'll have to walk me through it later."

"Gladly. Thomas, while I visit Anne, find out where Lady Eleanor's holed up, will you?" I knew Warren's instructions had been to find Eleanor, *then* Lisa, but screw that. Lisa was *right here*. What, I should ignore her or, worse, abandon her while I looked for someone else? No chance. "Then let's meet here in an hour, okay? And keep Lisa safe. She smells like bacon!"

Lisa let out a snort. "Naturally that's what you'd home in on. And don't worry, I'll stick with your boy here. If I could sew myself to Thomas without getting noticed, I would."

"Be careful, my lady Joan."

"I thought we agreed on just Joan."

He caught my hand, held it to his lips. "As you wish, my Joan."

"Slick," I said.

"Aw. You guys are cute," Lisa cooed, which was as alarming as anything that had happened that week.

The Lieutenant of the Tower looked relieved to see me, and greeted me with, "Her Grace the queen has been asking for you."

"And here I am."

He escorted me up to her sumptuous suite, the same one she'd stayed in for her coronation three years ago. Which was staggering when you thought about it. Almost a decade to woo her. Three years to turn on her. If it seemed unreal to me, how much worse for her?

I knew these chambers had been renovated specifically for her coronation, all part of Henry's "if I say she's my queen, and make her look like a queen and make her rooms like a queen's rooms, all of England will buy into her being queen" plan which, given where we were now, had been an expensive disaster.

Though Queen Elizabeth I might disagree with that assessment.

Henry had Cromwell, that velvet-clad snake, spend the modern equivalent of over a million pounds on her rooms, and the one thing I liked about the Tudor era that the shows and movies hadn't been able to nail were the colors. When you're flipping through a history book, or watching *The Private Life of Henry VIII* with your mom for the 20th time, you start to think everything back then was drab, all blacks and browns and grays. But there were bright jewel colors everywhere in TudorTime, from the apricots in the yellow tart stuff at the deceptively bland-sounding Gray Horse Inn, to the stained glass windows and bright tapestries of the Tower.

Gone in my time. All gone. Anne's apartments were just a grass lawn now. (Wow. I was having Tudor regret. If I went back in time—well, forward in time to my present, then back in time to ten-year-old me—she wouldn't believe it.)

The Lieutenant escorted me to the Queen's Great Chamber, rapped sharply, then swung the door open. I went in and swallowed a gasp at the enormous room—one of six!—and then saw her attendants, most of whom were hostile to her. Anne, who had never been able to make and keep many friends—being popular was *not* the same thing, just ask Regina George—was to be surrounded by enemies all the way to the end. The most treacherous being, of course, her own family. Her uncle, who had shoved her at the throne, passed the death sentence on his niece *and* his nephew. Her parents had made themselves scarce. Other

Boleyns were cozying up to Jane Seymour. And Mary Boleyn would steer clear, thanks to my warning.

But here was her aunt Elizabeth Howard, and another aunt, Lady Shelton, and neither of them were Team Anne. They were there to encourage Anne's confidence so they could play informer for Cromwell. I had no idea that trick was so old. And I imagined the other two ladies weren't put in Anne's rooms to make things easier for her, either. All this to explain why we were all giving each other side-eye without speaking. And then, to ramp up the awkward, Elizabeth Howard made the sign of the cross at me.

"Lady Joan, the king's holy fool, to see Her Grace, Queen Anne," the Lieutenant announced, and then got the hell out of there because he was a smart fellow.

Without a word, Howard and Coffin led me through watching chamber to the presence chamber, where Anne was waiting for me. "Ah. Lady Joan."

"Queen Anne."

"Not for long."

I winced as she repeated the first thing she ever said to me. "No."

"Ladies, I shall see the Lady Joan privately."

Elizabeth Howard was already ruffling up like a hen and bustling toward us. "Those are not my instructions. You are not to be allowed to see people without a chaperone."

I put up a hand to stop her. "She's still a queen. Which means you're still her subject. She wants to talk to me alone, now back off."

"How dare you!" Rustle, rustle. I half expected her to paw the ground like a bull. "The king will hear of this!"

"Great. Go tell him. Right now."

There was a sound behind me, like Anne was trying to stifle a snicker, but that could have been wishful thinking.

Howard tried to come forward again and I planted a hand on her narrow chest and pushed back. Gently. "Do you think I won't knock you on your ass?"

It was like everybody gasped at once—half the air was sucked out of the room. I waited, and was actually a little disappointed to see Auntie Howard think better of the plan that would end with her being knocked on her lying spying Howard butt.

I heard her mutter something in French as she turned away, something that made Anne Boleyn smile. "She called you a barbarian."

"She's right. Shall we?"

"Indeed."

I won't lie. Shutting the door on their astonished faces was damn satisfying.

CHAPTER SEVENTY-FOUR

"I actually don't mind if they overhear." Because this was a most luxurious prison cell, she had a throne-like chair right beside the window and the table. It wasn't even a dining room table—she had another whole room for that. No, TudorTime's idea of a small end-table was an enormous hunk of wood at least six feet long and three feet wide, which Anne was using as a bookshelf. There were rich, gorgeous tapestries on the walls, fresh rushes on the floor, and the room was dappled with yellow and orange light. "I'm not planning to say anything to get anyone in trouble."

"There does not always have to be a plan," the queen observed, "to find trouble."

Well. Not much to say to that. So I just sat there.

"I like those."

"Pardon, Your Grace?"

"Awkward silences. Would you care for some wine?"

"No, thank you."

"Some cheese? A pasty?"

"…no…"

The queen of England rolled her eyes at me. "Bring a tray of dainties for our guest."

Ooooh! Dainties!

Anne smiled to see my expression. "Have your holy travels taken you yet to France?"

"Not yet." And hopefully not ever. I didn't know anything about the French royal family, except that Marie Antoinette didn't actually say 'let them eat cake'. I couldn't even say who was running things over there right now. Well, Francis I, but I didn't know if he was a Medici or a Valois or what. Just that he irritated the piss out of Henry. And the guy who played him on *The Tudors* was mighty cute. Long, strong forearms, mop of curly black hair… "My work keeps me busy right here."

"I am sure."

I studied her while pretending I wasn't. She was wearing a gown so dark a green it was black in some light. It brightened her sallow complexion, but didn't hide the purple shadows under her eyes, or the fact that she looked like she was on the hard side of forty, though I knew she was in her early thirties. TudorTime was hard on faces, and a lot more so when you could hear them building the platform on which you would die.

There was a quick rap and then one of the ladies came in with a tray and set it on the table beside us.

"After you," I said, the two worst words when I was hungry—it felt like hours since I'd gobbled the tart Lee had given me. But the queen waved me ahead, so I put the linen pillowcase Tudors called a napkin in my lap and grabbed one of the small brown balls.

"This is a French dish as well as English, which is why I wondered if you had visited. Délices are spiced roe testicles."

That gave me pause. Not much of one, though. If anything, her still-affected French accent was more off-putting. "When it comes to food, I'll try anything." Testicles, get in my belly! I took a nibble and it wasn't terrible. The haggis truffle I'd tried last winter had been worse. "Are you sure you won't have a delicious deer ball, Your Grace?"

"Quite." Anne's smile soured as she took a closer look at the tray. Maybe she had pie for breakfast?

"Is something wrong, Anne?"

She nodded at the small unassuming tarts, which had been baked to a golden brown crust. "That is humble pie, a common dish of the poor."

"Wait, that's a real thing? It's just a saying where I come from."

She indicated the tray with her long, pretty fingers. I thought about how her daughter was famously vain about her hands and smiled. "This is what passes for wit in my chambers."

I snorted. "Subtle. What's in it?"

She shrugged. "Whatever is left of a deer once the best of it is gone. Heart, kidneys. Perhaps the liver, or the lungs. I myself have never had it."

"And never will, since I'm the one who should be eating it." I reached out and yanked the tray toward me. "Humble pie, down the hatch. And I'm sorry I assumed the worst about you, and couldn't be more help to you."

"You have a chance to be so now. Because you did not spin me a fable, did you?"

"Unh?" All right, humble pie was never going to make my top ten, because those slots were reserved for custard and prime rib and chocolate and *chawanmushi*. But it wasn't awful. "A fable?"

"You once told me to 'give it up in Calais'."

"It's wonderful but weird how you can do a Merkan accent." A *Midwestern* American accent. That would never not be hilarious.

"You said 'the future of the greatest monarch England has ever seen depends on it'."

"Yes. You're right. That wasn't a fable."

"Tell me." She leaned forward and for a second, she looked like a beautiful bird of prey. Caged, still dangerous. "All of it, this time."

"Tell me your plan first."

She raised her eyebrows. "My plan?"

"You'll have one, Anne. You didn't get to the throne without one." Not to mention a Plan B, C, D, and E through M, probably. "I'd like to know what it is—oh, this is good!"

She blinked at my happy gasp. "Surely you have mead in Merka?"

I shrugged and took another sip. Sweet but not thick, honeyed but not syrupy. Mmm.

"I swear, the oddest most common things put a smile on your face, Lady Joan."

"We barbarians like to keep things simple."

Anne laughed. "That puts you one up on me. As for my plan, 'tis nothing dangerous. I'm not fool enough to attempt an escape—where could I go where I am not known? There are those who would kill me on sight. I am as the old Princess Dowager once called me—the scandal of Christendom. To think I once pitied her. As she pitied me. I knew I would outlive her, but I could not have guessed it would be by less than six months."

I didn't say anything. Because she was right—Catherine of Aragon *had* pitied her. Had foreseen her end, even. After a few more seconds I couldn't stand it anymore. "I think you ran an audacious campaign and deserved that throne. It wasn't your fault the king couldn't give you a son."

Her dark brows arched, but she was too couth to let her jaw drop. "Take care, Joan. Suggesting the king is not capable is treason."

"It's biology, not treason." Although at this point in history, it was both. "My point is, you couldn't have anticipated your pig husband turning on you quite like this."

She smirked at 'pig'. "But you could have. You did."

I shrugged. "I have to follow my instructions. I explained all this to your pig husband."

"Ah. The infamous hailstorm you conjured up."

"Whoa!" I nearly choked on a testicle. "I'd rather not get burned alive, so take it easy on the conjuring talk."

"I have spoken of it to no one. Indeed, Henry forbade it. My sister Mary wrote me about it from whatever sad little farm she's languishing on. I forbore not to write back." She rested her small chin in her hand. "I regret that."

"That's—that's not why Mary isn't here. I told her to stay away. I couldn't go into specifics at the time, but she's obeying my instructions, not abandoning you."

"Both of those things can be true. But I cannot hold my sister up to blame. For any of it. She knew him of old and warned me. But I was determined to have him. *Aisi sera groigne qui groigne.*" She correctly read the blank look on my face and added, "Let them grumble, that is how it is going to be."

"That's the spirit. You yourself said that you were resolved to have him, even if it cost you your head. Y'know, 'if the realm be made happy by my issue'. Which it will be."

Anne froze in the act of reaching for her goblet. "My maid and I were the only ones who knew about that."

Obviously not, since it made the history books. "I'll tell you what I told *el puerco*—what if I told you when we met that you'd have one living child, a girl, and never any more and Henry would fall in love with Jane Seymour and kill you within three years of your coronation? At best, you would have laughed your elegant butt off. At worst..." I didn't have to elaborate. Not long ago, talking trash about Anne was treason. These days Henry loved to trash Anne and decided trash-talking Jane Seymour was treason because he is the *fucking* worst. "But we were talking about your plan. Specifically, whatever Lady Eleanor has talked you into doing."

"No one 'talked me' into anything," she said sharply. "And certainly not that witch, that false friend and fornicator."

I weighed the satisfaction that comes with calling her out for hypocrisy against the necessity of talking her around and went with the latter. "Yes, she's awful and she burned you."

"*What?*"

"Not literally. And she planted an idea in your head all the same, didn't she?"

"Not escape." She was staring pensively out the window, drumming her fingers on the arm of her chair. She was a living illustration for plotting. "I would never run away, though I would have accepted exile. But to dose Henry with a tonic guaranteed to make him ill? A posset of humiliation? That I shall do."

"I'm not following you."

"Few can."

"Boo."

"When I stand on that scaffold, I should make a pretty speech full of praise for the king, as my brother will, as my friends will…" Her voice broke a little on 'brother'; I read the room and pretended not to notice. "…but I shall not. The world will hear what their king has turned into: an impotent ogre who will kill me rather than live in a land where I no longer want him. All his nasty little secrets, all his fumblings in the dark, all his lecherous panting that nearly always came to naught, the feel of him, the *stink* of him… everyone will know."

So there it was. It wasn't enough for Eleanor to supplant Anne as Henry's lover and then get pregnant. She also talked Anne into taking a radically different path that could prevent Elizabeth I from taking the throne. I really was starting to suspect Warren's wife was Satan.

"That would be incredible," I admitted.

She leaned back and grinned. "Indeed."

"And probably unprecedented."

"Unprecedented should have been my motto."

I took a breath. "But you can't do it."

She wasn't surprised, and I counted myself lucky that I, at least, had never underestimated either Boleyn girl. "And here you are to tell me why."

"You'll jeopardize your daughter's throne."

Anne slumped and looked away. Talk of her impending death made her angry; talk of Elizabeth made her afraid. "I doubt it. What chance has she? She has been declared a bastard, and is lower now than his other bastard, the Lady Mary. And the Seymour is likely to give him a son. And if not her, someone else. We cannot *all* be incapable."

"It's not you. It's him. You know about Catherine's troubles, your troubles. Madge didn't get pregnant, either, right?"

"Madge?" Anne's brow wrinkled. "She has nothing to do with this. She has not been with the king. She left the city months ago. After I miscarried my son. You should have *seen* them tripping over each other to remove themselves."

"Right, sorry." Okay—this was fixable. Before Lady Satan put her nose in (among other things), Henry *did* stray, but he did it with one of Anne's cousins: Madge Shelton. So while Eleanor took Madge's spot in Henry's bed, it probably wouldn't result in a nuclear cataclysm. "I got his mistresses mixed up."

"A not uncommon error," she replied dryly. "The best I can do for my daughter is to tell all of Christendom that Henry is an impotent remorseless hypocrite." Wow, she was a little hung up on the impotent thing. "She will know her mother died protesting an unjust fate. If I do not speak out, she will live her life thinking she is the daughter of an incestuous witch, a traitor her father was right to have done away with. It is my only option."

"No, it isn't. Listen—Henry deserves every rotten thing you could say about him, and also a kick in the deer testicles, but you've got to play nice or he'll take it out on Elizabeth. And you must know she'll have a hard enough time as it is."

"I 'must' know? No. *You* must know. And you will tell me. You asked for my plan and you heard it. Now tell me why I should abandon it."

"Okay. See, the angels told me—"

"*Arrêt!*" She smacked her hands down on the arms of the chair; the sharp sudden sound made me jump. "The angels told you nothing; you're just a fool, and not at all holy."

"Rude. What I mean is—"

"What you mean is you have a machine, a strange machine from your land that you do not understand and which you have used to travel far back to the past. You have no visions; you merely read old texts. You are not guided by God, but by science. And you will tell me my daughter's future *at once*, and in its entirety—no inconvenient gaps this time—and then I will decide what to say the morning of my death."

I stared.

"When you gape like that, you look like a fish landed on the dock."

"Mean!" I shook my head. "How—I don't—"

"Do not deny it; your face tells me everything."

"Is my face telling you I'm about to have a heart attack? Because that's what's happening. How could you know that? I understand not thinking I'm a holy fool, but how did you make the leap to—oh. Lady Eleanor." I buried my face in my hands and moaned into my palms. She couldn't just start an affair with Henry, she had to make Anne—another abandoned wife—as miserable as she was. I was beginning to think the perfect revenge would be to reunite the Warrens, so they could unhinge their jaws and devour each other. "She told you about your death. And when and how you'd die. For spite."

"She overreached, and did not take kindly to being slapped."

"Ha! Tell me it left a great big welt she couldn't cover up. No, don't, we're getting off track. But see—that's why Eleanor is a repellant skank. She only told you the bad because that's all she cares about."

"What is 'skank'?"

"Bitch. Slut. Bitchy slut. But see, there's good in your execution. I know that sounds screwed up, but from your death comes a golden age. This, all this?" I motioned to her, the Tower, TudorTime in general. "Everything you did, all that you sacrificed, it really did have a great purpose. You won't die in vain. And eventually, people all over the world will know it. People in my time know your name, and your brother's name, and that you were wrongfully executed by your husband. It's not even a matter of debate; everyone understands you were railroaded because Henry Tudor was a monster."

She'd relaxed in her big chair and even smiled a little. "Tell me."

So I did. I explained how the red-headed toddler at Hatfield would eventually inherit the throne and do such a good job—and would have such incredible PR—that the Elizabethan Age would always be synonymous with the Golden Age.

I told her Henry's son by Jane Seymour would die young, that Mary would ascend but only reign for five years before dying of cancer (and a broken heart, but that was a tale for another time), and that Elizabeth would take the throne at age twenty-five and rule for decades.

"She's still considered England's greatest monarch," I said. And sure, there were arguments that Victoria was a bit better, but that was for another time and another queen. "And the pope? He *hates* Queen Elizabeth." Why was I telling this in the present tense? "He hates her but he admires her, too, he says 'She is a great woman and if she were Catholic, the greatest'." Something like that, anyway.

"And she's lovely. She's got Henry's hair and coloring, but she has your pretty hands and big dark eyes." And the vanity of both her parents, but never mind. "And she's brilliant—even Mary Tudor notices, and she makes a point of telling Henry all about it in her letters."

"Mary... Catherine's daughter? She is kind to my Elizabeth?"

I nodded. "It starts because she feels sorry for her, but Mary does grow to love her. It doesn't last forever—when they're grown, they clash over the throne. But right now, while your daughter's vulnerable and everyone's distancing themselves, Catherine's daughter is looking out for her."

"That is a kindness I had not expected."

"Anyway, Elizabeth's brilliant and even Henry gets that. So she's young and vibrant when she takes the throne and people. Are. Thrilled. Mary was a disaster—she spends her entire reign trying to put the clock back to 1520."

"Ha! As well to drop a bucket of water into the sea, then try to get back precisely what was in the bucket and no more."

"Sure, okay—anyway, they're not crazy about another queen, but she's so charismatic she wins them over." Mostly. "Even though the Pope declares her a heretic. Even when Spain declares war. She defeats *Spain*, Anne. She kicks the Spanish Armada's ass so hard, they scuttle back to their homeland and pray to God to forgive their arrogance."

Anne was listening with her eyes closed, smiling, and we weren't going to talk about the tears running down her face. "More."

"The best part? She never marries. She says she will—well, first she says she won't, that she's married to England and all her citizens are her children. And no one knows it at the time, but she means it. Still, she pretends. Whenever they need an alliance, she'll pretend to consider marriage with whatever country they're wooing. Whenever they're trying to hold off an invasion, she'll make a big show of considering *that* monarch. She keeps everyone on a string for years. No one ever knows what she wants at any given time, she plays them *all*—sound familiar? And after a while, she's an old woman and it's too late for babies, so they give up.

"So Henry's line dies out with your daughter, she's the last—and greatest—Tudor monarch." Anne was giggling *and* crying by now, but I couldn't stop. Not having to pretend these were visions, being able to tell her exactly how it was going to be, was exhilarating.

"And everything *he* did? All it got him was a reputation as an obese tyrannical wife-killer. He did some good things, but it's all forgotten in my time. *He's* not the one honored and revered to this day—your daughter is. *He's* not the one they named the Golden Age after—your daughter is. He's not the one who set a standard for a long peaceful rule by a woman—your daughter did that. And people know about him, sure, and there are books and plays about him. But every actor who plays him is fat." Almost every actor. Jonathan Rhys Meyers was too vain to put on the fat suit, so he decided makeup, a salt-and-pepper beard, and a raspy voice were exactly the same as gaining two hundred pounds.

"There are books and plays about you, too, and ironically, you're a lot more popular right now that you ever were, since everyone knows you're being railroaded. Even the people working for your fall know it."

"I do not understand."

"They know it's not true. They know Cromwell's making up lies and coaxing confessions to get rid of you on Henry's orders. Who's making a spectacle of himself over Jane, naturally. He's fooling himself, like he always does. But he's not fooling anybody else."

Anne tilted her head. Considering. "Is it so? And to think I once wanted my people's regard more than anything."

"You have it now." I sat back, almost out of breath. "So. That's why you have to be nice on the scaffold. You just have to suck it up one more time, Anne. Just this one last time."

"Holding my tongue," she observed, wiping her face, "has never been my strength."

"No, I hear you. But it'll pay off. Not only do you make a *quick* and *painless* dignified death, most people know you're being legally murdered because Henry's mad at you." She grinned at that, which I found simultaneously admirable and creepy. "They don't really believe you were with all those men, especially when you were in one castle on a certain date and whomever you were supposed to be having sex with was a hundred miles away." Seriously. Cromwell had been in a hurry, and subsequently sloppy. "No one with any sense thinks you had sex with your brother while you were still recovering from childbirth. So when you die with pure class, everyone watching will see it. And talk about it. And write about it. People in the 21st century know about Henry's madness, and your daughter's great skill as a ruler. And they know you changed the world to suit yourself through force of will. There's a monument to you on Tower grounds in my time."

There. That was all of it. Well, all I was willing to tell her, which was almost the same thing. I was spent, and all out of deer balls. I poured myself more mead to soothe my throat while Anne sat there and thought so hard I could almost hear the gears grinding.

Finally: "Very well. I shall do as you say, and secure the throne for my daughter. I will let Henry keep his reputation. Will you tell me one more thing?"

"Depends."

"How does my family? After?"

"Well." I put the goblet down. "Boleyn and Howard stock goes low, as you can imagine. The Seymours run things for a few years, just like the Boleyns did when you were in the ascendant. And I'm sorry to say your parents will be dead in a couple more years. But George's wife will pay for betraying him. And your uncle Howard will end up in the Tower."

Anne actually gurgled with laughter. "Truly?"

"Oh yes. Along with his son, whom Henry will execute. But your sister? She gets the happy ending. Even better, her children and grandchildren have prominent influence as well as places in Elizabeth's court. Your daughter takes care of her family." Except for Mary, Queen of Scots. And another Duke of Norfolk. And the Grey sisters. But again, not the time or place.

"So that's it," I finished. I stood, shook the pillowcase free of crumbs, folded it, put it back on the table, and glanced at the door. "And I've stayed too long and said too much."

"Yes, but that's your thing."

"I *love* when you do the accent." Now, what was the polite way to take leave of a woman headed for an unjust death who will die surrounded by enemies? "Wow, look at the time. God bless?"

She snorted. "Stop that, you are clearly at a loss."

"Right. Sorry. I'll go."

As I started to move to the door, she reached out and snagged my hand. She didn't rise, just looked up at me with those eyes. "If you ever have a chance to do my daughter a service in her reign, I pray you do so."

"Don't even *say* that." I tried to rein in how appalled I was. "This is supposed to be my last trip."

"And a decade ago, Wolsey was supposed to secure Henry his annulment within a year, yet here we are."

"Point. Anne, it's hard to imagine Gloriana needing anyone's help, least of all mine."

"Gloriana?"

"Gloriana, Good Queen Bess, the Virgin Queen... she's got more aliases than a vigilante superhero."

"Pardon?"

"If I'm ever in a position to help her, I will." That wasn't likely to come back and bite me in the ass, right?

"Thank you, Joan," the Queen of England said, and let go of my hand, and thank goodness, because Anne Boleyn had a grip like a beautifully garbed dark-eyed pit bull. "And God bless you."

"Goodbye," I replied, and left.

And I didn't cry for her. Not even a little. Tower's dusty. That's all it was.

CHAPTER SEVENTY-FIVE

I was exhausted, though I'd spent less than an hour with Anne Boleyn. And I wasn't done. But at least Lisa and Thomas were in the hall where I'd left them, and since I'd fulfilled the queen's request, nobody was bothering me. In fact, they were going out of their way to avoid me.

Lisa and Thomas had managed to form a little group of two in the far corner, studiously pretending they were calm and at ease, and when she saw me, Lisa perked right up. "How'd it go?"

"Another day, another one of Henry's sorrowful queens."

Thomas shook his head. "Poor lady."

Lisa took that in, and then asked, "Plural? You've met the first one? Catherine? What'm I saying, of course you did. Okay, when we get back, I'm gonna need you to tell me the whole story again and this time I promise to keep an open mind and if I feel the urge to laugh at you I'll do my best to squash it."

"That's more than I could reasonably ask for."

"Damn right."

"Can I give you the really quick Cliff Notes version? Anne knew about Merka. Where we're from and *how we travel.*"

"No shit?"

"That's what I thought! I'll tell you the rest later." And I had to hand it to the queen. She knew about time travel, but had no curiosity about it beyond culling whatever information she could use. No "how did you get here?" or "is it a job or a hobby?" or "how is any of this possible?" or "what's the future like?" or "did you bring something from the future that I could look at?" You had to admire the focus. She couldn't do anything about time traveling weirdos, so she focused on what little she *did* have control over.

"And we should drink a lot when you're regaling me. So much—like when you wake up crying because the hangover's that bad. But that's for when we get back. And speaking of that glorious time in what I hope is in the very near future, now what?"

"Now we find Eleanor and I try very, very hard not to strangle her. And then we go home." Piece of cake! Or humble pie. I stifled a belch; those deer lungs did not go down easy.

"And what's the best way to do that?"

"There isn't one," I admitted, because it was nothing but the truth. It wasn't like I could track the sneaky wench's whereabouts on social media. "And I have to warn you, the thing with these trips is, nothing is ever easy."

"Nooooo." Lisa somehow formed her face into the most limpid expression that was ever on a face. "But whyever not?"

"Shut up. A lot of times to get one thing done I have to agree to three other things. So I don't know how we're going to track her down, but it's definitely ... not ... going to ..."

An unmistakable voice rang out. "What have you meddled in now, you inconvenient bitch?"

"... be easy." I blinked hard but she didn't waver or disappear. In fact, Lady Eleanor, Warren's soulmate/Gorgon, was striding toward us, the perfect picture of wrath, and suddenly the great hall seemed a lot smaller. "Nice to see you again, Eleanor. All right, I'm lying."

"Lady Eleanor." Thomas did the not-really-a-bow burn, but she had no eyes for him.

"What did you do this time?" She was dressed in vibrant yellow, an unfortunate shade that made her look like an angry sunflower. "Did you talk to the queen? You did!"

"Of course I did."

"Of course you did! I should have put an end to your meddling years ago."

"That's your second use of 'meddle' in twenty seconds. You know you sound like a cartoon villain, yes?"

"Joan, what is—"

"Not now, Thomas," Lisa hissed. In fact, she seized Thomas by the sleeve and guided him a few inches to the left so she could step forward and level a full-on glare at Eleanor. "We're here to take you home, you ungrateful troublesome assmunch, so how about you shut your yap hole and come with us?"

"You know, Lisa, I couldn't have put that any better myself."

"Oh, stop it," she replied, waving me off with *faux* modesty.

"Sheer poetry."

"'Twas nothing."

"Stop clacking and get your servant in line," Mrs. Dr. Warren managed through gritted teeth.

"Given all the meals I've prepared for her," I replied, "and the times I've cleaned up after her experiments and the occasional explosions—"

"That was maybe four times! In sixteen months!"

"—you could make the case that I'm actually her servant."

"No way," Lisa insisted. "Partners."

"Come with me," Lady Mrs. Dr. Warren hissed, which was impressive given the lack of sibilants in that sentence. "*Not* you, bastard."

"First of all, Eleanor, his name is Wolsey's bastard. Second—"

"Forgive the interruption, my Joan, but I should like to answer that one myself." To Eleanor, "I am charged to protect Lady Joan and her companion. Which means wherever they go, so too do I."

"It's true," Lisa marveled. "Chivalry *isn't* dead. Well. *Now*."

"Fine!" Eleanor snapped, and motioned to the two guards I only just realized she'd brought with her, because I am dumb sometimes. "All of you come along then. We must talk."

I opened my mouth to throw sand in her gears because obeying Eleanor in anything was a terrible idea, then held off. I'd gotten to Anne relatively quickly, Joan and Thomas were all right, Eleanor had found *us* (which was a rather large timesaver), and going somewhere private to hash all this out was an excellent idea. Especially since I suspected Eleanor was a yeller.

"She's right," I decided, and fell into step behind the odious wretch. The guards, dressed in identical livery with gold and blue checkerboards emblazoned on their chests, were right behind us. Everyone kept out of the way. No one wanted to so much as make eye contact. I'm guessing Henry's new mistress was just as volatile and capable of vengeance as the last one.

Or perhaps they were all sick of the drama and wanted to keep their heads down. When I thought of all the upheaval they'd suffered over the last few years, I couldn't blame them.

Eleanor stomped her way out of the Great Hall, into a covered walkway that ran parallel to the Queen's garden, then along the curtain wall until we got to a square-ish tower on the southern rampart. (I still couldn't get over how strange the Tower seemed without tour guides and souvenir shops.) She led us inside through the lower chamber, which was quite nice—I found out later that the infamous Princes of the Tower had been lodged there before they disappeared (*cough* were murdered *cough cough*). And the tower she led us to was the Bloody Tower, which also should have tipped me off.

We followed her down a claustrophobic hallway lined with stone to spiral stairs that led to the basement, and from there into a large chamber that was chilly even on a sunny May day. In terms of privacy, it was first-rate. There was even a display of knives and short swords on a nearby table—was this a satellite of the royal armory?

Eleanor seemed satisfied, too, because she nodded to her guards and before I could move, or even think, one of them clubbed Thomas on the back of the head hard enough to send the poor guy right to the floor, out cold.

"Jesus Christ!"

(I can count on one hand how often Lisa and I have screamed the same thing in unison. This was number three.)

"Oh, are you silly twats religious? Don't worry; you'll be with Him directly."

If that was supposed to soothe us, it had the opposite effect.

CHAPTER SEVENTY-SIX

"**Y**ou're making a terrible impression on my roommate!" In terms of thundering denouncements, it wasn't great. But I had something more important to worry about, and turned to Lisa. "In retrospect, I should have seen this coming. I'm sorry."

"Maybe. But you've had a tough month. I should've been paying more attention, too. And not just today."

I threw my arms around her in a hug of mutual respect and forgiveness, which she tolerated four seconds longer than usual, then wriggled free.

"Pay attention!" This from Dr. Lady Eleanor Warren, whose guard had taken up position between us and the door. The table of knives was closer to him than to us, a silent, glittering rebuke to my naiveté in following someone I knew to be unstable into a room full of knives.

She'd ordered the other guard to remove poor conked Thomas (I hoped 'remove' just meant 'remove' as opposed to 'dump the body in the Thames'), so it was down to the four of us. "You're in trouble, if you American simpletons haven't realized, and pardon the redundancy."

"You're wearing a dress the color of an unhealthy urine sample, you don't give a shit about the timeline, you're making the worst mistake of your life—which is really saying something—*and* you're tedious in your bitchiness." Lisa shrugged. "We're focused."

"I told you before, get your servant—"

"Cut the shit, Ellie."

"*Don't* call me that!"

"Cut the shit, fuckface. You know I'm not her servant, just like you know she's not Lady Joan. I didn't get the whole story out of your piece-of-shit spouse before he booted me here, but I got most of it."

"You talked to my husband?"

"He talked *at* me."

"Yeah, he does that," I muttered.

"Three of the four people in this cell have no business being here," Lisa continued, arms crossed over her chest. Her hood was crooked, but it didn't take away from her natural authority. Much. "Joan's here to help you go home to your shitpoke spouse, and you sic your dog on her ally? Lock us in a room with your goon? What the fuck is the matter with you?"

"*She* is the matter with me!" I'd been studying the other guard and noting his weapons—and wondering if we should be talking so freely in front of him—but assumed without looking that she meant me. He was only about an inch taller than me, looked to be in good shape, wiry rather than bulky, and I counted one sword and one knife. No mail. If I could get on him without telegraphing my movement, I might disarm him. But I had to pick my moment. "She's been getting in my way for years! Since Blackfriars!"

"Been here a while, havencha?" Lisa smirked. "I noticed you picked up some gray hairs and crow's feet. It's been...what? Fifteen years or so?"

Wait. What? A decade and a half? Lisa accurately read my expression as 'huh?' and elaborated. "There was a picture of her in the lobby the first time I went to I.T.C.H."

I nodded—I'd seen the same pictures in Warren's hotel room.

"You glanced at a wall of framed group shots and recognized me?" Because she was awful *and* vain, she was actually smoothing her hair and rubbing her eyes, like *that* had ever worked on crow's feet.

"Lisa's got a near-eidetic memory. She ruined every grading curve. And she was *never* sorry. Not once."

"Fuck you, do your homework."

"Don't you dare speak to me about ruin!" Eleanor shrieked.

"Is Warren into older women?" Lisa was giving her a critical once-over. "You'd better hope so. I mean, you could get work done, sure, but even modern medical science has limits."

"*Shut up.* Do you think my man here won't hurt you if I order it? He will."

"Sorry," I said to the guard, who was doing a remarkable impersonation of a statue, "but I'm going to do that thing where I talk about you like you're not in the room. Eleanor, should we be talking like this in front of him?"

"He doesn't speak English," she snapped.

"*Vous savez la vieille femme en juane est un voyageur du temps, oui?*" Lisa asked. To me, she added, "I just asked him if he knew the crone in yellow was a time traveler."

"Shut up!" the crone shouted. "Even if he understood you, he couldn't understand you."

"Huh?" From me. (I'll admit it, I was having a hard time keeping up.)

"Because we sound like hillbillies with head colds," Lisa reminded me.

"Oh. Point. Now what were you on about, Eleanor?"

She whirled on me, flushed to the eyebrows. "How could my husband come to me with your constant interference?"

"Why didn't you tell me who you were?" I countered. "I would've brought you back after Calais. You could have had a passionate reunion and gone back to destroying each other instead of the timeline."

"He needed to come to me."

"That makes *no* sense, but even so, if you'd explained who you were, I could have given Warren a message, told him you were okay."

"I didn't need a messenger, I needed my husband! I knew they were getting close to being able to see through the gates. I thought if he observed the lengths I was willing to go to in order to get his attention, he'd come through— he would fix the problem I created and—"

"Fix you," Lisa finished.

"Exactly! Except there's nothing wrong with me."

(Our silence was eloquent.)

"Henry should have died at Blackfriars," Lady Loon went on. "I salted his meal with enough poison to kill an ox."

"Oh, Christ." I rubbed my forehead. "The poison made him choke—"

"And you Heimliched it out of him before he could die!"

"See?" Lisa asked. "I told you taking that class would come in handy. Nice work."

"Thanks, actually it was horrible, the entire experience was horrible. I'm lucky he didn't crack a rib when he took me down." I snapped my fingers and pointed at Eleanor. "You were at The More, too! Catherine of Aragon said she'd seen you twice in the same month. You talked Catherine into getting the Emperor involved and making war."

I could see how she'd done it, too. All sympathy, all kindness, visiting the exiled and lonely Catherine of Aragon and telling her exactly what the queen wanted to hear: that she was in the right, that England was with her, that Henry was headed for Hell but she could save him *and* protect her daughter's inheritance. That she could be like her esteemed mother, the warlike Isabella, who had waged war and presided over empires and made it look easy.

"Emperor Charles was going to bring 30,000 troops and put Mary Tudor on the throne at sword point."

"Holy *shit.*" From Lisa. "You were willing to consign thousands to death to get your husband's attention? The gate's not the latest tech toy for you to play with, for fuck's sake. Anything could have happened!"

"Nothing happened, because of *her.*"

I smiled. "Thanks."

"So then," Eleanor continued, aggrieved, "I had to waste time befriending Anne—"

"But you turned on her. You gave evidence against her; you're one of the reasons Cromwell was able to bring her to trial so fast. And now you're pregnant with Henry's baby because ... you think that'll make Warren come for you after nothing else worked?" That couldn't be the plan. Was that the plan? No way was that the plan.

Lisa was starting to snicker. "Wait, Catherine nixed the army, so—ha!—so next up was Operation Bang Henry? Because you thought *not* having to fuck Henry punished *Anne?* How does your mind even work? Is it like one of those old Bugs Bunny cartoons? Is your mind just a whirl of dust and fury like the Tasmanian Devil?"

"*Warren is not supposed to come for me.*" She paused, probably for effect, but really, it just made everything take longer. "He's supposed to come *to* me."

Silence. I even glanced at the guard, who was po-faced. No help there. "Sorry, what?"

"He comes to me and sees what a fine life I've made for us here and stays with me and we're happy here! It's not complicated!" Eleanor threw her hands in the air. "*What* is so hard to understand?"

"All of it. From beginning to end—so you got pregnant—"

"I, um." She was still flushing, but wouldn't make eye contact. Accessory to assault and kidnapping? Meh. Attempted regicide? No biggie. An unplanned pregnancy? Huge social *faux pas*. "I didn't plan that, actually. I wasn't able to, with Warren…"

Ha! Even Warren's wife called him Warren. Did she even remember his first name anymore?

"…but Henry is over the moon, which protects me."

"Protects you? You might want to check with Queen Anne on that one."

She ignored me. "He loves me. Not that I want *him*." Eleanor waved away the king of England: shoo! "But I like to have a reserve. And it might be a boy—think of that."

We were; Lisa's appalled expression mirrored how I felt.

"What a clusterfuck."

"Well put, Lisa." To Eleanor: "So you never wanted to be rescued?"

"From *what*? TudorTime is wonderful."

"You can't use that!" I shouted. "That's mine! I'm trademarking it and everything!"

"Whoa. Joanie." Lisa patted my arm. "That's a weird thing to get mad about. Simmer."

"Do you know how far gold goes here, you insipid wankers? How low the cost of living is? The rich can get away with quite a lot in our time, but in the 16th century? You can be a queen in all but name," Eleanor declared. "They don't have all those tiresome government regulations here. You can own people, or as good as, you can do anything, say anything… provided you can buy anything. Did you think I ingratiated myself with the Tudor regime out of boredom? This is a far less complicated time, we can be happy here."

"Because I.T.C.H. isn't here," I guessed. "So if Warren came for you, he could be a—what? Gentleman of leisure?"

"Less complicated?" Lisa nearly shrieked, cutting off Eleanor's answer. "Jesus! 'Less complicated' is the last phrase I would use to describe any part of this abortion! What. Is. Wrong. With. You? That's not rhetorical, you deluded cow. I genuinely want to know what the hell your damage is. So far I count narcissism, pathological lying, histrionic personality disorder, possible borderline personality disorder, the early stages of tuberculosis—"

"And there's none of *that* in this time, either," Eleanor sniffed. "Labels."

"Yeah, I'll be you heard a lot of them before you quit the 21st century, you psychotic noodle brain. And why are you rich here? It's not like you jumped with a treasure chest."

"Good question," I said, surprised. And speaking of rich, was it time to tell her Warren wanted her back mostly because of her money? And if not, then when?

"Well." Eleanor looked taken aback by the question. "I've had years, you know, and—and that is none of your concern! Why am I answering your questions? I wanted to get you in here to tell you to your face what an insufferable interfering blight you've been on my life."

"Noted. Then what?"

"I beg your pardon?"

"Well, you got to yell and do the 'I would have gotten away with it if it wasn't for you meddling kids' speech—"

"I *am* getting away with it."

"So what now? Warren sent me to bring you back. Forced me, actually—the only way he could do it was to trick Lisa into jumping, then let me go after her. So I was supposed to come back with you, then go back for her."

"Really?" Lisa asked. "Why'd you get me first?"

"Why wouldn't I? You were right there. Warren should have come himself if he wanted things done a certain way. And now's probably a good time to mention that if I try to come back without Eleanor, Warren threatened to pull the plug and strand us."

"Well, shit. Guess we're bringing her back."

"What?" Eleanor gasped. "No! He never. He would *never.*"

"Oh, take it easy, I'm not even sure I believe him. He said it himself—our absence was going to arouse 21st century attention that I.T.C.H. can't afford. It's a miracle they've kept the lid on this long."

"They do seem to be a bit of a confederacy of dunces," Eleanor admitted. "Not my field, though!" she added, as if worried we'd judge her for it. Because *that's* why we'd judge her. "And you're one to talk, aren't you one of them? I admit I don't recognize you, so I presume you're an expert they brought in to—"

"She's an intern," Lisa pointed out.

"What?"

"Independent contractor. That's what I'm going to put on my tax return. It's not my field, either. I'm studying for a different degree."

"You don't have a college degree? Then why are you— why would I.T.C.H.—"

"Because they don't know what they're doing, Eleanor! It's odd that you're not internalizing this. They're reacting, not acting, and they're out of money and Warren's out of money." Huh, I guess now was the right time for that conversation. "And they're just flailing around. They haven't been proactive and they seem to be collectively allergic to doing the right thing. I'd barely cleared the willow tree before I spotted the holes in his stupid plan."

Even worse, there was still so much we didn't know. Why did one jump drop me in 1520, and the next in 1532, and the next barely a year after that? Why was I in Calais for one jump and London the next? Could someone go back further than 1520, or did the gates only open forward? If the gates could be brought under control, was there a way to track people searching for Losties? And plenty more besides, those were just ones I came up with on the fly.

"Your husband isn't coming for you, Eleanor, and I seriously doubt he wants the life you've prepared for him. So your options are limited."

"I'll say," Lisa muttered. "Be insane, or go *more* insane."

"Not helping. Eleanor, if you don't come back with me, you'll have to live here. And eventually die here." Except that wouldn't work, either. Eleanor's sanity had clearly taken a sabbatical; if Lisa and I left her here, she'd keep pulling audacious crap in the misguided hope of Warren leaping back through the centuries to 'save' her. The definition of insanity had taken human form and was right in front of me.

"You don't know anything about my husband *or* me. And the choices are all mine. I only wanted to tell you to your face what a pain in the arse you've been and how I won't be putting up with you one moment longer. *Tuez-les!*"

"Bond villain bullshit," Lisa said, and stabbed the guard with the knife I'd slipped her from my sleeve during our hug. This made it easier for me to kick him off balance, get a hand on the back of his neck, and sweep him down until his forehead connected, hard, with the edge of the table.

His head made a satisfying 'bonk!' as he rebounded, hit the floor, and didn't move.

Huh. Thought that'd be harder.

Eleanor was not keen on any of it, because she'd rushed the table, snatched up a short sword (or a long knife), and lunged at Lisa with a mad slash. Lisa staggered back and clapped a hand to the side of her face, and I was horrified to see blood start streaming through her fingers.

So I shot her. Twice.

Eleanor, not Lisa. Just to clarify.

Chapter Seventy-Seven

"Jeez, Lisa. In the armpit?"

"I didn't want to kill him." Her voice was muffled as she put pressure on the slash in her face. We were staring down at the unconscious guard, whose blood had started to seep from beneath his doublet. Lisa handed my knife over with her other hand and I snapped it back into place beneath my sleeve. "What if he's important? Or is the father or grandfather of somebody important? Also thank you very fucking much for shooting that loon. Now tell me you've got a first aid kit in that ass-pack of yours."

I yanked up my skirt and tugged my pack free, then whirled as there was a tremendous racket outside the door as Thomas hurtled in. He took it all in with a glance, then slammed the door shut and got down on one knee to examine Eleanor, who had died glaring at the ceiling with an aggravated expression: *I can't believe this shit.*

Where to start?

"For God's sake, Joan, a .38?" Thomas looked up at me with a rueful expression. "Why not just throw rocks at her?"

"Whuh." That was it. That was my snappy rejoinder. Wait, I'd try again. "..." Nope. Couldn't even vocalize.

"Are you kidding?" Lisa cried, pawing through my meager first aid supplies. "All this time you've been one of Joanie's—one of her—um—"

"Losties," I managed.

"—and you never said? What the *fuck*?"

"Since I came through before she did, she's *my* Lostie. But Lisa, lass, we'd best get you to the apothecary."

"None of you hacks touch me!" She was pressing gauze to the wound, blood immediately blooming on the white, and backed away from Thomas as if he was going to pin her down and drop leeches on her face. And not the delicious kind. "I want a maxillofacial surgical consult with Dr. Anand at OHH and I want it right fucking now!"

"Noted." To Thomas: "Whuh?"

"I promise to tell you everything, love, but we need to go. No telling when my guard is going to come to."

"Love?" I hadn't even gotten a handle on the fact that Thomas was a Lostie, and now this? "You called me love? The way the British do? You know how they use it like we use 'dear'? Or did you mean love-love?"

"Really, Joan?" Lisa gritted out. "Now? Right now?"

"Of course it's love-love. I love you. Have done since Calais." Thomas Wynter—or whatever his name was—told me that like it was a fact of life. Lisa was bleeding, Lady Eleanor was dead from two in the chest, I loved chocolate, he loved me. "It's fine." His bright blue gaze clouded for a second. "I understand you don't reciprocate my feelings."

"Whuh. Nuh?"

"Holster your sidearm if you please. Time to go."

"Where?"

"To the willow, of course. To go home."

Well. Couldn't argue with that.

"You get migraines."

Thomas looked relieved as I broke the silence. He'd let me ponder, again offered to bring Lisa to the apothecary, got a verbal ream-job for it, and now Lisa was riding pillion behind him while my Hertz horse was abreast of his.

"Yes, Joan. Not often, thank God. I don't suffer them as frequently as you do."

"That afternoon we took a nap at the Inn. I was telling you about migraines but I didn't use that word. I just described them as really bad headaches and you said—"

"That I had suffered one or two myself. Yes. My first one was in Calais."

"That's the connection?" Lisa asked. The bleeding was starting to slow, thank God, though she still looked like she'd been in a war. Or had been slashed from temple to cheek by a crazy lady. "The Losties present with migraines? Well, hell. That's why most of 'em are women."

"I don't understand, Thomas. You're Wolsey's son. Nobody ever questions that, *I* didn't question it."

"One person questioned it. The same person who knew Wolsey better than anyone."

"Thomas Cromwell," I guessed.

He chuckled. "Cromwell knew I was full of shite, he knew my background was all wrong, my accent was wrong."

"Wait, so you're really Scottish? And what's your real name, for God's sake?"

"My first name really is Thomas. Thomas MacRae, born and raised in Edinburgh," he replied, smiling. He pronounced it the way the natives do: Ed-in-burr-uh.

So I messed with him. "Do you mean Ed-in-berg?"

He actually shuddered. "Please don't."

"You deserved that, you sneaky bastard." Was he even a bastard? "Be resigned; you're going to hear me mispronounce that a *lot*. Now talk about Cromwell."

"He knew I was an imposter. But he also knew I posed no threat to the cardinal or the king. He didn't realize I was from another century, he just assumed I needed a fresh start after an eventful childhood."

"Like Cromwell himself did." To Lisa: "Apparently Thomas Cromwell's dad was a real thug, so li'l Cromwell ran away and became a mercenary and worked his way up to the number two slot in the kingdom."

"I don't give one shit, Joanie."

"And this was a man who hated boredom," Thomas added, "so it suited him to keep a walking talking mystery around. I made myself useful to him, but I never forgot who he was. If he had ever needed something from me, he would have brought the hammer down."

I rubbed my forehead as pieces fell into place with near-audible clicks. Calais, at the Field of the Cloth of Gold, when Wolsey got close: *If he sees me I'll be in rather a lot of trouble.*

Yes. He would have been. Because Wolsey wasn't his father.

Who could miss this, if there be any way to attend? Who would ever leave, if they could but remain?

But Thomas wasn't just talking about that day. He was talking about that time period. Because he could have told me his background anytime, and never did, since he had no intention of returning.

"And when I complimented you on your outfit, you said the clothes weren't 'technically' yours. So you showed up in Calais, stole somebody's clothes, then hung around for the spectacle, ran into me, and…stayed?"

"It sounds insane, doesn't it? And it's difficult to explain. I'll give you the short version: I'm a confirmed Luddite with no family—"

"So no MPU report," Lisa interjected, which was a good point—I'd been wondering about that very thing.

"That's right, lass. And the NSPCC—National Society for Prevention of Cruelty to Children—had a hard time keeping up with me, so at best, any report of my disappearance would have come in late."

"I don't actually hate his background story," Lisa said to me. "Plus, he's an orphan like we are."

I rolled my eyes. *Golly, an orphan like us! Why, I guess it's meant to be! All is forgiven!*

"No family, but what I did have was a background in Medieval Studies, as well as the distinction of being the only lad in the system who never e-mailed, used social media, owned a tablet phone, or frequented a dry cleaners."

"I get most of that, but the last one's just dumb. What do you have against using perchloroethylene to clean suits?"

"So here I was," he said, ignoring Lisa's sensible question, "with a literal once-in-a-lifetime chance. And I took it. I knew enough about the period to make myself useful and well-off—I think we can all agree that this is a terrible place to be if you're a peasant."

"Anywhere is a terrible place to be a peasant, you big dummy."

"And I never caught on," I groaned. "Not once."

"Be fair, Joanie. You weren't looking for someone who *didn't* stick out. Tommy Boy here had a great cover story plus Cromwell on his side. So why would you question it?"

"Because I should have." The clues had been there. Giving me the holy fool cover story. Telling me "it's the linen" when I was surprised he didn't reek. Giving me the fever = haircut cover story. Giving me advice about my accent. And always, always dropping everything to help me.

"Help me with this," I said. "So Eleanor makes the first jump. She's fighting with her husband and there's a tussle and she falls into 16th century Calais. And wherever you were in the 21st century on that day—"

"Tower of London," Thomas said promptly. "The *Ein deutches Requiem.*"

"Okay. So you found yourself in 1520, and then I came right after. Is that how the gates work? You follow whoever went through just before you did? Eleanor landed in Calais so you did, and then I did? But later she was at Windsor, which is why I ended up there? And are the gates prone to open where significant amounts of people have gathered? Not just a random crowd?"

"Otherwise anyone attending the Super Bowl would be vulnerable to a gate."

"Or a random unprecedented crowd? Like at Blackfriars?" Ugh, none of it made sense. No idea why I was trying to science my way through any of this.

"So I stayed," Thomas finished, as if that was an actual ending to the story.

"So you stayed." Yes, that was incredibly unsatisfying. Although we'd been rehashing events for half an hour, I was still startled to see the Inn come into sight. "You must be excited."

"I'm happy I could finally tell you the truth."

"That's not what I—well, first, there wasn't ever anything preventing you from telling the truth."

"Just fifteen years of careful camouflage and self-preservation," he pointed out dryly.

"Yeah, yeah. I meant excited about going back." By now we'd pulled up, Thomas had dismounted, helped Lisa down, then turned to help me down. I held onto his shoulders even after my feet were on the ground. "You're coming back with me, right?"

He just looked me. "You know I won't, my Joan."

I knew. He'd been too careful, worked too hard, built a life he loved, been witness to some of history's most significant moments, knew he was ringside for several more, to toss it and roll the dice that I.T.C.H. could send him back to his carefully constructed existence in TudorTime if he wanted a do-over.

I rested my forehead on his chest. "It's not fair." The lament of a child, sure, but it covered *so much*. Virtually every aspect, in fact, of my adventures over the last few weeks. "And now I have to go back home where you're a bag of bones buried in a box somewhere."

"Actually, depending on where he's buried, he'd be closer to dust than actual skeletal remains and forget I said that, not helping, I'll go over here and stand under this random willow tree."

"How can I leave you?" I murmured. "You've been looking out for me for years. You've done so much for me and I've never done one thing for you."

"How can I let you go, my Joan?" he countered. "You hold the world away from your true self, but you allowed me to see you. You risked your life for strangers when the slightest misstep could have meant an ugly death. In this I'll take my cue from you: you're strong enough to leave, and I'm strong enough to see you off." He brushed his thumbs over my cheekbones, then leaned in and took a kiss. I clutched his wrists so I wouldn't cling to his forearms and do something deeply dumb like not go back. "And I doubt this is our ending."

"Why?"

"I feel it. I know it. Like I knew I'd always love the addled American at Calais, like I hoped I'd be worthy of her when I was at last a man."

"Hey, that's right, you were a teenager when you guys met! Joan had almost ten years on you! And what kind of supergeek teen has a background in Medieval Studies and now that I think of it these comments could have waited for later, sorry, sorry, carry on."

"Jesus Christ," I said under my breath, and Thomas dissolved into laughter. I stepped away from him then, because it would never be easier to leave him than in that moment. Did I love him? I wasn't sure. I considered him a good friend, certainly, and I was hot for his forearms, definitely. But in terms of time, I'd only known him a month. I wasn't prepared to make a permanent life-altering decision just now. Even if it meant I might never see him again.

I adored him, but I wasn't willing to give up my life for him. Or risk further brain damage. So I had to respect his choice not to give up his life for me.

"Goodbye, Thomas." Then I unceremoniously walked away and took my place beside Lisa under the willow.

"That was super tender and sweet and all, but what if it takes an hour for a goddamned gate to open?" Lisa waved at Thomas, who was standing beside the horses, watching over us. "It's just gonna get more and more awkward while you two gaze longingly at each other and I try not to exsanguinate."

"Incorrect." I closed my eyes. *I need a gate. I want to open my eyes and see a gate. Because they're always there, it's just most people can't see them. I can, though. I'm the only one so I will open my eyes and I will see a gate RIGHT NOW.*

And I did, I opened my eyes and there it was, wavering like a shimmering picture frame.

I took Lisa's hand. We stepped through and Lisa glanced back for a last look.

Not me, though.

CHAPTER SEVENTY-EIGHT

"**M**iss Howe. Dr. Harris." Instead of Warren, there was a tall, dark-skinned, gray-haired woman standing a few feet back from the platform. In her tailored tweed, pulled-back hair, and crisp pressed lab coat, she looked like she was answering a casting call for 'classy older female scientist'. "Welcome back to the 23rd century."

"*What?*" (What do you know? Lisa and I had now yelled the same thing *four* times in a decade.)

"Sorry, sorry." She snickered and pushed her glasses up. "Time travel humor."

"Jesus Christ!"

She stepped forward and held out her hand, which I shook out of reflex, then smirked to see Lisa spitefully shaking with her bloodiest hand. "My name is Cheryl Tennen—yuck, let's have someone take a look at that, Dr. Harris—of the department of Quantum Temporal Investigation. And I have an ungodly number of questions for the two of you."

"Department of Quantum Temporal Investigation? Please tell me you don't pronounce that acronym as 'cutie'." When she didn't say anything, I groaned. "That's almost as bad as I.T.C.H.!"

"I have a number of questions about I.T.C.H. as well." When I opened my mouth she anticipated and added,

"Dr. Warren is in government custody with a number of his colleagues."

"Cavalry's here fucking *finally*."

"Yes, Dr. Harris. And as it's only the two of you, is it safe to inform Dr. Warren he is a widower?"

"Wait, you know about—yes. Safe bet."

Three things. One: After a brief discussion about whether or not we should lug Eleanor's corpse back with us to fool Warren, we had decided that there had been enough lies and misdirection. That regardless of the consequences we would tell the truth about Dr. Lady Eleanor Warren: after several attempts to reason with her, I had been forced to kill her in self-defense.

Two: We also decided Warren was too gutless to strand us.

And three: If you need to stash a body before time traveling five hundred years to face an unknown future, the Tower of London is uniquely suited to that.

"I'm going to have to see so much I.D.," I told Dr. Tennen, helping Lisa down from the launching pad. "And references. And possibly a fingerprint match and a DNA test before I believe you are who you say you are. And all that only *after* my friend gets her face fixed." *Also, you're doomed to disappointment since I don't know a thing about anything: how it works, why it works, why you can be dumped in Calais in 1520 and in London almost a decade later. But first: Lisa's face.*

"Of course." She must have pushed a secret button or everyone's coffee break was over at the same time, because several people were streaming in, and I could already hear one of them calling for an ambulance. Another had grabbed a first aid kit the size of a Samsonite and was trying to coax Lisa into sitting down and letting him take a look. Several others were taking pictures of the equipment, consulting with each other, then taking more pictures.

"Cheryl, have you seen the calibration on some of these instruments? And don't get me started on the radiation." One of the picture-takers looked simultaneously horrified and intrigued. "Were they *trying* to kill everybody?"

"Document *everything*, Paul." To me: "Sorry. Listen, we owe you a debt, Miss Howe."

"And me! You're in my debt, too, don't forget—ow, goddammit! Give it up, fuckhead, butterfly plasters aren't gonna cut it!"

"And we might have to ask still more of you."

"Much has already been asked of me," I deadpanned as the unmistakable sound of Lisa hitting someone over and over with a pack of gauze filled the air.

"I can only imagine." Tennen, who'd been staring at Lisa with not a little interest, wrenched her attention back to me. "To be blunt, Miss Howe, you're not only my new best friend, but I need to keep you on my side."

"Start working on your list of demands right fucking now," Lisa called, wrestling a hemostat clamp away from the tech trying to help her. "That's my advice."

Yes. And it was good advice, because I think we all knew the experiments would continue. Certainly Lisa didn't seem at all surprised, and I couldn't imagine department QTI had any interest in unringing the bell. And there were still Losties back in TudorTime. Presumably ones I hadn't kissed. Or shot.

In fact, there was one in particular who, it seemed, had been right: our story wasn't over.

"Miss Howe, are you all right?"

"I know she looks like the Before picture in an ant-acid commercial," Lisa said, who had by now thoroughly cowed the tech trying to help her, "but that's her biggest, happiest smile."

"Are you sure?" Dr. Tanner didn't seem reassured. "Do you need something to drink?"

"No, no. C'mon, Lisa, the paramedics will be here soon. I'll go with you."

"To eat, then?" Dr. Tanner persisted.

"Oh. Well … now that you mention it …"

EPILOGUE

Before my parents died, I journaled almost every day. But in The After, I didn't think it was a good idea to write anything down. *April 28. Got an A on the vocab test and got the rest of the lightbulbs in the attic changed. Mom's still in the freezer.* Years ago, Lisa pointed out that I had cleaved my life in two: the years Before my parents died, and the years After. But now I was starting to see a third section: Before the Before. What better way to describe my TudorTime adventures?

And maybe it was still a bad idea to write down my adventures, but I no longer gave a wide shit.

"Why are you talking like a narrator?"

I closed my tablet. "Shut up. I'm not. I can if I want to!"

"Wow." Lisa plopped an armful of charts on the table. "Y'know what, I'm not gonna engage. On a totally unrelated topic, I'm taking you off the Maxipan study."

"Well, yeah. I mean—the brain damage."

Lisa, who had spent half the day immersed in lab reports, started sorting charts into an order that meant something to her and nothing to me. We were in the office/dining room and I'd just started thinking about the French Silk pie in the fridge. "No, that was never a problem, I told you. It was pre-existing, from when you had the flu as a kid."

"Not that brain damage. I mean the damage caused by all the time travel." How scary was it that I had to specify *which* brain damage?

Lisa didn't say anything, which was wildly, insanely out of character.

"Uh—remember? You were super-pissed at I.T.C.H.? I figured out the reason I could see the gates was because I got aura migraines *and* was taking Maxipan?"

"Joan, I want you to sit down."

"I *am* sitting down! " Calm, sympathetic Lisa was terrifying. "If I'm dying, just tell me."

"You're not dying. But—about the study…"

"Listen, I'm not mad. I know you guys have to cover all the side-effects in the paperwork, but you couldn't have known that an experimental medication would react with my migraines and help me see wormholes."

"That's the thing, Joanie. That was the first thing I checked after I got my stitches. You were in the control group getting the placebo. They're sugar pills."

I waited, but she was done. Oh. That indicated it was my turn to talk. Too bad I couldn't think of anything.

"Joan? Do you get it? You've essentially been taking TicTacs for your migraines. It's not the medication. It's just you. And it's not brain damage. It's—damage was the wrong word. *Change* would have been more accurate."

"I'm sorry, what are you saying? Other than I've been enjoying minty-fresh breath as part of this study?"

"I'm saying I don't know why you're the only one who can see and call the gates, and QTI doesn't know, either. But it's not the Maxipan, because you never took any."

I blinked, thinking it over. "I don't know how to feel about that."

"Confused? Try confused. That's what I've been going with the last two days. Your brain chemistry has changed in some significant way, the analysis of which requires further study and possibly booze. But you're no more brain damaged than you were before the medical trial started. I wanted you to know that. And something else." She opened one of the files and pulled out a little packet of papers, then handed it to me.

At first I had trouble understanding what I was looking at—it had been that kind of month. But then the words *Le Manoir aux Quat' Saisons* jumped out at me.

"Aw, Lisa, you didn't have to get me a gift card to—whoa." On closer inspection, it was *better* than a gift card! "You got me in one of their cookery school classes. Secrets of Eggs! Not only will I get to cook eggs, I will learn all their secrets?" I rose and flung my arms around her bony shoulders. "Thank you thank you thank you!"

"Hands to yourself, dumbass." By silent agreement, we weren't going to talk about how she hugged me back with desperate strength. "Are you really gonna do it, by the way? I saw the brochures. You're changing your major?"

"Yes, I can't *wait.*"

"That's more enthusiastic about school than I've ever seen you."

"Well, before now I wasn't studying to be a food historian. Well, a social historian of food culture."

"Didn't even know that was a thing."

"It's a wonderful thing. You should have eaten something when you were back in time; the food's incredible."

"Pass."

"I'll recreate some of the recipes here; they'll be perfectly safe. You'll love leeches, I promise."

"*Hard* pass. But I'm glad you like your gift. Figured I owed you something nice after the shit I put you through."

"What you put *me* through?" I drew back and looked at her. "Lisa, if anything it's the other way around. You could have died back there. I put you in danger by telling you the whole story, and then it was compounded by Warren's treachery, and you could have—I mean, you were almost—" I gestured to her face. Twenty-six stitches, but the doctors told her she'd have a full recovery and little to no scarring. But we'd been incredibly lucky, and no one knew that better than Lisa, who saw death in one form or another every week.

"I don't regret bleeding for this," she said, tapping her cheek. "Ow! That hurt, why did I do that? But seriously, I don't regret any of it. I'm glad I went—I needed to, in order to get it. And I know Thomas doesn't regret any of it, either. 'Better to have loved and lost than to etcetera'. But he hasn't lost you. Like he said, your story's not done."

"Why do you guys keep saying that?"

"Because we know you. Because your test results bear that out. Also, if I'd been paying attention I could have told you Thomas was a Lostie."

"How?"

"He used the word *patois*. It bugged me until I looked it up—it's French, but it wasn't coined until 1643. Thomas was using it over a hundred years before anyone else. Stupid of me to miss that."

"Being a little hard on yourself, don't you think?" Though I made a mental note to tease Thomas Wyn—uh, MacRae—about it when I saw him. Because if the smartest person I knew was confident we'd meet again, and the man with the greatest forearms I'd ever seen also thought so, who was I to say otherwise?

It would be difficult, no question. But no one ever said long-distance space-time relationships were easy.

THE END

About the Author

MaryJanice Davidson is the bestselling author of many novels, including the UNDEAD series and the FOSTERWERE trilogy, and is published across multiple genres. Her books have been published in over a dozen languages and have been on bestseller lists all over the world, including USA Today and New York Times. She has published books, novellas, articles, short stories, recipes, reviews, and rants, and writes a column for USA Today. A former model and medical test subject, she lives in St. Paul, Minnesota, with her family.

You can reach her at contactmjd@comcast.net, follow her on Twitter (@MaryJaniceD) and Instagram, find her on Facebook (https://www.facebook.com/maryjanicedavidson), and check out her website at https://www.maryjanicedavidson.org

Like a book autographed, or personalized as a gift for a loved one? Well, too bad, what do you think she's running here? She doesn't have time for that crap. You probably don't, either. Have some self-respect, dammit! Kidding! Send it to MaryJanice Davidson, P.O. Box 193, Hastings, MN 55033. Autographs free; snark is extra.

ABOUT THE PUBLISHER

This book is published on behalf of the author by the Ethan Ellenberg Literary Agency.
https://ethanellenberg.com
Email: agent@ethanellenberg.com

Made in the USA
Monee, IL
08 January 2021